Edwin Ahearn

The Arbhal Sequence

DOLVID

The ARBHAL Sequence

The tug of history, often very ancient history, is felt throughout these works. A large amount of information about the past is disclosed in the narrative (and a chronological tabulation is an appendix to ARBHAL*), but for the purposes of these extracts a reader needs to know that long before the land was Arbhal it was Owan, and the Owanil, a gifted, energetic, but often arrogant people conquered and then lost a vast empire on both sides of Arnan, the inland sea.*

After some centuries of obscurity, during which their island-based priesthood, the Atarlum*, was essential to the preservation of the Owani culture and language, the Owanil, through a series of opportune events, were able to regain control of their old realm, imposing themselves as an aristocracy on a numerically superior mixed population of Other Races (their own slighting term for all those without a pure Owani pedigree). Their old speech, however (the Owanilú), has become a scholar's language, surviving mainly for ceremonial and religious purposes, and in titles and proper names.*

Until relatively recently knowledge of the Owanilú was part of the elaborate system, Preference, by which the Owanil maintained control, practically excluding the Other Races from high office, and from many crafts and professions.

For half an age these exclusions were a source of unrest and rebelliousness among the Other Races, while many Owanil came to view the system as incompatible with their people's historic love of justice. At the time when Dolvid *begins, Preference has been abolished for the best part of a century; the exclusive Owani grasp of the realm's rewards has been loosened if not broken. With the extinction of the former reigning house even the* rabhsai *(the supreme, though by no means absolute ruler) has a mixed strand in his ancestry, and a conciliatory Patriarch has moderated the* Atarlum's *dogmatic insistence on the natural superiority and special fitness to rule of the Owanil.*

Nevertheless, the old conflict is muted rather than permanently silenced. The much-intermarried provincial aristocracy still preserves the purity of its bloodlines, and the same is largely true with the landowning class of the Heartland ("the Families"). Book III of Dolvid *is essentially a novel about the early manhood of its title character, and* Arbhal *an epic adventure, the theme which runs right through the entire sequence is the desire (often the schemes) of this stubborn Owani minority, with the support (often the covert assistance) of reactionary elements within the* Atarlum, *to reestablish their former unchallenged dominance, and beyond that to somehow bring back the supposed glories of a legendary Owani past.*

Edwin Ahearn

III

xiv

Homecoming

"More than a few years," Bolan said, "since Kadon Dinul had a victorious captain to cheer home."

Dolvid only grunted an unreadable response. Half a century, in fact; the day they had crossed the frontier into the wilderness of Naëni had been exactly the fiftieth anniversary of Saidhan's defeating Tobhsila to end the War of the Widowed, but he was not going to hand that comparison to Bolan, whose remark was a little unctuous, better left for someone else to say.

Even about being back at Kadon Dinul, Dolvid's feelings were unsure, and there was certainly no other reason for looking forward to tomorrow's ceremonies. Their victories had already been amply hailed, at Sebira, where Daënakh had unearthed what were said to be songmakers in the olden style, and his son, drunk, had revealed an unexpected talent for imitation, giving his own irreverent versions of the treaty talks with Ott, and Bolan's first meeting with the *Kímukan* Indhil.

More celebrations, less formal, had been waiting at Dônshei. With not enough ships available at Sebira, and many men to be returned to their garrisons along the way, the entire army had gone overland. With Bolan and Shumat Dolvid had spent a night at the *margú* on Luskran Bay, enchanted to find Embhu as a *nôd'yanu* there, his tutor and guide, years before, at the *Mankh'*. Nearing end of her service, she remained anyone's dream of the desirable, and no longer spoke in rote-memorised sentences. She giggled with Dolvid recollecting that first tentative encounter, each of them shy of the other's knowledge, and he left her in the morning with tender feelings of gratitude, and what could pass for real envy of the husband she would soon be looking for.

Then, yesterday, the diminishing army had reached Dônshei and crowds in the streets. They were greeted formally by *Foi'kani*, an official whose title and ceremonial dress came down from the First Empire, welcomed boisterously by the city with beer and embraces; many who took to the streets could have only the vaguest idea where Narn was, or what might be the significance of Bolan's triumph. Never mind; few did any sleeping, and the enthusiasm of the women of Dônshei made Bolan remark that given two more such nights the Victors of Narn when they reached home would be a bitter disappointment to their wives.

Having once reached a strength of fourteen hundred, Bolan's command was now not just above five squadrons, mainly Household with some General Cavalry, earliest of their recruits no longer distinguishable from the regulars in their riding, their discipline, nor (as Bolan observed) the trail of second-hand perfume they left on the air, as the column made south out of the city. The rest of the army had peeled away in stages, the Provincials at Sebira, men borrowed from other garrisons, recruits who decided not to sign for a full term of service. Some had chosen to remain in Narn, to help train and provide a stiffening for the new force being raised there to defend the port. Astonishingly, Onebhal was chief of these; seeing the Bowl of Narn in peaceful conditions, after a thoughtful thumbing of the rich soil he grudgingly allowed it was not bad country, considering its distance from Bathrâd.

Dônshei Bridge, it had often been said, was named to confuse travellers coming from the south, always annoyed to find Dônshei itself was still a good half-day's ride away. Formerly there was no town, just the big stone bridge, only one to cross the broad Paowan River, but a small group of dwellings, with a good hostelry, had grown up around the south end of the bridge and the cavalry post there.

Here they were met by an officer of the Household, a man Dolvid knew slightly, Kizhunai, one of those who had declined to step forward as candidate for command of the Northeastern venture. The prudent option, but he wondered how Kizhunai felt, bringing the *rabhsai*'s personal greetings to the Victor of Narn. Perhaps he did not mind; he might be happier in lesser roles (what Bolan once would have called a maggot by choice, not a fair name for Kizhunai's unexcitable competence).

Bolan was put under *rabhsai*'s direct orders; river barges were waiting to ferry him and his men down to Owan Sai, so in the morning they could make the traditional ride, up Harbour Way and in at Harbour Gate to traverse the whole length of the Avenue to the New Residence. To be there to greet them, the *rabhsai* had made an early end to his summer at Tan Lughsai, already interrupted once by the Pledging.

Rowers on the barges did little more than keep the blunt vessels in midstream, dipping occasionally to carry them through a stretch of sluggish water. For the most part the river's current took them, high hills of Dramal to the right, the hospitable meadows of the Paowan on the left. The sun was warm, but evening came sooner now, and heat of the day no longer hung in the air as at midsummer. Forward on the wide deck, Dolvid and Shumat found their voices hushing to the quiet of their progress. Shumat, eager for the festivities tomorrow, for once was undistracted; his attention, with his moods, had been unpredictable since the last round of tearful farewells at Yuvakh Din. He had an understanding of some kind with Manda, short of any promise (and privately derided by Bolan), but the relief he admitted to at having escaped formal commitment could not be mistaken for happiness.

"I shan't ride with you in the morning." He had an idea of slipping quietly into the city and finding Faëdhal, though guilt over not having kept in touch made him nervous about that reunion.

"You must. You're a subject of Lambarr's, too."

"Not a soldier. The royal directive was to *officers and men of Captain Bolan's command*. That's you with the breastplates — what would I do, hang a side of salt beef at my saddle?"

The off-centre face became sly. "If you refuse to ride with us, I'll tell the *rabhsai* all I've heard about the Pass of Perus and storming of the *drin'loi*, unauthorised persons issuing orders to soldiers of the realm — and having Bolan sign his name to a falsified account of the action; shocking."

"Every word of that dispatch was true."

"Oh, aye, but a lot of words were missing that might have been there."

"I don't know where you have been hearing tales — " doubly shy of being praised for discovering a part of his nature he was not proud of, a battle-frenzy he would as soon forget.

"From Ott. Also I do discuss things with my squadron officers on occasion, does that surprise you? Why the big secret? If I had led that charge I would have been bellowing like a stud bull."

"I do not want to talk about it."

"Then no more nonsense about not riding with us. Is it true you knocked out wagon-shafts with arrows combing your hair, and forgot to draw a blade till you had one leg over the parapet? Ott's son says you made a dozen enemy drop their weapons just by glaring at them — how is that done? Do you have *jinzai* blood?"

"For the love of Hrafi, shut up." Dolvid punched him lightly in the chest.

"Say you will ride with us, Hero of the Pass." Shumat punched back, and Dolvid caught the wrist, using a circling leg to sweep his feet away. He dragged Dolvid down as he fell, and they wrestled, laughing.

"Ride with us, O slayer who needs no sword. Ride with us — "

"Stop." A knee on Shumat's chest, Dolvid used a forearm to block the mouth.

"What's this?" Bolan was here. "No question he'll ride with us."

"But I'm not — " Looking up, Dolvid was sent spinning by Shumat.

"Bolan — " Shumat was up on one knee. "You remember the dispatch after the Pass of P — " and Dolvid again knocked away his legs. Still trying to explain, he was hit by a tightly-rolled blanket Dolvid had found and thrown.

"Ho, now — look." Bolan was in the impossible position of wanting to end horseplay, while showing he had nothing against high spirits. "Our escort of honour. They're going to think we are an army of clowns. What sort of example — " but the last word came out as a cry, Bolan going down, tripped by Shumat, who then, with Dolvid, pinned Grenaspaluk's conqueror to the deck.

"What about the dispatch?" Bolan managed to

demand, between spasms of laughter and useless attempts to struggle free.

"Tell Dolvid where he has to ride tomorrow."

"Stop, wait," Bolan gasped, then, firmly, "Stop, now."

He propped himself on elbows, rolling up his eyes to say what he thought of his senior advisors. "You have no choice," he ruled. "You're needed, to explain our plans for Narn."

"I can come to the Residence by myself."

"No." Bolan was decided here. "You'll speak with a better voice once you've been seen riding beside the captains, that's how the world is, with or without your approval. Not ride with us!" Allowed to rise, he brushed at his sleeves. "You must be mad."

Seated to Bolan's left on a good *pefrai*, he reluctantly agreed to strap on a sword, though he had never worn a longer weapon than his Froghuli knife throughout the campaign. He was ready for a quarrel about putting on a breastplate, but Bolan, realising his men could not hope to outglitter Household squadrons that would go before and behind, shrewdly decreed their plainest and most war-worn campaign clothes, faded and in some cases stained outshirts to proclaim (as he said) real fighting men.

There was already a crowd, largely of dockworkers and their families, by Plakhan's Arch in Owan Sai, where Harbour Way began, but in a little while, when the riders breasted the slope with the city walls rising immense on one side, on the other the familiar ripeness of the Bronze Residence lifting above the shoulder of its grassed eminence, they could see and hear a far larger throng, lining the way, fringing the broad open square, clumped around Harbour Gate. Dolvid pulled his horse just a little, for a quick glance across to the shop of the goldsmith, Vulakh; Bolan at once rebuked him for being out of line. In the crowd he had glimpsed a face that might be Valnoi's, and after six immense years it did not matter. His eyes started tears, but not of sorrow; Yoëlladhu's Spear was burnished in autumn sunlight; the Household squadron ahead split into files to pass the warriors in through the central arch of the gate, to a sudden blaze of trumpets that wrenched at his heart.

On the dark rose-coloured stones of the Avenue, there was the wonder of having become what was once observed, made sharper as they approached the Disc of Aëlovoi and Dolvid saw a tight knot of children pressed round its base, just as he had stood to watch the Great Families ride in, what seemed many years ago. Shumat on the far side was nodding and grinning to the crowd, raising a friendly hand when his name was called, while Bolan's face was a mask, eyes to the front. Where the Avenue swept to the foot of the steps a welcoming group of horsemen was standing; Dolvid quickly picked out Merovas, the Captain of the Household, and the *Bôdhrai* Rhunsilakh, drooping sacklike in the saddle. A pair of trumpeters with the flanking soldiery sounded a brief flourish, and Rhunsilakh unrolled a document, his horse twitching ears in annoyance.

In abrupt silence from the crowd Rhunsilakh began, "Bolan Bakir, Captain, *Narnai-Kindhri*, before whom the realm's enemies abase themselves, it is decreed by Lambarr *Deghi*, *Rabhsai*, that you shall be known as Bolan of Narn."

Fresh cheering broke out. Since hearing that *Narnai-Kindhri*, four syllables to range him alongside all great captains of history, Bolan's eyes had kept looking inward, and in the same tranced mood he accepted his scroll from the *Bôdhrai*, and exchanged salutes with Merovas. He, too, had partaken of history, a young lancer at Kir when Saidhan brought Laluvoi from the nightmare of the Ní-Tilagh. His creviced face showed humour, and there was strength left in the short neck, the trim, erect body.

Thoughts went drifting to last night's talk with Shumat, who, tired, had spoken about Bolan's luck. He himself was too much indebted to that luck for any bitterness, but he recalled with wide-eyed awe how Bolan's fame began with the marketplace incident that could easily have ended in a massacre, and how he had been decoyed by the two of them into fighting the Yuvakh Din campaign, alliance with Ott put in his hands as a fragile goblet he did not dare let fall, his (and Shumat's) reputation saved at the Pass of Perus by what Shumat called Dolvid's ridiculous conduct. Then, at the Gates of Narn, handed a flanking position any commander would sacrifice squadrons in mere hope of achieving, and then sailing unscathed through the thick of the enemy to kill Grenaspaluk unrecognised — a numbing recital. Yet Dolvid had insisted on a thesis he only now saw whole, that luck was part of leadership, and all famous captains had possessed it. And if Bolan had been trapped into success, triumphant with plans not of his own making, at least he had not beaten himself by rejecting the ideas of others. That, too, was captaincy, of a sort that might make a man better leader of an army than of a half-squadron.

After greeting Shumat, and, rather more dubiously, Dolvid, Rhunsilakh motioned for them to dismount, and in fresh din that greeted appearance of the *rabhsai* and others of the Family at the head of the Steps, Bolan was mouthing, "What a day, hah?" On the far side, Shumat was mumbling about Odis Combe, perhaps that he was less nervous there, being ambushed by bandits.

Bolan a step ahead, they mounted the central course between the rows of gilded figures. Lambarr was enclosed between his two eldest sons, Tholat the Heir now his equal for height, Banak-loi short and square as ever. Laluvoi, tiny and bright, not noticeably older, was with them, and not far behind, in the shadow of the Residence, many lesser officials and their families.

Reaching the top, Bolan swung a hand across his body in the royal salute, and dropped to his knees to draw and offer his sword. Lambarr accepted it, only to hand it back, then stooped to raise Bolan. Also motioned to rise and come forward, Dolvid, unwarned, was looking into the eye of *Menadhi*. The eyebrows were raised in familiar ambiguity, face unchanged, spare figure with the same alert stance. The charge of theft that had nearly kept him from joining the expedition had gone out of Dolvid's mind, but came back now to chill the face he showed *Menadhi*.

Then, quickly, there were introductions, to Lambarr, to Tholat, peering enviously from great height, the short, dull-faced Banak-loi. A little back from the bustle near Bolan and Shumat, Dolvid perceived Rhunsilakh's fussing insistence on proper forms for everything gave private amusement to Laluvoi, whose mouth and eyes, at close range, were after all beginning to show signs of age.

Down below, Household troops had permitted the crowd to come on the Avenue, surging forward right to the foot of the Steps. Lambarr gave his always boyish wave, and the day's heroes kept arranging in fresh groupings as cheers of the crowd brought them back again and again. Lastly, with all the others drawn back into shadow, Lambarr stood between the two soldiers, one arm round each, then gently pushed them forward, standing back beaming as the warriors received the acclaim alone. As they turned away, Shumat's face flushed with delight, Bolan's hectic with what could as easily be fear or drunkenness. Banak-loi had gone to stand next to *Menadhi*, who had a hand resting on the boy's arm. Again, Dolvid met *Menadhi*'s eyes, and with a shock recognised the muted challenge as one he had seen before, in the face of Valnoi, when she seemed to defy him to do anything about her flirting with other men. Banak-loi was six years younger than Dolvid, hence just his age that last year at the *Mankh'*.

It was *Menadhi* who stepped forward to close these ceremonies, raising both hands and beginning to chant the *kudhanoi-kolukezh'*, an invocation to joy. Dolvid bit his lower lip when he caught himself mouthing the words. The voice, well-remembered, was in dreams confused with his father's.

That was not the end. Inside the Residence, silvery cool and quiet after the glare outside, they all climbed to the Great Window Chamber, where they were joined by more of the royal offspring, the two eldest girls and the third son, Lambakh. The *rabhsai*, Laluvoi, Bolan and Shumat had to make fresh appearances to appease the insatiable crowd below. Notable how much of Laluvoi's public radiance was a careful effect; the smile left her as soon as she turned away from the window. Clearly she was becoming impatient, and was the one to suggest it was time to go on to meatier things. Quite soon, some of them retired to the General Audience Hall, much better known as the Oak-Wall Room.

A large, high-ceilinged hall with a floor of polished stone, and the Chair of State on a low dais, with a wrought stone canopy above. Many *ôdul*, in niches, others hung from chains, added to light from the high windows, yet the place was always shadowed. Except for the top section of light stone pierced by windows, one entire long wall consisted of a wood-carving in deep relief, *Plakhsila Receiving News of His Accession*, an event that had occurred in the Colony, and craftsmen of the West laboured to commemorate in Kamsilat oak. A serious-faced twelve-year-old mounted on a complacent *pefrai* was depicted being hailed by an improbably large deputation of horsemen. Many of those represented probably never crossed Arnan in their lives, and certainly could not have been there on this occasion in 2737.

The meeting was set in the midst of big trees, overhanging leaves carved with much realism, and the nameless chief artist must have preferred animals to men; the horses were more alive than the riders, and there was an eager squirrel up with the acorns, affectionately detailed. Amongst clustered legs of the *pefral* were slender hounds, eyes and mouths alert, and off to one side an unlikely spectator, a magnificent long-furred cat with a disdainful nose. Through the trees there was distant view of a city, supposedly Kamsilat, then the line of Arnan, with the conical summit of Karg' Kamanta on the horizon. Though the Mountain was said to be visible in clear weather from the Colony, its prominence here was plainly pious exaggeration.

All this was seasoned oak, and the two trees in the foreground which framed the scene, right and left, had been sliced to retain exact contours of the single massive tree from which they came. When new, the Oak Wall must have had a golden glow, but years and smoke of lamps and candles had turned it to a richer brown, lovely in itself, but drinking up all light in the room.

Lambarr was said to use the State Seat only on the most formal occasions and then with an uneasy reluctance. Today, chairs were grouped in front of the canopy, and after waving his mother to take a seat, the *rabhsai* also sat, with Bolan virtually facing him. Dolvid took the chair on Bolan's right, noting the company was carefully chosen for serious business; Rhunsilakh remained, and Merovas, and they were joined by the Master of Revenues, Arvus. He had been a friend of Dolvid's father, and time had not taken away his headlong, breathless manner.

Lambarr rubbed his long hands together. "Stirring deeds, Bolan — the Gates of Narn, hah? Nothing to match it since my father's day." He waved exuberantly. "And you simply rode right through the press. I would have given a lot to see that."

"I should have been there," Tholat, with a different emphasis. The big-browed Heir resembled his father as horse-chestnut does the sweet, coarsely. Tholat's hands, as a fact, were not unlike the splayed leaves of a horse-chestnut. He had on a Household tunic, and was wearing a sword. His father gave him a brief smile, and came back to Bolan. "It has been my fate to stay close to the Heartland; in two of our Six Provinces I have never set foot. What do they say about their *rabhsai*, there in the far Northeast?"

Bolan, uncomfortable, muttered that all looked to Kadon Dinul for justice, and Shumat rescued him with the true story of a woman in the streets of Narn, who had recited all her troubles, ending with a plea that they tell her tale to the *rabhsai*, who could mend everything.

"Well," he said. "We have sent help, as was asked of us. Are they not grateful for their deliverance? Can we count on firm loyalty?"

This was a clear opening, but too soon, Dolvid thought, for the business he had helped plot. Bolan gave him a savage jog, and reluctantly he took his part. "By your leave, *Deghi*, the soldiers were welcomed for the banner they carried." Impolitic to report that east of Yuvakh Din not many were at all certain who the present *rabhsai* was; some continued to believe Great Banak was alive, and Laluvoi, of living persons, was most often asked about. "Yet, in the nature of things," he went on, "Narn looks outward on the Ocean, rather than to the empty lands behind. If they are going to look to Kadon Dinul, they will have to have a reason that does not ride away."

Standing by Lambarr's seat, the *Bôdhrai* Rhunsilakh thrust out his lower lip. "*Rabhsayani* is *rabhsayani*, at the Residence, at Owan Sai, or a thousand miles away. Are you saying, young man, the seeds of rebellion linger at Narn?

Are we not hailing victory today?"

"He means," Laluvoi's soft voice was still arresting, "loyalty is a luxury that may be beyond the means of a starving man. Yes?"

"*Asayu*," bowing grateful acknowledgement. "What is needed at Narn is an assured livelihood."

"Who is this man?" Having presumably seen *Menadhi* off, Banak-loi had come into the hall, and approached stolidly.

"Who is this lad," his grandmother countered archly, "with the manners of an eel-salter?"

Lambarr chose not to see his son's angry glare. "This is Dolvid, ah, Vidukhat, chief author, as I am told, of those most vivid dispatches."

"And also a criminal, escaped from the *Atarlum*," Banak-loi, not meeting Dolvid's eye.

Rhunsilakh cleared his throat. "It is true, *Rabhsai*, charges were made that have not been entirely — "

"Nonsense," Laluvoi interrupted. "*G'Asalladh'* Himself has gone into these allegations, and pronounced them without foundation. If that were not so, Dolvidh Vidukhati, whose father is well-remembered, is no longer obliged to answer to the *Mankh'*, since he is with the personal retinue of the *rabhsai* — " She looked at him to be sure he was taking all this in. " — who desires and commands him to write the complete history of this year's campaigns in the Northeast."

"Hi-history." Dolvid had not stammered since he was a child, but he was stupefied by the suddeness. Laluvoi was enjoying the rout of her grandson. No wonder she was adored; she forgot nothing: mention of his father had touched him deeply.

"History," she said, "need not be, with smoked eel or *raminat*, a monopoly of the *Atarlum*." Banak-loi pressed his lips together.

"In past ages, so I understand," Lambarr said, "there was always a writer of history at court."

"*Uzh'freladhai*," Dolvid confirmed.

Rhunsilakh objected. "An *uzh'freladhai* was a maker of songs. Is, if it comes to that."

"Or a maker of history, *Bôdhrai*," Dolvid said. "Formerly, to say great song, *olu'rai*, was to say history."

"The doings of our age," Lambarr said, "deserve recording, I suppose, as much as any other." This might be a faintly wistful reference to the larger fame of his father, but Merovas used it as an excuse to begin questioning Bolan and Shumat about the fighting. Neither Rhunsilakh nor the restless Arvus wanted this, and it could be seen Laluvoi would rather put it off for some other time, but he admired her acceptance of the inevitable, and the way she then fastened her attention, asking one or two keen questions about terrain, and the supply of troops in the field. It dismayed Dolvid the historian how Bolan and even Shumat could put events in the wrong order, or omit vital facts, but clearly none of this was pure history; everyone had points to make about strategy or tactics. Even Merovas, showing special interest in Ott and his bowmen, was plainly reopening an old debate about the vulnerability of cavalry to concealed archery, his desire to add permanent companies of bows to General Cavalry garrisons. Arvus, shuffling invisible accounts, worried about what this would do to the cost of maintaining the armies, saying auxiliary bowmen could always be recruited when needed.

The Heir agreed, thumping his hilts, saying *péfrapravádal* would always remain lords of any battlefield, an

opinion which became another of Laluvoi's private
amusements. Merovas and Arvus would have continued the
discussion, but Lambarr wanted to hear about troops for
Narn. "You say we are training a force for them, their own
men?"

"For defence of the port only, *Deghi*." Bolan gave
Dolvid a hard look to be sure he saw this was the real start of
business. "Not the road which joins it to the realm."

Laluvoi said, "Your dispatches spoke of goods moving
westward from the port in safety."

"*Asayu*, our troops were also moving on that road.
Even a loyal province needs cavalry to keep its roads safe.
The wilderness of Naëni is larger than any of our provinces."

Arvus was quick to answer. "Captain, provinces
manifest their loyalty in loyal remission of their taxes. No
realm can afford to garrison wastelands."

Banak-loi, chin to chest, said, "Saidhan is allowed to
raise armies to garrison Landegh. If one wilderness, why not
another?" The *rabhsai* chuckled at what he decided to hear as
an innocent witticism, but Laluvoi frowned. To Arvus she
said, "There is more to loyalty than gold. It was not for profit
we sent our armies to Narn."

"*Asayu*, I did not mean that. But there can't be a new
provincial cavalry without a province to support it."

Bolan was starting to look cornered, but these were
questions he could hardly pass on to subordinates. "It must
be a royal force, General Cavalry, not answerable to the
Elders of Narn. From Yuvakh Din eastward should be a
single command, with the addition of not less than twenty
new squadrons."

"A Captain of the Northeast, then," Rhunsilakh said.

Merovas was dubious. "The Army of the West guards
our frontier against invaders — " His intended question was

obvious, but he was forestalled by soft-footed arrival of a servant, who rumbled at the *rabhsai's* ear.

Lambarr queried Bolan: "He says your men are here...?"

"With your leave, *Deghi*." In obvious relief, he sprang up, and with a gesture for Dolvid to stay, followed the servant to wide double-doors at the far end of the hall.

"In the Northeast, too," Dolvid picked up debate with Merovas, "the troubles came from across the frontier. Clearly, there was unrest, but no revolt, till the out-men began coming in. For years in the Yuvakh Din country, subjects of the realm have lived next to an undefended frontier, as would never be tolerated in the West." This was surely a comparison worth making; it went without saying the Colony would be defended, partly because the Army of the West gave the realm its most famous soldiers. Partly, too, because there were *jinzal* on Landegh.

"Are you saying we can't defend the frontier at the Pass of Perus," Merovas was sceptical, "unless we can subdue the wilderness beyond?"

"Our position, Captain Bolan's position, is that they must be considered together, frontier and lifeline to Narn. Rebels can live in the wilderness only by ambushing the road, or raiding the Yuvakh country. They would have to turn to lawful pursuits, if we denied them the fruits of lawbreaking."

"Speaking of which," Lambarr broke in. "That huge fruit you sent us from Narn, pine-cone on the outside, with yellow meat inside — most delicious." He beamed at his mother and his sons. "We also enjoyed the smoked fish."

"Very well," Laluvoi said. "But you won't raise a new army so as to bring smoked fish and this pine-fruit to Kadon Dinul."

Lambarr shook his head, and explained at length the

rabhsai could guarantee only access to a port, not its prosperity. In connection with the Narn expedition, he had published a proclamation in support of trade with distant lands, but had been obliged to mention other ports, such as Thenimala in the south, El'tuf in the north. "Our cousin Vinilat of Dramal," he revealed, "complains every kerchief of the Paowan shipped overseas from Narn is one less for El'tuf to handle. No doubt there is something to that."

"Unless Narn sends it somewhere El'tuf has never heard of," Laluvoi observed. "Then it is all gain. But Vinilat has always been jealous of his prerogatives."

The doors at the far end of the hall had opened, and men were carrying in heavy cases; Bolan was back with what ought to be the clinching argument. Dolvid had been about to observe no port can live on exports alone; ships had to unload a cargo to make their trading pay. Now he would have left the telling to Bolan, but he sat down with finality, low on his spine. "*Deghi*, this can best be explained by Dolvid."

Who stood, clearing his throat. At Pledging, men on the Avenue who sold love-charms and similar nonsense loved to attach their dubious wares to a well-known figure from history or legend, and he was ready to borrow from their showmanship.

"*Deghi, Asayu*," he began. "We have all heard the tale of Pir Perus, and how, among many marvels he possessed a remarkable jacket." Laluvoi at once recognised the style, and tucked a smile down into the folds of her chin. The *rabhsai* was indulgent, but with both his sons there was astonishment and contempt. Interrupted in his prowlings, Banak-loi said, "A riding-shirt like peacock's tails, now one colour, now another, warm as fleece, yet so thin it could be hidden in his hand. Made of worm-skins, was it not?"

"That is what the *Song of Tales* says." With the

winning tile to play, Dolvid could ignore sarcasm. "But not
every detail is exact."

Amusement came again; Laluvoi and Arvus both
smiled openly. Rhunsilakh puffed. "My dear Dolvidh, it is
fable from start to finish — and I am speaking of the *Mankh'*
edition, which managed to excise many of the most
outrageous absurdities."

"No, but this is fascinating," Lambarr said. "Do you
mean there is something to this about the worm-skins?"

Dolvid had considered perhaps dragging in the
swallow-riders, and Daënakh's discovery of bones, but
Laluvoi's eye warned him not to carry his toying too far.
"*Deghi*, it appears worms' *nests* would have been a better
reading. A copyist's mistake, perhaps; the two words are
similar in Old Gabhanilú." He was standing beside one of
the big wooden cases the men had carried in, and bent to pull
up the lid. "This marvellous fabric worn by Pir Perus is now
called *shuzi*."

Lid up, he silently cursed how the box had been
packed; all that could be seen was a mass of black and white.
"Fur?" Banak-loi asked. "Worms make their nests of fur?"

Bolan got up to rescue Dolvid, and explained this was
a different coat, one belonging to the rebel leader,
Grenaspaluk. He lifted it, a bulky cape pied in deep furs,
snow white and glossy black.

"Then this is yours, by right of despoliation," but
Lambarr's wistfulness was detectable, and he was innocently
delighted when Bolan humbly begged that he accept it, best
of all the furs they had seen in the Northeast. Only Dolvid
and Shumat knew how reluctantly the gift was made; they
had laboured to persuade Bolan he could never wear the
cape without provoking envy.

Lambarr draped it over his shoulders, preening, and

invited Rhunsilakh to feel the depth and softness. Arvus said, "This is not your shuzi?"

"No," dipping again into the box. "This is."

As he drew out the sleeveless surcoat made for a woman to wear, everyone gasped. Illuminated by *ôdul* it glinted blue and green, shot through with purple shadows that rippled with the twistings of the fabric. "This," gathering it in his fist and releasing it to show how it sprang back to fluid life, "is shuzi."

Laluvoi was first to reach out and take the tunic, and the others in turn felt the strange, slippery texture. The old woman let the tinted mist cover a forearm and spread fingers, and ran the other hand over it; she may have sighed. Then, as the garment passed from one to another, Dolvid was answering questions from every side, and telling everything he had learnt about shuzi since discovering a shipment just unloaded at the Narn quayside. The ship-owner told him the fabric could be treated with oil to keep out rain and wind, and a double thickness so prepared made an outshirt warm as fleece that could be stuffed in a pocket. It could also be woven far finer than the surcoat — and he began pulling from the packing case a length of undyed shuzi, an unwinding river that fell sinuously into gleaming heaps. Once again everyone wanted to fondle the stuff, and Dolvid noted the same effect he had experienced at first touch, thoughts of mating were in the air; Lambarr in his mind was draping the form of his Saëdhu with this enticement.

"Worms' nests... " Banak-loi was running shuzi through his hands. "This must be kept secret, or every *ran'ghai* in six provinces will be out in the woods, worm-nesting."

"*Asai*, it is a particular worm — " a little shocked at the word of contempt; *ranaghai* meant wretch, rascal, but was most often used by the Old Blood of Others, and was

unattractive in the mouth of Banak's grandson and
namesake. "A very particular worm, since it lives on leaves
of one sort of fruit-bush, and nothing else."

"This is finer than our best teased linen," Laluvoi said.

"And costlier, I'd guess," Arvus said.

"At Narn," Dolvid replied, "the price, as I make it, was
two to three times that of fine woollen cloth in the
Heartland."

"Much more could be asked," Laluvoi decided. "Have
large quantities been brought?"

He told her; almost all so far landed was here, but the
man who had carried it was no adventurer sailing from port
to port in hopes of a cargo, but owner of a fleet. He had been
secretive about where to the far eastward shuzi came from,
but certain he could guarantee a steady supply, both lengths
and garments, if buyers could be found. Laluvoi remarked
the difficulty was more likely to be finding enough shuzi for
the buyers.

Not Arvus, but Lambarr was the one to initiate the
question of a royal monopoly, and Bolan proudly announced
he had presumed to take the first steps by securing future
shipments and establishing the *rabhsai*'s first refusal at Narn;
it was only a question of proclaiming the actual monopoly.
But Arvus asked if shuzi could not just as easily be brought
to a nearer port. El'tuf, for example, was already well within
the ordered realm, and was not cut off from Kadon Dinul, as
Narn was, during winter months.

Inventing the means of keeping a prosperous Narn
part of the realm had turned into a personal ambition for
Dolvid, he could not say quite why. By itself the trade in
shuzi might not be enough, but just what was needed, a
reason for the port's existence. He reminded this gathering
that to dock at El'tuf, ships coming from across the Eastern
Ocean had to round North Cape, difficult at any time, seldom

even attempted in winter; cargoes of shuzi would be better warehoused at Narn for the cold months than lost in pack-ice trying to reach other ports.

He tried to hint at the further advantage for *rabhsayum* of using Narn, which would be a royal enclave, not a province, and Lambarr at last saw the point; there would be no provincial overlord to take a share of the proceeds.

The Heir, Tholat, complained, "This is fine talk for the *rabhsai*'s court, trade and profit."

"Finer than swords and death," still fondling the shuzi, "Your mannish notions of honour and glory."

They had indeed all become merchants, discussing who would be eagerest to buy. The Residence Quarter, everyone agreed, but when Dolvid suggested the *Mankh'* for a good customer, Banak-loi objected. "Are *atarlal* going to clothe themselves in this? I think you know better."

"*Asai*, I do not presume to be in the Mind of *g'Asalladh'*," scoring a clean hit. "But the *Nôdhilum* will surely want robes of fine shuzi for the *nôd'yanul*." One, in fact, had already worn a slender shift, pale rose in colour, Dolvid's gift to a delighted Embhu.

Lambarr rubbed his hands together in joy, murmuring it would be good to have something, for a change, that the Island needed, to offset the heavy cost of *raminat* and *ga-ôthu*.

The *rabhsayum*, of course, would not actually be in the shuzi trade; as with other royal monopolies favoured investors would be allowed to buy shares. Granting the right to invest was purely the *rabhsai*'s prerogative, and Dolvid left it to Bolan to explain how the shuzi trade already had one participant, his patron, Khelagh. At Narn, when the importer had demanded some payment to secure the *rabhsai*'s exclusive right, Bolan had produced from an inside pocket a wash-leather bag containing half a dozen large and exquisite emeralds, carried all through the campaign, and given to him by Khelagh against just such an opportunity for timely investment.

Bolan had not had much to say when it came to details of business, and Lambarr saw a kindred soul, putting an arm round him. "You and I are the same in this, eh, Captain? When I was ten I could add a page of numbers well enough, but it makes my head spin when traders start in with their net this and compound that. We'll leave all that to the Treasury."

There was to be a feast tonight, he said, and the heroes of Narn must have some respite. Clothes to fit them would be provided, and for the present they would be the *rabhsai*'s guests here at the Residence.

Bolan, hearing dismissal approaching, tried to reopen discussion of military matters. "*Deghi*, this new Army of the Northeast — "

"Is going to need its Captain," Laluvoi supplied.

"Let us give it to my grandfather," Banak-loi sardonically recommended. "He and Uncle Sebhal can raise enough extra squadrons, east and west, to hold the realm in their tongs."

"Your second son is a lout," Laluvoi told Lambarr.

"Oh, boys are," vaguely, avoiding Banak-loi's face, which had darkened with anger. "I was."

The Court of Nasilú

The Rose-Stone Wing had been added after completion of the New Residence proper, expressly for housing visitors not of the Great Families. When the Avenue of Treaties was made, matched stone had been carefully selected, and stone rejected as too pale or too various in shade used here, giving a gentle, mellowed appearance, so the wing seemed far older than its century-and-a-quarter. It was built on an open square enclosing a garden court, flagged walks separating plots of small trees, hazel and birch both silver and black, with a plashing stream flowing down from a small fountain, leaving under an archway into the spacious grounds behind the New Residence. This court was named after Nasilú, wife to the third and last *rabhsai* named Plakhat, known as `*Afoi*,' the Old, having been sixty-seven when he succeeded his long-lived father Plakhsila.

Pillars lined the court, and beneath the colonnade were doors to the apartments, each having an upper level with a balcony supported on the columns. Those staying here had easy access to the Residence proper, to the grounds, and, passing through a south-facing archway, into stable yards, the Court of the Ram, and so along the south side of the Residence to where Pefrai Gate next to the Great Steps opened on the Avenue. Beneath the colonnade a double door led into a corridor not far from the Personal Suite.

A light rain had begun, and a few brown leaves were flattening to the flagstone walks of the garden court. Dolvid was expected at Bolan's rooms, where Shumat was also coming, to discuss the meeting with the *rabhsai*. Washed, he turned over several suits of clothing laid out by a servant, and chose moss-green breeches, a good fit, and a loose tunic of earthy brown, picked out with black brocade. Not counting an officer's outshirt with signs of rank removed, these were the first good clothes he had worn in three years.

He answered a tap at the inner door by which the servant had come. Faëdhal was there, lean as ever, a little older, smiling. "Dolvidh, how good it is to see you. I come now from Rhunsilakh, who told me about your appointment. An honour well-deserved, if I may presume so; I have read every word of your dispatches, and found them most graceful. And what a warrior you made, riding with the cavalry! I was there, as you will have guessed, on the Steps."

"I looked for you, but there was too much confusion." They clasped hands, then hugged.

"Ah, well, a simple Master of Tongues is not given a station, and has to jostle with stablemen and linen-keepers. How well you look! Your father, if I may say so, would have been proud today, very proud..." the voice trembled for an instant. "Well, you are going to be great in the realm, and an old pedant can only say he always said. It is true, just the same — that day we first met and you spoke out in the Old Tongue, I remarked to Zhival that day, an intolerable man, and his son is going to be the fattest officer in the history of the Household — I told him, watch! Dolvidh will be a name in this realm."

"It is so good to see you again."

"You are to sit in honour at the feast, and there is to be a *frela'olu-rai* sung, not made as it should be, though I was able to correct some of the grossest errors of diction. I fear Nilradh was last poet indeed. Between us, Dolvidh, learning is in decline, I am delighted you are to be teaching young Lambakh *asaloi*, a good boy, weak in the Script — he thinks more of swimming at Tan Lughsai, and his weapons. Not to slight those accomplishments. I myself never went beyond staves, but in my day, let it be said, I was seen as more than acceptable with those."

Dolvid was uncertain whether he was to be retained as permanent *uzh'freladhai*, or only while he wrote up the Narn Campaign. "I haven't been told I am teaching anyone. Where did you hear this?"

That was a cue for Faëdhal to lower his voice and bring him up to date with Residence gossip. Rumour said the *rabhsai* had for once gone against Laluvoi in permitting the *Mankh'* a part in Banak-loi's education, and the results had reinforced her resolve no more of her grandchildren would be taught by the *Atarlum*. Faëdhal, whose teaching was confined to languages, thought Dolvid would be a splendid addition.

For wider news there was the Great Pledging. The Kamsilat contingent had included not only Saidhan and his wife Doleni, but Sebhal with his, the celebrated Aëlu. Faëdhal never had much use for women, but even he had been charmed by the grace and serenity of Aëlu. "Not to say, if one may use the word of one so young, her wisdom. That cannot be said of everyone who marries into the Great Families."

A meaningful sniff went with that, and Dolvid got out of him the explanation that Petakoi, wife of Tovakh baKargul, had failed to make many friends with her high-handed ways. Public explanation for the early departure of Sebhal with Aëlu was trouble at the Frontier, but the whisper was that Petakoi, herself of Island birth, had infuriated Sebhal with curdling references to Aëlu's lowly origins on Kamanta. The two wives were in fact indirectly related.

"A sad and curious thing. There was fear someone of Other Race, knowing her past, might fail to respect Aëlu — " he meant, because she had been a *nôd'yanu* — "Yet it was left for Petakoi, whose descent is of the purest, to spoil this reunion."

She and Tovakh had not yet left Kadon Dinul; perhaps they still hoped to end the long exclusion of baKargul from royal positions. Great Banak had made that policy, but had not said forever. The War of the Widowed was fifty years in the past, and Banak, if alive, would surely have lifted his ban long ago. A sudden, chilling thought came; if there was to be a new Royal Captaincy for the Northeast, and Lambarr wanted to be conciliatory, Bolan might not get his reward.

"I chatter on to excess, you must pardon me. This period, I am afraid, offers all too few opportunities for, as we may say, interchange among men of understanding. Tan Lughsai is the true court, and the diversions there are no spur to scholarly pursuits. Not, I must add, that this *rabhsayum* is in any way hostile to them. But in former reigns the Residence was a more steadfast beacon; the *Mankh'*, I fear, has by default become the only home of learning."

"Perhaps it is time to challenge that monopoly." Asked what he meant, Dolvid had to admit there was no plan in his mind, only a powerful premonition of struggles to come.

"With an adversary not unknown to you, I believe. Your *Menadhi* is growing stronger. He will certainly be next Patriarch, but he already has more than a little influence in the realm. With the Families especially, I am afraid. However —" nearly shy. "I would hope to be part of any challenge you contemplate."

"I would be honoured to have you beside me, Master." Saying that, he was assailed by the strangeness of time and change. Why should it be that going to Narn and keeping track of supplies made him the leader here?

Shumat was doing a headstand on the bed, and came rolling down to say, "The Northeast has to go to Bolan." The only appointment to come from all the morning's discussion was Dolvid's.

"Don't count on it." Bolan tried to sound indifferent. "The Household, as second to Merovas, wouldn't be bad. He's seventy, and I'd be the only full captain."

"You're the only one with experience in the Narn country," Shumat insisted.

"There is one other. If they gave the Northeast to one of the lordlings, he'd want you for his under-captain, and you'd be real commander for the troops."

"I wouldn't mind going back; there's not much to keep me here." Manda was back with his ponderings. As he said with transparent off-handedness, she would be quaintly out-of-place in Kadon Dinul, no wife for an ambitious man, but if he did return to her country it might be different; he would have to make up his mind.

Bolan lowered his voice. "I can tell you, it's not going to be the Heir. The story is, the *rabhsai* asked Saidhan if Tholat could serve in the West. Sebhal said he would sooner have Rodlakh."

They all laughed; Rodlakh, Lambarr's youngest son, was six.

"Where did you get that story?" Dolvid asked.

A complacent face. "If you're going to be part of this whispering house of glass, you'll have to learn its ways. It's fine to be invited to the Private Audience Chamber, but I can show you bedrooms where you'll hear more that's useful. Serving-maids are always ready for gossip with a handsome officer, if he remembers to bring small presents — small presents and a large middle leg. Not much that goes on here is as private as they might hope. You'll need an edge on your weapon tonight, too."

Thinking of Daënakh's feast at Sebira Dolvid groaned. "Another long tedium of bad minstrels."

Bolan kept grinning. "Oh, the strumming is a good mask for what we whisper in dainty ears. For conquerors, maidenheads will go for an eyeblink; we'll have our pick of all the darlings of family within a day's ride of the Residence. A day's gentle ride, let us hope."

The Great Hall, where the feast was held, was even more spacious than the Oak-Wall Chamber, and a complete contrast, polished walls and high, airy ceiling, a home for light. Food was lavishly abundant, and there were many splendid wines, the company was richly clad and in the mood for pleasure.

Great Banak had adopted customs from his father's father's side; passing of years and the changeless ways of the Residence had smoothed the corners, but in style the event remained a memory of an ancient Gabhani feast; the horseshoe of tables with the central one raised a little above the others, bringing in of cooked dishes throughout a long evening, with entertainment, music, song and dance, going on between and even during courses.

With Bolan and Shumat Dolvid was at the high table amongst other notables. Amazingly, Saëdhu appeared on the *rabhsai*'s arm; she was rarely seen at public functions. She had lost their last child in the sixth month, and calculation said this was her first year in twenty without a either a pregnancy or a child under four. By comparison with the Residence Quarter women Saëdhu was unfashionably dressed, her face pale. Not yet forty, she was moving into plainness, but Lambarr's singleminded devotion to her, as hers to him, never changed. On one famous occasion a street-wit had bawled out *long life to the everlasting bridegroom*, and Lambarr, pleased with the title, had given a good-humoured wave.

The gathering was not so informal the royal couple could sit holding hands, or fence with their noses, but Saëdhu's gaze was seldom far from Lambarr, and their glances often met and held. But her behaviour was improbably shy, and when Dolvid was presented he wanted to offer a few words of encouragement. Laluvoi, by contrast, relished everything, friendly and alert in a robe the exact bright colour of a wildflower country people called blue-beggar.

As well as the Heir and Banak-loi, some of the younger children were here, and the betrothed Laloi in a resplendent robe of ruby-red, next to her soon-husband, Brodhai of Ân, not as big-boned as his brother, and with a face showing impermeable boredom. Rightward of that couple sat the baKargul without their children, broad, bearded, big-voiced Tovakh, bored in a more dangerous way, impatient for action, and his wife Petakoi, lean and stately, the very Owani face with its long arch of narrow nose striking rather than attractive. She kept her chin high, mouth a determined line. Rhunsilakh had brought his tall son of eighteen, Rhunilat, while with Arvus were his daughter Tellis in a very low-bodiced gown, and his rather silly-seeming son, Arvat.

"I hear you're going to have an apprentice," Arvus, indicating by tilting his head the ten-year-old Lambakh with his pleasant, uncomplicated face. "Would you care for one more?"

"*Bôdh'loiki*, I have yet to find out what my duties are."

Arvus was grim. "I would never blame anyone for not wanting to tutor him — " meaning his son. "Beating does no good." Arvat was making grotesque faces in Lambakh's direction.

"By the way, there was a curious arrangement made with the *Nim'* of Ân, where Daënakh *Asai* sends us our own drafts in lieu of remitting taxes."

"Just a convenience," blandly. "We needed goods and other help from Daënakh, and this saves the Treasury the trouble of taking in money with one hand and giving it out with the other."

"Very thoughtful," Arvus murmured with grinding gratitude.

He might have said more, but Rhunilat, long-necked, not at all his father, had come down from the high table and was about to begin a recitation, accompanied by a girl, also of family, who played finger-drums. It was a traditional celebratory piece from the Island years.

"Has he a good style, Master?" a low voice asked, and Dolvid was slow to identify himself in that title. Notwithstanding much exposed throat and shoulder Tellis Arvus-daughter was only fifteen, and could scarcely be inventing questions just to get his attention. Without a word about Rhunilat's stiff, conventional manner, he said quietly what he thought of the stiff, conventional song.

"Everyone says he is a most accomplished writer," the girl said, pleasant face youthfully sincere. Again, he questioned who, Rhunilat? the anonymous Island poet? and then realised he himself was being referred to in deferential mode.

"I have no gift for song, but I can tell good from bad."

"Of poets, I love Bronal," and with the same low voice Tellis spoke in Owanilú a pairing from one of Dolvid's favourite lyrics. The accent was good, and he wondered where she had learnt it, or the poem. Surely not from her Deniant father.

Rhunilat finished, and received the same patter of polite applause he had been welcomed with. Flutes and skin-drums sounded, and with a rush dancers came.

To Dolvid's joy they were Froghul. What they showed was (as it could only be) their 'outer' dance, the leaps and somersaults all the more impressive in the limited space the tables enclosed. They were good, and would have been better in flickering firelight instead of the pale quiescence of *ga-ôthu*. Three men and a girl, and the corners of eyes kept seeing old friends; they were very like Huro-Nam's people, though the girl was too tall for Tini-ra, who had never been one of the dancers, and in any case would be past twenty by now; this girl was not above sixteen. Yet the dark hair whipping across her face as she turned was a stabbing reminder of Tini-ra when she stood in the wind with a slight anticipating lean of her supple body. On nimble feet, this girl spun in a tightening circle, leaning as if held by invisible rope, and the end of the dance came when each man in turn sprang, one forwards, one backwards, over the crouching girl, spinning with knees hugged to chest, to land lightly on their toes.

For half an hour the Heir had been behind one of the lower tables, attracting a rainbow of Residence Quarter girls, and Bolan was off in a corner using his hands to explain the Battle of Narn Gates to a knot of admirers. Dolvid took that to mean he too could leave the high table, and did so with a faint bow to the Family, in the thunder of approval for the dancers.

Near the side doorway he caught at the arm of their leader, and as the near-black eyes came on him made the Froghuli sign of pleasure, palms rubbed together with a twisting motion. In their language he said, "You made good fun-dance."

The face, a creviced and leathery forty, showed surprise. "You say, fun-dance." In what should be his own tongue he was about as hesitant as Dolvid was.

"I saw before blood-dancing, also."

"Ah." Polite surprise veiled disbelief.

"You know the people of Huro-nam?"

"The people of Ka-Nam. That other name is free."

"Ah." As he had seen Tini-ra do, long ago, he made the grief-gesture, right thumbnail scoring left forearm. A name never belonged to one who had died, but became `free' till someone else took it.

"All hear about that people, the clan of open path."

"They stay now at Tan Dramali?"

"They'll be at Dramaru when there is snow. All can use the path Ka-Nam won in no-knife-fight with the Lord of Dramal."

The one-who-guts-game in Dramal; Vinilat should hear that. "They have a well-woman." He hoped she was alive, but would not risk repeating his mistake.

"Inghi." The name spoken with deep respect.

"I saw before her blood-dance as Mocker."

"You had good meat — " this was what others meant by `blessed,' specially rewarded. "I myself never. That dance is said about under all sky."

Guests seated nearby were curious about Dolvid's talk with the Froghuli. He considered whether he should give the dancers money, and the mere notion put distance between them; he saw it come into the man's eyes. Just then Rhunilat came up and actually did thrust silver into the dancer's hand, saying, "quite wonderful."

The man thanked him, and turned back to Dolvid with practised diffidence. "We thank you for your praise," going into ordinary language.

"As I thank you for your dancing," bowing back, lacerating himself with curses over the callous and stupid grown-up he had become since the days when Huro-Nam's people made him one of them.

Faëdhal came up, tall, blinking. "Ah, Dolvidh. There is a kinswoman of mine, anxious to meet with you." Drawing him by the arm he added in an undertone, "Linaëyu, wife of Khelagh."

He led Dolvid to near the head of the side-tables. A woman stood, dressed in deep green fitted close to her body. "Have I chosen the wrong time, Master?"

"Not at all, Madam," making half-deference. Linaëyu was a word not exactly beautiful, though her skin was of a soft ripeness that seemed to invite touching; she too was in the fashion with a low-cut bodice. The style was not wasted on her, and the slender hand she kept at her bosom was pretence of a pretence, not meant to be taken for modesty. The face was lean, her lips full, light eyes able to trouble, even frighten Dolvid, who felt appalling danger. She was amply aware of her effect. "My husband was eager to meet you, but could not stay for the feasting. He leaves for the north at dawn. My daughter Khalú." Next to her a girl of perhaps fourteen, too bony for the dress she wore, looked up briefly and went back to food in front of her. The mother must have been a girl herself when Khalú was born; she was not much above thirty now. Khelagh, in fact, had divorced an earlier wife to marry a much younger woman, this one.

"I have a son, too, who would have been allowed to come, if we had been told his playmate would be here." She meant Lambakh, and meant to impress.

Throughout the campaign Dolvid had been relied on for Great House talk, and now he was at a loss, finding nothing to say, but not wanting to go away from this perilous woman.

"My husband, from the beginning, Master," her voice was cool, but also had its dangers, "took a keen interest in the question of Narn, and its value to the realm."

"So I have heard."

"What about this shuzi? Is it as desirable as they say?"

An interesting choice of words, but before he could answer the *Bôdhrai* Rhunsilakh stood, calling for attention. Into the abrupt void came a plump young man dressed in the robe of minstrelsy, and a very pretty young girl carrying an *olútaloi*, the traditional stringed instrument. The man set his stool opposite where Bolan and Shumat were sitting, and the girl knelt on a cushion beside him. She might very well be one of the apprentice *nôd'yanul* borrowed for the occasion from the *Mankh'*, long hair flowing over lovely bare shoulders to the upper edge of her white tunic.

Linaëyu motioned Dolvid to take the empty seat next to her, and he could only comply. It was irresistibly funny, dividing a poet in two; in former times no song-maker would have let someone else try to guess at his rhythms and pauses and mark them with appropriate runs and flourishes. Worse when the young man dug into the bosom of his robe and produced a sheaf of small parchments, shuffling them to find his beginning; once, any song-master would have a score of epics by heart, and certainly would never read his own.

The girl struck summoning chords, and the minstrel, using the Owanilú, made his dedicatory address, praising Aëlovoi *Yoëlu*, then the *rabhsai*, descended from Yoëlladhu, Regent of Raëdh, where all began. This would be the *Frela'olurai Naënali*, the Epic of Narn. Lambarr was portraying absorbed attentiveness; Bolan spoke to Selnoi, wife of Rhunsilakh beside him and she, a pleasant, calm woman, covered her mouth with a hand. Laluvoi was sitting catlike, eyes enigmatic, either alert or focused on nothing. The poem began.

It lasted the best part of half an hour, a fanciful account of the expedition, the feats of Bolan and Shumat, twice interrupted by an ovation when listeners believed or hoped that must be all. Every so often Dolvid could catch the translated echo of a passage from his own dispatches, but most was high phrases worn null by centuries of use, a casting of real events into formulas outworn before the Night of Owan came, lifeless as a stuffed eagle. Archaic constructions and all, there could not be many here to follow closely; of others who knew anything about the campaign, Bolan probably understood little more than Shumat.

The eventual end brought a big and swelling ovation, the poet standing with formal gesture, transferring all praise from the maker to the subjects of his piece. Those, Bolan and Shumat, who had been in understandable doubt as to whether they should join in the applause, stood, urged by Lambarr, and were loudly cheered.

"And was that how it was, the campaign?" Linaëyu

asked as the noise began to die down.

"No — " remembering Shumat, after the Pass of Perus, telling him how it would be better in recollection, and he supposed it must be his sad gift not to forget what was cruel and petty, so as to see a more praiseworthy whole. Delivered and receipted, it was a bundle of fragments, difficulty of pegging down hurdles in sandy soil, chalk in the flour sold by a dishonest miller in El'tuf, a threatening shortage in oats that turned out to be an error in recording, a yellow-headed sore where breeches chafed the inside of a thigh, when water for washing was scarce. Grenaspaluk was dead, and so was Under-Captain Antrovai, and chanting of stale epics did not make a difference, or help the good men on either side who died, or lived on crippled. Men he had joked with, jerked from the saddle by an arrow, or dying in dust that turned to purplish mud, and he would not think about others tormenting a dying captive at the *drin'loi* — and yet Shumat was right, too, and there was no other glory to match battle, not if he could solve the mystery of Plakhan's Bride-Quest, discover the origins of *jinzal* — nothing, ever.

He recalled how ragged men and women were, captured in the Yuvakh Din country, thinner, surely, than anything that could be alive. At Narn, too, hungry men, women and children on both sides or no side, beggars mobbing troops in hopes of stale bread, bony women baring shrunken breasts in would-be enticement, small boys and girls who went through the leavings of the army like cankered rats. Dolvid remembered a gaunt, hauntingly beautiful face, a girl kneeling at roadside over the decomposing wreckage of — something that had been dear to her, that much was certain.

"The others we saw, the ones you spoke with, I have heard they dance their stories — was it a story we saw?"

Shaking off ghosts he told her about the two kinds of Froghuli dance, with Linaëyu watching his lips as he spoke.

Tellis Arvus-daughter had come and sat down next to the hungry girl. They nodded to each other, but Linaëyu's daughter went on eating steadily, and Tellis was attentive to his discourse.

"How do you know so much about Froghul' ways?" Linaëyu next asked.

After all, she might be more friendly than formidable, and he gave a brief and incomplete explanation, no Tini-ra. An eagerness spread gradually into the large-eyed face with its planed cheekbones. "Would it not be joy to follow such a life — not to trouble with fashion, property, the boredoms of the Heartland."

Here the daughter glanced up, but she had heard her mother in this vein before, and soon went back to a dish of stewed apples. Tellis was smirking privately.

"Is Shumat as brave as they say?"

"Braver, unless they say a great deal."

"They say he is very brave. He's very young."

"He and I are the same age."

A soft laugh. "I did not say too young. If I joined with a band of herders, I would take ripe young husbands and cut their hearts out when they came to be — what is the age you share with Shumat?"

"Twenty-two."

"I would cut their hearts out when they were twenty-three. A year is long enough, do you agree?"

This was either invitation or a trap to mortify him; he felt clumsily out-of-practice for this Kadon Dinul word-play. A long bout with eyes wrestling, but he was saved from any decision when the *Bôdhrai* Rhunsilakh stood again at the high table. "Hear the will of Lambarr *Rabhsai*," he proclaimed. Faëdhal, standing not far from Dolvid, shook his head despondently, holding all such ceremonial should be in the Old Tongue.

"There is created," Rhunsilakh went on, "by the *rabhsai*'s decree, the Army of the Northeast, and as its captain, in gratitude for his feats and achievements, recognising his fitness for command, the *rabhsai* names and designates — " a small pause, "of the Household, Shumat Shurris-son."

Astonishment of one kind or another was general; Shumat's youth, his hitherto subordinate position, his obscure origins all made this the unlikeliest of appointments.

At the high table Bolan recovered fastest. Prepared for a modest smile of acceptance, his face had frozen white with the naming of Shumat, but he forced it back to life and a broad grin. Standing, he used one hand to bring the bewildered Shumat to his feet, the other to pound the younger man's back in congratulation. Everyone else rose as the *rabhsai* stood to hang a chain with a heavy pendant about Shumat's neck. Still dazed, he acknowledged words murmured by Lambarr, and let Merovas grasp his hand.

"Know him!" Rhunsilakh proclaimed, unaware, probably, he was using a formula of the old Gabhanil clans when they confederated to nominate a High Captain, who might indeed be unknown to many. A crash of drinking cups and pounding of hands, and Shumat at last smiled.

With a change of tone Rhunsilakh went on to explain factually that while Saidhan *Asai* was Captain-General, a lifetime post, he, preoccupied with the Colony's affairs, recommended, and the *rabhsai* concurred, that there should be a Captain of Armies for the General Cavalry here on the Mainland. As this captain, the Captain of the Household, Merovas Miruvakhati, was named and designated.

This received the polite applause the manner of its announcement called for, and Merovas only half-rose in salutation. Fascinating; a space had been made, but would Bolan fill it? His alliance with the influential Khelagh could help or harm his chances, and Tovakh baKargul was there at the high table, pretending only a detached interest in these proceedings.

Reminded of law, Rhunsilakh used a near-apologetic undertone to mention all royal captaincies were subject to approval in Council, then resumed his declamatory style. "To be Captain of the Royal Household, the *rabhsai* names and designates — " again, the pause, "Bolan Bakir of Narn, Captain, *Narnai-Kindhri*. Know him!"

A fresh crash of acclaim, and Merovas stood as well, taking from his own neck the chain of the Household with the *rabhsai*'s wheat-sheaf token pendent, which he handed to Lambarr to loop over Bolan's head. Amid congratulations and handclaspings Bolan was sober, as if reflecting how far he had come; he might be the only one not entirely of Owani blood to hold this post, and was youngest, except for Saidhan, who had been twenty-three at Banak's investing, and had for a while held two captaincies, before going to the West.

For Dolvid, he had earned all respect for his dignity in the moment when Shumat was named Captain in the Northeast. The wonder of it all struck suddenly, all three of them raised to these heights, and Bolan with the post he had claimed when first met at the Bronze Residence seven years ago, his captaincy then about as likely as Dolvid being chosen Patriarch.

As the hall quietened Petakoi, wife of Tovakh, said in a clear, firm voice, "By your leave, *Rabhsai*. My husband has petitioned for a royal captaincy. Where does that stand?"

In suffocating silence someone — Tellis? — muffled a nervous giggle. Bolan's smile, and Lambarr's, faded slowly. Saëdhu turned, arching her neck, to stare in horror at Petakoi, while Rhunsilakh took the opportunity to look for leaks in the ceiling. By Petakoi Tovakh kept his great head bowed; he might be digging at the claw of a crab, and maintained the air of one not much concerned. That he was here at all, however, when Vinilat's yearly hunt was beginning, measured how much he wanted this captaincy; Tovakh was famed for his fierce love of the chase — and the ferocity of his hunting.

Laluvoi now appeared; having settled amongst cushions she sat up straight, eye glittering. Petakoi's hard stare faltered a little.

Only those near the high table heard Lambarr's words, spoken sadly; "*Asayu*, this is not the time."

"Is it permitted, then, to ask when that will be?" Petakoi's chin was firm, and Dolvid, who should be as annoyed as anyone at how she had marred the celebration, felt grudging admiration for the woman, who was not unaware of the enormity of this. Her body was rigid, arms straight down, hands hidden. Tovakh picked at his crab.

In a voice even softer than her son's Laluvoi said, "Kinsman, Tovakh *Asai*, do you have a question?"

Tovakh, chewing, made an abrupt motion of dismissal or disgust. Laluvoi's face was pert. "Then it is for yourself, Lady Petakoi, you want this captaincy?" Those near enough to hear chuckled, and Laluvoi let them, before adding, "I would have led armies, if there had been body-armour in my size. Our day is yet to come, *Asayu*."

She reached out to touch the arm of Petakoi, who met her eyes and then admitted defeat, shoulders sagging as she brought up her hands to reach for a piece of bread, and start reducing it to small fragments.

Eyes luminous, Laluvoi swung a circling glance to forbid laughter. Rhunsilakh finished his study of the ceiling and signed for musicians to begin playing. Ignoring the buzz of comment under the sound of plucked strings, Laluvoi leant to Sai-Nivu, prettiest of her granddaughters, and pointed out a peach worth eating.

Shortly, Tovakh asked leave, and together with Petakoi withdrew. Soon after, Laluvoi and Saëdhu also left, taking the smallest of the royal children, and Lambarr looked very much as if he would prefer to go with them. On his way to congratulate Bolan and Shumat, Dolvid was accosted by Rhunilat.

"Dolvidh, there is no badge for *uzh'freladhai* — if there ever was, it has been mislaid. But it is the particular wish of Laluvoi *Asayu* the post be ranked among lesser counsellors. Accept this token, *Bôdh'loiki* — " and over his head he looped a slender chain with the *rabhsai*'s wheat-sheaf cast in bronze.

As Rhunsilakh grasped his hand, Dolvid, a little stunned, found room to admire the tact that had not made his appointment a tame public tailpiece to the more glorious ones, although as a *bôdh'loiki* he was one of less than a dozen with that rank. Evidently he was to stay on after writing the history of the expedition.

Having seen the warriors he returned, as was wordlessly expected, to Linaëyu. Now his journey was intercepted by Faëdhal, with no trace of envy in his good wishes. Rather, he shared in the honour, saying in a near-whisper, "Time, well past time, for a man of scholarship and learning to be given rank."

Linaëyu, as he came up, said, "What were you smiling at?"

"When?"

"When the Epic of Narn began."

"What did you think of it?" He was tired of airing his opinions about poetry.

"Fitting to the occasion, it seems to me, neither better nor worse than others I have heard. It was correct, wasn't it?"

"Oh, irreproachably." He wanted to burst out with all his loathing for a false tradition, artificially created out of polite misunderstandings, to say real epic had none of that smoothness and polish, that no song-maker of the First Empire could have earned his keep without the gift of `dipping from the stream,' inventing half-lines as he spoke. He was shy about caring so much, never having encountered anyone else who did. "When I was little, I met the Poet Nilradh, who would have banned all recitations of his *Frela'olu-rai Banaki* if he could — the style was lost. And Bolan's horse at the Gates of Narn was not called Zhavukran." A part of the mouldy tradition was to give that name, Black Storm, to the mount of any victorious captain, because that was what Larghai's *pefrai* was called, at least in the *Frela'olu-rai Larghayi*. Sickening.

"I would be pleased to hear some of your own songs."

He bowed his head slightly, then was abashed to see that Tellis, with whom he had denied any talent for verse, was still listening.

"Are you staying here at the Residence?"

"In the Rose-Stone Wing."

"I have spent pleasing hours in the Court of Nasilú."

What might be heard there was pointed by her darting look into his eyes. Through an obstacle-course of well-wishers Shumat came to meet Linaëyu. He took her hand, and there was a tiny off-guard moment, a flicker of absolute desire in Shumat's face, at once smoothed into calm courtesy. For as brief an instant Dolvid had a twist of anger, as if Shumat was trying to take away what was his; so quickly come and gone he hardly felt he had been jealous, but was certain he wanted Linaëyu, now muddling Shumat into false modesty about his lance-work, into a confession he had understood about every fourth word in the epic.

Dolvid reached a hand to weigh the chain about Shumat's neck. "This changes all the questions east of Yuvakh Din."

He knew what was meant; ambition no longer came into whether or not he would marry Manda Otts-daughter. He did not recognise Dolvid's ruthless cunning, but to Linaëyu's questions about the size of the new army his answers were preoccupied. He saw a man he wanted words with, the Royal Stud-Master, breeder of *pefral*, and quickly excused himself, mounting of his troops to be considered.

"He is a fine-looking young man, the Captain."

"So I have heard more than one woman say. We have been friends since we were children," he added, explaining his lack of enthusiasm.

"It is becoming stuffy," Linaëyu led. A glance to the high table, where several notables were no longer to be seen. In the body of the hall the feast was breaking into smaller gatherings.

"Would she care to see the Court of Nasilú again?"

Not offering an answer in words, Linaëyu bent over and quietly instructed her daughter. Khalú gave Dolvid cool appraisal, nodded to her mother, and went back to food; she had begun all over again with spiced beef. Beside her deep-eyed Tellis seemed ready to speak, but instead reached for a crystallised plum.

There was an almost imperceptible feathering of rain. Very close, Dolvid and Linaëyu had taken only five paces on flagstones before she asked, "Where are your apartments?" He stooped to her, and she looped an arm to bring him nearer, and began a kiss which ended as a firm bite at his lower lip.

He recoiled a little, and then was startled by the wanting rage of his response; he had to catch at her waist as she staggered back against a low curb by the tree-beds. He had her cloak underfoot, his right hand was gripping her hair near its roots, and the other moved up to slide the robe from a shoulder that gleamed in faint light from the Residence. Linaëyu gasped what could have been a reproach, but her body was thrusting up against his.

There was no such thing (not for him) as uncontrollable; that was an excuse. He took a vast breath, and stepped back, retrieved her cloak, and led her to his rooms, counting doors with care, and all the while shaking like a sick man. Inside in near-darkness she turned to him, and he felt and heard her head thud against the wall as he kissed her. On the floor here was a mat of woven rush, and he saw small hope of reaching the bed upstairs. The first taking was greed on both sides, forceful and untender, till in the swift ebb, trembling, they could kiss with their claws and fangs resheathed.

"Has he no bed, then?" after long, breathing stillness. Dolvid could feel on his elbows the ridged patterning of the rush carpet, and all the smells of this space were coming to him, dust, oiled wood, the bleak odour of just-disturbed vacancy. The window under the colonnade was a dim square.

"Come." Getting to his feet he reached down to help her up, guessing where her hand might be. Forearms brushed each other, and he was far from finished.

Upstairs an *ôdu*, which must have been brought and set in its niche by a servant, gave pale light. Linaëyu, properly happy to possess the body she had, accomplished her undressing, and he his, all the while marvelling at her lithe brightness. Naked they were scarcely less urgent than before, but with less selfishness and more savouring.

Much later when he saw they were not going back to the feast, he said, "What about your daughter?"

"She can find somone to escort her. Or she may spend the night with, oh, any kin, or with a friend." Her calm suggested this was by no means the first time the girl, Khalú, had seen her mother vanish from a feast. Certainly, there was nothing unpracticed in any of Linaëyu's actions — a reflection which, past anything, gave a sense of his new eminence, not a pride he could be proud of. Only a short while ago, Linaëyu, wife of Khelagh, would have been beyond his reach.

She brushed hair back with a forearm, and looked down at him, eyes shining. "Is this how you are, the men of Narn?"

"I can only speak for myself. Linaëyu, I have never —
"

"Yes you have — " rebuking a sentimentality that would express gratitude in false superlatives. "I taught you nothing you have not learnt before. I prefer men who already know how to please. Well, Dolvidh, shall we go and join your herding-folk, and make hard love on hard ground, till you are tired of me?"

"Would you cut my heart out after a year?"

"If I had not already eaten it — " pretending to gnaw at his chest. "Do those people beat their women?"

"I never saw that."

"You are not afraid of me now."

"I never was," he lied. "Only afraid you might say no, or just walk away, after — "

"After what?"

"When wanting you had made a fool of me."

"You can no more master foolishness than Khelagh can a simple dance."

"What about him?" feeling the stir of ignored complications.

"Khelagh? What? Khalú was born on his forty-sixth birthday, and? When we married I was not quite nineteen, and Ghuradh is three years younger than Khalú. He was born in my fifth year with Khelagh — there is a puzzle in numbers a *manadu* of the *Mankh'* might set. What else?"

He took note she knew about his past. "Won't he miss you?"

"He is going north tomorrow, as I told you." Linaëyu explained her husband had already left Kadon Dinul, because the horses he needed for hunting were stabled at their country house.

"Would he miss you?" Dolvid insisted. "I mean, does he mind?"

"If I do not come home? We have servants. I do not wear the sash. When wind and weather are just right, and he has had a good dinner, not too heavy, a skilled *nôd'yanu* can stir up Khelagh even now. All you men want these delights as a bargain paid for and done with."

"Do we?"

She leant away in mock-astonishment. "I have won your devotion for all eternity, have I? Standing by my side, you wanted to bed the girl who played the *olútaloi*. Why didn't you? All you had to do was arrange it with Rhunsilakh."

"Then I would not be here with you."

"If not this occasion, another. And if I were not here with you, I would not be alone."

This gave an odd stab of pain. Yet he had wanted the minstrel-girl (and now would always want her).

His hands went on stroking smooth skin. He had told himself he was out of practice; the truth was he had never learnt Kadon Dinul ways. "Your pardon, I have not lived amongst the Families. The Residence Quarter is far more foreign to me than the Froghul. No, it is true."

She pondered this earnestly, and thought about the *Mankh'*. "Things you have to learn, Master. When a woman, I mean a grown woman, not a girl, says she wants a bout with you, if you say no, you must leave her. She may want to try elsewhere."

"I did not say no."

She put a hand to his cheek, first indication of the dozen years between them. "I am glad you came back to me, if that is

what you mean. But you refused me three times. Oh, come —
" as he started to deny it. "At least you must have guessed
women of the Families do not say, *would you go behind the barn
with me?*, like a farm-girl with a dyer's son." Her laugh became
tender. "We are not that blunt. Perhaps that is how we save
ourselves from the foolishness you were afraid of."

He struggled against feelings of untutored ignorance; no
help that he had been to Narn and kept up the appearance of
nerveless competence, dealing with Daënakh, Ott, the Loyal
Elders: not even the Pass of Perus mattered here. True, he had
known in his first five seconds with Linaëyu that she wanted to
be bedded; the trouble was, he often was able to recognise
people's desires sooner than they did themselves, or than they
would admit. What she said might seem true for her, but he
was not ready to believe here at Kadon Dinul was a world of
fearless frankness that left no pain behind.

"Your pardon," nonetheless. "I would not have refused
you once, if I had known how not to."

"Never mind," soothingly. "You have made handsome
atonement." She sank down, giving herself with a kind of
generous greed.

The Bronze Residence

"I would not want to be Bolan," Shumat said one day in Dolvid's quarters. "He has to go everywhere being *Narnai-Kindhri*. They want to see him kill Grenaspaluk after dinner."

Fame, it was true, appeared as worrying to Bolan as the chance of failure had been, and all the energy that went into attaining his eminence was becoming fear it could not last. With Khelagh for ally he had become a fashion of the Residence Quarter, but only a week after the feast at the Residence he had confessed how much he envied Shumat, who would be another Sebhal, preserving renown a long way from Kadon Dinul. For Bolan there was something unfair about Sebhal; he performed his feats glamoured by distance, came briefly to Kadon Dinul (now with a dazzling wife), then was gone again, long before his mystery began to wear thin. It must be a trick.

Shumat, however had no leisure for nursing a reputation. A long, mild autumn, but he was in a race against winter, struggling to put together the core for his new army before snows came to the Northeast. In the month since being named to his captaincy he had signed a few officers but come to admit most of his troops would have to be recruited and trained at Yuvakh Din and Narn. Yet he would not leave without assembling mounts and most of the equipment needed for a dozen squadrons; he would visit Dolvid to shoot a dozen rapid questions about supplies and their purchasing, and then be off again to see a saddlemaker or armourer.

"It'll be too narrow for you here, with your nose in books," he goaded. "Come with me." A serious offer, made more than once before, but not to be taken seriously; Dolvid, as well as working at an account of the campaign, was tutoring royal children in several skills, and could not very well tell the *rabhsai* he was leaving to take a post with one of the royal captains. Besides, while his mind often drifted lovingly to the excitements and even remembered hardships of the campaign, he was doing work that satisfied him, and scheming to do more.

Shumat, for once in no hurry, was lingering over cool *raminat* when Bolan arrived with news confirming all his suspicions about Sebhal, astonishing news. After a thousand years the lost ruby-mines of Shâl had been found again.

Dolvid had often thought a study of old documents might give clues to their whereabouts, but Bolan told him to save his eyes, there was no doubt; the messenger with the dispatch had also brought a leather bag of rubies, some big as a slinger's pebble.

Not easy to get the whole tale out of Bolan, who very nearly believed this latest feat of Sebhal's had been designed primarily to eclipse the fame of the *Narnai-Kindhri*, and diminish shuzi as a gift. Sebhal, patrolling Landegh, had reportedly given chase to a group of raiders from the tribes, and somehow become separated from his troops, who later encountered his riderless horse. A search lasting as long as they had food and water failed to find him, and for days it was feared he must have been captured, even killed.

The acting commander at the Frontier fortress, one Wanildhai, had made up his mind the terrible news must be sent to Saidhan, when Sebhal, having crossed waterless, pathless and hostile terrain on foot, appeared there with a broken arm and a pocket full of uncut rubies.

Even how he had rediscovered the mines was an annoyance for Bolan; Sebhal had fallen in through a thin crust of hardened salt, finding himself in a sloping entranceway. He managed to clamber out, but only to gather brush for making a torch. Returning, he found his gems amongst bones of men who died an age ago.

Much more than rubies, Dolvid wanted to hear whether Sebhal had seen any remains of the ancient town, Eshaël Asumun, where there might be valuable relics of the First Empire.

Bolan was pitying. "He was alone on foot eight days where the *jinzal* roam, sucking plants for his thirst. Rubies lying about like rubbish — they're not going to make ballads about a ruined town."

Beyond that, he predicted this was the end of the long conflict about the Army of the West. "Saidhan, naturally, doesn't desire a share in this wealth; the rubies are his loyal offering, and so forth. But the Mines are days outside the Frontier; miners will have to be guarded, and the way there. Kadon will let Saidhan have any numbers, ten new squadrons if he wants them, you see. Twenty."

He turned to Shumat. "You'd better pack your arms and

armour up, and get your *pefral* on the road, or Sebhal will steal them from you. You still mean to race the snows?"

He nodded. "If I'm not gone soon, it will mean waiting for spring. I wish there were experienced men to rely on."

This was an indirect renewal of the invitation to Dolvid, who reminded him the reliable Onebhal was at Narn.

"Such a pity," Bolan said, "you can't have the *Kímukan* Indhil, to make sure all the breastplates are polished right."

"You need him more." Indhil in fact was no longer in royal service. A strange case; his terror of being murdered had begun with disappearance of Stanni, the stableman, shortly after amnesty was announced. Indhil was certain Ott had killed the man in revenge, but when it transpired Stanni was quite alive, and looking for work in Sebira, Indhil's fear of being Ott's next victim only changed to certainty there were several people who wanted him dead.

Now Shumat grinned. "I am going to be lord of winter, no?"

It was clear what he meant; for the coldest months when nothing moved on the roads east of Sebira, that army beyond the Pass of Perus would be effectively an independent command. Momentarily Dolvid supposed that might be an additional reason why Shumat, not Bolan had been chosen — but absurd to conjecture a man would be made Captain of the Household because he was not altogether trusted. Possibly *rabhsayum* preferred having Khelagh's influence over Bolan kept here in the Heartland, rather than taken to the Northeast, especially with Khelagh the biggest investor in the shuzi trade.

Bolan made one of his rapid turns. "I would sooner be

here at the centre. The General Cavalry may have six times my squadrons, but it would take Merovas or any man a month to collect two dozen of them together. Readiness, not size, is what matters to an army."

"Readiness for what?" Shumat taunted. "Another uprising of the Craft Families?"

"All you have to do is send your squadrons back and forth on that cursed road." Bolan shook his head. "It may be our rise was too steep for the colour of our eyes."

Where had that come from? Dolvid found it exasperating. "I am here with two of four royal captains, and one of them has a seat at the Council of Thirteen."

"I want to get your thoughts about that. What do I know of policy?"

"Vote *aye* for confirming Shumat's captaincy. Other than that, follow Laluvoi." He imagined that would not always be Khelagh's advice.

Shumat said, "And if you want to be sure of your position, marry Sai-Nivu." Lambarr's second daughter.

"Not for a year or two."

"Well, while you're waiting, find a wealthy magnate's wife to sport with."

"This place is worse than any market for gossip," loudly. Shumat was all unconscious of awkwardness here; with Bolan there had been, so Dolvid thought, an unspoken treaty on this subject.

Or perhaps not; he joined the game: "What did you expect? The lady is a prize. Not everyone who asks shares in her pleasures."

"It would please me," Dolvid blustered on, "if the Residence had smaller attention for small things, and more for large ones. Look! this messenger comes with news about Shâl's Mines, and no one sends for the *uzh'freladhai*. What am I here for?"

Bolan was not put off his scent. "Is it true, as I've heard, the lady has more than a few ways to please a man?"

"You would do much better asking the lady."

"In time, in time. I want to hear a little of what to expect."

"Nothing to be afraid of, Bolan."

"Ha. You challenge me to take her away from you?"

"She is not mine to take away. She'll do what she decides to."

"Could you ever be that sort of husband?" — struck with the gulf that opened between him and his Residence Quarter friends.

"No," Shumat, thinking of Manda. "Those women are the cause of murders. They drag their men down, make fools of us."

"Their men make fools of themselves if they expect what isn't in the bargain." Valnoi had told him that, years ago, but it was easier to understand when the woman meant happy diversion rather than howling madness. "Not many at Kadon Dinul wear the sash."

"Listen to him." Bolan recovered his worldly pose. "A true *atarlai* of the *Mankh'*, everything settled by the rules. Take sporting lightly, and crow over your conquests, that's Kadon Dinul. Oh, she'll tell you how delicately we manage things here, and meanwhile every wife in the Residence Quarter will know to a fingerspan how much you have to offer. You may as well make a boast of her while you can."

There might be experience behind this, though Bolan, in what could be seen of his real life, seemed to feel safer with serving-girls.

Talk became fragmentary, not striking a common subject. They were not three alike, and had divergent futures; unlikely there would ever be another single enterprise to bring them together in harness. The expedition was really over, and when Shumat made a last token attempt to persuade him to go to the Northeast, he said, "I have my own campaign to manage, here at Kadon Dinul. You remember I told you about falsehoods in the *Song of Tales*."

"Yes. Yes," trying to be definite, but Dolvid talked about so many books.

"I am going to bring out a corrected version."

Bolan said, "The *Mankh'* is not going to cheer about that."

"That is the campaign."

Laluvoi's glance told the *rabhsai* Dolvid should be seated, and Laluvoi spoke. "The *Song of Tales*. I have heard there is already a book extant under that title."

"*Asayu*, I have chosen a somewhat different title." Best, he had found, to be forthright with Laluvoi, stopping short of disrespect. "*The True Song of Tales*."

"Thus calling the *Mankh'* edition, praised everywhere, untrue."

"My father loved the *Song*," Lambarr said.

"*Deghi* — " They were in the Private Audience Chamber, and Dolvid was close to both hearers. "*Asayu*, there was ridicule when I brought up the marvellous outshirt worn by Pir Perus. Now we have shuzi."

"Young boys often scorn what they do not understand," the boy's father placated. "I don't believe Banak-loi intended any offence, *bôdh'loiki*."

That was not Laluvoi's opinion, but she kept to the subject. "As the *rabhsai* says, Banak-rai was among admirers of the *Song*. I still have his copy, well-thumbed, with his comments in the margins."

"That would be worth studying, *Asayu*," calling on all his tact. "But if I may presume, Banak-rai of honoured memory would, I am sure, be first to hail restorations conferring new dignity and coherence on Gabhani history."

Taking a deep breath, he told the story of the excised portions in the swallow-riders episode, linking it to Daënakh's discovery of bones on Sebira Bay. He did not identify Pir's ruthless enemies as the Army of Owan, nor suggest the true tale had been deliberately suppressed. Lambarr said it was all most interesting, while Laluvoi sat regarding Dolvid with an expression halfway between smile and frown.

"Dolvidh. You have been made *uzh'freladhai*. Aside from your duties, aside even from your recreations, you surely have time to take this on, if you say it is worth doing."

So she had heard about Linaëyu. "I have, *Asayu*."

"Then why do you need special permission? Do we have enough parchment at the Residence?"

"It will not have escaped her attention my relations with

the *Mankh'*, and with those of the *Mankh'* having particular interest in history, are less than cordial."

"We have dealt with that," dismissively. "If loss can be measured by rancour, you came well-recommended. West of Treaty Stone the man is a power, but this is the New Residence."

"A great deal of the material I would need for the *True Song* is at the Bronze Residence library."

Lambarr looked up. "Yes, we share that collection. But you are not a prisoner here. The *rabhsai* is, perhaps, but not you." The year was latening for Tan Lughsai, and Saëdhu had not managed a pregnancy to take them south for winter. Discontent was hovering, and Dolvid went hastily to his reason for being there.

"*Deghi*, there is the question of admission."

"To the Bronze Residence? It is ours, the Household guards it. You can speak to Bolan, surely?"

"The Household guards the grounds, true, *Deghi*. The doors are kept by the *Atarlum*."

"Armed men? Of the *Adanum Plakh'*? Never, it would contravene the Treaty." A weak laugh. "Unless *g'Asalladh'* is living there. Even He would need our permission."

"In my years, door-duty was shared between auxiliaries with short-weapons, as the Treaty allows, and the *atarlal* themselves, or apprentices, with no weapons at all. They are enough to keep out anyone without a token from the *Mankh'*, unless he wanted to start a fight."

"You are of the *rabhsai*'s suite, and the Bronze Residence is his property," Lambarr said.

"Yesterday, the distinguished Master of Tongues was refused entry." Faëdhal, an eager confederate, had been boyishly delighted to provide the test-case.

It was, Lambarr said, scandalous if true. To his mother he repeated, scandalous. Laluvoi sat fingering the ruby she always wore on its fine chain.

"The *bôdh'loiki* could not know, could he," softly, "*G'Asalladh'* had just returned from the Island, and in all likelihood will soon visit us here?"

Dolvid did not speak.

"We were hoping not to trouble His age with fresh disputes. In the old days we were cat and dog, fighting — oh, yes, Dolvidhai, in those years Banak often was the voice of moderation; he feared I would go for *g'Asalladh'* with my claws. That is thirty years ago. The past is silliest of dreams." Swiftly she had turned inward.

"The *Atarlum*," Lambarr pronounced, "cannot be left to forbid the *rabhsayum* access to its own property. How can this ever have come about?"

Either Khelagh's name or her own gave Linaëyu ready entry to the New Residence. Not long after their feast-night together, Dolvid came back from tutoring Lambakh, and found her waiting for him in his quarters. She kissed him without a word, then took off her clothes, which were few. There was fierceness and also languor, and then she tried dangling bait, wanting him to demand more meetings. Contrary to her assertions about the frank ways of the Families, nothing was to be taken at face-value. Telling her to come when she could started a new game about whether he would not rather have a warning, in case he had another woman here. Her subsequent visits had been filled with pleasure, but she did not stop trying to get control over him.

"Next week it may be I shall go to Arbhu Hills." Where Khelagh had his vast estates and reputedly opulent country house.

"Then I should not expect to see you."

"Nothing is fixed. Should I be missed?"

He kissed her. "Yes. But I've got reading to do."

She gave a seductive squirm. "Aren't I better in bed than a book?"

"I am not going to give up reading so as to miss you better."

That caused reflection. Then, "Should a scholar be made so well for pleasing?"

"Your beauty inspires men to give pleasure."

"In the Court of the Ram, I nodded to your friend. He has a boy's smile. He looks very strong."

"Shumat? He is gentle, too. In Narn I saw him pick up a small child who had fallen in the street."

"Dolvidh?" on a note of enquiry, head on one side, chin tucked in. "I need not be only yours."

"That's true." Absurd; to begin with there was Khelagh. Was it because she was married that the sparks of jealousy were so easily snuffed?

"I follow my nature. When I begin to hate you — " she was affectionately stroking his chest — "I shall hate you, not say, no, Dolvidh has always been — what it is you have been."

"Why should you ever hate me?" disturbed by bland acceptance.

"You don't need me."

"I enjoy you, as you enjoy me. Isn't that better?"

"You're right. If you needed me, you would be boring. Does Bolan ever ask about me?"

"Why?" She must see more of Bolan than he did.

Hugely, she hugged him. "You are so ancient, and such a baby."

He answered her tenderness, knowing the fencing would begin again. But his side was nothing but parries.

All power was a riddle. Eight years, more than eight years ago Dolvid had first met *g'Asalladh'*, and seeing Him now marvelled that this frail old man could be in control of the *Atarlum*. He sat in the Oak-Wall Chamber gripping the arms of a highbacked chair as if to save Himself from drowning; the few strands of hair outside the close-fitting cap had gone from white to a shabby yellow. His forehead was shrunken, deep wrinklings around the eyes like crumplings of soiled rags, brown and dead grey. The lower face with its bird-boned jaw was stippled and blotched with dull discoloration, but the cheeks above their hollows were unnaturally smooth, with neither the fresh gleam of a baby's skin nor the muted glow of a woman's, but the shine of a painted wooden mask. The blade of nose jutting from the time-wrecked face was like a spar of bare rock in the wilderness of Naëni.

He was very nearly blind, and had needed an attendant to both guide and support Him to his seat. The *rabhsai* was there, and Laluvoi; Dolvid and the *Bôdhrai* Rhunsilakh, though not presented, were permitted to sit, and the *atarlai* who attended *g'Asalladh'*, one from his personal retinue, known by the dull-blue robe with its gold whorls, also acted as recorder.

Dolvid could not think there would be much to record, the more so seeing the Patriarch's fragility. Likeliest outcome here was to have the question referred to *Menadhi* for a later meeting, where the real struggle over the Bronze Residence would be.

They spoke in ordinary language, probably a habit acquired in early years; Great Banak had never become comfortable in the Owanilú. The Patriarch was vague and halting in reply to Laluvoi's enquiries about His summer on the Island, and did not make any reply when Lambarr said He must visit Tan Lughsai soon.

After *raminat* had been brought (*g'Asalladh'* slipped a little-finger into his cup to test the level), Laluvoi said, "We want to talk about the Bronze Residence."

"An emblem...emblem of sharing," Kamanasalladh said.

"It was meant to be," Laluvoi agreed, and recounted what Dolvid had told her, and how Faëdhal had been kept out.

"This," the *rabhsai* said, "should not be."

"No, no — must not be." Going briefly into the Owanilú, *g'Asalladh'* told the recorder His Will should be made known.

Laluvoi was far from satisfied. "Not enough for servants

of *rabhsayum* be permitted entry to the *rabhsai*'s own. The *Bôdh'loiki* Dolvidh is here, and he needs access to books and manuscripts."

This was harsh, and she softened it, laying a hand on the old man's sleeve. "A spirit of sharing grew between Himself and Banak-rai, and that should not be lost."

Hearing Dolvid's name, *g'Asalladh'* had frowned, groping for a memory. Now He sat in silence, breathing shallow. "Lost," He said slowly, "We wonder. In seeking accommodation, We might have lost the Way."

"*Shanu akan ga-Shaëdhu b'Asalladhit ôl.*" Dolvid had not meant to speak before invited, but had said it as a response many hundreds of times; *the One Way is the Way of the Father.*

Undead, the eyes came on him; it might be they could still discern shapes and movement. "Perhaps, but it is not unheard-of for the Way to change from Father to Father, and We may have taken for maxim what was meant as admonition: *Shanu akan ga-Shaëdhu-na b'Asalladhit y'ôl* — so long as the Father's vision is clear."

He laughed, an arid sound, but He was gathering renewed strength from this. "When I had my eyes they said I, with all Patriarchs, had *aën'modha*. Now, when I hear about the *aën'modha* of the blind it seems a thing people like to believe, so they need not feel guilty about having *modhum*, their ordinary sight."

"But He sees something," Laluvoi said.

"In sunlight, a stone thrown at His face, too late to dodge it. With a good lamp, a page of bold writing, held close to Our right eye, but I don't often do that; people are disgusted by such peering. If He had His eyes again, I trust He might watch less and see more. I do well enough without the suspicion and wariness I am deprived of."

"Better than most of us," affectionately, "He has used His eyes wisely."

"Laluvoi," Kamanasalladh changed course. "If you attain age, you'll find its consolation is not peace and the softness of what they call serenity, but being able to say exactly what you think. You, it is true, have had longer practice than most at that exercise. But what pleased you about Our Patriarchate was not its wisdom, but that it could be bent to the will of the Residence."

"Come," she objected. "I reverence His Enlightenment, but He surely has not forgotten how we bickered over every question."

"We agreed to call that sharing." The old man tasted it on His brown lips. "Very fine, but the concession was already made; others who had the Seat would not have let their *aën'modha* be argued-over, as it might be an ordinary opinion. Oh, yes — " He held up a hand, though no one was about to break in. "You can say Our *aën'modha* was to permit such debate. The Golden Seat is a cage, with blamelessness its bars. Your pardon, *Rabhsai*. Old friends have to have their gossip."

Lambarr stirred and coughed a little. With Dolvid, Rhunsilakh was hardly breathing.

"Change was past due,"

"Change, yes. But your Residence must stand for something, or lose any purpose. So, too, the *Mankh'*."

"Why should it not stand, as your *Mankh'* has, for conciliation?"

"Even a very long life is a short season. Any farmer can tell you what happens if good seed is not planted where weeds have been cleared."

Laluvoi said, "But there is the *Ramadilum* for healing, the *Nôdhilum* for joy, and the *Edhrodilum*, His own first home."

This was cryptic, and Lambarr might have thought old wits had gone wandering. Rhunsilakh was restless, too, but Dolvid caught the meaning, and shivered. From Laluvoi's list of Orders the *Manadilum*, the *Manadilum* of *Menadhi* was heavily absent; the Patriarch's reminiscences had turned into a warning; the weeds were the views *Menadhi* advocated, the glories of a past age of Owan, where pure blood ruled, and the Others were subject races. Dolvid detested and had rebelled against those views, but even *Menadhi* as Patriarch could hardly make history run backwards, except at the *Mankh'*. There were laws now for everyone, and the old system of Preference which gave all the best posts to those of unmixed Owani descent was dead; Shumat and Bolan proved it, and so did Arvus at the Treasury. So did the *rabhsai*.

Rhunsilakh brought them back to present business. "By His gracious leave, *g'Asalladhâo*, the library... "

The Patriarch came sighing back from wider speculations. "*Bôdhrai*, the Bronze Residence library, joint-property since Plakhsila's day, should be for all men of learning. The *uzh'freladhai* has been there, I wonder; does he want it all to himself? The Memory, surely, is ours too. Some say, not only at the *Mankh'*, ours alone."

Dolvid, encouraged by a look from Laluvoi, said he saw no reason why the *atarlal* who cared for the library should not continue there, side by side with his enterprise, auxiliaries of the Household for door-guards. "*Rabhsayum*, too," he could not help adding, "tries to preserve true Memory. Where Memory is false, preservation is no prize."

Laluvoi frowned at that, but *g'Asalladh'* cackled. "It may be more of a job than you expect, to set right what you see as false Memory." Then He moved Dolvid by saying, "As We told you before, take good care of your eyes."

"What then is decided?" Lambarr, impatiently.

The old man turned up his dry palms. "All that you want is yours."

"Forthwith?" Laluvoi asked. "His Will is to be known today?"

"As soon as We return to the *Mankh'*."

"Meanwhile, His servants at the Bronze Residence are to be informed of His intent?"

"My well-loved Laluvoi," a touch of asperity here. "Just as with your Residence, the *Mankh'* has its due forms. This is *Menadhi*'s particular concern, and he must be informed."

"Bolan has auxiliaries ready at this moment to act as door-guards," lying a little; her glance at Rhunsilakh meant Bolan should be so instructed.

The vitality was ebbing again, Kamanasalladh weary and sorrowing, at the same time petulant. Laluvoi was implacable. "He admits there is a wrong, then why delay an hour righting it?"

"Very well," the old man said at last, and again spoke in

the Owanilú to His attendant, telling him to write out an order for His signature, establishing the new arrangement.

He faced Dolvid again.   "He wishes this was an undertaking where the *Atarlum* could join you, assist you. We are a disappointment to those who think of Us as omnipotent."

Five years, he answered Faëdhal's question, and frightened himself, five years with all help they could hire or cajole, training their own apprentices and scribes. Since they could not expect much from the *atarlal* who knew the Bronze Residence library far better than Dolvid, they would have to master its arrangement, and bring together every scrap of writing belonging to the *Song of Tales*; preserved fragments in the score-alphabet, transcriptions, in Old Gabhanilú but using the letters, translations into the Owanilú, some in the Script of Shâl, first versions of retranslations into ordinary language, before the *Mankh'* editors began their work of shortening and falsifying. Much material was out of reach in the *Mankh'* library, but Dolvid, in his surreptitious early researches, had found mainly edited tales there, the ones appearing in the published book; the Bronze Residence had most of the fuller, often more coherent versions. Other sheaves were in the library of the New Residence.

That whole mass of manuscript would then have to be put in order, and all versions compared, to determine the earliest, or where no early version could be found, the best. What were simply variants, what differences were due to translation (and often, no doubt, as Faëdhal said with pursed lips, mistranslation), whether any particular omission had been made to avoid contradictions or with a darker purpose — all this would have to be threshed out, and the results put into the final language and as near a single style as could be achieved. Five years was not generous, yet a larger slice of his life than Dolvid had ever set or imagined setting aside for a single purpose.

When it occurred to him *Menadhi* might try to have much of the most valuable material carried off to the *Mankh'*, Dolvid told Bolan on his own authority the *atarlal*, in their comings and goings, must be prevented from taking manuscripts from the Bronze Residence — and discovered the ruthless Laluvoi, in her original instructions to the Household men, had anticipated him.

Necessary, the measure was resented, and there was an initial coolness between the *Mankh'* and Residence contingents. So as not to interfere with living and sleeping arrangements of the *atarlal* Dolvid installed his enterprise in the Old Audience Hall on the floor below the library, and did his best to make friends, seeing to it *atarlal* got small presents of food from the New Residence kitchens to enliven their *Mankh'* fare. Possibly instructed by *Menadhi*, they kept aloof, and on occasion indulged in a pettiness the *Kímukan* Indhil would have admired, such as refusing to let *Atarlum* ink be used, even to make a hasty note.

When Arvat Arvus-son heard that he had a number of ideas for retaliation, such as restricting *atarlal* to one inconvenient staircase, but Dolvid, recovered from initial anger, said they would go on being friendly, and had Arvat mix a large batch of ink. Arvus had suggested his son as an apprentice, and Dolvid had taken him on, assuming a portion of the father's intelligence and sense must be lurking under the boy's infuriatingly prankish manner. He showed spurts of energy but was easily distracted, and his elder sister Tellis would have been a better recruit. She came sometimes with her brother, and proved a patient and accurate copyist, but could not be there all or every day; she kept her father's house, the mother having died giving birth to Arvat.

Through a mild winter and into a long spring they laid out their task. Never having worked beside Faëdhal, he found their methods of tackling translation quite different, Faëdhal dogged after the single right word, where he was readier to trust context. It exasperated him occasionally that Faëdhal was so reluctant to go outside a text for illumination that might make a passage clear, just as his conjectures, based in knowledge of history or customs, occasionally scandalised the older scholar. But conflict was blunted by mutual respect and the relish they both had, for the work itself, as well as its distant goal.

In somewhat the same way the continuing struggle with Linaëyu for possession of himself was muted by shared pleasure. His life was going well, except he had no money.

As *bôdh'loiki* and *uzh'freladhai* his salary seemed generous to him; he spent nothing for lodging, and had no full-time servants. But it was all being swallowed up by the Bronze Residence, and as need for helpers grew he was less able to pay respectable wages. Faëdhal had his salary, and Tellis refused payment for her irregular services, but for all the searching and copying at least five trained scribes were needed. Rhunsilakh, anxious over cost of the eternal building work at Tan Lughsai, could not commit any funds. Bolan, hearing Dolvid complain, offered to approach Khelagh, but he vetoed that, and not only because he was bedding with Khelagh's wife. The *True Song* was not going to be flattering to the Owanil, and no one of the Families would help finance it without trying to influence its content; Linaëyu had often tried to find out exactly what this large book would be, and whether there was any truth in the rumour it was filled with blasphemies against the *Mankh'*.

Instead, he went to Laluvoi. In her suite at the New Residence, in a chair the years had made overlarge for her, she leant forward eagerly, discussing expenses with a keen appetite for detail. "This is a fine reward for the man who brought us shuzi." With spring large shipments had arrived from the Northeast, hungrily bid for by dealers and garment-makers; outshirts and gowns of shuzi were being worn in the Residence Quarter, where Khelagh would be richer than ever, and, as he heard from Linaëyu, Dolvid was seen as an extraordinary simpleton not to have made a fat profit for himself.

"We need not trouble the *rabhsai* with this. A little money remains at my disposal, salaries of people I have never needed — a keeper of accounts for my private expenses. We are pleased your *True Song* is going to give the Gabhanil their due, Master, but we Owanil still have things to teach the Others."

"*Asayu?*" — suspecting this was not the digression it appeared.

"The strain in our well-loved Banak-rai was father-to-son, and he managed to preserve notions from his grandfather's store of wisdom about what women were and how they should be treated. They, you may have heard, have grave suspicions of any woman who can divide twelve in four equal parts. Long ago, I told Banak I could keep my own accounts, and he said *then spend those wages on your frills*. On my frills! That very day we had been considering the aims and limits of the Pledgings, and also whether the *Mankh'* would ever meet our conditions for reopening the *manal*. And with that one-quarter of a Gabhani eye — less, his grandfather's parents had some admixture — he saw me as only a woman, pleased by *frills*."

"My impression is that even amongst the Gabhanil, those ways are changing. Slowly, though," he added, as she glared.

"Slowly, yes. Is it not true your friend the Captain of the Northeast was all-but forced into his hasty marriage, because he'd had the girl's maidenhead?"

"There, *Asayu*, I would venture Captain Shumat let old ways force him into what he already wanted. He is good friends with the girl's father." News of the winter wedding had come with the first shuzi.

"Sport before wedding spoils a girl — what savages! Unless she is marrying for position or property, any girl who takes a man before she finds out if he can please her is a fool."

"*Asayu*, I have heard men say the same about their own pleasure."

She sniffed. "Very well, but you men will find a way to have your little spasm, with any woman, or without one. You are pleased more or pleased less, but do not go undelivered. With a woman, not to reach finish may be less pleasing than never to have begun — am I making you embarrassed, Master?"

"Not so, Madam."

"I'm old," belligerently. "The old often become lascivious in their minds. Well? If Laluvoi names Dolvidh Vidukhat as the Keeper of Accounts she has never needed, will he use the wages for what is needed at the Bronze Residence, and keep his nose out of my expenditures?"

"*Asayu*, I shall account for every tobhai spent."

"Don't trouble me. If you had wanted to steal, you would probably have begun with the four tobhal it would take to have your shoes heeled. You are certainly not spending your income on frills."

He blushed, having meant to have the shoes mended. Linaëyu, also, had noticed them, and the general shabbiness of his wardrobe.

Having evidently bullied him enough in revenge for Banak's remark, fifty years ago, she complimented Dolvid on the excellence of his little history of the Northeastern Campaign, and asked if there would be other works while the *True Song of Tales* went forward. She was almost coquettish, asking, "Words, perhaps, about the War of the Widowed?"

That, too, he told her, was a large work, but one he had always wanted to write, beginning with the last three rulers of the House Gabh'Owan, from the death of Plakhsila to the death of Thral-Sivu, and of her son, Valplakh. History blundered into here and now; Valplakh was Laluvoi's first husband.

"A silly man," she reminisced, eyes inward. He wished

she would say more about that long-ago marriage, its end in the horror of the Ní-Tilagh, and how she, of purest Owani blood, came to decline her baKarguli suitor, and wed the tanner's grandson — whether it was true she and Banak had fallen in love years before, when he commanded the escort bringing her from the South for her wedding to the feeble Valplakh. Of those directly concerned in the War of the Widowed, fewer and fewer were left: Merovas had been a very junior officer, Saidhan did not often come to the Mainland and Dolvid might never have the chance to question him. Besides, with Banak dead, there were things only Laluvoi could tell, and still he could not break in on her private contemplation.

She looked up. "I shall bequeath my journals to you, *Uzh'freladhai*. They will come to you after my death."

"May my sight of them be long delayed."

"A lot there about the War. I lied less, writing to myself. Hardly at all, except where I could not tell what was true. Feelings, I mean, and the lies they make in our brains."

The interview did not so much end as peter out; Laluvoi abstractedly gave her leave, and Dolvid withdrew, taking a new and meaningless title, a new and useful income, and long thoughts about Laluvoi's complexity.

Arvat was twelve, old enough for an actual apprenticeship. Although there was no indenture, and the rank of half-master at sixteen was not Dolvid's to confer, he paid him as a full apprentice. He might not deserve it, and, with a father who lived simply despite high rank, did not need it, but Dolvid could well remember the pride of the first money he had earned on his own. The sister, Tellis, again declined any payment, with one of the smiles that came as a sunrise to her face, grave in repose. She never refused any task, and unlike her brother seldom waited to be told what needed doing. Besides Laluvoi she was one among few of her sex Faëdhal had ever been heard to praise, though in summer he once or twice deplored the frivolity of her dress, which displayed the litheness of the young body.

The father, Arvus, on his visits to the Bronze Residence, enjoyed renewing old dog-fights with Dolvid's father. What he was told about how the new *Song of Tales* would differ from the extant one became with him part of his case for abolition of the *Mankh'* and all its teachings, which, he argued, were nothing but the charter for injustice. Even today, he said, no one dared speak out against unequal division of the realm's wealth and privilege. A claim refuted by his own outrageous speeches, which could be offensive to Faëdhal, about Owanil magistrates giving judgements favouring their own race, the tricks by which the Old Blood maintained control of the best land, and for those outside that bond of bloodlines, the unattainability of high rank.

"Such as Master of the Revenues?" Arvus could be tedious in this vein, but he was never less than animated, and made everyone laugh with his tales from the Treasury, the landowner who tried to pay his taxes in flaxseed, of which he had bought cartloads on a false rumour of scarcity.

Others came to the Bronze Residence for the talk there, lovers of books, painters of pictures, one or two song-makers, including the plump, inoffensive cobbler of the Narn epic. Dolvid did not need telling the Bronze Residence was supplying something the New Residence lacked, but while flattering it also took away time and privacy. The Old Audience Hall was spacious and well-lighted with space for copyists and apprentices to work. Beyond an inner door was the smaller but still ample Old Throne Room, mantled in dust when first seen, but as everywhere in this edifice, with stonework richer and more skilful than the New Residence. With trepidation — this was, after all, where Plakhsila *Kímukoi* had sat in state — he installed writing desks for himself and Faëdhal. In choking billows of dust he had the heavy hangings removed, except at the end, flanking a low dais where the Chair of State had been, and concealing the archway to a small, narrow chamber, perhaps a place a *rabhsai* could have withdrawn for a few gulps of *raminat* in the middle of hearing suits.

Now he was no longer restricted, as in his *Mankh'* years, to surreptitious forays into forbidden subjects, the Library, on the floor above, was filled with potent seductions. Of his Three Mysteries, besides the Rise of Banak, which would wait for Laluvoi's bequest, and the Origins of *Jinzal*, not likely to be solved with documents, there was the puzzle of Plakhan's Bride-Quest, and the stranger sequel that left the Sword to his monstrous brother, Kanavakh; tempting to wonder what the library might contain from those years.

Other distractions were ready to leap into his hands; rambling, petulant letters of Plakhat the Exile, Dromladh's grandiose plan for a new port on Arnan, a memorandum in the hand of Plakhsila discussing the famous Oak Wall carving; Dolvid, keeping narrowly to his set subject needed sterner discipline for himself than he ever had from *Menadhi*.

When autumn came again the *rabhsai*'s daughter, Laloi, married Brodhai of Ân, and Kadon Dinul was filled with great of the realm. Ominous that *Menadhi* spoke the invocations at the ceremony, not *g'Asalladh'*, who was in ill health, and had not returned from the Island; there was open speculation He would never leave the Summer Palace again, except in death. Another absence was Sebhal, again due to unrest at the Frontier, and that was threatening only to Bolan, as always looking back over his shoulder, wondering how long his fame could last, resentful of Sebhal's elusive magic.

The troubles in the West were not grave enough to keep Saidhan and Doleni away from the marriage of their granddaughter. Saidhan was the same unaging, upright figure, weathered and smiling, cheered everywhere. Dolvid was present at the Residence when he complimented Bolan on his conduct of the campaign in the Northeast, and also praised Bradhinal, there for his brother's wedding. Saidhan was not lessened seen close, and Laluvoi ten years younger while he was in town.

"They may have been bed-friends," Linaëyu conjectured.

"When?" Dolvid challenged. "Saidhan worshipped Banak-rai. They were closer than father and son."

"Has a son never wanted to bed his father's woman? But she was not always Banak's wife, and Saidhan was of the Household. All women have eyes for young Household officers."

"She was Valplakh's wife then. It would have been treason. And what about their ages? Laluvoi was nearly thirty when Saidhan was barely twenty."

She coughed softly, and he felt foolish; there were more years between his age and hers.

"They say he was a handsome man. He still is." Dolvid let silence concede. Outside in the Garden Court a steady rain was soaking. Not many leaves were left to be beaten down, and afternoon was cool enough, after exertions, to lie together beneath a coverlet.

"What are you thinking about?" thrusting up on an arm to look down on him. "Another woman? A Deniant baby, perhaps?"

"What?" baffled.

"Tellis Arvus-daughter is about to blossom. She told my daughter she is going to marry you."

He dismissed it: "She will have several other plans before she gets to eighteen." Actually he had been recalling his doomed venture with Darborr in the fleece business at Dônshei. As never before to anyone he recounted for Linaëyu how Darborr's violent jealousy had made their partnership impossible.

"The wife of a Mixed? A sash-wearer? Dolvidh," she reproached.

"Radis was often taken for an Owaniyu. It was at her insistence we bedded together, while Darborr was off buying oats."

Linaëyu found that funny, too, but it was true: Dolvid had kept his distance for months. "I had known her before, here at Kadon — " and he told about the newlywed Radis, living next door when he and his father came from the South.

"And then, when you came to Dônshei?" she was enjoying all this. "The little boy had turned into a big boy, well able to please. She was then — ?"

"Not thirty. Darborr, too, was often drunk." Radis had claimed Dolvid with fierce passion, and then, threatened by her husband, ended their beddings with a chill abruptness that left him numb. The disaster of Darborr's speculation in oats, the destitute stranding in Irbat, had been things happening to someone else, and he had kept that wakeless sensation of being walled off from life, though Bolan's arrival in Irbat had taught him how to distract himself with work, a chosen goal.

He would have wished Linaëyu to understand: this was the reason he never demanded when (or even whether) she would come again, could not be provoked into jealousy when her eye wandered, had at a cost become proof against illusion of need. After Valnoi, after Radis, he would never again put his whole life in a woman's hands.

"Now I see. I see why at first bedding you wanted to know whether Khelagh would be annoyed. I used to think because of Bolan." She stretched her whole body, and with the closed face of a cat said, "There is a new officer in the Household, Dorrmas."

"A file-leader, who will soon have his half-squadron. He is short."

"He is very muscled. They say his swordplay is a wonder."

He gave a loud guffaw. The pleasures here were enough, without *tomorrow, forever, only,* all those invitations to misery. The time for Linaëyu to cut his heart out was already a month past.

One cold morning the *atarlal* were gone. Dolvid learnt there had been a minor disagreement over working space, not enough to explain the disappearance.

"I for one," Faëdhal proclaimed, "am not shedding any tears. There are men among them of laudable learning, but on the whole, as soon as we can train helpers of our own in care and repair of books, we are better off without them." He gave the smile of someone who wants sentimental communion. "Your father's craft, I may say, would be useful today."

Dolvid gave the rueful assent he wanted, but did not linger there. "The *atarlal* have been in residence here for a century, and coming to study for an age. The man who is in charge at the Paowanu *Mankh'* has not removed them for our convenience."

With *Menadhi* there was always a strategy, but the year tapered down with neither return of the *atarlal,* nor any clue what their absence meant.

Not long after Fire Days, the *rabhsai* came with no warning to the Bronze Residence, a dark afternoon, skies a dead weight over the snow-stippled fields of the Heartland, obscuring the whitened heights across the Estuary. Lambarr sauntered in affably with the unaccustomed stamp of booted feet and clatter of Household pikes, feverish buttoning of shirts amongst Dolvid's crew, hiding of half-eaten food.

"Grim weather," Lambarr remarked with a shudder,

stretching his hands to a small brass stove. "Tell me, Dolvidh, or you, Master Faëdhal, do you know of anyone who understands fireplaces? We might spend more weeks at the Cape, but when they light fires the Wooden Residence fills with smoke. The updraught, so they say. You would think a realm that has brought forging of steel and cutting of gems to new perfection might manage a fireplace, wouldn't you? Stonework is a craft we once knew better," he conceded, looking about. "You won't find this class of work today, eh? You could not get a horn razor into the joints by the entrance. A history could be written about stonemasonry."

Dolvid duly acknowledged the suggestion. Perhaps Plakhsila, in a curious way, had caused the decline. His immense rebuilding projects called for more masons than there were, and master-masons had been obliged to pass on part of their craft to many apprentices, instead of all of it to a few.

"They said I had lost my wits, building in wood," cheerfully. "But carpenters have not forgotten any skill — a Gabhani craft, mostly." He went on to sound quite learned on seasoning, matching grains, various kinds of joints, then winningly admitted his expertise came from Master Untimarr of Burantal. "You have met the man? A wonderful carpenter, despises nails. We were lucky to find him."

Dolvid at once remarked, when no work was going forward at Tan Lughsai, this Untimarr might come to the Bronze Residence, where various shelves and furnishings were needed. Faëdhal frowned, but the *rabhsai* was not offended, and nodded, though not making any promise.

"Books," gesturing at the piles. "How could anyone read them all in a lifetime?"

"These, *Deghi*, are just the ones needed for our present work. The entire Library would be beyond the reading of any life-span."

"It was of the Library we wished to speak," and the sudden plural was a signal-trumpet. "Banak tells me you have expelled the *Atarlum* from here."

Initial confusion was worse for failure to recognise *Banak* as Banak-loi. Lambarr's second son was nearly seventeen, but the diminutive had become part of his name, and Banak meant *Banak*, Banak-*rai*, not *Menadhi*'s dour friend.

"With all respect," working it out, "Your son, *Deghi*, is misinformed. If the *atarlal* return tomorrow, they will not be denied entry, or interfered with in any way."

"Why were they ever denied admittance?"

"Your pardon if my words were unclear. They withdrew voluntarily, we assumed under instructions from the *Mankh'*."

"Our son has it from *Menadhi* their position here was made untenable."

If the object of quitting the Bronze Residence was to cause trouble, *Menadhi* might well consider he had succeeded, just with this uphill effort for Dolvid. "*Deghi*," measuring phrases. "I would request to be face to face with *Menadhi*, in your honoured presence, to hear just how we have inconvenienced the *Atarlum*. This space was cleared to avoid encroachment. A speedy hearing, such as I ask, would prevent these vague and groundless charges from taking root."

He felt Faëdhal silently applaud, while Lambarr pondered from his height. "Oh, I don't see that is needed. If you tell me, and we can assure *g'Asalladh'*, through *Menadhi*, we have been more than fair, then that is our answer, and the *Mankh'* must make a meal of it. Nothing will be done here to hinder their return? No? Our son, I am afraid, can be too credulous, listening to Frog — to *Menadhi*. Naturally, I reverence His Enlightenment, as we all surely must." He made the pious sign, but there was no doubt he had almost used what must be his private name for the Patriarch-in-waiting, *Frog-face*. "Do you look for any break in the weather, Master?"

Bolan lingered behind to hear what the fuss was about; apparently he had taken personal command of the escort with that in mind.

"Banak-loi," he said, given the facts. "And *Menadhi*. But your coming here was approved by *g'Asalladh'* Himself. We do these things better in the army."

"At Yuvakh Din, you outranked the *Kímukan* Indhil, but he managed to cause trouble for you."

"It would be different now, I would be firm with him from the start. Firmness is all they understand, men of that sort. Firmness."

Across the room Tellis, copying, paused and caught Dolvid's eye. Bolan had struck a pose, one fist clenched, and Tellis looked ready to burst with suppressed giggles.

The Song of Tales

He enjoyed his work more than others did their recreation, had good friends, standing, enough money; he could always borrow a Household *pefrai*, and summers when his royal pupils were at Tan Lughsai he came to know the province better, and love its rich variety. Later he called those first three years back at Kadon Dinul his own *shuda'loi basibadhum*, little Blossoming Age.

Never as happy as memory, and change, came to make it seem. Then, he could never quite shake off a feeling of menace deferred; he derided the rumblings of Arvus about Old Blood and injustice, but was uneasy about how they dovetailed with the warning *g'Asalladh'* had hinted to Laluvoi. The friendship between *Menadhi* and Banak-loi was worrying; a distant glimpse, when riding, of the *Mankh'*, brooding beside the Inland Sea, reminded him there was a Will that wanted everlasting subjugation, and its main adversaries, the good and great who were aging, and would die, had no apparent successors.

Yet against all surmise *g'Asalladh'* got well, as well as could be hoped in a man of his age, and came back to the Mainland. Bolan questioned what difference it could make when the man was blind and nearly crippled as well as wandering in the head. Dolvid, correcting the last, had no real answer, except to note that Laluvoi could not ride at the head of lances, either, and never had.

One immediate effect was reappearance at the Bronze Residence of the *atarlal*. Nothing was said about their absence, and nothing more was ever heard of *Menadhi's* accusations. Later, chief of that *Mankh'* contingent was at-Dhanurai, one of Dolvid's former teachers. He was plumper than he had been, but not much changed, friendly, glad to tell tales about the old days, as if he had never swung a leather strap in his life.

A favourite ride each spring was eastward. The Royal Way, the Great Stone Road, ran on a sort of shelf, northward sloping down to rich pastures, pleasantly untidy brakes and patches of newer woodland, with the water-meadows of the Paowan beyond. Or, having crossed the short bridge across the Kadonu, foaming with the last of the thaw, a turn to the right led across fields into rougher country, mounting to the line of the Arbhu Hills, domed and welcoming. Here there were green vales with streams winding idly after their scamper from the uplands; he made his way among farms where a cup of milk bought at the dairy door was sweet with yellow cream, across pasture where cows feasted after doled parsimony of winter. Mares stood bemused while their young wobbled on treacherous stilts, or as muscles (it seemed) were swelled by soft huffing of the breeze, went bounding, dipping and tossing slender heads. He loved to find quiet, mysterious passes that sidled through the hills, or climb till he could look southward across the whole Heartland, in the direction of an unseen higher range he meant to explore someday along its whole length, from Burantal in the west to its eastward end near the golden city of Kanzan Tâl; Kafan Burantali, with the perplexing marshes of Shemugrân on its farther side. Or he might make a yet longer ride to the source of the Paowan River, and the wild mountains of Asekh, the empty province. Keeping to the narrow inhabitable strip to the north, he would come to more and higher mountains, and little-used, perhaps lost trails that clung to cliffs and threaded between peaks. With luck he could find his way into Lower Ân, and surprise Shumat by appearing at Yuvakh Din. This was only a dream-journey, when work was going slowly at the Bronze Residence, or he and Faëdhal could not agree on a word.

Once, he followed a grassy path leading him in long curves upward. He watched a speck that circled slowly against islands of white cloud, trying to determine whether a kestrel, or perhaps a peregrine, far afield from its haunts in the Hills of Burantal, where there were men who made a living trapping hawks.

Hoofbeats came hurrying behind him. By habit he reached back to touch the haft of his Froghuli knife, then twisted in the saddle to see a good-sized saddle-horse, no *pefrai*, urged hard by a small rider, a slim girl with light, billowing hair. She was dressed in what was the fashion for horsewomen of Family, a divided skirt, fluttering back, over close-fitting breeches. She had good hands, but used more crop than Dolvid approved. Farther down the hill there was another rider, a man, who gave a shout and started after her.

"Master Dolvidh, *Uzh'freladhai*," as she came up. He had no idea who she might be. She must have seen him at Kadon

Dinul.   She was Owaniyu, pretty, delicately made, with exquisite wrists, her face both proud and (as it struck him) sad. Yet the sidelong look she flashed put him in mind of Laluvoi in the mood for mischief.

"But I know all about you," answering his expression. "May I ask a favour, Master? Ride with me down the hill."

He jogged his big mount forward as the girl made her turn, movements quick and impulsive. The other rider was only a short way from them, a smooth-faced youth, perhaps eighteen. The girl was certainly not older than that. When he saw she was returning, the young man sat leaning forward a little, keeping his lips tight as they rode past him. They came to the hawthorn-brake at the foot of the hill, and the young man was plodding behind.

"Will you canter?" Wordless, Dolvid nodded, and they let their horses out, heading downhill on a long, smooth run, where turf was dotted with cowslip, celandine, and a small reddish flower he could not name. The girl knew riding, and he was on a big *pefrai* of the Household, tirelessly powerful. Light air slid by their faces, and when the girl whipped her horse into a gallop he stayed with her, the horses impersonating a runaway team, heads working, yet in hand, so that one will might control both. They skirted a patch of woods where leaves were fresh, and ahead was the Great Stone Road. Not slowing they reached the embankment together. The girl chose east. Hoofs rang on hard stone, pillars with the *ôdul* marching past. If she wanted he would ride to Kred Bakali and beyond.

At last, at a long curve overhung with lindens, she

slowed, glancing back. Finding no one following, she skittered to a walk, her hands sure, the horse plunging and threshing its head, as if angry to be slowed. Dolvid also pulled up, turning back to the girl.

They stood in the shade of the trees while a ponderous wagon went groaning by, heading for Kadon Dinul. "Good. I thank you for the run, Master Dolvidh."

"I should thank you. I do not have your name."

"The new cap becomes you." A leather one, Linaëyu's gift.

"As the breeze does you." Bright-eyed and bright-cheeked from the gallop, she was like a kitten when it looks up suddenly from a tussle with string.

"When I'm in Kadon Dinul, can I come to the Bronze Residence and watch you vanquishing parchment?"

"It might be hard for you to pass the doors, unless I can give the guards your name."

"I'll get in." The smile made dimples as her eyes flashed, and he thought, yes, she probably would. He was groping for a distant recollection.

"We have met, I am sure of it."

"Oh, yes. We've met. I have to go now. You'll see me at the Bronze Residence, but if you can't guess my name you will have to serve me four years and four months and four days and four minutes." This was from a nursery tale everyone knew.

"I shall learn it from a silver frog." In the story the

answer was *Yagha-Yeghut*. The girl's smile was very contagious.
"My thanks again, Master." She would ride due south.
"You'll be safe?"

"Oh yes. That was only my cousin. He wants to build
water-gardens. Farewell, then." She crossed the road and
picked her way down into a ferny dell, where he soon lost sight
of her. Dolvid gave a mental whoop, hoped she would keep
her promise to visit him, and started westward. He decided
this meeting was one of the happenings he would mot recount
to Linaëyu.

The young told time. Unchanging Faëdhal, seen every
day, Linaëyu, the other grown-ups met often, could make years
stand still, but not with the royal children, his chief pupil
Lambakh, learning lances on a full-sized *pefrai*. Or Tellis Arvus-
daughter, suddenly tall and graceful, even-tempered and
patient as ever, though more reserved, at least with Dolvid.

When he could, the master-carpenter Untimarr of
Burantal had been coming to the Bronze Residence, to make
shelving and work-tables they needed, and to oversee some
repairs. Dolvid had taken immediate liking to the man, a
Mixed in early middle life, broad-framed and broad-fingered,
but with a loving touch for the texture and finish of woods, a
cheerful man who had chosen (or been born to) the right craft,
and was assured in his skill, but with no vanity. Married, with
small daughters of his own, he was warm friends with Tellis.
When he returned that spring to make, for the walls of the Old
Audience Hall, large maps of the realm, copied in contrasted
woods from drawings made at Dolvid's invitation by at-

Dhanurai, the change in Tellis was easiest to read through Untimarr's eyes. He treated her now with a mixture of fatherliness and half-joking lechery, and there were moments of passing envy, seeing how easily they made fun together, sinewed hand often resting on slender shoulder.

When Tellis next came to the Bronze Residence, the puzzle of the chance-met rider, remaining with him as a pleasant sort of irritation, was solved. With her was the light-haired girl, older than before in a long summer cloak, hair clasped with a silver band. Dolvid saw who she must be.

She said, "I would not interrupt your labours, Master." The girls had passed through into the Old Throne Room.

Tellis said, "That would take more than us, than a hundred such as us." Dolvid took this to mean, young, attractive, and surely Tellis was becoming prettier, or became so beside the other. They made an appealing contrast, Tellis taller by a head, long-limbed, frank-faced, her energy all repose, while the other's taut readiness made standing still into an event. But she had mystery, too, and a danger. Softened by youth, the restless eyes and changing face, it was not as assailing as his first meeting with Linaëyu. But there, with her mother, the daunting self-possession originated. He mocked himself for the resolve not to tell Linaëyu about the horseback encounter. "Welcome," he said, "Khalú Khelaghilayu." Faëdhal, who had just mentioned they had gone a long spell of work without food, was trying to greet this interruption with courtesy appropriate to one of Family, in some way his kin.

"So, you have saved yourself my service."

A younger Dolvid would not have been able to resist the flattering reply; his greed was more cautious now.

At Faëdhal's suggestion they sat down together for food, and Arvat was permitted to join his sister and her friend. There was yellow cheese and fresh bread, no wine but cold fruit-drink, and Tellis had brought a few apples. Faëdhal amused Khalú and himself by tracing half-a-dozen ways they were related. Genealogy was a favourite hobby of the Families, as if the plotting of matings and cross-matings could wring a permanence from grudging time. Faëdhal's interest in bloodlines was altogether innocent; his own descent, he claimed in all modesty, was equal to anyone's outside the Great Families, but he did not believe that gave him any special privilege, and his conviction that to be Owani was by far the best existed happily alongside admiration for Untimarr, wary respect for Arvus, and real affection for Tellis.

Khalú was hungry, but without the voraciousness she had brought to the feast for the Victors of Narn, going on three years ago. She had also lost her bony look; when she loosened her cloak she was wearing a gown of light, flowing stuff which did not entirely come together almost to her waist, leaving exposed a startling stripe of young body, inner curves of her breasts smooth and separate. As they talked Dolvid wondered how he ever could have missed the resemblance to her mother; they tilted their chins in just the same challenging way, and both, listening, put on a serious face, head tipped to the left, his right. By accepted standards Khalú was more a beauty than her mother, whose face was too long for the ideal. Strange; amused by a remark of Faëdhal's about counterfeit bloodlines, she put a curled wrist up to her teeth; Linaëyu did the same when seized by unbearable final pleasure.

"We passed Captain Bolan by Harbour Gate," Khalú, a giggle in her voice.

"She doesn't have to tell everything," Tellis, gravely.

"He told me, cloaked or not, I would break the heart of a province. We see him at our house for dinner, quite often."

"No doubt an intended reference to the sobriquet, *Heartland*," Faëdhal offered.

"I'm sure he meant the compliment," Dolvid told Khalú. Amazing for Bolan to say such a thing to a woman of standing, his patron's daughter.

"But he knows so many lovely women," Khalú insisted.

"Flattery can always be doubled," Tellis observed, "with craft."

"You can't think how I had to build up my courage for this visit." Khalú had risen to wander about the room.

He got up and went to her. "Not many have seen this in the last century or so." This year was in fact the centennial of Plakhsila's death.

"Is this where *Kímukoi-Rabhsai* had his seat?" Horrified, he was afraid she would mount the dais, which no one did. She merely ran a hand lightly down one of the slender columns supporting the canopy. He told her the same Seat was at the New Residence, then as now resting on the ancient Axis of Owan, line of the shadow cast by the Spear of Yoëlladhu on Midsummer's Day at sunset, the straight course of the Avenue.

Carried westward the same line would pass through Treaty Stone to the Hall of the Patriarchs at the *Mankh'*, and also, it was said, to the Hall of the Golden Seat at the other *Mankh'*, the True *Mankh'* at the knees of Karg' Kamanta. Building the New Residence, Plakhsila had taken pains to be exact about the Axis, *Traëvu ba-Owanu*.

She paid attention, polite but not kindled. Soon she was bending to see the documents on Dolvid's desk, and spoke about learning to write the Owanilú "in olden style."

Tellis said, "The Script of Shâl, you mean."

"No, not that. Isn't there a different one?"

Faëdhal gave the list: "Besides at least one writing no one alive can read, there were the glyphs, ancient and middle, then the syllabary glyphs. Next came two modes of the true syllabary, which we call Pure and Broken, and after them the Script, primitive and perfected. There was a transitional script, before the writing we use today was adopted."

"Mainly borrowed," Tellis said, "from the Gabhani invention."

Khalú shook her head. "I'm sure it is not a Gabhani writing I want to learn. I was taught our letters were given us by a scribe of the Island."

"So it is said," Dolvid agreed. "No one can be certain, but his letters were probably influenced by, if not imitated from, the Gabhani mode which replaced the old score-alphabet."

"Then it must be the Script of Shâl," abruptly. "Is it hard to learn?"

"Middling." But important, because scholars of the

Atarlum had continued to use its fluent forms for many years, and still did, for ceremonial writings.

Faëdhal said, "Tellis, if I may say so, is not unskilled in the Script. Others would do well to follow her application." He stared hard at poor Arvat.

"I've said I would teach it to you," Tellis told Khalú.

"I can't learn it from you." Whatever this was meant to imply, Tellis did not show any offence. Dolvid tried to recall when he had ever seen her annoyed, or out of humour. Khalú, now; easy to imagine her in a fury, thwarted or denied.

"Come," he said. "I'll show you the Library, and some of the other halls, then I must get back to work." Tellis had said she could stay to do sorting of pages.

Khalú chattered as he led her through the sober old building, and made him laugh with faintly malicious, clever mimicries of self-important persons of the Residence Quarter, though not her father. Last, they came to the Square Gallery, near where wide steps went down to the principal entrance, tall bronze doors folded back. In a sunlit wedge of pavement the shadow of a Household pikeman could be seen.

She gathered but did not fasten her cloak. "Thank you for your courtesy. When I talked about needing courage to come here, I did not mean the building. A chance meeting with Master Dolvidh riding across our lands is not the same as going into the bear's cave. You have a soft growl." She touched a cool hand to his cheek.

"I was not making idle chat when I said I wanted to study the Script of Shâl, Master."

"Khalú," but with misgiving. "You may come when you want, and study with the apprentices, if you will give me a promise."

"Which is?"

"Your pardon, to dress in a fashion less likely to make our young men forget their studies. They are — young men."

"He is not past his prime himself," archly, very much Linaëyu. Penitently, she made him full deference. "I am the one to ask pardon. Tellis said I should wear soberer clothes."

"I don't mean this does not become you."

Again she bowed to him. "A man I met said the breeze becomes me better. Do you often ride eastward?"

"When I find leisure." The pointed reference to `our lands' lingered in his ears.

After a wait she said, "My father is amazed by my riding. It's a knack I take no credit for — I have always loved horses."

A pity one so delicious needed to fall into that preening mood, supplying and answering her own compliments when none came. Seeing his restlessness to be back at work, she fastened her cloak, saying, "When would you wish to school me?"

Whether she was aware of the other use of those words or as innocent as her eyes, he felt a stirring. "I can't teach tomorrow, we'll be busy with other things. Let us say, tomorrow a week."

"I'll be serious as an *atarlai*." She briefly pressed his hand, and went down the steps on quick feet. As she emerged into sun her smooth hair answered its gleam.

"To learn the Script. Few women, to my mind, have the application for these learnings."

"Don't say so in Laluvoi's hearing."

"Ah, Laluvoi *Asayu* is apart from any rules. There is little, if I can say so without presumption, that she could not do, if she chose to; that mind is good metal. These others with their scents and their rustlings — what is their place in our labours? Their strengths, it seems to me, are quite otherwise."

Faëdhal's favourable comparison of Tellis with her brother was evidently no threat to his general principles.

"I hear you have a new pupil." Linaëyu stretched sinuously, with the smug face that made him a prized possession.

He had not been looking forward to this conversation. With Linaëyu the right level of unconcern was practically impossible to find. He could hardly fail to agree her daughter was beautiful, but once he acknowledged that, she would charge him with making plans to bed Khalú. Or if he was stupid enough to say he had not noticed, she would ridicule him as a very bad liar. Last year there had been a pretty hair-dresser at the Residence whose moist-eyed infatuation he pretended not to see, and Linaëyu mocked him, virtually, into the girl's bed. Which he had enjoyed, certainly, but with the uneasy feeling of losing choice. Too reminiscent of the *Mankh'* and *Menadhi*'s condescension, pleasure provided to confirm ownership; best to say the least he could.

"You are very silent. Has Khalú's blossoming struck you dumb? It all happened in just this last year, not even that; she doesn't feel her power yet. She was full of your courtesy, and she admires your strong neck." Linaëyu caressed it.

"Does she know you and I are friends?" He thought he could detect both pride in what the daughter had become, and envy of her youth.

"Who does not? I have not recommended you to her, if that is what you mean."

Nearing their allotted year three times over, Linaëyu was a profound enigma. She never had the smallest intention of leaving all the comforts she enjoyed as Khelagh's wife, yet it amused her to behave as if Dolvid was the one deficient in devotion. He had adopted her way of cool distance in considering matings, and could not tell whether these conventions stood for her real feelings, or masked them. For himself he often questioned what he had ever needed with yearning songs, vows of eternity, the pain they guaranteed. For bodies, he and Linaëyu were wonderfully suited.

She had often told him he must find a wife, but always in terms of property and position, and he could agree tongue-in-cheek, not setting a date. She also liked to talk about leaving their smoothed paths, riding off together into the wilds, bruising passion with nuts and berries for food, but those were only noises that pleased her, a tug at the halter to be sure it was still there.

Now she teased him expertly into a new assault, and he knew he was being expertly pleased, while wondering what had happened to him, that his thoughts could continue to go in circles as he worked on Linaëyu's wet body. When with a slew of eyes her wrist went to her upper teeth, his eyes played a strange and even frightening trick.

"What, Dolvidh? Not good?" In the afterstill he was sad enough for a realm's misfortunes, but he reassured her with a forced smile, and asked forgiveness: he was preoccupied with a hard choice. He was going to have to dismiss one of the Bronze Residence apprentices who simply had no aptitude for the work.

That tale was real, but its use here was a lie. The truth was much worse. Somewhere almost out of his sight, as certainly out of Linaëyu's, he must be keeping the desire for obsession, abject madness, scorch of necessary kisses.

Slipping her summer gown over the new shift of pale-yellow shuzi, she said unexpectedly, "You must not publish your *Song of Tales*."

"Oh? That will disappoint the *rabhsai*, and Laluvoi."

"As you now plan it. Khalú found out from Tellis how far you mean to go. Too far, Master. Perhaps the *Mankh'* can't harm you now, but it will ruin you with the Families."

"What have the Families got to do with me?"

One foot half into a shoe, Linaëyu froze, with incredulous looks chasing across her face. "Don't make foolish boasts with me. You cannot count on Laluvoi's protection for ever. Give up your *Song of Tales*."

The summer was like his last at the *Mankh'*, hot and

rainless. With half his pupils at Tan Lughsai there was time to go riding with Khalú, recalling again the summer of Valnoi, though now he did not share the saddle of one docile and aging piebald. A dozing giant, thunder snored often in the afternoon, while distant ghosts of clouds towered grey and silvered blue in masked blue of the hot sky.

Partly because of the heat of the day, partly to make up time spent with Khalú, he began working deep into night, awed by the shifting silences in the vastly empty Bronze Residence, but not uncomfortable with his awe. He installed a camp-bed in the narrow chamber behind the dais in the Old Throne Room. After brief sleep he would wake to refresh himself with cool fruit-drink or *raminat*, then going downstairs to heat water for washing before walking across to the pie-shop for a breakfast, with Harbour Way still waking under pink and pallid blue. Apart from a mattress and well-worn sheets, a single plain chair, his bedroom had no furnishings, and Faëdhal, after one sight, decided to pretend it did not exist. To him, Dolvid's failure to keep up dignity fitting a *bôdh'loiki* of the *rabhsayum* was a perpetual vexation.

There, on a still evening, Dolvid first bedded with Khalú, not long after her third — and, as it happened, last — lesson in the Script of Shâl. He had wanted her ferociously; just the fidget of a knee under a summer gown was an urgent thirst for him, and when, as her habit was, she rested fingers lightly on his forearm, the print of them burned. But it was not easy to admit his feelings, and especially while he assumed she had not yet broken the colt. Once she had given him a plain hint that was not true, it came clear how far imagination for him had galloped ahead of events or sober expectations, and when he asked if she would stay she gave a simple, placid answer, "If he wants that."

He ended puzzled. Not passive, she did not pretend to be an adept, but was eager to give pleasure. Signs of her enjoyment appeared, but no matter how long he deferred his sprint there was no signal from her, no gathering of joyful urgency to which he could match his own. He felt accepted, and rediscovered for the hundredth time his best pleasure was in pleasing. He did not mistake this for unselfishness, seeing how easy it would be to blame Khalú for not allowing him the gratification of giving her joy.

While his mind wrestled in silence, she sat up to say, "Now you have to tell me your secret." That made him laugh, but tenderly; she was very young. She gave no signal of a wish for renewed sport, and at last said reticently, "It's the knowing that matters, isn't it?"

"No." His answer was forceful; not what he believed, not even Khalú's own thought; the tone was echoed, he could imagine from where, a spotty Residence Quarter youth, indifferently armed, mouthing a wise-sounding motto to divert attention from his own ineptitude, or lack of sustained enthusiasm.

"It can become better, if you'll tell me what pleases you best." That in turn he had heard from others; Bolan talked boldly of catching a filly young and training her, but Dolvid had almost always been with women older or more experienced than he. With patience, there might be an answer in Khalú to the upheaval she made in his blood. Patience would be easier to find if that appetite came from or had anything to do with liking her.

"Does my mother satisfy you better?" Her eyes were guileless, but the question was not, could not be. He turned away; she must realise this was unfair.

"Does she?" she persisted.

"It seems I please her more," coolly.

Khalú made a vigorous lunge, to start collecting clothes. "I'll go. I am nothing but a burden to you, with my dullness."

It would indeed be a release for him if she would go back to her Residence Quarter, the slack-necked young men, their simple enjoyments; to be drawn into Dolvid's finicky world was misfortune for a girl whose smile, nothing else, would make any other man grateful. She should follow her mother, marry wealth, live in complacent, easy railing against the narrowness of her existence.

He caught her wrist. "No, stay. It's getting late."

"I do not need your kindness, Master."

"My kindness!" He drew back to contemplate her nakedness. "Are there no mirrors where you live, then?" Arching her neck a little, she could not fight off her pleasure, and he felicitated himself; it was nicely said. For his sane remnant, however, she was quite right; it was not enough.

She stayed, and in the end fell asleep, his hand under her, so he did not dare get up, though there was a point in the Annals he wanted to verify.

Because he seldom slept there he had been making arrangements to meet Linaëyu at set times in the Rose-Stone Wing. One afternoon he was delayed by Bolan, who wanted private talk.

It was shortly before the provincial gathering that took place six years of every seven, the Little Pledging. As Captain of Household he was expected to sit on various councils, and at first Dolvid was sure he wanted advice, as usual, about laws or customs.

Instead, he spoke about the open magistracy for a district just this side of Kred Bakali. The name of the tax-gatherer Forrlas was before the *rabhsai*, but Bolan produced the copy of a plea, framed with care in proper legal terms, praying the magistracy should go instead to one Ladh-Sivai.

"How is it," Dolvid asked, sounding to himself like Arvus, "only nomination of an official of Other Race is ever challenged? And the rival name is always Owani. This Forrlas — wasn't there a petition against it when they made him tax-gatherer? An army man."

"That's him. He was an under-captain in the General Cavalry. Merovas supports him, as you would expect."

"Who would not?" having just identified the other name. "Ladh-Sivai — that's the one Arvus had to fight a duel with, and wounded. He refused to drop his absurd accusations of theft, even after Arvus had been completely cleared."

Bolan nodded, observing he could not count on much support at the Treasury, either.

"How can he even be thought of to administer justice?"

"All that was long ago," thrusting out his lower lip, and with a shock Dolvid realised he was supporting Ladh-Sivai. "He is widely respected. Rhunsilakh is not opposing this plea."

Is not opposing, Dolvid noted. It must be an awkward matter of kinship. Brighter light dawned. "Isn't he married to Khelagh's sister?"

"No. To the sister of Khelagh's sister's husband. He is cousin again, a different way, to your Linaëyu. He's got a lot of powerful friends."

"Apart from being born with the right relatives," more Arvus than ever, "what qualifies Ladh-Sivai for this post?"

"You know how these things are. No one is trying to take away the post Forrlas has. But as they say, it would make things fairer, with one of their own for magistrate."

To redress, understood, assessment by one not of their own. He had often listened to Arvus complaining about the madness where rich men were magistrates over their own lands. The district Ladh-Sivai wanted would adjoin Khelagh's.

In his rooms, surely, Linaëyu was waiting, and it was a puzzle what was wanted from him. Not support for this plea?

"I can remember," he told Bolan, "when you were the one trying to persuade me Preference was not yet dead in the realm. Perhaps not, but it could be, if officials were not influenced by wealth above justice." This stopped just short of calling Bolan corrupt. Quite possibly he stood to gain nothing material here, nothing but continued acceptance and approval by Khelagh's circle — but that was a corruption more profound.

"I stand against Preference, all right. How could I not, with my face? This is a particular case, where those who have aided me want my help. But the Captain of the Household can't openly support Ladh-Sivai, and my friendship with Khelagh is certainly no secret. Once we get this plea in, you could take my seat on the Provincial Council the day this comes up." Back in his old manner, he grinned. "The Council and the Province would both benefit if you were there in my place on any day."

Flattery, but there was no chance he would support Ladh-Sivai. His reasons ought to be Bolan's, but instead he made a point Bolan could understand. "How is it better for me? I am equally suspect, for my friendship with Linaëyu." Which was in peril, as minutes went by.

"But you don't command an army. Besides, it's common knowledge this other *Song of Tales* of yours is a long love-letter to the Gabhanil. No one is going to say you're biased in favour of the Owani candidate for this magistracy. Between friends, it wouldn't hurt you do a favour for the Families. Hrafi's elbow, you're Owani, you could have an honoured place — "

"I thought I had."

"In their opinions. A little bending doesn't cost anything — you're too stiff-necked, always were. Look at me, I'm Captain of the Household, I'm my own man, and being in with the Families only helps that. With the best of the Families, it's not how Arvus thinks. They're not against the Other Races, only when it becomes Preference stood on its head, an illiterate lout in authority just because he's not of the Old Blood, anyone can see that's wrong. The best of Owan is what they want, whether it's found at the *Mankh'* or in a Mixed cavalry-captain."

All this was so completely unlike Bolan it could only

come from Khelagh.   Just the same, chilling to hear in this mouth the same cant *Menadhi* had spoken, years ago.

"What is found at the *Mankh'* is not what is needed in a magistrate. If I take your seat in Council, I'll vote against Ladh-Sivai."

Bolan started to become agitated. "When you sulked at Irbat, you weren't much good to anyone. The same with this book of yours."

The reference to Irbat was easy to read, a reminder of how he had come here, what he was when Bolan adopted him. How that resembled the *True Song of Tales* mystified Dolvid.

"You keep telling me all the good it can do for the Others. First it has to be brought out."

He covered quick anger. "Are you telling me Khelagh and his cronies could prevent publication of a book to be brought out with the *rabhsai*'s seal, and under Laluvoi's direct patronage?"

Bolan considered, but with a touch of the wild-eyed look he had in the Northeast when tormented by possibility of defeat.

"At least read the plea, you can do that for me. Bring it with you when you come to the New Residence. You can give it straight to Laluvoi, she will have the Council that day."

"Very well," tucking the controversy away with the pages, wanting to be with Linaëyu.

He was not far behind Bolan's half-file of Household on the Avenue, and entered the Residence courts on the same opening of Pefrai Gate. Leaving his mount at the stables, he hurried to his quarters.

The scent Linaëyu always wore to their beddings was on the air, but she was not there; she had come and gone, leaving a brief note:

I meant this meeting to be our farewell, Master, but

now words must say it. Be as kind to others as you

have been to me. My thanks, always, for everything.

May you prosper.

She signed only her initial.

He could hear those thanks in every tone her voice had, from tenderness to a shrivelling sarcasm; a light half-irony was perhaps the one, with the characteristic dip of her head. He hoped their nearly three years of afternoons had left memory to make gratitude sincere, but Linaëyu had capacity for rancour, and if he asked her why could answer in one word, a name.

A shock without being, as he weighed it, a surprise. An oddity was the purple ink, an expensive luxury not kept at Dolvid's quarters; Linaëyu had come here with her note already written. Determined, that meant, to say goodbye, whether she saw him or not.

He supposed she was right. Even in the Residence

Quarter a mother and daughter were not bed-friends to the same man, or if so it was a subject for shocked gossip, once known. Evidently what was scandalous described and discussed might be entirely otherwise when happening. If it were not, he would have seen in advance he could not bed Khalú, not once, without losing Linaëyu.

She was lost, there were no rewritings. Even if he broke off with Khalú (which, on its merits, he had already come close to doing), he could not bring Linaëyu back except by destroying what he wanted to restore, a pairing free from debts, demands, recriminations, unequal needs.

He wept a little, and stopped when he had to admit he was oddly enjoying his tears, as a sign he could still feel pain.

Pairing with Khalú was losing race after race with a last surge that fell just short; he was never quite good enough to make her happy, and not sure why he wanted to be. Her enthusiasm for his lovemaking never went beyond acceptance, and if mating meant so little to her he could not imagine why she wanted to be with him.

He had never been less deceived; Khalú was beautiful but that did not blind him; he could easily have made a list of what he disliked about her, as she should about him. Their being together was mad: if it had been the force joining stallion to mare, buck to hind, with no need for a match of tastes or opinions, proof would lie between sheets, and did not. Once, twice he truly pleased her, but she did not look for ways to make that more certain; he suspected she was afraid to depend on him for such potent joys. Yet with all his clarity, it was his words that most often brought them or kept them together; he would hear his voice tell her no, he did not want to be left alone with his studies, although that was exactly what he did want. In the northwestern corner of the city, Old Town, there were women who, for a payment, could take away an enchantment. Dolvid had always derided such things.

Laluvoi came back from Tan Lughsai, cheered in the Avenue by crowds that grew more affectionate each year. Dolvid saw her next day, and gave her the written plea left by Bolan. Something he did may have betrayed the hope she would put it by unread. Almost, but she glanced at the top page, tilting sheets to catch the light.

She half-lifted the page, frowned at later passages, and jabbed in Dolvid's direction with the sheaf. "Ladh-Sivai? You give me a petition favouring Ladh-Sivai?"

"I brought it here, *Asayu*."

"Dolvidh, do you know a flower country folk call blue-beggar?"

"Three years ago, at the feast for Narn, she wore a robe the colour of blue-beggar. It became her very well."

Laluvoi made the noise of a sneezing cat. "Flatter the old sack of wrinkles and she'll do anything for you, is that what they say? Well, do you know how the weed came by its name? You see, like any beggar, it keeps coming back, no matter how you mistreat it. Chop it down, burn it out, dig it under, pull its roots out, it comes back blooming. Preference is another blue-beggar, so I have found in fifty years of battling it. If the *Edhrodilum* could give us wheat as stubborn, we would never have hunger."

"In many regions, *Asayu*, the weed can't come back, because of the healthy crops sown by Banak and Laluvoi." This was, he remembered, the same metaphor *g'Asalladh'* had used.

She shook the pages of the plea. "So, the battle is won, is it? With the country folk I say just one season of neglect could let this weed overrun all our fields. I thought you were with me in this, when you told us how you would improve the *Song of Tales*."

"So I am, *Asayu*. It is my contention false Memory steals greatness from the Others. Restore Gabhani history to its rightful stature, and the theory of Preference is deprived of the lies that — "

"Its rightful stature!" She tossed the pages onto the table by her side. "And now you bring me that. Great Hrafi! the husband of that bed-friend who is stealing your wits has been trying thirty years to throttle the Heartland with his skein of magistracies. Besides, the other man, Forrlas, has good law, and has served honourably as a tax-gatherer. Ladh-Sivai, what is he?"

Explanation was overdue. "*Asayu*, I agreed to bring the plea here, that is all. I am not an advocate for Ladh-Sivai's appointment."

She screwed up one eye. "You oppose the plea, then?"

He had warned Bolan he would say so if directly asked.

"*Asayu*, I made plain my sympathies were all for Forrlas."

"To those who framed this plea you made it plain. With me, you would say nothing, let me assume you too favoured their man."

Dolvid did not speak; he would not give away Bolan's support.

"Master." Laluvoi sighed. "You must marry. It is time. After the knowing, as they call it, is done with, a wife does not lead a man by the bowsprit, as a bedfriend often can. I do not enjoy seeing you made into a fool, Master."

On Midsummer's Eve he was with Khalú on the Avenue of Treaties and she was light-footed and restless, clothed in airy fabrics the misted green of water-meadows at daybreak. Everything delighted her; there were not the dense crowds of Great Pledging, and not nearly as many entertainments — many of them, like the *rabhsai*, must have gone instead to the Great Pledging, this year at Nivu Din — but jugglers were here, sellers of trinkets and sweets and charms. The Marionette Guild of Burantal did scenes from Banak's life, especially the youthful exploit when, with a few men following, he left the Colony hoping to find shipwrecked Dromladh, riding down into the forbidding Lunu Tezh' by way of tall mountains and dense forest. Most episodes were pure invention, an encounter with a talking serpent, fighting with bandits, outwitting an evil dwarf, but after several of the traditional, slower-moving pageants from sober history, the fable was loved by the crowd — and did more to keep Banak's name alive, Dolvid reflected, than any history he could ever write.

In one scene the puppet-Banak accepted the guidance of an immense, garrulous raven with huge flapping wings. Amid the mirth Dolvid was watching Khalú. She'd had wine and in lantern-light her face was slightly flushed. Strands of hair curled over her forehead, and the eyes were wide with wonder, her lips parted. He was touched by trust, the childlike surrender to this spectacle; this defencelessness bound him to her, made him lie when she guessed he wanted to be rid of her. He had a sharp wish to lose himself in her innocence; if he could not be part of her amusements, he ought to be generous enough to love her enjoyment, cherish her as a lovely fact. It was surely worth desiring.

As she turned to him, eager to share her excitement, Faëdhal threaded his way through the crowd to greet them, and give the marionettes his conditional approval. Then he became confidential.

"Ah — you will pardon me, but there is a tale you declined to advocate the magistracy for Ladh-Sivai. There is, true, too much idle chatter, but Rhunsilakh would not deny the rumour."

"Bolan asked me, and I said no." Dolvid had been dreading this; Faëdhal, too, was related in some way to Ladh-Sivai.

And was nodding judiciously. "You were, if I may say so, quite right. The man is a fool, not fit to judge a foot-race. The other, besides, is spoken of as very worthy. Ah — there is no need to tell Rhunsilakh I said so. Although... " smugly amused.

"Yes?"

"I might venture Rhunsilakh is not altogether displeased; Ladh-Sivai would not have been, we now discover, his own choice. You have done well."

What he meant was that in an odd way Dolvid's standing with Rhunsilakh had been strengthened.

Faëdhal went away up the Avenue, and Khalú said, "You were the one who spoke against Ladh-Sivai?" The man had been asked to withdraw his name from consideration.

"What I say is of no importance. Laluvoi was against it. The man was not the better candidate."

"He is my mother's cousin."

"His kinships were not the issue."

"I see they weren't." She was actually offended.

"Preference, have you heard, was outlawed over fifty years ago."

"My father says Other Races own three-quarters of the farms, and never stop crying about injustice."

"Three-quarters of the farms with one-tenth of the good growing land. Arvus can tell you; the sixty biggest properties have more acreage than all the rest together, and almost are all Owani-owned."

"What else would a Deniant say?" she demanded. "But he's speaking out for his own, and you're not. When the *rabhsai* gave you your post, why didn't you tell him there must be someone better than you, a Gabhani?"

"Because I knew there was not, not of any race." His proud, angry answer startled him, and he was not sure he believed it: he had often wished the *True Song* could be altogether free of Owani condescension. "Three out of our five apprentices are Others." A fine example.

"Master — " Her use of the honorific was in sarcasm. "Are you wisest of all? Who gave you a warrant to rescue the Other Races?"

"Laluvoi, not only to me." True, but indiscreet. At the end of the discussion about Ladh-Sivai, she had told him to be alert for instances of what she called closet Preference, and bring them to her attention.

Khalú's face was experiencing the struggle Laluvoi always caused the Families in these questions; most revered living member of the race she was betraying (so they maintained).

"My mother said you had mastered everything but loyalty."

He did not seem to have any answer; his one-shoulder shrug, long thought cured, infuriated Khalú. They had been moving up towards the Disc, and she halted, gesturing down Market Way. "You could probably hire a week-wife of your favourite race. She might charge nothing, in gratitude for your noble works."

She wheeled and went back down the slope of the Avenue. Without loss of dignity he could go after her, saying it was not wise to go unescorted during Pledging. That was absurd; she was twenty paces behind a mounted watch who did not need torches on the amply lighted Avenue, and the pillared house of her father was not far.

There were many throngs, cheerful knots of farm-folk, a group of dancers, couples walking arm-in-arm. Khalú soon vanished, and he considered taking her last advice. The pleasant simplicity of mating and farewell would be very sweet. He could not remember why, when Linaëyu was his friend, he had ever been wistful for more consuming throes. And now, if she had really said what Khalú said, she had begun to hate him, as she used to say she would.

He must have dreamt about Linaëyu. Wakened by knocking at the inner door his mind, or the part of it where dreams writhed on, expected her to be there, though she never came that way, but always through the Garden Court.

No, a servant sent by the *Bôdhrai* to reinform Dolvid as a *bôdh'loiki* he would have a part (or an allotted station) in the day's ceremony, noontide declaration of *Shuda'sai*.

G'Asalladh' was mostly too infirm for these occasions, and Dolvid hoped the speaker for the *kolukezh'* would not be *Menadhi*. He was yet to work out a way of dealing with their encounters, usually brief and wordless. It was *Menadhi* who ought to be abashed, but that perception refused to translate into behaviour, and Dolvid was always the one who averted his eyes. He had a distaste for, nearly a horror of holding authority over others. Command, for a worthwhile object, was allowable; it was power for its own sake he recoiled from, whether as master or mastered.

After the servant left, a knocking came at the other door, downstairs. Bolan, in a crisp new tunic, who had come to jog him about *Shuda'sai*.

Dolvid brought him inside. "Mistrust of my ability to keep the calendar seems to be widespread."

"Now where could that come from?" glancing at pages on the work-table table that had kept Dolvid up to near dawn.

He accepted cool *raminat*; the day was going to be another hot one. "The comments I hear about your absence from feastings and dinners are not praise for your industry."

"Then I have something in common with Lambarr."

"No jokes, Dol, this is no joke. Who was the one they took the Sword from? With the nasty ways?"

"Kanavakh *Vakh'biSegh*."

"Aye. I'd give you odds he was no good at feasting. He could have been all gore to the waist, but he would never've been deposed if he'd known how to slap backs and look happy in company. Lambarr *Deghi* is no Banak, but he puts people at their ease. They'll forgive anything but gloom, shyness, being too good for them. Take it from me."

"All right, but I don't have a *rabhsai*'s duties." He was at his table, making a note. Bolan's point was overstated, but well worth remembering.

"I didn't say that to help you do more scribbling," Bolan growled, but was pleased.

"Not scribbling is the one thing an *uzh'freladhai* ought to be blamed for, never mind his hand on the wine-flask."

"You live in the same world as I do."

"Very well. As soon as the *Song* is finished I'll give a big feast at the Bronze Residence, and when everyone is there have the doors barred on the outside, and read my works to all my admirers."

"Be sure to wear the blue velvet."

"I've got new clothes for today, brown and silver. You won't see me through the crowds of women."

When warmed water came Dolvid washed. Good to be

in a lighter mood with Bolan, but puzzling what could have brought him. He was at the table again, reading Dolvid's note. "I've often thought, if I'd begun early enough — no, I could never be a scholar of your tribe. All that reading? Still, I do have ideas — I know what makes a man work, hah?"

A vague nod. The flaw in a clear view, Bolan's, of the world that is, was that it left out one very large thing that made men work, desire for a world as it might be.

After increasingly desultory remarks and another half-cup of *raminat* Bolan appeared ready to leave without ever coming to the object, if there was one, of this visit. At the door he said, "I was never strong for Ladh-Sivai, not for myself. I made the case for him, as I had promised, but the army man would have been my pick."

Not quite Dolvid's recollection, nor could he see how it was more creditable to be insincere than simply wrong. In any case, why bother to tell him? On that enigma, Bolan departed.

Ducking at the window to see the sky Dolvid wondered if the faintly-sketched clouds might bring rain later. In the Garden Court the stream was a listless trickle beneath leaves drooping from thirst, so soon in summer. Bolan, out of sight, had encountered someone he knew; Dolvid heard his laugh. At once there was a tap at the door.

Khalú was all in white except for a short cape and hood of dark green. She had a honeysuckle-blossom between her lips, and put one in the hand he reached to her. "Sweet," she said.

He sucked out the drop of nectar, and her fine hand went to tug at his neck. They kissed, tip of her tongue darting between his teeth, a faint sweetness lingering there, hers or his he could not tell. *Not knowing taste from taster, prize from praise.* Bronal, but better in the original, as Tellis could confirm.

Inside, she gave him a present, a game-sling, a leather thong with a handsome silver clasp, for hanging birds or small game from a saddle. He was touched by the very uselessness to him of the gift; Khalú could not imagine having no use for such a thing. He kissed her with a compassion springing into peremptory want.

"No, we can't." She pulled away with a two-handed gesture to say they were both dressed for the ceremonies. A drowning inbreath imposed control, and he led her by the hand upstairs. With a playfulness not confirmed, he suspected, by his gloom-hot eyes he began peeling off his new clothes. After a moment she took off the cape, and reached back to unfasten her gown. Following his example she carefully hung or folded each garment; not till they were both naked did they touch again, and they sighed to each other, like coming to water after a long, thirsty march. He took her, but with all her readiness and his restraint, wishing she would use him to perfect her own pleasure, knowing she would not, he could tell she was no more than moderately moved. She stilled as his urgency ebbed away. The feeling of powerless sorrow connected with her gift.

"Gabhani work," she said.

"The clasp is not." If he had been gazing at the sling, hung on the back of a chair, it was not to study the crafting.

"I wanted to bring you a nice thing not of Owani make."

That was contrition, but as he kissed her for its innocence, she spoilt it. "Everyone agrees they go beyond us in leathercraft and wood. Why do they want to be silversmiths and dyers, our skills?"

Not many days ago he had been saying the Craft Guilds, for all their devotion to excellence, were also the device of a few Owanil families to keep luxury trades under their control.

"Each should keep to his own."

Not wanting to turn this into a debate, he had to explain the difference between choice and compulsion; there was nothing to keep an Owani from working in wood or leather if he wanted. "You may never want to be a painter of miniatures — "

"I don't, but when I was little everyone thought I drew very well. It's not a thing I studied — I only drew what pleased me to draw."

"What if the Guild prevented you from being a painter?"

"I don't want to be, just that everyone said I had talent."

"But don't you see? That is your choice — "

"I thought you would be gentle today. It is *Shu'sai*."

The childish contraction caught him curiously between irritation and sentiment. Except at the solemn *Mankh'*, *Shuda'sai* was a happy commemoration of how the Promise came to Yoëlladhu, that these lands would always belong to his heirs. For Khalú, as for *Menadhi*, that meant, always, the Old Blood, but to Dolvid, who knew the original meaning of *Owan* was not the name of a race, but Being, it must take in everyone, or mean nothing. "I just want to explain — "

"What makes you so angry with me?"

"I'm not, not with you." Denying it, he nearly became so. "I can be angry with Preference."

"Preference does not exist, it's against the law."

"That is what I have been telling Arvus for years. He's right; it is creeping back."

"My father buys Colony timber from a Mixed merchant, whose kin own half the province, south of Shemugrân. Lots of them are wealthier than we are. They don't have the expense we have, here at Kadon."

There was no answer to this, and Khalú pressed on as if she had gained a point. "You don't see Craft Families idling away two weeks at Pledging. Others, some of them, come all the way from the Angle, and spend a week just on the journey."

"No," drily. "The Craft people do not close their shops in the year's best week for business. You know as well as I do only one in a hundred of the truly poor is an Owani." He recalled his life at Irbat: "And that one is poor because he wishes not to follow a trade, not because he has been dispossessed by a magistrate who is also a magnate."

She was incensed by this obvious reference to men of her father's kind. "You want to make robbers into magistrates," she flared. "Out of a hundred thieves, how many are Owani? We aren't waylayers and bandits."

"I don't call a starving man who steals bread a thief, any more than a thirsty tree that sends its roots across a boundary-line. Anyway, who has ever judged the big landowners for their crimes, for the slow murders their greed commits?"

He had not realised how much he had come to agree with Arvus's boring invitations to guilt. Perhaps this went too far, with Khelagh's daughter, but there was nothing Dolvid could retract. He turned to her, and rather clumsily stroked her bare back.

"My father — he is a thief; I hear him and his friends when they're together, boasting which is the bigger thief."

"All men of business do. It is called good business to twist law, and drive small farmers off lands you covet. It's only what they learn."

"Then he is not to blame?"

"I don't care about blame. I just want them stopped, everyone rich who makes the poor poorer."

Khalú looked miserable. "I hate it when you sound like a Deniant. They want to take away everything we've worked for."

"It does not fill me with joy." But the idea of her working for anything gave him passing amusement. Though he had not in years, he remembered the two louts, using slogans of Deniants, who had attacked and threatened to kill him when he was little. Arvus, true, often intimated darkly about giving the wealthy a taste of poverty, but that was talk, not the policy of his Treasury. "Belief is in no danger. The rich could be very rich, even in a realm where no one was hungry, or slept without a roof over their heads."

With no warning Khalú smiled conspiratorially, a naughty child. "I'm glad I am with you, Dolvidh." Defiance.

He kissed her. "And you brought me nectar. Honeysuckle and apple-blossom." The second was *khaëlu* in the Old Tongue.

Late in summer there was word of fresh troubles in the Northeast. Shumat was struggling with a new invasion of raiders turned invaders, who seized a stretch of coastline south and east of Narn. Their leader, taking the old name, Grenaspaluk, demanded tribute from the port. For Shumat's earliest dispatches the fighting strength of the enemy was not yet counted. Now, by contrast with the years of inaction before the Bolan expedition, with the shuzi trade to protect, there was immediate talk of sending reinforcements, even of a general levy at need.

If only for his familiarity with the terrain Bolan would be obvious one to command. He, certainly, was in no doubt, and came to ask Dolvid if he would serve in his former capacity if the call came.

At the Bronze Residence parts of *The True Song of Tales*, certain to be among the largest volumes yet brought out, were going into their final writing, though there were many additions and emendations ahead, as alternative manuscripts kept coming to light. Of all times Dolvid wanted to give it his complete attention now. He observed the magnates in the shuzi trade would see to it the next Narn Expedition was properly supplied — though they would surely ask their price from the Treasury — and he would have his choice of helpers. Nevertheless, Bolan wanted him, and when he began to drop heavyhanded hints about duty, Dolvid, with an inward groan for the *Song*, said he would go if there was need, and the *rabhsai* allowed. Though it might already be too late to gather an army and deploy large numbers east of Yuvakh Din before winter, Bolan meant to go at least to Sebira to have troops ready for a spring campaign.

Shumat had not yet asked for reinforcements. His next dispatch described a sea-victory; over the past few years Narn had constructed a small fleet of fighting-ships to deal with piracy, and these had met and defeated a fresh wave of invaders, sinking fourteen ships and scattering the rest. He was quite confident he had the forces on land to defeat the second Grenaspaluk.

A dry autumn followed parching summer, and the harvest would be a lean one; the *rabhsai* promised to release quantities of grain from royal stocks to hold down prices.

After Halving-Day the *Bôdhrai* Rhunsilakh held a garden-feast at his house, hard by the New Residence, for the twentieth birthday of his son, Rhunilat. In the metal cages that turned them into lanterns, *ôdul* were hung amongst crisp, twisted brown and yellow leaves persisting on the trees. Food was set out on long tables, and there was music.

Dolvid had been spending long days driving to do as much as he could in case a new war took him away. He judged Khalú, altogether uninterested in details of his work, was bored with him, but she thrilled to these gatherings, which he went to as an obligation. That evening she was a drawn bow; beside her he could feel taut tremulousness, and her eyes were live and unresting. All the Residence Quarter was there, and Khalú wanted to be where they clustered, so her mother's approach was unnoticed; she was in front of them without warning. A knot formed in his belly, but Linaëyu greeted them graciously, with a bow of her head. "You are very handsome together." No mockery was detectable.

Khelagh came from sampling cold meats, still chewing, and took his wife's arm. He was short-necked and wide, with a face Dolvid had always seen as brutal, made of pride, acquisitiveness and the habit of getting his way. He nodded, and made a neutral remark about work at the Bronze Residence, which was answered blandly.

"History," Khelagh said, "was once a pastime of mine. But it didn't mix well with everyday things — how I judged men, for example."

If not a reference to the Ladh-Sivai affair, it would be a fatuous remark. "Master, when I try to make judgements about my own age, nothing helps me so much as a little of the past, its follies and its failures especially." They smiled on at each other.

"Well, but history is always unfinished, not so? I find self-interest a more reliable guide, so long as you don't lose sight of a greater good. A fascinating subject; we must discuss it further. My house is always open to you, when you have leisure, *Bôdh'loiki.*"

"Khalú must bring you," Linaëyu said.

Dolvid thanked them, and they moved away. Khalú had begun a conversation with Rhunilat, whose birthday this was, and Arvus came up behind to mutter, "You scored a win over that magistracy. But you see what I mean? Half the people here call themselves my friends, but once let those wild bees start buzzing in their heads and they'd see me dead for the sake of putting one of their own at the Treasury."

"This is a feast, Master," reprovingly.

"Tell him." From a nearby table Tellis brought Dolvid a

custard. Her hair was worn loose, and in the light of the scattered *ôdul* she had a teasing look, till now wakened only by Untimarr. Catching the compliment in his eyes she bobbed a half-deference.

Faëdhal strode up in a new robe, brocaded above the waist, his belt of many enamel links chinking. "Pleasant, is it not, to see the young enjoying themselves? Not that you — that is, if I may say so — um. Your eminence, shall we say, is beyond your actual years. Only today I was reading over your reconstruction, so I might call it, of the Swallow-Riders episode. A masterly compilation from disparate sources, if you will accept the praise of one not versed in history as such."

"In the old *Song of Tales* it's just stupid," Tellis said. "It is tremendous now."

"But a terrible tale, terrible," Faëdhal shook his head. "Let me say I was shocked by the ending, tragic."

Dolvid stared. "You yourself were first to translate the leaves which include the part about severed hands and feet."

"Was I?"

"You let me see your translation ten years ago; I just recast it in a freer style to match the rest. They were the pages you used to show how the *Atarlum* scribes attempted to render sounds peculiar to Old Gabhanilú."

"Ah — "nodding recognition. "I recall the original, done in a very murky brown ink. The scribe kept vacillating between long *e* and closed *u* to represent that vowel we have no sign for even now."

"Yes, those sheets." Dolvid exchanged a complicit glance of amusement with Tellis. When wrestling with questions of translation, Faëdhal's indifference to content was a Bronze Residence legend.

Evenings remained warm, but it was late enough for cloaks and outshirts when a contingent from the Residence appeared, Rhunilat's nearest friends among the Family, Laloi with Brodhai of Ân, childless after two years of marriage, and the Heir, Tholat. He was two years older than Rhunilat, and at last outgrowing dreams of martial glory; he had not put his name forward when word came of the fresh troubles in the Northeast.

There was a persistent rumour the *rabhsai* intended to follow his father's example and abdicate when the Heir reached twenty-five. Dolvid refused to credit it: Banak had been near eighty and in poor health when he gave up the Sword, while Lambarr, though he probably relished the idea of retiring to a life even more private than his present one, had neither excuse; he was fifty-three and in his prime. Yet to think of Tholat ever becoming *rabhsai* was daunting; he seemed to have inherited all his father's limitations along with his height, but with none of his saving geniality. And in the normal course of events, by the time Tholat came to Sword there would be no Laluvoi to offer wisdom, or to duel with the Patriarch — who would surely be the man now called *Menadhi*.

Casting about him Dolvid was reassured by the stolid reliability of Rhunsilakh, the competence of Arvus and his friend Mirrat, Master of Coinage, the good sense of Merovas, whose exemplar, Saidhan, was firmly there in the West. Perhaps, after all, the realm was not teetering on the edge of a cliff.

Pipes and drums called foursomes to assemble for the traditional Owani dance always performed at such celebrations, consisting of simple sidesteps right and left, turns individual and paired, joinings of hands and stately bows, all at a deliberate pace, impressive for its sober dignity even while a little ridiculous.   Tholat, unwontedly decisive, lunged to capture Khalú who was inviting Dolvid with her eyes. Holding her hand like a cabbage chosen in the market, the Heir joined Tellis, who had been paired with Rhunilat.   A little irked, Dolvid was put in a maturer foursome, with Rhunsilakh, his wife Selnoi, and Linaëyu, who greeted him with a grave half-deference. Finger-drums gave out a shower of beats.

Clearly (the puppet-play of the dance left space for reflection), Rhunsilakh was making it plain Dolvid, notwithstanding Ladh-Sivai, was accepted by the Families. But he and everyone must know Dolvid's part in the affair was a minor one, and Laluvoi's mind had been all that counted.

Or perhaps — arm linked with Linaëyu's, he had a new notion that made sense of several oddities, including Bolan's pointless visit on the morning of *Shuda'sai* — perhaps they might have it backwards, and suppose his opinion had influenced Laluvoi. Linaëyu frowned at his small private laugh. A cool gust rattled dry leaves and made lanterns swing. The drum-rhythm shifted; how well this silly dance suited its dancers; as one turned, all turned.

Next day word came from the Northeast of Shumat's decisive victory in his war. Bolan, who brought Dolvid the news, was glad to see it settled with no need for a second expedition, and pleased by their friend's success, but he was also worried about how it would muddle and lessen his own standing in history, to have a second Grenaspaluk defeated in a second and far larger Battle of Odis Combe. Or so Dolvid judged; anxiety at first came out as niggles over the highhanded settlement Shumat and the Elders of Narn jointly proposed, where some of the defeated enemy, after giving hostages, would be allowed, if the *rabhsai* approved, to colonise empty lands as new subjects of the realm. The second Grenaspaluk had survived his battle to negotiate these terms, and would be permitted to sail away.

"People will say it was all a lie I ever killed Grenaspaluk — " forcing a laugh. The man likely to be the only historian of either war, reassured him. He wished there had been time to learn something about the invaders' language; he now believed, and would conjecture in his history, that rather than a name *Grenaspaluk* might be a kind of title, `supreme war-captain,' for example. If that were true there could be any number of them. No one thought `the *rabhsai* died young' must be untrue because one *rabhsai* lived to be 106.

With Khalú there was no ease. She certainly meant it when she said how deeply she valued his company above the shallow amusements and callow bachelors of the Residence Quarter, and yet never stopped trying to make him more like them.

"You are too harsh. It's not my cousin's fault he is not a master of learning, and has not been in a campaign."

"I did not blame him for it. I only said we had nothing to talk about." He had gone riding with Dolvid and Khalú.

"What you mean is, he is not worth your trouble."

"He has more friends than I have. He does not need my approval."

"You want to make yourself unhappy."

"I have my work." He always had.

"You would rather be at your work than with friends. With me."

Even when (as often) she produced remarks precluding any answer, she always wanted one. He began to tell her what he called a friend, but she had lost interest before he finished a sentence; this was also common. The silence that fell between them was an accusation, nothing of the peace there had been at afternoon's end with Linaëyu when the noise of voices was not needed.

Once when he was little and had earned money as a scribe he had gone to the shop on Harbour Way and bought no fewer than four pieces of pastry, unprecedented wealth. He ate one while waiting for his coin to be changed. By the gate to the Gardens he met Shumat, and instead of sharing one piece of pastry, which was normal, felt obliged to give him a whole piece of his own. Dolvid took another piece to keep him company, and all at once his endless treasure had shrunk down to one piece of pastry, slightly burnt at one end. As his gloom over Khalú deepened with the shortening days, he reflected that a year ago his happiness had been similarly inexhaustible.

Retreating from intolerable muddle to places where problems existed to be solved, he told Khalú they would both be happier apart. Archly, not aware she was almost exactly repeating words by Valnoi, ten years ago, she said she would not lack for company.

Faëdhal did not disguise his satisfaction with the change. Rumours from a distant country, Dolvid heard as he laboured at the *Song of Tales* that Khalú often rode in the Residence grounds with Tholat, who had also been part of a two-day winter jaunt by barge up the Paowan to Dônshei Bridge and back. A Residence Quarter poet made a song about her, mostly assembled from old poems about former famous beauties, yet able to sting with a sharp nostalgia not connected to any specific recollections of the actual Khalú.

One raw and dreary evening with another year begun, she came to the Bronze Residence, nose and cheeks shining, and he had missed her. The small peat fire was lost in the big fireplace of the Old Audience Hall; Khalú was shivering with chill, and to take her to his arms and so to his bed was practical as well as pleasing. But she wept, saying his name an enormous number of times.

Earlier that day, she told, Rhunilat had come to see her. After small talk he admitted he was there on Tholat's behalf. The Heir was contemplating marriage. To Khalú, as she eventually understood.

Using an intermediary was a custom of the highborn that had passed away, but while Tholat was often pained by his father's disdain for ceremony, it was not out of a desire to revive past rituals that the Heir had sent Rhunilat. His self-respect must be frail indeed; going outside (and therefore beneath) the Great Families, he must believe chances of refusal were slight.

The union would not please his grandmother, who would see it as a triumph for Khelagh. So would Khelagh, although Khalú had not mentioned him. She would not be eighteen for a month, and in theory Tholat could have made consent certain by arranging it with her father. Rare, however, for daughters today to wake up beside men they had no voice in choosing.

Great Hrafi, Dolvid exclaimed in his head, if Khalú this afternoon had given Rhunilat anything that might be construed as a formal undertaking, he, Dolvid, was committing treason with her; because there must not be any doubt as to the succession, a woman whose child would be the Heir's heir, a future *rabhsai*, was no safer to sport with than the *rabhsayu* herself. It was unclear what the penalty would be for him; although never formally adopted by the Council, the famous advisory of Banak and Laluvoi, *Against the Punishment of Death*, had been followed in all but a few cases, those of the worst murderers. He might even escape the alternative, a life salting eels on the Island, if it was clear he had not been told in time about her betrothal, but provincial exile was the least that could happen to him, to remain at least three dayrides away from Kadon Dinul, an outlaw anyone could kill with impunity if he broke the ban. Khalú could hardly expect much better; certainly her engagement would be over before it had really begun.

She said, "No, I gave Rhunilat no answer he could call an answer, only thanked him for bringing the offer. He kept badgering me, and said he couldn't go back to the Residence with that, so I kissed him on the forehead, and he went away very irked with me."

At last Dolvid considered how curious this evening was; she had come here alone, not unwilling to be bedded, anything but elated over a future as leading woman of the realm. "It is risky to toy with princes, especially when they have a fragile pride."

"It's not Tholat I want."

"Khalú, that is not sane. How could you do better? Your father — "

"My father has never laid a hand on me, but would have me beaten if told I had taken one breath before saying yes. I don't care; he doesn't, you don't know Tholat. I do."

The image of her perfection mauled over by those clumsy hands was revolting, but in Khalú's shudder there was more, and she told enough to make it plain the Heir's notions of mating were unappetising even by Residence Quarter standards; to Tholat's Gabhani great-great-grandfather they would have called for execution by methods equally distasteful.

Dolvid tried to stay sensible. Every prince, he supposed, would prefer the illusion he was the free choice of the woman he had honoured, but if he wanted Khalú enough there were numbers of ways short of overt commands that Tholat could practically compel her consent, and nothing could prevent him.

Not quite nothing. "If you dislike him enough to give up the chance of becoming *rabhsayu* — "

"I do. What is it to be *rabhsayu*? Saëdhu has no fun, only

babies and babies."

"Tholat would have to respect your understanding with another man." Or if he would not, Lambarr would, and there would be the end of it. That other could not expect a brilliant future, someday under a *rabhsai* who might want revenge. He was an abstraction, a faceless man of the Families, perhaps the cousin who had been pursuing Khalú the day they first met, riding in the hills.

Not for her. "My father will be furious. He doesn't own me. I'll be eighteen soon." She leant eagerly to Dolvid, and he, between smiles, tears and rapt murmurings of his name, understood he had made a proposal of marriage, not possible to retract, not where they were, naked together in bed.

The wedding was set for a week after Halving-Day. Never told about the Heir, Khelagh was adequately cordial. Faëdhal gave coolly polite congratulations, but Arvus, when he heard, bounced into the Bronze Residence to inform Dolvid he was an idiot. "You marry into the Families and you'll be their captive, or they'll break you in pieces."

"You didn't pay attention to your own advice, did you, Master." The long-dead wife of Arvus, Taësu, had been an Owaniyu of good family, a faithful Daughter of Yoëlladhu oddly married to a Deniant.

Arvus brushed that aside. "Tell me you don't know in your heart who your wife should be," he challenged, then rolled his eyes. "She would boil me for saying this."

Another day, Untimarr the carpenter, leaving for Tan Lughsai, where his work was almost finished, looked in to wish

Dolvid well. "And, by your leave, the lady, faithless wench," so his voice would reach Tellis, quietly working at copying. Untimarr was perplexed then immensely embarrassed when his mistake was explained, and Dolvid, though he managed to assure him there was no harm done, found it hard to meet the quiet face with which Tellis observed.

No, too late, and though he admired Tellis and hoped she did him, they were perhaps too alike. He was always pleased to see her, and that had acquired troubling meanings since the evening of Rhunilat's birthday, when he had begun to think it might be good to be in her bed. Too late, and life with Khalú was going to be quite endurable, a true marriage of the Residence Quarter, where passion and matrimony were considered an undesirable and even vulgar mixture, and merged estates meant more than joined lives. Tellis would have been other, a friend and colleague, with neither the distance nor the danger there was with Khalú; if he had asked her to marry him, whether she had said yes or no it would have been calmly and with thanks. But it really was too late. Khalú had chosen him, and he did not have courage to face her distress.

A voice, unidentified, in his head asked why he was so lukewarm when he had the envy of half the Heartland; Khalú had been admired in song, and had he not taken her from the Heir? In bed, her indifference to achieving madness would have been acceptable, perhaps preferable, to many men. He was a *bôdh'loiki* of the realm, supposed to have influence with Laluvoi, she was daughter to enormous wealth, how could there be a better match?

If their lives needed madness, no wife of Khalú's standing was expected to take sash, and once wedlock had been confirmed, perhaps by a child or two, she could imitate her mother and have manageable bed-friends, while no one would censure Dolvid for losing his head now and again, if the girl was below his rank, honoured by his attentions, satisfied with that and with presents, not supposing he would ever leave his wife. All this, he acknowledged, accorded better with real nature than any poet's dream of devotion eternally renewed by passion that never staled. Everything could be explained, nothing by any external measure was fatally wrong, and still it was an awful mistake. He accepted congratulations, made arrangements, went through ceremonies to make him Khalú's husband, all in a numb and baffled state, inside a distressing dream he could not stop.

No suitable house was vacant in the Residence Quarter, but Dolvid declined to see their need for one. Khelagh made available a whole suite of rooms at his handsome house on the Avenue, though Dolvid never used them, sleeping in the Rose-Stone Wing, or in his camp-bed at the Bronze Residence when he stayed overnight at Kadon Dinul. For dowry Khalú had received a strip of lands at the nearer, the western fringe of her father's empire of estates. Whereupon Laluvoi, who, whether or not she had heard about her grandson's attempt, seemed inexplicably pleased by Dolvid's choice, discovered she had a small villa in her gift, with grounds adjoining Khalú's, a well-built stone house in good repair. Its position, an easy ride from Kadon Dinul in the green beginnings of the Arbhu Hills, could hardly have been better, not far from where Dolvid and Khalú, riding, had met for the second time; her lands actually took in the hillside of that encounter.

Also three small farms, which he was expected to manage. It embarrassed him to be a landlord, but a second and comfortable house was vacant on the villa grounds, and when he heard Untimarr, back from Tan Lughsai, wanted to remain near Kadon Dinul for a while, Dolvid offered him a place rent-free in exchange for overseeing the properties. Untimarr readily accepted. His wife was Morú, a friendly, practical woman, experienced as a midwife, very motherly though not many years older than Dolvid; of their two daughters the elder was an earnest six-year-old, very much her mother. Pleasant as well as useful to have Untimarr there at the estate; he soon turned a disused storehouse into his shop, where Dolvid always spent more time than he meant to, breathing rich oak, rosewood and pine scents, watching Untimarr at his craft, strong, exact hands cutting, smoothing and joining woods, while he gave his laconic comments on the realm's affairs. That wet spring and early summer, too much talk everywhere was about shortages and rising prices, the legacy of last year's drought.

Khalú complained, "You would rather listen to some Gabhani carpenter than go riding with my kin." He had forgotten all about the planned ride, one of the sedate evening saunters the Families enjoyed.

"At least the carpenter doesn't call a man `lazy *ran'ghai*' because his crops have failed, on land your father would not use for nettles."

She turned away petulantly. "It's all nothing but the

injustice of the realm with you. You won't do anything for my sake. When your book comes out, I shan't have any friends."

"You knew when we married I was going to bring out the *Song*." But as publication came nearer, efforts to have him abandon or at least modify the work did not abate; warnings masked as friendly advice came from her father and other landowners, and she had evidently forgotten the spasm of rebellious defiance, her way of accepting a proposal he had never made. Khelagh's tolerance of the match had perhaps included the unspoken (and erroneous) understanding no one married into the Families could perpetrate such a scandal as the *True Song* was rumoured to be. But he did not see how his wife could be blamed for any part of a work so long in the making.

"No friends," she repeated. "I'll be disowned by my kin."

"Must friends all be of the Families? Tellis was your friend, Morú wants to be your friend." She stared, not crediting his simplicity.

In the utter darkness of his makeshift bedroom, Dolvid lay listening. From nights here during Pledging when there were rowdy crowds in Harbour Way, he was sure no noise from outside would rouse him; this had been a sound close by. There were *atarlal* in the building, but none of them should be on this floor. Heavy rain had caught him here after nightfall, and convinced him to stay.

Silence crawled on, and in the archway entrance he could discern along the floor the rim of faint light where the hangings ended; there were a couple of dying *ôdul* in the Old Throne Room. Another small, shifting sound came, and he knew there was someone on the other side of the curtain.

"Who's there?" Perhaps at-Dhanurai had crept in to see how the book was progressing; Dolvid concealed nothing from the *atarlai*, but *Menadhi* would never believe that.

No answer. Any alien sounds there might be could not be told from the night-noises of the city, faint stir of the Bronze Residence itself. Very quietly he slipped from bed, putting on a short robe, and taking down his long Froghuli knife from its bracket on the wall. Feet plainly made a scuffle.

"Who's there?"

The hangings were dragged aside, and against the pale was the figure of a man, poorly clad, a bared sword in his right hand. Realising the man peering into black could not see him, Dolvid gave a menacing growl, lunging forward with his empty hand to grasp the sword-arm. The man struck out wildly with his left hand, and by pure chance caught the side of Dolvid's head with a hard object, which fell to the floor with a metallic clatter. Dazed, Dolvid saw the sword-arm go back, and struck upwards with his knife, slicing into cloth, then flesh at the ribs.

The sword clashed to the stone floor, and its owner screamed shrilly, thrusting him back down with his left forearm. Hangings fell softly into place as the man retreated, and there was at least one other intruder; the gabbled whisper of words came, then a fresh crash as a heavy thing was kicked over.

Head clearing, Dolvid bawled out, "Stay and fight, scum!" He scrambled to his feet. Past the dais where the Chair of State used to be, he emerged into some light, to see the doors at the far end closing. Going back he scrabbled on the floor till he had the dropped sword, a plain, broad-bladed one, and with a weapon in each hand went after the intruders.

Cautiously he came into the larger space of the Old Audience Hall, where half a dozen *ôdul* quietly gleamed, and there were fewer shadows, or nooks that might hide men. Again, double-doors ahead closed with a smooth click; he followed, again wary coming through the doors.

The hallway was empty. He went a few undecided steps, and at the Square Gallery tensed as two figures came from the direction of the main stairs. One was carrying an oil-lantern, both were wearing robes; at-Dhanurai and another *atarlai*.

"What is it?" at-Dhanurai called, recognising him. "We heard cries and noises." He was carrying a stave, and Dolvid's suspicions ebbed; no one could have counterfeited the nervousness of the two men. His assailant, besides, had been in breeches, burlier than at-Danurai, certainly larger than his mousy companion.   Swiftly Dolvid outlined what had happened.

"Are you hurt?" the short one asked.

"The blood is not mine, I wounded a man." But his head was throbbing.

As at-Dhanurai started to ask a question, Dolvid held up his hand for quiet. From below there came the heavy thud of a door closing.

"The old guardroom," at-Dhanurai suggested. It had an iron door, below the level of the platform on which the Bronze Residence stood. The space was used only for storage, but Dolvid had assumed the outside door was kept locked.

"If bandits and robbers," at-Dhanurai complained, "can come into the Bronze Residence whenever they choose... "

"You are hurt," the other, smaller *atarlai* said. Dolvid had sheathed his knife, transferring the sword to his right hand to hold the left to his temple. "You should be seen to. Come up to our quarters."

But the word *robbers* had started new fears, and he refused to go. Parts of the *Song of Tales* not yet copied were out in the open in the Old Throne Room.

"Then I'll bring you healing. I began with the *Ramadilum*."

"Wait. Stay together. The two of you go down and tell the guards at the main entrance to send word across to Harbour Gate. A search must be made, though it's too late. Take this —
" proffering the sword.

"I am not permitted — " at-Dhanurai recoiled.

"Great Yoëlladhu, I know you are not permitted. Take it, the Treaty would be waived; you are not required to have your throat cut for the sake of Plakhat Gabh'Owan."

At-Dhanurai held the sword as a dangerous snake, but the two *atarlal* made for the stairs, and Dolvid went back to the Audience Chamber, unsheathing his knife again. He had in mind old rumours of secret passages within the walls of this edifice; beyond rumours, he had come across writings on the subject, and had put them aside to study when there was an empty hour.

It was very quiet. By the doorway to the Throne Room he found a large earthenware jar of lamp-oil, and supposed the clink of its being set down was what had wakened him. He could also guess what hard object had struck his head. Taking an *ôdu*-lantern he went back to his sleeping-space, and on the floor found what he expected, a tight-lidded metal box. Inside were a steel striker, fluffed strands of tinder-cord, and a piece of stone glistening with what looked like precious metal, fool's gold. Fire, not robbery, had been the object of this visit. He had already ruled out murder; even he had not expected to be here overnight till a few hours ago.

Had a blaze been set, it would not merely have put back the *Song* by a year or two. As well as uncopied manuscript, there was a great deal in the Throne Room quite irreplaceable, working drafts of translations, and even unique source-material; the book could never have been fully reconstructed. With all here that would burn, Dolvid, if he had not been wakened, would probably have had an unpleasant death, most likely suffocation, but was not sure that would have been worse than being alive to face what was lost.

Tomorrow morning they would begin making an extra copy of everything so far written, and copying in future would always keep pace with a day's work, no matter how certain what was written would be superseded later. More, copied sheets would be taken away every night; Arvus could probably find space for them at the invulnerable Treasury. Tedious as it was, working copies would have to be made of all source-manuscripts, and originals returned to the main library each day. He had long been fully aware of people who did not want the *True Song of Tales* published, but had scarcely imagined how far they might go.

At-Dhanurai and his small companion arrived, bringing cool *raminat* and a jar of the unguent made from *ga-raminat* and what smell said was oil from sheep's wool. Dolvid was grateful for this care; the faintly furtive manner of the younger *atarlai* told him their instructions from *Menadhi* were being contravened. Where the skin high on his forehead was broken the ointment stung fiercely, but he did not complain, remembering the virtues of the nasty stuff.

Bolan took it as a personal insult, coming in the morning as soon as he heard the night's report. "They'll say the Household can't mount a watch as the *Adanum* could," he forecast gloomily. Besides strengthening the outer guard, he arranged that by night half-pay veterans would walk the halls, armed and with cattle-calls hung on lanyards about the neck. The penetrating note of these fat little pipes would easily be heard outside.

Quite seriously, he also told Dolvid he should have a couple of Household men for bodyguard wherever he went.

"Then have armed servants of your own," when he exasperatedly declined. "Your father-in-law doesn't stir without his escort."

That was true; the private army on Khelagh's estates, many of them farm-workers most of the time, could be brought up to a couple of hundred, and even in Kadon Dinul he always had armed men with him.

"Linaëyu rides about all alone."

"She's not doing all she can to make enemies. Besides, Khelagh has her followed, at a distance."

He grinned to see this came as news. That Khelagh must have known in general his wife was seeing Dolvid was not the same as his being kept informed exactly when, and for how long.

"Words on a page," Bolan said, thumbing the edges of a sheaf.

"No one from the Families would do this," Khalú, big-eyed over the purpling patch on his forehead.

"Just what Faëdhal said." Interestingly, both minds had gone there instantly, answering an accusation never made.

"You can't believe they would."

"No." He was satisfied with the innocence, or ignorance, of at-Dhanurai and the other, but went on suspecting *Menadhi*. The intruders would never be found, but if they had been caught at the Bronze Residence there would be no possible connection to the *Mankh'*. There were hungry men at Kadon Dinul who would take on any job for a payment.

Now the realm of the present became a dream; sodden clouds rolled endlessly in off Arnan; there was flooding in the southern Paowan, a march on Kanzan Tâl by hungry people looking for relief, a riot in central Ân for the same cause, and all much more distant than Pir Kallikuk imposing his leadership on a shaky confederacy for the Wars of Cleansing, or his namegiver, a thousand years before, rallying defeated armies for another trial of strength with the disciplined might of the

Empire.   News came of Shumat's second child and first daughter, less real than even the Odi Kukkuk tales.

With officials of the *rabhsayum* occasionally too few, Dolvid was obliged to preside over some meetings in outlying parts, always to do with food supplies, long wrangles, full of useless recrimination, with local magistrates, town elders and self-appointed leaders of the people.   Good to escape back to the Bronze Residence and into other times; with the goal plainly in sight even the long task of reading for copyists was not unpleasant, and new strength came to cramped fingers when the copyists saw their piles of sheets sewn into fascicles, and those at last put together inside their covers.

At Zhôl's Moon, which, though it could come earlier or later, was by tradition midpoint between Midsummer and Autumn Halving-Day, he formally requested an audience with Laluvoi and the *rabhsai*, he unexpectedly in Kadon Dinul, while the roof of the Wooden Residence at Tan Lughsai was undergoing repairs. At Dolvid's insistence, for this ceremonial delivery, Faëdhal came too, dressed in his best, his chain-belt chinking proudly. After discussion they decided not to bring any of apprentices or copyists, "since to choose one were to slight the others — " Faëdhal quoted slyly from Dolvid's version of an Odi Kukkuk tale.

For Lambarr there was the holograph, vellum-bound in two volumes, dedicatory page lavished with ornament. "What a fine, what an excellent book," the *rabhsai* said. "I did not realise it would be so many pages."

Laluvoi gave her copy a brief inspection, then laid it

aside for more leisure, to discuss what was to become of the remaining books. Each of the provincial *nimul* was to get one, the *Bôdhrai* Rhunsilakh and most of the leading *bôdh'loikil*. A personal copy would go to *g'Asalladh'*, and another to the *Mankh'* for its library. The rest would be available for purchase; Khelagh, among other prominent people, had already spoken for a copy. With mischievous zest, Laluvoi tried to set the price.

"We can't ask our patrons of literature to defray the real cost of this long campaign. Your wife's father can afford it, but others less lucky may be just as deserving." In the end they set a price only about twice that of an ordinary book of romances.

The afternoon was warm, and rain-clouds were gathering again, as Dolvid walked Faëdhal home. He was still waiting for the surge of elation he had expected.

"Gratifying, is it not," Faëdhal remarked, "to see Laluvoi *Asayu* so well, and lively, if one may presume, in her interests. Lambarr *Deghi*, no doubt, is anxious over little Orbanak." The youngest of the *rabhsai*'s sons, now near two, was suffering from a nagging cough, but the implicit contrast was surely quite innocent.

The Paowan

Arvus, amazed at Dolvid's temerity, thought it was the best book in his lifetime, and maybe ever. "My clever daughter says I'm right, but for the wrong reasons. I am not supposed to praise a book because I salute what it does."

"What does it do?" After more than a month he felt as with the victory at Narn, wondering what was achieved with so much labour.

"Sets right an ancient fraud. Shows up the self-flatterers of the Old Blood for what they are, all praise an Owani did it."

"Well, so far I haven't found anyone ready to draw a blade to defend the glory of Old Owan."

"You want too much. They tried to burn you out, didn't they?"

Dolvid laughed at himself, and agreed that was honour enough for anyone. He had never expected publication of a book to change the realm overnight; minds, as g'Asalladh' said, were slow to alter. At best the *True Song* was dropping yeast into the mixture, to work silently in its own way. In logic, what the book taught should have moved the Families, either to surrender a just proportion of their holdings to the despised Others, or to defiance; all he had heard was polite compliments.

Many in the Families, making due allowance for regrettable episodes, seemed really to enjoy the book — and that must be for what Tellis would call the right reasons.

"Master Vulakh, I have work for you." The shop on Harbour Way was exactly the same after ten years, and the metalsmith was not much changed, except when he spoke his teeth were discoloured, at least one broken off or missing entirely. He did not remember Dolvid to begin with, but took the ruby, holding it up to the light.

"That now, that's no glass," nodding expert approval.

"I have good title to it — " never forgetting his first meeting with this man's daughter, when she practically accused him of trying to sell a stolen brooch.

"*Bôdh'loiki?*" Vulakh was puzzled, having noted the official chain Dolvid wore.

"It came from the *rabhsai* himself." Lambarr had presented him with the ruby to mark completion of the *True Song,* and perhaps to make up for not reading the book, a fine dark stone from the Farther West, all the more prized for the exploit of Sebhal's that had found the mines again. Since that adventure, a road had been made on Landegh to connect Shâl Mines with Drin Navuna, kept free of *jinzal* and human raiders by the Army of the West; all this was part of the ruby's value, and he had decided to have it put in a setting for Khalú to wear.

He handed the goldsmith a crude sketch of the pendent piece he had in mind. Vulakh turned the parchment over, took a slender stick of charcoal from behind his ear, and in a few sure strokes conveyed how he would interpret Dolvid's suggestion.

"Yes, exactly."

Vulakh turned and began unlocking little bronze-doored pigeonholes. At third try he found what he sought. "There are these earpieces, *Asai*, make a good match to that. Stones are less good than yours, but the colour is near enough — from the West they all have that dark cast, near blue at the centre, you see it?"

"Very good." The small studs would be ideal with the way Khalú was dressing her hair, which showed all of her neat, perfect ears. "I can give security for the metal, and your work — " reaching for his washleather purse.

"This, *Asai*," Vulakh held up the large ruby with a flourish, "is security enough. The metal is on hand, red gold, set off the stone just right. Pay me when it's all done, *Asai*."

"Not `*Asai*.'" The incorrect honorific was intentional flattery. "Dolvid Vidukhat." He expected Vulakh to note his name on a strip of the treated bark used by old-fashioned shop-men.

He did not. "Married, Master, are you?"

He nodded, and there was a pause. Abruptly Vulakh put on his broadest grin, again holding up the ruby between thumb and forefinger. "I'll show her this, Master, if I may."

"Valnoi's well?" Saying her name made a kind of test.

"Grandchildren are a joy to my wife. Shall I give her your wishes, Master? Pleased, she'll be, to hear about your rank." There was humour here, and Vulakh, oddly, was taking wry satisfaction in the untruth of what he said.

"Perhaps I shall see her." To his relief he was truly indifferent whether he did or not. Nothing was left, except to tell Vulakh to take the time he needed over the work, not required for any particular occasion.

Vulakh approved. "I never give less than value, but the great ones always try to hurry me. True master's work needs time; everything's better for some slow pondering — 'cept a fresh oyster, maybe."

A cool drizzle had begun. Halfway to Harbour Gate he was accosted by a raggedly clad and unshaven man, eyes bleared and cheeks hollow. "Something for my hunger, *Asai*." He was shivering with cold or sickness.

"Don't do your begging here, so near — " Dolvid had bent close to the man, and now recognised him. "Norlum." He had gone all through the Narn Campaign, fighting well at Odis Combe, before that at the Pass of Perus, where, behind the *drin'loi*, he had tormented a dying prisoner. He now seemed to have spent several nights, at least, in the open.

"Come." Grasping the man's arm he led him to the pie-shop. Norlum vaguely remembered Dolvid, but had yet to dig out a name. He was seized by a violent shudder as they came into the steamy warmth of the shop, where Dolvid's call for hot drinks met the beginning of disdain, till the owner noticed the chain of *bôdh'loikim*.

Drinks beside them, Dolvid had ordered and Norlum was spooning up marrow-broth before Dolvid, having heard the very hungry should not be allowed to fill up too quickly, began asking questions.

"Didn't you go back to the Northeast with the Captain Shumat?"

"I meant to stay there, *Asai* — "

"Not *Asai*: I am Dolvid."

"See, my service was up, two years since. I might've done another six, but my wife was homesick." Picking up his bowl, Norlum drained the last of the broth, then broke off a piece of bread to wipe out the bowl. Remembering his own lean years at Irbat Dolvid called to the serving man for a chunk of baked mutton, and could easily feel again the ache in his stomach, the near-drunkenness meat and hot grease brought on. Dismaying how much Norlum had aged: five years ago he was in early middle life, but that prime had been swallowed up, and he looked more than his years, which might be fifty-two.

Shumat, with empty farms to fill, and wanting to have a trained reserve he could call on, had been authorised to grant acreage near Narn beyond the small plot normal for eighteen-year veterans. But Norlum's wife had wanted to go back to her home country, the fenny land between Shemugrân and the River Lovu, and Norlum had accepted a lesser holding, not far from the place of her birth.

On good soil, in good growing weather, to live on a veteran's holding was just possible, but Norlum was not given either. Two years ago, the summer of the drought, the local tax-gatherer had not allowed him the usual option of "seeding back" his first-year taxes, and the money Norlum saved in service was exhausted. He raised a loan for fresh seed in the second year, but the wet spring had been disastrous for that low-lying country. Much worse, his daughter of seven had become ill, and tending the child, so had his wife. Both died in the same week; whether a *ramidu* could have prevented that was impossible to say, but Norlum had never been able to get one to see his family.

Despondency and apathy, no doubt, had then made Norlum's failure as a farmer more complete; he had abandoned meagre crops to his creditor and the tax-man, and come north in hopes of finding work.

"An appeal can be made for return of your first-year taxes."

"That's what I was told, Master. The point is, you see, staying alive long enough to do it, and you begin to be a thing no one would trust his piss-pot to." The mutton arrived; he tore at it, and swallowed greedily.

"I can help you get a hearing. You are due a sum in relief. No matter whether or not you intend to continue farming." It could be seen loss of his farm was all one for Norlum with that of his wife and child.

"Not a farm, that's the trouble. In that country you could put three of those garden-patches together and make a farm of it." Norlum used a crust of bread to scrub grease from his lips.

"You'll have a wait while the law works. I have been looking for a good stablemaster." Not strictly true, but Khalú was eloquent about their need for more than the half-dozen animals they kept, and Dolvid had recalled the careful and loving way Norlum had with horses. "My stables are not huge, and there would be other tasks, but I hate to see a horse mistreated."

"That's so, I recall you do, Master." Norlum's thoughts had gone elsewhere, and his shamefaced manner was embarrassing to Dolvid, who did not want any reference to those terrible few moments at the *drin'loi*. He had already troubled himself, although having stables there was no way to speak of them without sounding snobbish.

"The pay can't be much, but you'll have the stablehouse and your food." He spoke on, telling about the Arbhu Hills, Untimarr, the number and condition of the present horses and how Norlum could advise in purchasing of others — anything to hold back silence, in which the man would certainly begin to weep.

Today, as most days, Dolvid had begun in misery about his life with Khalú. Then, when he was setting out, she had come to his stirrup in a dressing-gown too thin for the cool morning damp, laying her head against his leg, as he leant to caress her neck. That dependent sweetness could go through him like a blade, and just now, reminded about Valnoi's insatiable vanity, he had left Vulakh's shop thinking perhaps he had not married so badly after all. Listening to this fellow-veteran of the great and triumphant Northeastern Expedition, seeing his broken condition, Dolvid marvelled at his own effrontery, ever having a complaint about any aspect of his life.

Bolan arrived at the Bronze Residence in a torrent of curses. On his way here to talk about hunger, a mob in the street had been at the edge of riot. A small mob, he admitted, and they had hurled only words, except for one who had added a rotted onion, but taken care it landed not too close.

It was the temper of the times; as in the years of Bolan's rise troops were needed to keep order in the streets, and disperse gatherings of unhappy and unruly townspeople. Bolan had added levies to the Household strength, but trusted only the discipline of regulars for the Market, where mobs were most inflammable. To judge by their captain, even Household good-temper was not endless.

"Always the same cry; `you won't go hungry, will you?' and every hovel-dweller spits it out as if he's the first one to think of it. You sit on a horse while they throw stinking onions at you, and see how long your sword stays in its sheath. `Go back to Narn, Captain,' one of them bawled out." His humour began to come back. "I said, `I wish I could, friend, there's fresh fish there.' Then another wag, with, `you won't go hungry, will you?' I said, `you see my paunch, don't you?'" He patted his stomach, flat as when he was a file-leader in his twenties.

"Something must be done."

"Something — what? With Laluvoi, it's always *no use of force.*   There'll always be trouble if troublemakers go unpunished."

Faëdhal was in agreement. "In my years there has been a tremendous decline, shall I say, in manners. Too many are now grown who as children never so much as saw the strap."

"Too many," Dolvid said, "have never had a full belly. Something must be done about feeding this realm."

"Aha," Bolan said. "That's what I'm here about. But you might begin by making the weather more reliable."

"But there's food. We could have plenty, even in bad years. So much of the best land runs wild, while the poor are battling with fen and gravel. We can't tell how much food there is, stored and on the hoof, waiting for prices to rise."

"Saidhan is in town," Bolan, with curious emphasis.

Not immediately apparent why he mentioned Saidhan in particular: several of the provincial *nimul* were at Kadon for meeting of the Council, with hardship and hunger as main topics. Most of the overlords had argued for an immediate rise in the maximum legal price for standard foodstuffs, grain and meat, and Bolan was quick to agree it was the only way to bring stored food out of hiding. "Just what Vinilat of Dramal said; a man has scraped and saved, borrowed, it may well be, to set aside a bit of grain against shortage, and he sees prices have to go up — it's only natural; the *rabhsai* can't hold them down unless he's got goods to put on the market. There's already private dealing above legal prices."

That was where Saidhan came in. Vehement as ever at seventy-seven, he refused to be a part of that trade. The Colony was nearer feeding itself, but the dry year had been especially hard there. With the *rabhsai*'s remittances for the rubies from Shâl Mines added to proceeds from trade in timber, Kamsilat had no shortage of money; Saidhan could have bought foodstuffs and sold them to his people at a loss, but would not do so, not that he was interested in profit, but because he said he would be bidding up prices that would never come down again.

Vinilat scorned that, saying one good harvest and farmers would all be lamenting falling prices. "You once told me," Bolan said, "how a man could lose money on plenty — no, don't tell me again, I'll only forget how it goes again. But if there was no law against your partner losing all his money, why should the law prevent a man making a profit on shortage? It's only natural."

"Then riots are natural, too,"

"They won't be, as long as we have weapons."

"Come on, Bolan — how many of the magnates have been paupered this year? There is no law against a man dying of thirst, but that's not to say one can dam rivers and sell water for any price he sets. Fair profit is not the same as hiding food away till the price doubles, while the poor starve."

"Very true," Faëdhal agreed. "What can one say about those whose answer to dearth is to put better locks on their barn-doors? Criminal."

Resignedly, Bolan admitted that was also the view of Laluvoi, who said the magnates were holding the realm to ransom. She and Saidhan, persuading the *rabhsai*, had forced through Council a measure against hoarding. In each province there was to be an official given extraordinary powers to purchase foodstuffs at or near legal prices.

In order to get enough support for her proposal, Laluvoi had to agree the *nim'* of each province would name this official and oversee his activities, and Bolan guessed such overlords as Vinilat, much less Tobhan of Kargul, were unlikely to make strong appointments.

"A minor issue," Dolvid said. "More food is grown within a dayride of Kadon Dinul than in any other entire province. The battle will be won or lost in the Paowan." He surprised Faëdhal and Bolan, even himself, with a sudden shudder. "Let us hope the cure is not worse than the disease. Extraordinary powers! He'll need troops behind him."

"Laluvoi saw that," not happily. "Merovas says he'll

make General Cavalry available."

"Forced sales, informers to tell where food is hidden, and men who'll bribe informers to overlook their stores — whoever gets the post will have plenty of temptations. I hope they find a good man — and one who will be ready to give up his extraordinary powers when the crisis passes."

Bolan's expression was his sly one. "Let me know if you think they've found a good man. I put your name forward."

"Mine?"

"They remember, or I recalled for them, the marvels you did with the campaign, dickering with farmers, feeding prisoners and the amnestied, as well as an army."

"That is altogether different. I never had to feed above three or four thousand. I was too young then to know the difficulties. This post needs one with rank, with prestige."

"Laluvoi seemed to like the idea."

Bolan remained a paradox. When he spoke of profit being the proper nature of the world, there was the voice of Khelagh, who certainly knew his son-in-law had not become an advocate of privilege by marrying Khalú. Yet Bolan was genuinely, proprietarily proud of having suggested Dolvid for a post which, taken seriously, would have to mean confronting the magnates, of which Khelagh was the biggest.

He hardly expected to be given the job, and certainly did not want it. Nothing would ever rival the *True Song of Tales*, but work had begun on more than one new book, and he had plans for others. What Bolan did not see, smiling as if he had done a favour, was that this new official could come to be the most hated man since Kanavakh, either among the rich, or the poor he was supposed to help.

When Arvus came to the Bronze Residence he took it Dolvid was already as good as installed. "Laluvoi was very pleased with Bolan. I don't think he's worked out just why. She wants somebody to go after the magnates, naturally, and he named the one man the Families can't say is out to ruin them — Khelagh's son-in-law? I told Merovas, he's going to have to keep on keeping you alive."

"My thanks," not really subscribing to the world of sudden murder Arvus liked to imagine.

Relish, and differing concerns, made his Council meeting both livelier and wider-ranging. For a start, Bolan had left out the inattention of Lambarr *Rabhsai*, distressed by the absence from Kadon Dinul of Saëdhu, and anxious about her condition. In nursing her youngest son back to health, she had mislaid her own, and suffered alarming failures of memory and spells of unsteadiness and fainting. She was at Thenimala in Ninkufu, where it was hoped the mild sea air would restore her.

Beside her silent, preoccupied son, Laluvoi was left to preside for much of the meeting. She was unable to prevent a lengthy and bitter wrangle between Saidhan and Vinilat, mainly over whether or not it was good for the realm to allow smallholdings, through failure and default, gradually to be absorbed into the voracious estates of the magnates. Vinilat maintained with new grants of land made every year there would always be enough small farms, but Arvus had tax-rolls to cite in support of Saidhan's view that the supply of wheat was being controlled by fewer and fewer large landowners, with the rest of the minnows counting for nothing when it came to setting prices.

Vinilat insisted the inept who could not make their farms pay deserved to be driven from the land, and larger farms could produce more food. Saidhan again appealed to Arvus, who could show that under the magnates more arable acreage was allowed to lapse into disuse each year than was awarded in new grants of land.

"Dramal doesn't love the Treasury. Vinilat doesn't think facts have any part in a quarrel. But if he and Saidhan had worn weapons, it might have come to a fight — and I'd back the old champion."

When Vinilat said again those who lost their farms were lazy *ran'ghal* the realm did better without, Lambarr somewhere found his attention and his voice. He spoke with feeling about the satisfaction of owning land, the importance as a reward for faithful service of the smallholdings, which must be seen as benefits, not miseries to break the hearts of their owners and fail in a couple of seasons. His demand for ways to aid smaller farms to survive was a direct rebuke to Vinilat.

"Amazing, isn't it," Arvus said. "We're all loyal *rabhsayanil*, good enough, but I don't have to tell you we never forget Lambarr is not his father. Then he says, help the small farmers, feed the hungry, and that's what it was, snap, and let Vinilat go home and hunt toads."

"*Rabhsai* is *rabhsai*, all else aside." The same thing entirely in the Owanilú had a natural play on words, but Arvus always pretended not to understand, and to be offended by Old

Tongue foolery.

"As you say. The one definite measure we adopted is, we won't collect any taxes next year from anyone who started farming in either the dry year or the wet year."

Bolan had not mentioned that. "Not enough," remembering Norlum's dismal history. "Back in Banak's reign, when there was flooding down by Kôbh-shore, loans were made, free of interest, to the ones who otherwise would not have lasted to next harvest."

"That could be done again. Gold is spilling over at the Treasury — all the big landowners bought their own food at tax-time." He meant they had chosen to pay their portion entirely in money rather than goods. "As who would not, betting on prices to double? But there's a general shortage of money out there, as money — even your adopted kin."

"Khelagh? That is not possible."

"Easy," enjoying his command of these arcane matters. "As well as buying in his own goods, he lent out healthy sums for others to do the same. Convince them there's not going to be any doubling of prices, and there'll be a calling-in of loans such as this realm's never seen."

"And a selling-off of goods to cover the loans?"

"Well, the ones with goods to sit on are sure the *rabhsai*'s nerve must fail. Now, I'm not one to say there could be faithful sons of Yoëlladhu who'd stir up unrest amongst the Others; we all know what the Residence Quarter thinks about unruly unbelievers. Howso, a decent riot or two wouldn't maim anybody who matters, and might scare *rabhsayum* enough to force our hand over food. Zhival, who's got a warehouse stuffed with wheat, says it would be fair if *rabhsayum* bought food dear and sold it cheap, if it wants to feed the hungry."

"How long could that go on?"

"Aye. We'd end up with the Treasury asking money-lenders for cash to pay the money-lenders' prices; the Residence Quarter will rule the realm instead of the Residence, and the Household will be your father-in-law's private army. To pay their interest they'll demand a tax on anyone who can't name the Four Ministers or tell you what the wild bees said to Yoëlladhu. Get it, too — that's why you have to take the provincial thing."

"It has not been offered," but he would have to accept if it was. Faëdhal protested his time was too valuable spent in scholarship, but while his life was frugal by Khelagh's standards (or for Khalú's), it was lavish in comforts compared to the poor of the countryside, many, like Norlum, drifting into Kadon Dinul, with the virtual certainty, if not the intention, of becoming beggars. Books might be, as Faëdhal insisted, a necessity, but only for the fed. As long as there were people starving, Dolvid was just another Owani working in a luxury trade.

Yet there was a difficulty no one had raised. While Tholat had never shown any interest in policies or politics, by tradition he was, as Heir, titular *Nim'* of the Paowan, hardly likely to welcome in this new and powerful post the man who had taken away his Khalú.

At a tense gathering, in Laluvoi's suite, Dolvid fought nervousness to enumerate points. "*Asayu*, a proclamation there is to be no increase in lawful maximum prices. Treasury loans, free of interest, to let smallholders buy new seed, and to tide them over till next harvest. This would also give them a little protection against any sudden calling-in of their present borrowings — Master Arvus can explain this."

"It is understood," Laluvoi, tartly. "Even an old lady may have the wits to see the magnates mean to have their money, or else add new foreclosures to their empires, before summer comes. They'll be patient, however, if they foresee we can't hold prices down. How are you going to bring food onto the market?"

Dolvid, very conscious of his company, and especially the calm and watchful Saidhan, clothed, whether he sought it or not, in his renown, suggested a law against storing beyond a set quantity of foodstuffs. Where those amounts were exceeded, there could be seizure and forced sale.

Saidhan was quick with approval. "Aye, smoke them out."

Beside him, Rhunsilakh said nothing, and puffed out his cheeks despondently, seeing these were going to be difficult days for a *Bôdhrai* of the Realm who was also cousin or in-law to all the magnates.

Laluvoi grunted. "Do you mean a law, a Decree in Council?"

"We have the votes," Saidhan said. "Let Vinilat squeal."

"I did not realise we were so eager for new wars to show our undiminished prowess," Laluvoi's reproach to Saidhan was affectionate. "We see the falcon can still hunt. People remember, as they should, the deeds of glory — " she was using the gathering for her audience. "They do not hear about the grey diplomacy that brought the War of the Widowed down to Saidhan Sainati and Tobhsila baKargul, sword to sword in a mountain-meadow. If Kargul had made allies, who can say how the war would have come out?"

"We would have won in any case," Saidhan stoutly maintained. "Kargul with any allies could not triumph, when Banak and Laluvoi were already proclaimed, in the hearts of their people."

"Hundreds more would have died," Laluvoi, simply. "It has been said of Banak and Laluvoi they were often too cautious, change was too slow; Preference is not yet dead, the Families still count for too much in the realm — you'll pardon us, *Bôdhrai*."

Rhunsilakh used a cupped hand to say his loyalty went always to the *rabhsayum*.

"Policy," Laluvoi informed, "has always been simple; not to force measures that unite factions in opposition; *Mankh'* and Kargul, Kargul and its cousins, Great Families and the Families; no one proposal must threaten all at once."

This was candid enough, and it was painful to realise the renewed wars Laluvoi envisaged were actual wars, not just a figure of speech. Rhunsilakh, too, was shocked.

As he had with Bolan, Dolvid insisted the Paowan, especially the Heartland, was where food to feed the realm's hungry could be found. "Each province," tentatively, too conscious of Laluvoi's unwavering gaze, "might be let decide for itself what measures are needed. In that way — "

"You mean, give you powers to compel sales as a provincial proclamation," Laluvoi said. "Without impinging on the leisure of the Council. They would still be able to meet and judge whether it was lawful."

"If they dared." Merovas had been subdued till now, in the presence of his old captain.

Laluvoi had her head on one side. "There may come a time when we shall regret this, when our cousins of Kargul or Dramal bring in measures we would rather stop. Well, one disaster for one day. The Heir always has welfare of his own province in mind," with steely humour. "I expect he'll see the need for bold actions."

Tholat's absence from the meeting was adequate comment. There was discussion of how hoarders of food would be warned, how much notice they would be given before their stocks could be seized. Saidhan wanted goods to be forfeit to the realm where a warning was ignored, but Laluvoi would not have that. "You don't want them calling us robber-princes," patting his hand. The difference between highest and lowest market prices was to be the only penalty for those who waited for seizure.

"Tholat, being a bachelor still," Laluvoi said, perhaps cryptically for some there, "will find this more palatable if we do not call it Dolvid's Law. And Dolvid would be well-advised, at least for now, not to take his rummaging into the Paowanu Loi."

Conjectural which reason came uppermost in Laluvoi's mind: the so-called Paowanu Loi, on the far side of the Kôbh River, had once been the easternmost region of Kargul, which kept petitioning for its return, and bitterly resented its new name. Because from there Kargul had launched its attacks on the Heartland in all three of the civil wars, Banak had stripped away the district, called Kovilanu by Kargul, when the War of the Widowed came to an end. The present *rabhsai* had made it a sort of consolation prize for his second son, Banak-loi, who among other titles was Prince of the Paowanu Loi. Dolvid would be glad to leave it alone, but the warning from Laluvoi only pushed him deeper into gloomy forebodings. The enemies this new post could make for him were without end.

His pessimism worsened when, following the Heir's obedient issuance of an edict against large-scale hoarding, the next proclamation from the *rabhsai* announced, after all, an increase in the maximum price for wheat. The rise, amounting to about one-eighth, was less than had been hoped on one side or feared on the other, but Dolvid, having left the meeting with the impression prices would be held, perceived another regrettable instance of Lambarr's indecisiveness.

There was also Khalú's distress to endure, her anguish he would engage in what she saw as war against her father's circle, but then Khelagh unexpectedly rode over from his estate, and in a cordial atmosphere offered to sell direct to *rabhsayum* at the new price. The amounts were far less than he was rumoured to have stored, but Dolvid happily bought all that was offered, though conscious Khelagh was simply insuring himself by converting part of his hoard into cash.

When he saw Laluvoi she said, "We have to use both spur and bridle," and he saw she was behind the increase in price: he had been blaming the vacillation of Lambarr, when he should have been praising Laluvoi's shrewdness.   Full enforcement, as she said, could wait its turn. Together with the new laws, the change produced exactly the effect intended, as others of the large landowners followed Khelagh, and with not a blade bared large quantities of both grain and flour were available to relieve immediate famine, some to go to the Colony.

With Merovas there was instant understanding. He had a habit of beginning a conversation with bad jokes or inconsequential gossip, as if he supposed a certain amount of idle chatter put people at ease, but he was at heart a serious man and a soldier of calm resourcefulness.   It had been comfortingly vague to insist loudly on the need for wide powers, but was a little frightening to have Merovas ready with cavalry for any task he specified; every garrison had been ordered to provide assistance, and fast-messengers were always available.

"When do we begin?" Merovas asked.

"Today."

"Ah, that's the way. Saidhan always said a swift move can be worth an added regiment."

"So long as the move is in the right direction."

"As you say."

What Dolvid had in mind would not find a place in the annals of glory. A fishing-village called Voruni, where he had never been, but said to be on the far side of the Burantali Gap, was reporting large catches, and he wanted to send an agent to buy all he could at quayside. "You have a man we can trust?"

Because of haphazard supplies there were no fixed prices for fish.

Merovas pondered. "A file-leader, Hinn, with the Burantal garrison. He comes from a merchant's family. You're going to make the dealers unhappy."

"There is more fish than they could handle. All we're doing is preventing waste — and keeping their prices honest."

"You're going to need wheels, then."

"Wagons can be had at Kanzan Tâl. I am going there myself in any case." The city was reputed to be a centre for illicit grain trading.

"I'll give you a half-squadron."

"I can get men from the garrison there."

"For the road," emphatically. "I hear you made enemies with that book, don't ask me why; fine set of yarns. But when you start interfering with people's greed — !"

"A file, a half-file, would be enough for escort."

"A half-squadron." Merovas was stubborn. "There are those who could find fifty to waylay you. Wouldn't be enough against a dozen *péfrapravádal*, but good men might be killed if they thought it could be done."

At the estate Norlum showed him a fine pair of Sebira stallions. "Sent, they were, sir. A gift, so it seems."

"Was there a message?"

"Mistress Khalú knows. Zhival, it was, him with the fat son in the Household."

"Aye, and a fat hand in the corn trade."

"Words about your new appointment working to the benefit of all good men, sir. Nothing wrong with that."

A sigh. "They'll have to go back. Send one of the boys in the morning." For Norlum, a heartbreaking order; his feelings for horses combined a mother's love with the jealousy of a miser. He no longer had any interest in regaining his farm. "I'm content here, sir. We followed you at the Pass of Perus, and so forth."

This devotion, verging on the abject, embarrassed even as it touched Dolvid. "I have entered a suit for recovery of your taxes. You might want to marry again."

Norlum's actions would have been rude in other circumstances; he turned his back and began rubbing down Dolvid's horse. He was muttering, as Dolvid left, about faint signs of chafe from a girth that could be a wee bit tighter.

Khalú said the horses were a lovely gesture. "You should be friends with Zhival."

"He once gave me a half-plakhi for writing his letter. I was only eight, and I took it for a fourthing." He smiled at the memory. "I am sending my thanks, but the horses must go back. In my position I can't take gifts."

"My mother said you would be the richest man in the realm."

"Your mother knows me better." This, lying between them, was more tactless than he had meant to be.

"She does not know you at all. Otherwise how could she praise your good sense? Is there even a salary for your new position?"

He had not thought to ask. "I already have two salaries. I can draw on the Treasury for my expenditures. The expenditures of my office — " seeing her eyes light up.

"What do we not have?" he asked, when she became glumly silent.

"We could be wealthy." For her, an end in itself, but it had many aspects: rough hunting, a house in the Residence Quarter and a villa by Shelum-shore, jewellery to match what she had brought from girlhood, a stable stocked to mount a houseful of guests, this house built larger to sleep all the guests they could then invite for riding.

Dolvid turned away feelings of guilt: she had every right to want what others had, but had married him undeceived about what he was.

When she finished her list, he came back to his point. "It's notorious, Zhival is storing enormous amounts of feed, which he sells at killing prices — farmers are forced to slaughter underweight animals because they can't buy feed, while others are going into debt to save their livestock, and may end up losing their farms. I cannot accept his gifts."

"We are all so unworthy." She was near tears and trying to be cold, a manner he pitied and loathed. "Why would a man marry into the Families, when he is out to destroy them?"

"I didn't — " He tried to grasp her elbows, held tight to her sides, but she shook him free. "I did not marry the Families, I married you."

"No. You're married to Laluvoi, and she'll let you break yourself in pieces. She uses you as a lightning rod, to draw off fury that would otherwise strike at her house."

"Yes." Calmly, not to show how he was shaken by the perception. "That's what rulers do."

Khalú, curiously, was fingering the ruby hung at her breast, just as Laluvoi often did the larger stone she wore. "You could be happy."

"I am riding for Kanzan Tâl tomorrow. I'll bring you a present from the Arcades at Bathrâd." That was absurd, but there was nothing left to debate. She tried to hide her face, but he would not permit it.

Their bedding disappointed hopes of profounder meeting, a mouthful of sweet wine, after which thirst comes back the sourer. In early morning he rode to the cart-track, and a half-squadron of cavalry was waiting, breath of the *pefral* steaming in the chill. Khalú had not risen to see him off.

Amongst soldiers he used, both regulars and auxiliaries, he soon uncovered men who showed every sign of honesty, had the head for prices and quantities, some from farming people far better than he at assessing quality. The most promising he removed from regular duties, to start what was effectively a provincial quartermaster corps, whose main object was to see no one starved. Early on at Kadon Dinul he asked for and obtained a new decree forbidding shipment without approval of any large quantities of food to any other province. This was to prevent men such as Zhival, who owned big estates over in southern Dramal, from evading the measures against hoarding. Other new rules, bound to be an annoyance to many honest growers and dealers, were introduced to regulate how food was bought and sold: it often came to mind he was helping to forge potent tools for oppression, if they came into the wrong hands. At the Residence, where he went to give reports, and to hear praise and encouragement from the *rabhsai* and Laluvoi, he kept hinting at these dangers, and recommended not merely his own tenure but the actual office should be terminated when conditions improved, in no case more than three harvests from the next. Except against dealers blatantly selling well above legal price, he had not invoked power of seizure; its threat had been enough to keep supplies coming onto the market.

Even so, as spring moved to a new summer he must have been to some a sinister figure as he made many journeys, always trying to arrive unexpectedly, after giving due warning of his imminence. As often as he could he dispensed with an escort, riding cross-country: Great Banak's favourite joke had been that no enemy could be prepared for him when he himself seldom knew just where he was. Once, on a clear, cool day near Bathrâd, an arrow buzzed near his head, but that could easily have been someone taking careless aim at a bird, who fled, seeing the near-accident. Again, beyond Burantal a falling rock crashed just ahead of him in a narrow defile, but the spring thaws could cause shifting, and when with his knife out he clambered to where the rock had stood, there was nothing to show anyone had been there.

That was a region he came to love, the folded, always mysterious hill-country between Burantal and Entun Shelum. He was fascinated by the deeper mystery below its tumbled backslope, Shemugrân, wide marshlands, desolate and treacherous, but not abandoned by birds, rabbits, otters, foxes, or venturesome men who hunted its fringes with their bows. For far longer than the dry years had lasted there had been trails through Shemugrân for men and their cattle, joining the Heartland to the Nambalus country in the south, now reached by an immense detour through Kanzan Tâl. Dolvid was convinced that with attention, skill and some luck, a way might even now be picked amongst sluggish streams and standing pools, the quivering bogs and innocent-seeming, green-skinned mires.

Once, leading his horse, he ventured through long marching lines of reed and marsh-grass, root-drowned trees standing lifeless, the ghosts of oaks. Living trees crowned mounds that shouldered up, firm islands in an ocean of doubt, and there were butterflies and moths, midges and gnats, many dragonflies, and a small whirring fly never seen elsewhere, with a shiny blue body. There was a mournful-voiced grey-blue bird that loved to gorge on those flies. Methodically Dolvid led his trembling horse through a band of slow-bubbling marshes to one of the larger islands, rearguard or vanguard of the Burantal Hills, rocky on the western side, with dark firwoods and a spurting, icy stream. Once this had been a camping place; there were shallow, dry caves, and he found signs of many fires, none recent. Just inside a cave he stooped over a mass of rust yet holding the shape of the hunting-knife it once was, and there were the calcined bones of a long-ago meat feast.

He had intended to sleep in Burantal, but could not reach there before dark. From this spot, with a little pushing, he could be in Kadon tomorrow. He made camp, building a fire of dead fir, and passed that night looking south across the darkness of an empty country, where moonlight made blacker shadows and glinted from the surface of sheltered pools. He was enormously alone, and made careful borders for the happiness that came to him. In the past months he had discovered more than he wanted to about dishonesty, duplicity and greed. Tomorrow it would begin again; he loathed the job of hounding men, introducing punishments for doing what people had always done. In his corps there had been falsified reports and faked accounts, attempted juggling with weights and measures, marvellous cases of abrupt prosperity. Normally, with (he believed) tacit approval of Merovas, he simply returned offenders to garrison-duty, confiscating obvious impossibilities, the silver-fitted belt and jewelled scabbard an ordinary file-leader had openly worn; such spoils, with presents given to Dolvid himself, were turned over to Arvus at the Treasury. Risking ridicule, he went on nagging his troops, telling them where they ignored a case of overpricing or left a hoard of foodstuffs unreported they were robbing the poor, perhaps starving some of the poorest.

Arguments with farmers were less exhausting, lines clearly drawn, and it no longer seemed incongruous he could better endure harsh abuse from a farmer's wife over fair price for carrots than habitual skirmishing with Khalú. Why not? the stranger knew him as nothing but a function, and could assail him only in general terms, such as the phrase that used to exasperate Bolan, 'you won't go hungry,' still a favourite. Whereas Khalú, it often seemed, taught herself what mattered to him only so as she could be more accurate with her woundings.

Filling his metal cup at the stream, he heated water and made an infusion of herbs. Through giant quiet there came a long, gathering sigh of wind. Nearby, his horse fidgeted, and blew a little. A burning stick snapped and sent a panic of red sparks rushing up.

During summer, with the Family again at Tan Lughsai, and Faëdhal free to be at the Bronze Residence, Dolvid tried to keep work going there. He continued making his journeys, but less urgently with livestock in live pasture, and meat and cheese, eggs and green vegetables to relieve besieged stocks of grain and root-crops.

Seeing no early hope for a book as demanding as *The End of the House of Gabh'Owan*, he started some brief monographs, not meant for a wide readership, but useful to makers and students of history. One dealt with various methods of reckoning the calendar, another with the many systems of weights, measures and moneys used through the ages on the shores of Arnan. Both threw down fresh challenges to the *Mankh'*, whose view, as with everything else, loftily assumed all coherency in such matters began with Old Owan, though a grudging credit was conceded Ancient Vrobhan.

But the *Mankh'* at present was curiously silent, and had contributed nothing to the making of policy during the hungry years. On his travels Dolvid often had friendly encounters with the *edhradul*, aiding and advising farmers, and they all spoke with pride and wonder about the venerable Patriarch, as if His having come from their Order gave them a special share in His longevity.

Menadhi had not been seen at Kadon Dinul, nor, according to at-Dhanurai, at the Paowanu *Mankh'*. He was assumed to be on the Island, renewing his devotional studies, and his absence doubly lessened his influence on the realm. Banak-loi, his apprentice, joined the Family at Tan Lughsai, as not for several summers. "His own mother hardly knew him," Bolan said, a cruel joke. Saëdhu was back from the South, much stronger, but there were distressing tales of her lapses in memory.

At Kadon, a softness had come with summer to mute all conflicts. As a visitor at his own house, Dolvid was able to establish a truce with Khalú; they were polite and ever so often carefully affectionate. Untimarr, never disconcerted, kept the estates in order, and she spent most of her days at one or another of her father's large houses.

On a journey to Bathrâd where a new smokehouse for pork was being built, he rode alone, leaving the Great Stone Road and taking byways through the hills. On the way he saw evidence that having failed to force up prices many big landowners were taking land out of cultivation. Treasury loans to small farmers elsewhere might help make up the shortfall, but it seemed very wrong that men were wresting oats and barley from thin soil while broad tracts of the rich Heartland were left to weeds and wildflowers. Small farmers east of

Bathrâd, others destitute at Kadon Dinul with stories not very different to Norlum's, would gladly become tenants on these lands just to keep their families fed, with no claim to share in any profits. Riding where sorrel and sparse new grass still followed the contours of recent furrows, he pondered an old law he had come across while looking for something else; Plakhsila *Kímukoi*, wanting to encourage planting, had introduced a measure whereby landowners deliberately keeping growing-land idle (excluding fallow) could be taxed on one-half the value of crops that might have been produced. Even Plakhsila, who normally called the Council together merely to approve what he had already decided, must have met resistance in getting that law adopted; it had rarely if ever been used, which perhaps was the reason why, as far as could be told, it had never been revoked, but simply lain forgotten.

A rioting patch of blue-beggar, starting to creep up over the thatch roof of an empty house, made him think of Laluvoi. He would have to discuss this with her when she came back to the city. As framed, Plakhsila's measure could be used to ruin the Families, but a judicious modification might put a lot of good land back in use.

When he came back to the city on a pleasant late-summer evening, he was jolted from quiet reflections by a hard chorus of jeering. Half a dozen youths of the Residence Quarter out riding had gathered to hurl insults at him. One was Khalú's younger brother Ghuradh, but their leader was that cousin of hers who wanted to design water-gardens: Dolvid now knew he was Lavsila, son of Ladh-Sivai, the would-be magistrate. He was a little older than the others, and would have been strikingly good-looking, if his face had not been twisted up with loathing and contempt. "Take care, *Bôdh'loiki*, when you ride all alone," he called, to forced hoots of approving derision.

"Tholat is no longer pining for your wife," Bolan said. A sure sign of autumn was his coming to the Bronze Residence with all the gossip when he brought the *rabhsai* back from Tan Lughsai. "He's gone south, to ride with his grandmother, they said, but he's also seeing home — do you know about a wench called Radaghi?"

Faëdhal's face portrayed outrage, and even Dolvid winced at the description. The wench, as he explained to Bolan, had connections with all the Great Families, doubly a niece to Daënakh of Ân and Laënakh of Nîv, with at least two clear lines of descent from the House Gabh'Owan. Indeed, with her elder sister Finú, she could claim to be nearest there was to a Gabh'Owan heir; if Banak (as might reasonably be maintained), in strict law, never had any right to the Sword, then Finú, considering both her father's and mother's bloodlines, was legitimist candidate for *rabhsaëyu*, and if declared incompetent (as rumour had it she probably was), then the choice would have to fall on the *wench* Bolan mentioned.

None of this was going to happen; the sisters, who had not inspired any movement for restoration of Gabh'Owan rule, were no threat to Lambarr. They were understood to be very often at Inilun Barabhi in Kargul, lair for bitter might-have-beens, but their home was in the South, near Thenimala, and from there Radaghi had come, and now returned, as Saëdhu's travelling companion.

For Dolvid, wanting to consult with Laluvoi, the most important news was that she had set her mind on what, at eighty-six, might be her last visit to Thenimala where she was born.

Bolan preferred to chatter on about the long days Radaghi and the Heir had spent together — nights, too, he said. As often his information must come from one of the serving women he liked to bed and blandish; he mentioned supposed evidence of a shared taste for pain as part of mating, and amused himself over whether the Heir might prefer inflicting or receiving. Faëdhal, scandalised, stalked away, and the only real interest was confirmation of Khalú's shuddering distaste, the night her panic to escape Tholat had made Dolvid propose without meaning to.

Possibly to show his eye was not only for servants Bolan offered that Radaghi was not much to his taste, a face with hard bone to it, though she had improved the Heir's temper. He also found Sai-Nivu less pleasing than before, saying conceit was a quality he could not stand in a woman. General opinion was that at nineteen the *rabhsai*'s second daughter was the one who most resembled young Laluvoi, either for beauty or for sweetness of disposition; evidently she was being blamed by Bolan for Bolan's loss of nerve.

He made Dolvid jump by asking brusquely, "What have you ever heard about a law taxing farmers on crops they don't grow?"

"From Plakhsila's century, seldom if ever enforced." This was mind-reading; he had not mentioned his reflections to anyone.

"I always heard Plakhsila was supposed to be wise. How can you tax a man on what he hasn't got? Arvus is talking about reviving this. He must be mad."

Dolvid now recalled exactly why he knew of the law's existence. Some years ago Tellis had made, for her father's use, a copy of a treatise on Plakhsila's land-reforms. At that period laws were inscribed only in the Owanilú, and she had consulted Dolvid on points of translation.

He told Bolan, "The law prescribed a full year's warning before the tax could be imposed, giving the landowner the choice of putting in new crops, or being taxed on half their value."

Bolan, arresting his scorn in full flight, stared. "You're not saying this would be a good law."

"Not indiscriminately applied. The realm needs ways to get more use out of the best land."

"If growers were assured of better prices," giving out the Residence Quarter view at its baldest, "nothing against what you've done, there wouldn't be any shortages. Why should they lay out good money, when there's no profit to be had?"

"Who asks them to? But as long as there is hunger in Arbhal they should not be allowed to keep the best land from farmers who know how to use it."

"That's Deniant talk, Dol — Arvus has been speaking about forfeiture when people fail to use their land. I tell you, when word gets out about a tax on what you haven't grown —

"

"I'll get together with him. I'm sure Arvus does not want to start enforcing the law exactly as it stands."

"My father always means what he says." In his usual light-footed, faintly surreptitious way, Arvat had come into the room. "Well, doesn't he?" Small, voice not darkening, Arvat had grown a faint moustache he often stroked. At his same age Dolvid had left the *Mankh'*, and was in a battle against Darborr's love for wine, his for Darborr's wife. Better, perhaps, to be son to a high official, allowed a childhood that faded slowly, although even those who did not care for the opinions of Arvus wished Arvat had inherited a little of his father's character.

"For once," Dolvid said. "What he says may have been misreported. Or over-reported."

But Bolan, this once, had it right. Just the same, the worst might have been averted if only Laluvoi had not been away in the South — and, oddly, if Tholat had not gone with that same riding.

Before there was a chance to discuss anything with him, Arvus took his recommendations to the *rabhsai*; imposition of the half-value tax on all lands recently fallen idle, after a year's warning. What happened next had to be put together from differing accounts. Rhunsilakh, prepared by rumour for this, at once opposed the measures, and had hot words with Arvus, who was supported by Merovas, only other appointed official there. Tholat's absence, though he was *Nim'* of the Paowan, would have meant nothing by itself, but Banak-loi took his seat, and he supported Rhunsilakh; it was agreed he also went well beyond anything Rhunsilakh could ever have said, with rasping sarcasms on the subject of Arvus's intelligence, even loyalty and personal honesty.

Everything conspired to bring about disaster; it could also be claimed *Menadhi*'s disappearance contributed; without that, Banak-loi would not have spent summer at Tan Lughsai. The *rabhsai*, even Bolan said, had once or twice shown extreme impatience with his second son, who had not only declined to join in the simple pleasures of the Summer Residence, but mocked them as childish and brainless, using exactly the same exasperating tone he now directed against Arvus and his proposal.

Added to all this, it might be the *rabhsai* wanted to show he could make decisions apart from his mother. Not that Lambarr went against what he would assume to be Laluvoi's views. Arvus told him there, as he later maintained with Dolvid, that he had already discussed this with Laluvoi, who had been all in favour.

Perhaps, but she would never have approved a proclamation as unequivocal (and tactless) as the one Lambarr had read on the Steps and posted in public places, a precipitate step he could take without convening the Council, since the needed law already existed. From the coming tax on disused land not even provincial overlords were explicitly exempted, an oversight, plainly, but one that provoked anger and a mood of defiance in all the Great Houses.

Even more damaging was a single phrase Arvus had

insisted on; the tax would be imposed on estimated potential yield, `whether or not lands lying idle have been dedicated to *ga-Yalum*.' Arvus said afterwards this was intended to show the tax was not directed exclusively against the Families, the only ones ever to have their fields consecrated with the chanting of an *atarlai* and proper ceremonial observances.   Dolvid suspected Arvus was also showing off a little, parading his knowledge of a faith he did not share.

The Families, however, aware who was real author of Lambarr's proclamation, heard this as the gratuitous sarcasm of a Deniant.   The *Mankh'*, too, was outraged, and a personal protest came from the venerable Patriarch, whose own *Edhrodilum* was the Order performing the rituals of *ga-Yalum*. In one stroke ill-considered policy had done what Laluvoi had always tried to avoid, uniting Families, Great Families and the *Mankh'* against the *rabhsai*.   Past harvest anger rumbled on; hard frosts came early, Laluvoi returned to Kadon Dinul on a raw day well short of the Fire Days. She had a grim face, and like an omen first snow came blanketing down to whiten fields and block the roads after her.

Circumstances kept conspiring against reason, putting the normally mild Lambarr in the most intractable position. Dealing with a local magistrate's foolish misinterpretation of law, Laluvoi, Dolvid had seen her do it, would set him right with sweet patience (contempt kept well beneath the surface), and send him away convinced he had been astute enough to catch the error himself, and man enough to admit his initial mistake.

She was tired from long journeys, and annoyed with her son; her skill failed and her tone made him remember he was the *rabhsai*. He dug his heels in, and nothing could make him budge, not even Arvus, who, after a long debate with Dolvid and a private audience with Laluvoi, was willing to admit there must be something wrong with a proclamation, however just, that could tear apart a realm. It was doubtful tempers could be cooled by a mere modification in its language, but Lambarr refused even to consider that, reminding Arvus, as he had his mother, that what had been proclaimed was an existent law, which only a full meeting of the Council could rescind or alter. General opinion at the Residence largely blamed separation from and continued anxiety over Saëdhu for this new, implacable Lambarr.

The new year came in a mild spell, and Dolvid, at home, had a visit from Khelagh, who rode up with only a small escort. He had put on flesh in the past few years, and was short of breath.

"You are known," he said, given a comfortable chair and a cup of wine, "as a man of moderation." Dolvid just prevented a smile; until the *rabhsai* rashly followed the rash advice of Arvus, the Families had seen him as maddest dog of the Heartland. They must have heard about his dismay over the proclamation. Through Faëdhal, perhaps, or Rhunsilakh.

"This proposed tax," Khelagh went on pleasantly. "Under a law long-forgotten, wisely forgotten. It can never be collected."

"It is entirely out of my hands," he took rather shameful pleasure in saying. His very first feeling when the law was revived had been personal pique, natural if less than laudable, that he, with his responsibilities for feeding the Heartland, had not been consulted.

"You are modest. You are said to have the ear of Laluvoi, and Laluvoi has always sought the just and peaceable solution to any question. You have seen her? They say she is showing signs of age."

She had not been seen in public since returning. "Laluvoi *Asayu* is tired from travel, but a long way from her retirement. She still seeks moderate answers to heated questions. But I don't believe this measure, taxing idle lands, is going to vanish entirely. One may be opposed to its full severity, yet see there is a need to encourage, if necessary force, increased cultivation."

"Force," the voice stayed affable, "may only provoke counter-force. I hear the Great Families are calling this new law intolerable, and I know people everywhere, officers of the Household, magistrates, all true Children of Yoëlladhu, even if they would never be touched by the tax, have been offended by the reference to *ga-Yalum*."

This long speech left him rather winded, and gave Dolvid a chance to measure out a reply. "I am told the Residence will soon make it plain this law was never meant to apply to provincial *nimul*. When *g'Asalladh'* — " he, with Khelagh, made the pious gesture — "is satisfied no slight to the *Atarlum* was ever intended, we'll be left with the real purpose of the proclamation. How rigorously the law is enforced may well depend on how much hunger there is this winter.

Between us, there can be no advantage in holding back foodstuffs. No further increase in prices can be expected." He had been informed Khelagh had purchased and was storing even more grain.

Khelagh, thoughtful, turned conversation to bland remarks about the unpredictable weather, and a new strain of cattle he had high hopes for.

At last he got up, buttoning his brocaded outshirt. "I should speak with you more often, Dolvidh. You're a busy man, true, but one as close as you are to the heart of the realm is well worth a visit. What you say about prices will be hard news for the dealers. Is this your opinion, or settled policy, then?"

"My opinion, of course," letting his face hint he would say more if he could.

Khelagh looked round the room. "I do not recall we ever made you a gift when you moved in here."

"My thanks, sir, but there is nothing I need."

A small laugh. "Tell me there is nothing Khalú needs"

"You must ask her — as father to daughter."

"Is she nearby?"

"I expect she'll want to see you to stirrup. If you will excuse me, I have to ride soon myself." After a stiff exchange of half-deferences, Dolvid withdrew.

While faint, the air of affront had been genuine. Yet even if he believed his dangling of gifts was innocent, the context of the offer made it unthinkable, even a gift to Khalú (which she would certainly accept) in Dolvid's presence. And of course it both was and was not innocent; for the Families there was no clear boundary between friendship and self-interest; bribes did not exist; friends were allies and allies friends, favours followed gifts in the nature of things.

Before that, what they had implicitly been discussing was sobering to contemplate. Khelagh's inclusion of the Great Families with those that would resist the new tax suggested, must be meant to suggest, civil war, while mention of army officers among those whose religion had been offended was a plain hint there could be mutiny if the *rabhsai* tried to enforce his proclamation. Dolvid saw his unruffled answers had taken off part of Khelagh's edge, but was distressed to see the settled, familiar realm change overnight into a terrain where loyal swords had to be counted, and words could start wars.

When Khalú came back in from seeing her father off, her cheeks were glowing, her hair ruffled by the breeze that declared winter was not done. She made a face, seeing him dressed for travel.

"I hoped we would have a meal together," looping arms loosely about his neck, and bringing her slender body up against his. When he kissed her, a small hand snaked between buttons of his outshirt, then shirt, scrabbling at his chest. He decided the realm's business could wait an hour.

When bedding came during a truce he always pretended not to see she pretended to be more pleased than she really was. "My father," she murmured in the quiet after, "says you deserve much respect." She made it sound a novel idea.

The wild vacillations of weather brought the heaviest snows in years. Merovas, saying he would turn the entire General Cavalry into a quartermaster corps, sooner than have food riots to deal with, had squads and companies of soldiers out to cut wagon-wide passages through the worst of the drifts. In one of their always-harried meetings he confessed that if there was unrest due to shortages, he would be half in sympathy with the rioters, which did not mean they could break things with impunity.

Thaw came, too early to call it the end of winter. While on the southern rim of the Heartland, getting animal feed moved to places hit hardest by snows, Dolvid took an afternoon to look into the rumour of an out-of-the-way farmer who had a large number of cheeses stored, not hoarded, but for the odd reason that he had not found buyers.

Taking to squelching grasslands less muddy than the roads, under the brightness of false spring but a sky that promised further showers, he soon concluded he had missed the way, spotting none of the landmarks he had been told to watch for, eventually seeking directions at a farmhouse on the top of a gentle rise in the middle of small, well-kept lands.

He had ridden through rain in his shabbiest cloak, so it was not rank that made him welcome. The farmer asked him in. His face was browned by wind, as if dusted with brown clay, and crevices at corners of mouth and eyes were sharp-edged like cracks in clay. The greying eyebrows were also sun-bleached, and the eyes beneath full of kindness and a glint of humour, a little of Ott, though there was nothing so daunting about this man, Urnirr. He swung back the battered-looking bottom half-door over which he had been talking, with a gesture Lambarr might have envied.

Like many poor farmhouses it was virtually all one large space, with a loft, and a couple of smaller rooms, scarcely more than alcoves, tacked on at the rear. Over the front windows part of the loft became a sleeping-space, with broad shelves serving for bunks, while much of the rear wall was an immense hearth with a broad swathe of burnished brick in front, kept scrupulously clean. There was a half-dozing peat fire, and as near as possible a huge, striped, copper-coloured tomcat was stretched out with a foolish grin, twitching tail-tip betraying dreams, or the fraudulence of his seeming sleep. On either side of the fireplace, set back, there was a slatted box, one a mass of variegated kittens and a black-and-white mother, all ecstatic to be sucking or giving suck. The other topless cage held dark, fluffy, very new ducklings, which kept clambering over each other to flop awkwardly to the brick floor. Urnirr or his shy wife Altis would pick them up and put them back in the box, watched by a smooth-haired black bitch, tail shortened in a long-ago accident, whose face conveyed pity mixed with contempt for the failures of some mothers.

"Warm yourself, master." Urnirr waved to the fire, or the low seat on the kittens' side. True, Dolvid's hands, having been wet, had turned delicate shades of lilac, raw pink and ivory.

A grandson of about three appeared, and stood staring without emotion at the stranger, till Altis, who kept her head averted, gave one sharp word, and the boy ducked away under a shock of dark hair. The glance he shot as he retreated was furtive but not hostile.

Outside, rain was pattering again on bare earth. Sharp animal smells mingled with acrid peat-smoke.

Urnirr was puzzled, but too polite to ask, so Dolvid gave him some idea of what he was, and what doing. The man nodded. "Yes, it's bad for the poor, winters, worse when they see others with fat bellies. I can say this to you, sir. But I wouldn't want to be at that Kadon."

His wife, not looking up, said, "No land can ever be as bare as an empty market-place." Seated across the hearth from Dolvid, between rescues of ducklings she was working at her mending, gnarled fingers still nimble.

"When I was a boy," Urnirr said, "we had to go up the hill and strip bark from trees for eating. It hasn't come to that again, not yet."

"Perhaps he would honour us," Altis, to her husband in a small voice.

"Ah, I'm all gossip — would you do the favour of taking a hot drink with us, sir?"

"That would please me."

Urnirr went outside. A wet slap, a mournful bleat, and a goat, its flanks steaming, pranced in. Altis had gone for a pewter pot, and she stooped to milk the goat with an experienced hand, Urnirr resting an arm across the high-ridged back. Long mouth kept working, eyes alert for things to chew.

For Dolvid there was immediate passage back to those days long ago in the encampment of the Froghul; not only the goat but the open hospitality here. Unbitter but baffled, he wondered how he could come to feel so welcome where he had no possible home.

Milking complete, the goat was given a wisp of hay, and driven unwilling out into the rain, light but steady. Urnirr quickly closed the bottom half of the door; instantly there was the heavy thud of a horned head, and the deep scarring on the outside of the door was explained.

Dolvid admired how this couple, without words, divided tasks; Altis put tiny twigs on smoldering peat, and broke small sticks to lay across, and Urnirr bent to huff up flame. At the sound of milk spurting into the pot the huge coppery cat had raised his head, and now Altis poured a small amount of milk in an earthen bowl near him. Back legs remaining sprawled, he twisted, then, deciding the warm yellow milk was worth it, rearranged muscles and stood completely, arching his back and bristling before crouching to the bowl. The mother cat, meanwhile, shook off her insatiable and shrill attachments, yawned, and jumped lightly from the box to circle to the opposite rim. The two heads made feints at each other, but on the whole they took sensible turns. The smaller cat's head had exactly the profile of Khalú's breasts.

While Altis was busy warming the milk Dolvid took over retrieval of the spilled ducklings. Necessary for the black dog to come forward and sniff at his hand, and apparently he passed the test; tongue drooped from a smiling mouth the dog went back to watching the endless task.

They drank a brew of nettles in milk, sweetened with crystallised honey, and he was given a barley-cake so dry he could hardly swallow it. Luckily the small grandson made a second appearance, and had most of the cake. Dolvid told about Lambarr, and about Sai-Nivu's famous new gown, made all of shuzi, inventing details he could not remember, while the squeezed face of Altis gleamed interest. She was even more attentive to parts about Laluvoi, how well she managed notwithstanding her age, how kind she could be, how brusque with any impertinence. Where they were sitting was less than a full day's ride on a good horse from Market Gate, and it was as if he was telling tales of a fabled city beyond pathless mountains in forgotten time. Urnirr and occasionally Altis talked about what was real to them; weather and planting, soil which could be wooed, but would never surrender. A son, a daughter-in-law and an unmarried daughter lived with them and today were all working at the linen-maker's in a nearby hamlet. An older son had married and Altis made it sound as if he had moved away to the Colony (or the moon), till she admitted he came to see them, now and again, from his farm this side of Burantal. His bride, it seemed, was gradually learning how a man's house ought to be kept.

The rain stopped and watery sun came through the doorway. Dolvid had his directions, and no excuse for loitering. He had not realised how weary he was of the envies, suspicions, restless discontents of Kadon Dinul, how little he wanted to be part of policies, plottings, rumours of civil war, how much he longed for simplicity. As long as he lived, it appeared, he would be turning back to watch Tini-ra make the sign of grief with her thumbnail.

He would offend his hosts with offer of payment, and so pressed a whole plakhi into the small, fat, hot hand of the grandson, who stared at the coin in absolute amazement. Dolvid plunged a hand pleasurably into the nest of jumbled fur where the mother cat was back on ecstatic duty, picked up and replaced a final duckling, stroked the strong-necked head of the great tom, who yawned rudely and formidably. He bowed to thank Altis for the drink, and with Urnirr beside him went out into cool air. The farmer sniffed. "Be dry for your ride. We're not out of winter yet, not by a month or more."

He hoped their guest would pass that way again, and Dolvid agreed, knowing how unlikely that was. Behind the half-door an Altis, ducking away, gave a half-wave. Turning his horse in the direction of a man who made more cheese than he could sell, Dolvid ambled down the slope, leaving that happy time behind him.

xix

Ban-Sila

"Who would have believed it," Bolan said, "after last week?" False spring had gusted away, and the capital was under a fresh mantle of snow. After Halving-Day any snow that laid was unusual in the Heartland, but Bolan was anxious about Tan Lughsai, where a much heavier fall was reported. Days with the soft warmth almost of early summer had taken Lambarr with most of the Family on an early visit to the Cape. The same freak of position, winds and Arnan currents that gave Tan Lughsai its swift spring and warm summer also exposed it to sudden storms, and while riders from Kadon Dinul could without much difficulty reach the hamlet of Rhutalai, the peninsula itself, just to the south, was buried, *rabhsai* cut off from his capital.

"At least Laluvoi, praise Hrafi, is here. I came to tell you we've borrowed your work-crews from Burantal. That road is open; by one way or another we should be able to dig through to the Estates."

"Lambs and kids will be lost in this," despondently. "I was hoping this would be the last year we would need a quartermaster."

"Aye, wear your balls out to see the rabble fed, and they're never satisfied. How do we stand, as against last year?"

"A little better." The smokehouses they had built in outlying parts meant farmers got some return on animals that otherwise might have died for lack of feed. Saidhan had been glad to pledge fuel-woods from the Colony, in exchange for preserved meats.

"You'll be well out of it. There's going to be the bloodiest battle over Arvus's new tax. Still — " Bolan became thoughtful. "We can't go back to leaving it all to chance."

"The *rabhsayum* could guarantee grain-supplies." What Dolvid said would probably be reported to Khelagh, but it did not matter; the policy could accomplish as much if it only scared magnates into virtue. "It is not a hard sum to see enough wheat sown; there may be poor years and good ones, but over three or four years warehousing would maintain supplies, and then prices would be no worry. What I am sick of is all the prying and spying, the threats. It's no better for the ones who do the intimidating — Hinn was a good officer a year ago."

"Hinn? Isn't he honest? You said he'd done a good job at Kanzan Tâl. Have Merovas replace him, then."

"Oh, he is honest. Replace him, and the next one may take bribes or falsify reports." Men could be ruined other ways; in gratitude to Hinn two merchants had given Hinn a saddlecloth of white shuzi; he let women reach up to kiss his hand, and though apparently incorruptible by money, could be bribed by flattery.

"What power does."

"Don't tell me. Everyone fights to be in the personal

escort; when I pick men for Tan Lughsai every half-squadron wants to tell me I'm the cleverest captain since Larghai. One thing, I might send a ship from Owan Sai." Struck by this new idea for communicating with the Cape, Bolan left to go across to Harbour Gate, where someone might know what ships were available at the royal port.

Faëdhal was patiently waiting to compare notes on a translation, but work had scarcely begun when there was a new interruption. A half-squadron leader from the Household, Perimas, a man Dolvid knew by sight, came into the Old Audience Hall, looking dazed. He was near exhaustion; easy to guess he had come from Tan Lughsai, first since the heavy snow there.

"*Bôdh'loiki* — isn't Captain Bolan here? His standard is by the entrance. I was told he was with you."

"He'll be back." He had come by the side-entrance and left through the main doors. "Have a seat." Dolvid sent Arvat to the kitchens to fetch warm *raminat*, if there was any, otherwise any other hot drink. Perimas was cold and trembling, barely able to speak.

"You have ridden from the Cape?" More than fatigue in the face; pain, fear, a crushing anxiety. "What is it?" Dolvid said.

"There has been a fire — " in a near-whisper.

"At Tan Lughsai?"

"The Summer Residence. Burnt to the ground." The vast structure of wood, fireplaces never made for winter weather.

"Is anyone lost?" — feeling fear start.

"Everyone," beginning to weep in shuddering sobs.

"Not the *rabhsai*?" Faëdhal asked sharply.

"Everyone."

The tale was told in agonising fragments, and had to be started again when Bolan came in, to listen with a dead, ashy face. It was filled with terrible confusion, but the facts were terribly simple: fire had begun in the bitterly cold night after the big snowfall. Most of the troops were quartered in the older stone building nearby, where nothing was noticed till the blaze was lighting the sky. With head-high drifts hampering movement, there was never any effective attempt to fight the fire. A few from lower levels were rescued or saved themselves, mainly servants, but also Selnoi, wife of the *Bôdhrai* Rhunsilakh. Not Rhunsilakh himself, none of the Family, and the Wooden Residence ended by collapsing in a fierce core of flame.

Having had to fight his way through snow to bring the news, Perimas was muddled in his time-sense, but must have remained a full day and night before setting out. When he left, ashes on the mound of the Summer Residence were still smoking. A few more survivors had emerged from the trees surrounding, and all were now at the Winter Riding School with the soldiery. Everyone not found must be dead: Lambarr *Rabhsai*, the Heir Tholat, Laloi with her husband Brodhai of Ân, Dolvid's former favourite pupil Lambakh, the pretty Sai-Nivu, their little sister Telura.

"There is no *rabhsai*," Perimas went sobbing on.

Also weeping, Faëdhal said, "That, if you will pardon me, is not possible. The realm is never without a ruler."

"In the South, with Saëdhu," Dolvid began. "Young Rodlakh." He was about twelve, and his reign would begin with a *Moradhilum* till he came of age. Saidhan, perhaps jointly with Laluvoi, would be obvious choice for *Maëdhrai*, Protector.

"Surely," Faëdhal said, "Banak-loi was not with the Family at Tan Lughsai." The distaste with which he spoke the place-name touched on its old reputation as ill-omened, and the peculiar, sombre exultation of the superstitious when grim events came to confirm their folly.

"He was going," Bolan said. "Then word came *Menadhi* was back on the Mainland. I sent a half-squadron with Banak-loi as far as Treaty Stone four or five days ago. He is at the *Mankh'* now, unless he left on his own and went south."

"Banak-loi *Asai* never came," Perimas said.

"Banak *Deghi*," Dolvid corrected, and Faëdhal stood. "The Second Banak, Banak *Iftaki, Rabhsai*."

Not only Lambarr but Lambarr's *rabhsayum* had been destroyed at Tan Lughsai; as well as Rhunsilakh, several lesser counsellors had been lost. Dolvid counted up those who survived with the rank of *bôdh'loiki*; Arvus, Mirrat, himself, and two Royal Captains, one of them here.

"You must send word to the *Mankh'*," he told Bolan. The Captain of the Household had, for this hour, the realm in his hands. Bolan sat down dully on the edge of a table; Faëdhal was alternately clasping each long hand over the other.

"Are we certain?" Bolan said. "Some of the Family may yet be alive." Perimas, who had seen the fire, shook his head.

"The news has to go to Laluvoi." Dolvid felt sick. The faces of the others told him who would have that job.

"You have to act," he urged. "Remember what happened in 2876, when news came out of Ní-Tilagh. We have some powerful lords who never have accepted the House of Banak."

"You mean, someone might try to grab the Sword?"

Surrounded by grief and numbness, Dolvid recognised his own clarity as either praiseworthy or monstrous, but it was too soon to miss Lambarr or mourn him, too dangerous to spend minutes searching for right feelings.

"Merovas is away in Dônshei."

"You have to act," Dolvid repeated. Arvat had come in with hot *raminat* freshly made, and Dolvid sent him to fetch the Household men from by the side-entrance, thinking if they were brought here Bolan would have to start issuing orders.

As he did. Once begun, using Dolvid as his scribe, and often consulting with him, he was furiously active. An order was written to cancel off-duty hours. Kizhunai, whose rank was now under-captain, was sent to the main barracks of the Household to give the alert, then to secure the Treasury with an extra squadron. Guard on all city gates was reinforced, and two squadrons left for the *Mankh'* to fetch the new *rabhsai*, under Acting-*Kímukan* Zhinladh, corpulent son of the wealthy Zhival. They had unresolved discussion about the advisability of a curfew, and Bolan soon left for the General Cavalry barracks to concert their plans, leaving Dolvid to take Perimas to the Residence and Laluvoi.

Late afternoon; they rode with a half-squadron under Dorrmas, celebrated beyond his age or rank for his swordsmanship. The sky was dull, and on the Avenue, where patches of trodden snow remained, small gatherings of townspeople called out for news as the soldiers rode past. All the comings and goings of troops must have started rumours.

There was no talk with his companions, and Dolvid was pondering not the death of Lambarr and the others, but the accession of Banak-loi. With his glumness, contempt for his father's mild rule, his close friendship with the next Patriarch, he was least appealing among all the offspring (of that large family only three survived, all boys; besides Rodlakh, six-year-old Orbanak was with Saëdhu in the South). Banak-loi was *rabhsai*; a sudden, unanimous conspiracy at the Old Bronze Residence might have decided otherwise, but if you challenged his succession, it did not bring anything better, merely restarted all old quarrels about his grandfather's right to reign, opening the field for any imaginable challenger.

It was often taught no one could predict what a man would be when he came to power; the young Plakhsila was said to have been full of stupid jokes, and even Great Banak's fame as a fighter had not given any hint of the subtlety and calm forbearance of his reign. Banak-loi, if he was astute enough to accept it, could have help from the same companion who had brought out those virtues in his grandfather; Laluvoi was hope.

No *rabhsai*'s rule was absolute. The Treaty of the Wind Caves had established the Council, and there, Banak-loi at present did not have the two weapons needed for any *rabhsai* to dominate, widespread general popularity, and prestige with the armies. Yet Banak-loi, after so many deaths, would have greater say than most rulers in initial composition of his Council; there survived, besides the *rabhsai*, only seven certain members, though the Royal Captains, Bolan and Merovas, would be reconfirmed in their posts by silence. But if *Menadhi* had found in Banak-loi a more faithful disciple than Dolvid had been, only Saidhan and Laluvoi in the Council could be counted on to resist *Menadhi*'s vision of Old Owan reborn, the return of Preference, religious tests for office-holders, subordination of the Other Races.

Coming up the slope to the Disc he frowned; to think of Banak, grandson of Banak, he grandson of Rodelam, a Mixed tanner, as advocate of pure Owani blood and ancient aristocracy was hardly sane; more sensible to worry over his own future, and whether *Menadhi* still felt vindictive; Dolvid's days as office-holder with *rabhsayum* might be approaching an end.

As they dismounted, Dorrmas, a compact, effective figure, was shaking his head. "It'll never be the same without Lambarr, *Bo'laki*." It had evidently become a point of honour with younger Mixed officers to mispronounce words of the Owanilú in everyday use.

Attended by two serving-women and a *ramidu*, Laluvoi was in the Great Window Chamber, where for seventy years she had looked out on the Avenue of Treaties, long enough to tell a happy crowd from a puzzled or discontented gathering. With Perimas dry-mouthed beside him, Dolvid made deference. By some means Laluvoi already had the news.

"*Asayu*," he said, "*bi namakil shudal yi-butraghal ul.*"

"*Y'olagh' am*," she returned. The eyes were giving none of their lively glances, and the voice was of a very old woman.

Dolvid wrestled with the question of holding out hope, probability it would be false. While technically true the *rabhsai*'s death was not certain till identifiable remains were found, that, by Perimas's description of the fire, might be never.

"Poor Saëdhu," almost inaudibly, Laluvoi's eyes blank and tearless. "She would have chosen to be there, and shared Lambarr's end."

That could even be true, though not understood; death was a personal enemy, against which alliance had no effect.

"What steps are the captains taking, *Bôdh'loiki*?" sitting straight to ask that, voice stronger. He told her about the squadrons riding for the *Mankh'*, redoubled guards, the proposed curfew.

"The auxiliaries should be called to the colours."

"*Asayu*, Bolan insists his strength of regulars is adequate."

"That may be, but bowmen and pikemen gathered under the Bronze Sword are not under other colours, or none."

Shock and grief had not driven out her shrewdness. Perimas was enormously relieved when, telling him she would hear his full story later, she dispatched him to find Bolan and bring him, or failing that one of his senior officers. But as Perimas was withdrawing, she did ask one question; "It was all burnt, the Summer Residence?"

"*Asayu*, to the ground. The snow boiled."

With his reason for being here gone, Dolvid also would have taken leave, but Laluvoi waved back her other attendants, and beckoned him near. She put out a dry, crinkled hand to tug on his arm. "Come closer. *Bôdh'loiki*, you have written about famed lives, and read many more. Do you think life is to be valued? We honour those who save lives — would it not be better if we punished anyone who tried to prolong this fraud?"

She had ended in a strained whisper. He said, "I do not have any wisdom, *Asayu*."

"Saidhan should be here — he is the only one left. Banak and his captains, all gone. Kamanasalladh goes on living, as a rotted stump of himself — for what? You know what I have always worked for?"

"Justice, *Asayu*," awkwardly conscious of the serving-women, the *atarlai*, trying to appear preoccupied, and guessing at talk they could not quite overhear.

"Oh, certainly, justice." Her sardonic mouth came, but she kept her voice at the same throaty whisper. "Prosperity, liberty, happiness for every man, woman, child and household pet. With every ruler through the ages, the general good has been my constant preoccupation."

There was nothing to say. The clutch on his arm tightened, as yellowed lips started to tremble. "A family — " she began, and swallowed. "A family is life."

Tears were there, but did not flow. Dolvid dared to bring his free hand across to close over hers where it gripped his left arm, the loose, arid parchment-skin unpleasant to the touch. Laluvoi pulled in her lower lip, and bit down with front teeth that were still strong and white. She closed her eyes for a long second. Then the hand disengaged, and went to rest in her lap with the other.

"My thanks, Dolvidh." She meant he should stand back a little.

Rhunilat came in, looking both youthful and ill; he heard as news that his mother was alive, and was afraid to seem glad of that. Arvus arrived together with Bolan; a different Laluvoi, surmising no word would come back from the *Mankh'* before dark, issued instructions for a curfew, and the calling up of auxiliaries first thing tomorrow.

Turning her back on everyone she went to the Great Window. A colourless evening was near, and clouds were lower. "No. No object to declaring a *Moradhilum*; there isn't any hope. We shall proclaim the Second Banak, and send them home to bed."

A light cold rain was falling, as the people pressed forward against the cordon of soldiery across the foot of the Steps. News of the Tan Lughsai disaster had been announced in the streets, and the crowd was a sober one, many weeping.

It was no resplendent gathering on the Steps. Laluvoi, tiny and forlorn was at the centre, sole representative of either Family or Great Families. Arvus and Mirrat, with Dolvid, were highest civil officials, and amongst the others Faëdhal's presence made absence more conspicuous; with Lambarr and Tholat gone he was tallest there, stooped a little, and blinking in the rain. Bolan had assembled a number of senior officers, and the rest were wives and offspring. Khalú was there, pale and serious: Dolvid earlier had asked Bolan for a half-file to fetch her from the estate, and had barely greeted her arrival before trumpets sounded to begin the ceremony.

He was the one to proclaim the new *rabhsai*: there was

no one else to do it. He had no chance to rummage documents for a precedent, and no exact one came to mind; in the end how Banak-rai had come to Sword, with no legitimist claim, created the need for this makeshift and fevered haste to instal an absent *rabhsai*.

Till he stepped forward, trumpets giving the royal salute, he had only vague ideas what to say. His knees were trembling, but that was only his body; there was no nervousness in his mind, or his voice, which came clear and strong, not loud, but it would carry.

"Lambarr *Rabhsai* is gone," cold afterword to a gentle life and a terrible death. "The Heir having also died, succession lawfully falls upon his second son." Pause; small mouthfuls were best for large gatherings. "Know your *rabhsai*, Banak *Deghi*, Banak *Iftaki*, Banak *bi*-Arbhai-Navu, Prince of the Paowanu Loi, Prince of the Paowan, Lord of the Whole." This accorded in turn the titles of elder brother and father, but it was uncertain how readily the crowd recognised this Banak as Banak-loi.

"Know him!" Dolvid cried, and this was the juncture where a new *rabhsai* would normally step forward. "Honour him! Obey Him!"

"*Olagh am!*" came a voice louder than his, and there beside him, riding cloak over grey robe thrown back, arms outstretched, was *Menadhi*. Trumpets again gave the royal salute, and a deep sound of assent came from the crowd. Dolvid was glad to step back and let *Menadhi* use his practised craft to play the new mood, hushing it to solemnity as he pronounced a brief *kolukezh'* of hope for the new *rabhsayum*.

Then Bolan strode out to tell the people they could greet their new ruler in the morning, and they should go quietly to their homes.

Just inside the Residence doors, near the foot of the gleaming stair, *Menadhi* detained Dolvid. "You did well, *Bôdh'loiki*."

The deep-scored face was friendly, and Dolvid, forefinger to breast, made quick half-deference. "At sad need, *Menadhi*."

"But I shall not reign in that name." There by the stair was Banak-loi, accepting everyone's obeisance and words of condolence. He was in plain riding-clothes, but it was an oddity he had not shownn himself to his people. As with his being here; there were several possible ways to enter without riding the length of the Avenue (including a very hidden one only Dolvid could find), most improbably, circling the entire city on the southern side, to reach the well-guarded eastward gate to the grounds behind the Residence; the question, rather, was why Banak-loi had chosen to.

He had his hands resting on Laluvoi's shoulders. "With you, *Asayu*, this realm can only ever have one Banak." The often glum face had an expression hard to read, a melancholy near-smile. Not a bad beginning, but no one asked in what name he did mean to reign.

"As you say," *Menadhi* kept Dolvid, after most others had mounted the stair, "a sad day for the realm, for Arbhal." The conventions masked the sting of ambiguity; the realm for *Menadhi* had always been Owan, and Arbhal a name used only in contempt.

"You have been permitted to attend Laluvoi *Asayu*? We do not mean to intrude on her grief; you can, if you will, convey our profound sympathy, and wishes for her health."

He felt laughter swell, a bubble in his throat: perhaps the day's strains were making him hysterical. He could not decide which was more absurd, an *atarlai* (as *Menadhi*, however grand, undoubtedly was) who did not want to intrude on grief, or a powerful man who evidently shared the delusion of the Families about Dolvid's special influence with Laluvoi.

Khalú came, and after making *Menadhi*'s sign gracefully leant into Dolvid's side, as she had not for a long time.

"At the *Mankh'*," *Menadhi*, with all the old suavity. "We have studied your *True Song of Tales*. A remarkable production, and remarkably written."

"My thanks. I had remarkable teachers."

They parted on that exchange of two-edged compliments, Dolvid feeling he had passed a self-set test. It had taken the horrors of this worst day to let him face *Menadhi* on equal terms.

Khalú said, "You will have to be a courtier, for a while."

"Not one of my skills."

"Dol — everyone can flatter. It doesn't cost anything. Just follow Bolan — he'll surely be Captain of the Household."

"Oh, yes." There were puzzles in this.

With Khalú beside him he mounted to the Great Window Chamber. As dusk came the townspeople had dispersed, and on the Avenue not much was moving except half-files of watchful soldiery.

A numbed quality held the days that followed, a

waiting, while rains shrank the snow to diminishing islands, to nothing. The brown banner of mourning hung limp over the New Residence, where the *rabhsai* somewhat surprisingly put off his formal investiture till midsummer, making the Pledging, in effect, into a Great Pledging a year before due, since the provincial overlords would come to witness the robing.

The robing of Ban-Sila. Reasonably, he could hardly be blamed for wanting a new name; as Banak he would always have been Banak-loi, with the implied comparison to *the* Banak, Banak-rai. But Ban-Sila was an Owani form, appropriate for the grandson of a Baniukh or a Banival, but ominous (or so some found it) here.

Rabhsayum waited: allegiance was taken, but except for the captaincies of Merovas and Bolan the *rabhsai* confirmed no titles, and gave only one new one, generally applauded; Rhunilat, to honour his father's memory, though with no specific duties, was raised to the rank of *bôdh'loiki*. Strictly speaking the only one now, although Dolvid and Arvus continued their work, and Mirrat soon prepared a new issue of coinage with the portrait of Ban-Sila.

Bolan, as Khalú had forecast, moved rapidly to establish credit in the new *rabhsayum*, and led escorts in person.

"Tew," Faëdhal observed drily, "have not heard about his swift, decisive actions when the news came from Tan Lughsai. Actions, I might say, for which part, surely, of the credit belongs, um, elsewhere."

"He has earned his boast. He didn't make any mistakes that day."

"He had you, if you will pardon me, at his elbow giving advice from beginning to end."

"Giving advice is not the same as issuing orders, and bearing responsibility for them."

"One might observe," pertly, "it may be less harmful to advise without acting than to act without counsel. You have not yet met face-to-face with Ban-Sila *Deghi*?"

"Not alone. He has not summoned me, and I have no reason to ask for an audience."

"Ah. Then the *rabhsai* could learn about your part in his orderly accession only from the Captain of the Household?"

"Banak-loi, Ban-Sila was truly the Heir."

"He has followed custom, and pardoned criminals, all but the most vicious."

"They say he is fond of *zhabhu*, and plays very well."

"The *Menadhi* has not been in Kadon very much."

"He smiles more than he used to."

"He treats his grandmother with a courtesy that is good to see."

These crumbs were served up proudly, and eagerly devoured amongst those seeking consolation for Lambarr's departure, some hope in Ban-Sila's rise.

Not Bolan. "How long have I been petitioning for an independent grant? It's always been, we'll pay the wages and supply the food; if I needed a new sword-knot for an officer or an extra saddle, I had to go a-begging, to see if we could afford it that week."

"Ban-Sila sees your point?" a little shocked at Bolan, who was very near mocking the dead.

"A sum to be fixed yearly, and spent as I determine. I know, I know — but, Hrafi, it's good to hear some straight answers. When are you coming to court?"

"I was at the New Residence just yesterday."

"Oh yes, scuttling about in the Library, like a mouse. Anyone who didn't know you — well, there is Khalú, after all. She must be anxious to pay courtesies to the new *rabhsai*. Pardon, Dol, but a woman needs to be sure where her man stands in the realm."

"Khalú, if she wants, has her own access to the court."

Bolan, having failed to offend, decided to take offence himself. "Forgive me. I was giving friendly advice. There are changes in the realm, and no use pretending otherwise."

Hunger was the same, and Dolvid, ignoring lack of official rank, made a journey to Kred Bakali, thence to Kanzan Tâl, where army men still followed his orders. But several of the officers who had been with him longest were worried by what they perceived as a more defiant attitude among the ones hoarding or illegally dealing in food; this was not because of any word from Kadon Dinul, but from a feeling Ban-Sila's reign would bring a change of direction. Everywhere he went, under dappled, unpredictable skies of early summer, he was asked for impressions of the new *rabhsai*. Even Hinn, till now complacent in his petty empire of supplies and praise at Kanzan Tâl, was uneasy.

"All very well, *Bôdh'loiki*," he piped, voice absurdly

high-pitched for a large and fleshy man, "when you are the right race, but what about the Others, if the *Atarlum* tests are brought back? They say they might be."

"Bolan's captaincy has been confirmed. The *rabhsai*, after all, has Banak's blood in his veins."

"True, true enough." With many others, Hinn was not quieted, and could not have said why not.

The *Atarlum* tests! It was a marvel how rumour could gallop on so far ahead of any event. Unless he had changed completely over the past ten years, *Menadhi* would certainly be all for restoring them, and he had been Banak-loi's teacher, but even if Ban-Sila wanted to bring back the former tools of Owani control, it was hard to see how he would dare attempt a step to instantly disqualify half the realm's magistrates, and two Royal Captains, Bolan and Shumat. Together with most officers in the Armies of the West and the Northeast: those armies, at least, would never stand for it. The worry was it might be tried.

Khalú had scolded him for leaving Kadon at such a time. She meant, when he had not yet made friends with Ban-Sila. Jogging the rim of the Heartland, eyes filled with fresh green, Dolvid had other reasons for wanting to be back where the future was being wrought.

On the return journey he stayed overnight in the *margú* between Bathrâd and Kred Bakali. He did not take a *nôd'yanu*, though he had meant to, and there was a slender girl there who reminded him of Embhu, surely a wife and mother by now.

He was learning to turn aside from thoughts about

Khalú, so avoiding a kind of panic, when their dissatisfaction with each other was the steady bleeding of untended wounds, and their unspoken conspiracy of well-mannered pretence only let more unlived life slip away.

In the morning, having buttered oat-cake and spiced *raminat*, he was startled when Merovas came into the common-room. Making tours, the Captain of Armies would usually have a squadron escort, and stay with local commanders or other officials.

They greeted, and Merovas said he had come in late, and heard Dolvid was here. From Kadon Dinul here was a long day's ride for a man of seventy-five, although Merovas was in sturdy health. He was making a short tour of inspection, as far south as Kôbh Crossings, returning for the Pledging and the investiture, for which, he said, everything was in readiness.

"Somewhat early." Merovas was talking as if he, Dolvid, had been away from the city a month.

"I mean, the soldiery." He leant forward over strong clasped hands. "As you know, we have no Provincial Cavalry."

As he and everyone knew; this was a strange thing to say. With the Household at Kadon Dinul, and nine General Cavalry garrisons (no other province had above four), the Paowan did not need a provincial force.

"Well," Merovas again tried to convey more than his words, "there's this special force Bolan's raising, none of them trained men. I was not consulted."

"For the Pledging? Auxiliaries for the Household, you

mean?"

"They say for the Pledging, but who ever heard of auxiliaries being signed up for twelve years? And they're going to have *pefral* for mounts."

Dolvid, mystified, said he had heard nothing about it, and Merovas described a force that, for a start at least, would have six squadrons, three hundred men, the offscourings of Kadon Dinul and Owan Sai, being recruited, he complained, mainly from drink-shops. A number of lawbreakers freed by Ban-Sila's amnesty had also been signed, also to a full twelve-year term. Merovas, as an afterthought, had been asked to name a few junior officers to help with their training, so far mostly to do with keeping order amongst crowds.

"Some of them," sourly, "need training on how to stay on the back of my lady's ambler, and they're going to be given *pefral*, robbers, the ones who snatch combs and kerchiefs from the stalls on Harbour Way."

"You have been told they are to have *pefral*?" It seemed very odd.

"No. I haven't been told anything. But there is going to be a new barracks, outside Royal Gate, with stablings for several hundred *pefral*, and the Stud-Master's been told he'll have to find four hundred soon."

In this grumbling way, Merovas came to what might be his main subject. "I wondered what Laluvoi *Asayu* might think about all this. Not my job to wonder, you could say. She is not seen much. They say, if she's downcast, she's not cast down. At Pledging, I should be seeing Saidhan *Asai*, but, well... "

He was not wondering, it dawned, he was asking

Dolvid to ascertain what Laluvoi thought. Dolvid's old friendship with Bolan might also be in his mind, and another reason he had contrived this chance meeting.

What a condition they had come to already, when the Captain of Armies had to leave Kadon Dinul and hunt down a minor official for information on a military decision. "When I return, I'll discover all I can."

"How do you find the garrisons?"

"Their spirits? No one can quite believe Lambarr is gone, and so many of the children."

"Their spirits, yes. Their loyalty, you could say."

"To the *rabhsai*?" A startling question.

Having resisted it so far, Merovas had a quick look to either side. No one was interested in their conference. "Well, it would be to the Captain-General, to Saidhan *Asai*."

"He is honoured, as ever. But it should be the same thing, shouldn't it?"

"Always, always," with fervour.

"We'll do all we can to keep it so."

Bolan was in his quarters at the Residence, being fitted for a new tunic and breeches. The special forces, he explained airily, were to deal with disorders. Not just for the Pledging, he conceded, when Dolvid brought up the twelve-year enlistments, but for subsequent ones, and wherever else they might be needed. It would save the necessity of always training new auxiliaries, and the force would scarcely be larger than some private armies of the Families.

This was very much a prepared answer, but not a plausible one: if there was fear of new measures Ban-Sila might introduce, it was not among the Families. But there was also the question, as raised with Bolan, of the kind of men he was signing.

"Well, it's only what we did at Yuvakh Din in '28, isn't it? Ott was a lawbreaker, wasn't he, when we enlisted him and his men as auxiliaries. It serves a double purpose — men charged with keeping law aren't breaking it. And we can be sure these men won't question their orders."

More ominous yet. "What orders would there be that the Household would not follow?"

"Orders of mine? None. That's not the same, Dol; this is a new age. One thing I can tell you, anyone making trouble is going to find less softness. Not severity for the sake of it, but the *rabhsai* says, quite rightly, leniency for lawbreakers brings injustice on those who keep the law."

"What could be more lenient to a thief than signing him up for twelve years, and giving him a *pefrai* to ride?"

"What about Ott?" imagining he had triumphed, and it was useless to enumerate all the faults in the parallel: Ott had been provoked into outlawry by unfair taxes and a personal assault by a cavalry officer, the Paowan was not in revolt, or threatened by an invasion of out-men.

He did say, "When we amnestied Ott, it served a larger purpose."

"So does this," Bolan predictably answered. "So does this."

He asked blandly whether Dolvid had run into Merovas on the road, and Dolvid just as blandly answered, yes. Sad not to trust Bolan, and worse to know he, Bolan, suspected

Merovas's loyalty, but suddenly this had become such a realm.

Perhaps his imagination was out of control. Faëdhal, anyway, was losing his misgivings about the new reign. He was reconfirmed as Master of Tongues, again without the rank of *bôdh'loiki*, an honour he desired, as he had been explaining as long as Dolvid had known him, not for his own sake, but to acknowledge the importance of scholarship in the realm.

Was it only to Dolvid's mind, too, that the provincial *nimul*, when they rode in, displayed a new arrogance, an indifference to the crowds on the Avenue, as if their day had come? Vinilat when he came with his Dramali cavalry did not even raise a hand as he rode by.

"Is it wise for an author to go unescorted?" He had drawn aside under slender lindens near Harbour Gate, and the question, coming from behind his elbow, was asked of and about him by Tellis, earnest-faced.

He gestured at the Household squadron following Vinilat's riding. "How often, at Pledging, can we be far from soldiery? Besides — " he made a rueful face. "Your father has made people forget the *True Song*."

She nodded understanding. He had heard last year she was going to be betrothed to Rhunilat, but there had been changes since then, and it might be the decree Arvus had insisted on had spoilt his daughter's chances with a son of the Families.

"My father is afraid — " she began.

"Of war?"

"War, Master? Where?"

"Nothing." He really must restrain his imaginings. "What is your father afraid of?"

"That the *rabhsai* intends to call in all Treasury loans. Immediately."

"You mean, after harvest. Even so — " The loans had been granted for three-year repayment. To demand the money at once would ruin farmers who had relied on them.

"Nothing has been said about waiting for harvest."

As in the meeting with Merovas he felt a paralysing despair begin. This could be conjecture by Arvus, or a misunderstood word or two, but there had to be the climate for such rumours to flourish.

"Not possible. It would cause an uprising." And Bolan was enlisting men who had no scruples, training men he bragged would follow any orders.

"I'll have a talk with your father, soon." He saw Tellis was worried to be the cause of anxiety.

"Is Khalú well?"

"Yes. Well, but not happy. Many things, policies I have to follow, she can't approve of. Then, too, I do not give her much of the life she would enjoy." A mystery why he picked Tellis as hearer for things he never said.

"When she married you," evenly, "it was no secret, what you were; she knew, or should have known, you were not going to turn into someone else."

Her grey eyes met his without flinching, and it was not conceit that told him she would have taken the Dolvid that was. They parted cordially.

For one of his titles he did not need reconfirmation from the _rabhsai_, Keeper of Accounts he had never seen, Laluvoi's. Leaving Khalú sleeping he rode for the city through early light of a soft summer's day, and asked for audience.

He was afraid she would not receive him, but after a wait a servant came and led him to her personal suite. She was drably, somewhat carelessly dressed, small in a large carved armchair.

After he had made deference she motioned him to take the high, padded footstool. There was a low table with a pot of warm _raminat_, and a number of fruits; strawberries, apricots, apples cooked with figs.

"We thought you had forgotten us, Master. What brings you now?"

"To pay my respects, _Asayu_."

"I am past these flatteries. I've even given up the last of them, to make me imagine I am still worth lying to." She lifted her forearm up near her nose. "I start to _smell_ old. Pffa!" She blew exasperatedly. "Only for a while, in the morning. But, you know, it might be I just become accustomed to it, and it clings there to disgust others, like garlic you can't smell on your own breath. You have a suit?"

Dolvid stammered. He could not say he had come hoping for an ally, and the comfort that would give him. Nor could he be the one to bring up fears of where the new _rabhsai_ might take the realm.

He had a lame tale in reserve, about a delay in moneys, "which have now been paid, so there was no need for me to trouble *Asayu* with this."

Not reassuring that the keen look faltered, to leave her gazing for a while on nothing.

"Indeed, Master." She came back from where she had been. "I can't see there was much need to begin with. Eat some of this fruit — I cannot face food before noon. I shall take a little *raminat*."

He poured small cups of the amber drink, which was honeyed. Laluvoi took hers, but did not yet taste it.

"Policies," she announced. "Can we understand each other, Dolvidh? We might both have the same questions. For me, they come down to: did Great Banak live in vain? Has Laluvoi lived for nothing?"

Alarmingly, she drifted into another reverie, a state beyond reverie; her face became empty, as if thought was being washed away by the steady lapping of the past.

"*Asayu*, no responsible writer of history could ever say so. For centuries there were evils that could go on, because they were the way the world is. If they returned, they could never be the same, now we know them for what they are, intolerable. Banak and Laluvoi, more than anyone, taught us, and showed us we could be free of these injustices."

He was not sure she had heard him, and then there was the old, spirited snap of her eyes. "Then you would say a prisoner was better off for having had a day of freedom? Captivity might be so much harder to bear. Is that your fear, return of old evils? Mine, too."

Now they were there, he fumbled. "There is not much

real to point to, *Asayu*, to explain this fear. To believe any *rabhsai* would — not, as I say, Ban-Sila *Deghi* has given any sign — "

"The *Rabhsai* is our *rabhsai*, and we are all true *rabhsayanil*." She tried her *raminat*, and made a face, though it seemed good to him. "We may take that as spoken, Master; a question about policy is no dispraise of the Person, and so forth. Now."

He spoke about the Special Forces Bolan was raising, and the twelve-year enlistment came as news to her. Not saying where he had heard them, he mentioned the various rumours; reintroduction of the *Atarlum* tests, the sudden calling-in of Treasury loans.

Laluvoi nodded. Leaning forward, small cup held in both hands, she reminded him irreverently of a squirrel. "In a word, Preference."

"But Preference is no longer possible, *Asayu*. No rule and no number of swords can ever bring back the old realm."

"Then there can be nothing to fear," as challenge, not statement.

"*Asayu*, the age of epics is past, and can't be brought back. But we have had the *Frela'olu-rai Naënai*, the *Frela'olu-rai Sebhali* written, and heard them declaimed."

A grimace; apparently the memories pained her, too. "A fool can always attempt what cannot be done," she summed up.

"Attempting to bring back Preference would destroy us." He did not have to speak about the armies Sebhal and Shumat led, or the landowners and office-holders of Other Race who would have to fight.

"Yes." She was there already. "I ask you again; would it not have been better if we had never reigned, Banak and I? We hoped they would see reason; we never meant to store thunderbolts for shattering the realm."

"*Asayu*," bringing her back from another escape into emptiness. "Justice has to be followed, no matter where it leads."

A chilly smile. "The realm is the vessel that holds justice. If you break the realm, justice runs away."

He had come for comfort, and was comforting her. "We can never know how many were unjustly put to death, thrown off their lands, left to starve, when all magistrates were of our race, and only our race could get justice. Your realm, madam, includes all those who lived out their lives because Banak and Laluvoi lived, and fought for what was right." The sleepless author hoped he could remember that for his book, if he ever could write it.

"You are no fool." He suspected she was commending his tactics with her, not agreeing with his history. "The Council meets tomorrow, Banak-loi's, Ban-Sila's first. What is going to come of that?"

"I had hoped to ask you, *Asayu*."

"Bitterness," simply. "Kargul warring on with the man who killed Tobhsila. Vinilat, at least, will stand with them, and *Menadhi* for the *Mankh'*. They say *g'Asalladh'* is dying. But Saidhan has me for an ally. As always."

Unnerving how quickly she went from full vigor to tranced vacancy. Afraid she was going to spill *raminat* on herself, Dolvid rose to take the cup, and as on the day when they heard of Lambarr's death she gripped his arm. "Stand by me, Dolvidh."

"I shall."

"No, in Council."

"*Asayu*, I do not have a seat there." He had sat at lesser meetings, but this was a Great Council, the Council of Thirteen, and he lacked even the rank held under Lambarr.

"You can stand, then, beside Laluvoi, if Laluvoi says so. But my body is starting to betray me." She released him, to look with curiosity at her trembling right hand. "I would not much care, except it affects my will. Moments come when nothing matters except that Laluvoi does not disgrace herself, and then I might give in where, strong, I would fight. I need young muscles near me, you understand?"

He bowed his head. He was no nearer understanding power, and was powerless himself, but if Laluvoi believed she got strength from leaning on him, seeming was being, and he gained by giving what he did not have.

She was smiling. "We could deploy our squadrons better if we knew what battle we were fighting, or were certain there would be a battle."

"I would be surprised if the last proclamation made by Lambarr *Rabhsai* were not debated, *Asayu*." Acrimoniously, he foresaw.

She nodded concurrence. "They say I have been loved."

"No one more so, ever." Her vanity was immense, and excusable.

"I have to keep earning it." This was plaintive. "Not just once, twice, but over and over again, till I fall out of my chair.

I don't know why, when some live lives of honour on one youthful deed."

Unthinkable yet unmistakable, that mischievous reference to her oldest friend, Saidhan.   "Not Laluvoi," yawning.

The Great Hall was overlarge for this gathering, opening like a cavern from where at one end the long table was placed for the meeting. Dolvid had not been there since the evening when, on that same spot, a plump poet with the assistance of a pretty musician had declaimed the *frela'olu-rai*, Bolan's and Shumat's.

The long lapse of years was emphasised when Daënakh of Ân came up to greet Dolvid cordially, and commend the *True Song of Tales*. The *nim'* was proud of being mentioned in a note there about the find of bones on Sebira Bay. He accepted condolences on loss of his elder son at Tan Lughsai, and congratulations for the marriage of Bradhinal to the youngest daughter of the Warden at the Port of Sebira (the insatiable Sholu, Dolvid remembered). From a short distance his own younger brother, Laënakh of Nîv, looked on, standing beside Vinilat of Dramal, who always appeared to expect conspiracies, small, suspicious eyes set above flat cheekbones. Bolan was prowling, nodding a preoccupied good morning to Dolvid, hearty with the bearded Tovakh baKargul, who was there for his father, the *Nim'* Tobhan.

Conversing half-mindedly about Shumat, whom

Daënakh seldom saw, and about the new prosperity the restored health of Narn had brought to eastern Ân, Dolvid was trying to assess the composition of the Council, and how it would behave. With four members and five places yet to come (the *rabhsai* counting twice), he made it eleven. Rhunilat, graver since his father's death, was there, but would not be in the *Bôdhrai*'s seat, and the other vacancy was the Heir's, as *Nim'* of the Paowan. Rodlakh, presumably, now had that nominal title, but was just thirteen, and half a realm away in Thenimala.

Eleven votes changed all the usual sums. The Council of Thirteen had first been established largely to protect the newly-created provincial overlords and the immemorial *Atarlum* from any arbitrary use of the *rabhsai*'s power. Ordinary laws and new policies were approved by simple majority, and since the *rabhsai* could generally count on support of his Heir, the Royal Captains, and the *Bôdhrai* he had chosen, seven votes (including his own two) were not hard to find. But for matters affecting prerogatives of the *Mankh'* or the provincial *nim'*, a two-thirds vote, normally nine, was needed, which meant any four *nim'* voting with the Patriarch or His representative had, at least in theory power of veto. But the *rabhsai* had other powers not subject to the Council, granting of monopolies, or his supreme magistracy over all legal rulings, and with a strong or a vindictive *rabhsai*, it took endless courage or an issue of overriding importance for the provincial lords to defy his wishes.

Today, then, if the rule held, eight votes could overturn the law empowering *rabhsayum* to tax ungrown food. Dolvid's sense was that Laluvoi would prefer to retain and modify it instead, but did not see what support she could enlist beyond Saidhan and Merovas. That must leave her one vote short.

Accompanied by a recorder, one more of the mask-faced, tightlipped young men the *Mankh'* could endlessly supply, the slight, robed figure of *Menadhi* appeared at the far end of the hall, and came to the long table with the familiar cat-silent, cat-exact pace. He acknowledged the pious gesture made on all sides, but did not speak, positioning behind the chair at the foot of the table.

Laluvoi and Saidhan came in together. She, walking with a straight back, seemed rested, and had put aside mourning brown for a gown of muted blue. No one would have guessed the alert, resilient Saidhan next to her was past eighty, and he was almost boyish greeting the other lords, kinsmen but not allies. Behind this pair came Arvus, his face very sober, and there was the shadow of an unpleasant feeling tracked down and identified as jealousy. Foolish; Laluvoi had already caught his eye and smiled, and must have a good reason for keeping Arvus next to her.

Lambarr had always sauntered into these meetings as if the main object was for everyone to be together making good talk. Ban-Sila's appearance was preceded by the day's escort-officer, Zhinladh, self-important as his wealthy father and much fatter, who took up his post just inside the door. Then Ban-Sila came, escorted by pikes of the Household, who stationed themselves a few paces behind his chair, and remained watchful throughout, as did Zhinladh. Nor did Ban-

Sila copy his father's habit of moving about and greeting everyone, asking about wives, children, the state of iron-working in Ân, the size of the plums this year in Lower Nîv. The new *rabhsai*, glum-faced, went straight to his chair.

The others assembled, the four Mainland overlords occupying the left side of the table. Bolan was opposite Tovakh, Merovas across from Daënakh, leaving the upper right as Laluvoi's enclave, Saidhan facing Vinilat, Laluvoi immediately to the *rabhsai*'s right, with Arvus and Dolvid hovering behind.

He was agreeably impressed with how Rhunilat handled unfamiliar responsibilities, using a list to introduce questions to be considered, and calling on the appropriate member. It began quietly in formalities, with Saidhan getting nine votes (the *rabhsai* abstaining) for the declaration Ban-Sila's succession was lawful and regular, and that he should henceforth preside over the Council. Next, *Menadhi* asked for a moment of memory for Lambarr and his service to the realm. When everyone was seated again, Laënakh of Nîv proposed each anniversary of the Tan Lughsai disaster should be a day when no business was transacted. This brought the start of dissent; Laënakh was being seconded when Laluvoi acidly observed that in a few years, when the reason was no longer well remembered, it would not honour the dead to have men mark the day by stupefying themselves with wine and beer. She suggested instead the affectionate nickname for the Tan Lughsai road should become its official designation, *Lambarr's Way*, and Laënakh was quick to allow his proposal to be superseded. He was taller than his brother, but with much the same square-shouldered, compact build. He had a passion for breeding dogs, and had successfully crossed various strains to produce a new hunting companion, called Laënakh's hound.

With other smaller matters disposed of, *Menadhi*'s soft, arresting voice announced a change of tone. "*Yoëlladhuyil*," he began, a form of address, 'Children of Yoëlladhu,' that brought in everyone, with no slight to the *rabhsai*. "If I understand the will of Ban-Sila *Deghi*, we are here to discuss *edhrodi-dhanayol'*."

"Husbandry," Saidhan put in. "Harvests. In the Colony, your pardon, *Menadhi*, we don't often use the Old Tongue."

"Its *nim'*, at least, has no such deficiency," *Menadhi* answered, with his familiar, ingratiating smile. "To come *from* the Colony is not necessarily to be *of* the Colony." He won a few chuckles around the table.

Not from Saidhan. "Surely we can speak about farming, not using words which, of themselves, bring in the *Edhrodilum*?" Like a big, dark cat stretching and yawning, conflict had roused.

"But concerns of the *Edhrodilum*," *Menadhi*, but softly, "are part of the business that brings us together."

Next to Dolvid, Arvus shifted his weight from one foot to the other. *Menadhi* was alluding to the unfortunate phrase, in Lambarr's last proclamation, about *ga-Yalum*.

Laluvoi was ready. Before His present illness, she had talked with *g'Asalladh'*, who was now satisfied. While no affront had ever been intended, the reference to *ga-Yalum* would not be repeated; the matter was settled.

"Stilled, perhaps, *Asayu*," *Menadhi* said. "As for settled — "

"Are you questioning His *aën'modha*?" she demanded.

Menadhi turned up his little hands in modest concession. Perhaps he was confident he could afford to be patient a little while; soon all trappings of the Patriarchate, including the infallibility of *aën'modha*, would be his.

Ban-Sila only watched this exchange. "When I was ten, I was told how someday the Colony would feed itself." When he was sixteen, Dolvid could remember his sarcasms about Saidhan, and Laluvoi calling him a lout.

Saidhan would not let his grandson bait him. He spoke about recent fighting on Landegh, and how Sebhal had compelled submission of a Froghuli tribe. Established policy, reaffirmed by Banak, made the Frontier open to all who wanted the protection of the realm, and would come peaceably; the former enemy had been settled near Kreshavu. Though the Vale of Banakit was growing more food every year, there were always added mouths to feed.

"So," the *rabhsai* said, "Kamsilat comes as ever to the Heartland, begging for its bread."

"The Colony, *Deghi*," evenly, "has never taken a single bag of flour unpaid for. We might as well say the Mainland comes to Kamsilat, begging for its fuel-wood and its timber."

"We may have less use for your long-timbers now."

Saidhan's face went stony; Daënakh of Ân drew breath sharply between his teeth; not even Vinilat was comfortable. Everyone knew the use Lambarr had for Colony oak and ash.

Ban-Sila ignored shock. "The Colony's needs could be reduced at once, by bringing your armies down to limits originally set."

"They are the armies of the realm," Saidhan, all dignity.

"The limits were set before the Mines were found, well beyond the Frontier. With captaincy less skilled, the Army of the West would need twice the squadrons it has."

"Sebhal," Ban-Sila said, "does not hold any captaincy ever submitted to this Council." He cast about the table, inviting support.

"Your uncle, *Deghi*," Saidhan replied, "is a loyal subject, and my chosen commander in the field, with the rank of captain. Would you want me to tell his officers they must on no account think of him as Captain of the West? Guarantee him that title, and I'll resign it today." Lambarr had been made the same offer on Saidhan's seventieth and again on his seventy-fifth birthday.

"What if I ask for that resignation, with no conditions?"

"That would be taken note of, *Deghi*." He was on firm ground; a Royal Captain was so for life, unless treason, other gross crimes, or incapacity could be shown, and this Council was not going to unseat Saidhan. Here, a glance may have passed between Ban-Sila and Tovakh baKargul, his hopes for a captaincy renewed by the change of *rabhsai*. But realities were against him if he wanted the West, with Saidhan as *Nim'* of the Colony, and the army, largely of Other Race, ferociously loyal to Sebhal.

Vinilat, in his bustling, bullying way, ended this particular clash of wills by reminding all the chief subject was a proposed tax on unused lands and their ungrown crops.

"A decree," Ban-Sila said, "which we do not desire to remember."

"A proclamation," Laluvoi corrected.

"All the easier to forget."

Arvus was the one to tell the *rabhsai* it could not be done. He knew he was supposed to seek permission to address the Council; Laluvoi turned to frown and Vinilat began a rebuke, but Ban-Sila found or feigned some of his father's easygoing manner, and motioned Arvus to explain. Less precipitately, Arvus did so: Lambarr's proclamation rested on a law of Plakhsila, made and adopted in the Council.

"We are going to reign a century, too. In so long, perhaps, we shall acquire enough wisdom not to make mad laws. But what one Council approved, another may revoke, not so?"

"If it votes to, *Deghi*," Arvus said. "But that has not yet been done."

Once again Vinilat was impatient, ready to vote at once, but Ban-Sila again quieted him, and turned back to Arvus. "This is interesting. We shall have to find more work for the Treasury, there is too much leisure for study there. Are you saying as *rabhsai* I can do nothing about it, if the Treasury has the whim to collect a tax, lawful or not, that I oppose?"

Now enmity was palpable, and this was a bait, not a question. Any *rabhsai* could put his own man in charge at the Treasury to carry out his wishes within the law.

Laluvoi rescued Arvus. "If the *rabhsai* is not bound by law, then anyone, magistrate, official, even provincial *nim'*, is nothing, a flag on a *zhabhu* board, to be removed at will or whim."

Not precisely relevant, but an effective way to change the mood. Jealousy of his prerogatives, conviction the *rabhsai*, any *rabhsai*, wanted him as an obedient puppet, were never far from the mind of a *nim'*.

Vinilat tried again. "Well, then, the Council can change the law. No one here wants to keep it — no one with a place here." Arvus did not flinch at this stab.

"Kargul, from the beginning," Tovakh growled, "intended to ignore the cursed proclamation."

"Now — " Ban-Sila wagged a cautionary finger. But it remained true, after three defeats in civil war, and nearly sixty years of healing, that Kargul was in many ways a realm of its own, naming its own magistrates, playing host to no garrisons of royal troops, maintaining, on the contrary, as everyone knew, perhaps double the provincial cavalry permitted by law.

"Haste," Bolan spoke for the first time. "Overmuch haste, *Deghi*, went into your lamented father's proclamation. No one says the intentions were bad."

Some there would. Into gathering agreement *Menadhi* brought his practised voice. "I am instructed by *g'Asalladh'*, of Whose wisdom Laluvoi justly speaks, to use all influence to set aside this ruinous measure."

Laluvoi said, "Who here has ever read the law?"

"I have read the proclamation," Vinilat, derisively.

"Then no one would know," she said, "the private lands of provincial *nimul* are explicitly exempt from its provisions."

Even Arvus, so it seemed, had not known that, though it might have been deduced: the Council that passed the law for Plakhsila had been composed as this one was.

It changed everything. Saidhan could find willing

listeners, as he urged the need for some means of encouraging those with arable lands to put them in cultivation. By what must be prearrangement with Laluvoi, he invited comments from Dolvid, who, conscious of Ban-Sila's cool stare, recited what he had often said, with wise use of lands a single good harvest could insure against two or three poor ones. He was careful to stay away from the question of which people held the unproductive lands, but watching the faces of the four *nim'* to the left side, he realised they cared only marginally what race was affected, so long as they were not threatened. Some of them must share his conviction the big Owanil landowners were too wealthy, and the *nim'* would, as always, retain the provincial portion from any new taxes collected.

Menadhi was the only one to bring up the possibility of general overproduction ruining all the farmers, but when Saidhan suggested excess could be dealt with when it came, if ever, both Daënakh and Laënakh agreed.

"If the Others," Vinilat said, "knew how to work their lands — " This was only a token, as Arvus should have known, but he was determined to be the champion of the Other Races, and tactlessly disputed Vinilat, beginning his familiar offer to prove with tax-returns how the big magnates produced less food on lands they took over when smallholdings failed. This, from the known Deniant, could only bring support for Vinilat's view, and annoyance was gathering against Arvus when Saidhan intervened.

"Give the Others your rough-hunting to farm," he told Vinilat with a loud guffaw. "They could feed your province and my Colony by themselves, in the hands of growers I know near Kreshavu."

Vinilat reddened with annoyance, but the laugh went against him. Here, the *rabhsai* abruptly chose to end discussion with no vote taken, using the traditional formula, *Ul an' yalil botadhayin*, we shall seek advice. He was unhappy, and evidently wished to avoid the humiliation of having the Council reaffirm the law he wanted to repeal.

Except for desultory discussion of minor questions, also finish of the meeting. The calling-in of Treasury loans was never mentioned, and soon Laënakh moved an appreciation for the *rabhsai*'s conduct of his first Council, which his first Council carried unanimously. Again, *Menadhi*, perhaps unhappiest of all about how it had gone, rose to give a short *kolukezh'*. The *rabhsai* rose, and nodded his head here and there, conspicuously omitting Arvus. With a quick turn, flanked by his pikes, he went out, and Zhinladh followed.

Next to leave was *Menadhi* with his scribe, and as the remainder drifted into small, separate groups, there was no feeling of victory in the one about Laluvoi. She had a rueful face for Arvus, who was defiantly aware he had said too much, too forcefully. Merovas stood next to Saidhan, hoping for a word to help him cope with an unfamiliar realm. If Laluvoi's chief purpose had been to show her grandson he needed more than his will to rule by, she had succeeded, but at uncertain cost. Nothing had happened but a drawing of battle lines.

"These debates easily tire me now," Laluvoi confessed to Saidhan, and he took her small hand between his large, gnarled ones.

One reason not to make a sweeping announcement

about loans might be so as to foreclose piecemeal, a single small region at a time. In that way, relatively small numbers of reliable troops would be enough to enforce seizures, without causing widespread resistance.

The soldiery that came to mind, Bolan's special forces, had not yet been given *pefral*, but could be observed during the rest of the Pledging weeks, mounted on smaller saddle-horses, and keeping order with greater force, using their staves with more relish, than was called for. One evening Dolvid saw an unruly but good-humoured mob sent cowering and howling by a unnecessary charge, and when he sought out Bolan next morning to protest, was told he was a good fellow who should stick to his books.

"As a friend," Bolan added. "Let me tell you, be careful. Last year's opinions aren't in fashion. You should consider Khalú, if you don't care for your own sake."

Coldly angry, Dolvid next went to Laluvoi, who received him. There was a meeting he was not asked to attend, with Bolan, Merovas and Saidhan in the *rabhsai*'s presence; what Laluvoi said he never heard, but afterwards order was maintained with less force by regular Household men, special forces kept in reserve.

With Kamanasalladh reported near death, the investing, on the eve of *Shuda'sai*, was accomplished by *Menadhi*, who robed Ban-Sila, placing in his hands the tablet and the Sword, the plain blade which had been used since loss of the true Bronze Sword, sixty years ago. Packed into the Avenue between the Disc and the Steps, the crowd acclaimed the ceremonies and the *rabhsai*, but with nothing to match the outpouring of enthusiasm that had greeted, for example, public appearance of each new child of Lambarr and Saëdhu. Perhaps Tan Lughsai, after a quarter-year, lingered in their minds, but undoubtedly an intuitive sense of change had spread through the city, a feeling the new *rabhsai* would be a friend chiefly to the rich and powerful. The Midsummer rites on the following day struck a new note of solemnity, like echoes of the *Mankh'*, Dolvid shivered to think.

"It is a change," Khalú said.

"A darkening."

"Don't say that, Dol. I was told you did not please the *rabhsai*. If you lose your appointments, we'll have nothing."

"The harvest should be good this year, despite everything. After, I could resign my provincial post. Not much more for me to do." He wanted to make a start on the book about the rise of Banak.

"Then you will be at Kadon Dinul more. Here more."

At the estate Untimarr came to see Dolvid, in wary half-apology; at Burantal his father was about to retire from the family trade, for which his fingers were becoming too stiff. He wanted Untimarr to come home and succeed him, both as the city's master-carpenter, and an Elder of Burantal.

"We have been happy here, the girls too. Morú, though, wishes she'd had work to do here."

Dolvid thanked him. The reference was to Morú's skill as a midwife.

Somewhat excessively, Untimarr elaborated; it had always been understood he would follow his father and live in the big family house, with the other Burantal people of consequence on Utalai Course; Morú had her kin and friends there, too.

"And the Heartland seems less hospitable than it did last year."

"For my sort. My nose says a storm's coming."

"Maybe only a squall, in the end." But he did not blame Untimarr for wanting to be away from Kadon Dinul; he envied him the chance.

"You will be missed here," he said.

He, too, often thought wistfully about escape, or his unthinking mind drifted without instruction to distant scenes with all muddles left behind; he would go to Narn, change his name, and work for Shumat, or to the remote South, where he was born.

Saidhan, having left Kadon Dinul immediately after the investing, was there, seeing his daughter, poor Saëdhu, who (as was said) had not spoken a word since comprehending the news from Tan Lughsai. He, Saidhan, became with familiarity more likeable than you would expect in a figure of legend, but neither the humour nor the habit of belittling his own brain did anything to diminish the hero. He would pass through Kadon again on his way back to the Colony, and Dolvid seriously considered asking him for a post at Kamsilat. Saidhan was one man who would not be intimidated by threat of the *rabhsai*'s displeasure (which would have nothing to do with how much or little Ban-Sila valued Dolvid's services).

Khalú, a Heartlander whose realm was the Residence Quarter, would not want to go to the West, would probably refuse to go, expecting that to change Dolvid's mind.   In ruthless moods he would admit she was as much a part of the misery in his life as the accession of Ban-Sila, and to be rid of her a necessary part of his dreams of a new beginning, free of all the muddle.

It could be seen as an omen, and a cheering one, when in a bundle of documents from Great Banak's reign in the library of the New Residence, most of small importance, he came across one that should not be there and he had assumed must be lost, the original report, in the young Saidhan's own hand, of the events that precipitated the War of the Widowed. The parchment had never been good, and was flaking at the edges; Dolvid carried the pages away to the Bronze Residence, and, not trusting them to any scribe, made his own careful copy.

Not a happy tale. The history that led there was fairly well-known. About eleven years before this report, Laluvoi had come from Ninkufu to be married to the Heir, Valplakh, the sickly (some said, half-witted) son of the *Rabhsaëyu* Thral-Sivu. On that occasion the escort was commanded by Banak, already a seasoned and famous warrior. She was seventeen, and most renowned beauty of her time; a part of folklore and perhaps fact was that their deep friendship began on that long northward journey, at the end of which Laluvoi became Valplakh's bride, and soon a familiar figure, popular among all races, known as a friend of justice.

More than ten years went by before she conceived. She wanted to bear the child, due at midwinter, in the milder climate of her original home. With the realm tranquil, two unsuccessful rebellions by Kargul now a good few years in the past, the aging Thral-Sivu decided to go south with her son and daughter-in-law. Banak by now was in the Colony, Captain of the West, and the escort was captained by the youthful, well-connected Saidhan, a favourite apprentice to Banak, like a son, despite differences of their blood.

Easy to imagine, the joyful beginnings of that progress to the south, the way through the cities of Paowan and Nîv — Kred Bakali, Bathrâd, Kanzan Tâl, Nivu Din — strewn with autumn flowers, as crowds gathered to witness and to cheer. The unpromising Heir might have caused alarm about the future, but there was hope that after Thral-Sivu's passing Laluvoi would become the real power, and still have Banak to serve her. It must have seemed all worst evils were in the past.

The account by Saidhan began with departure from Kir, the fortress town near the northern fringes of Ní-Tilagh. There were no towns in that arid wilderness, but there were favoured spots for making camp. Saidhan's intent was to make use of one, long ago fortified, set on a low rise, with the remnants of strong walls for protection. Because of Thral-Sivu's age, however, the start was delayed and the column moved slowly. When the *rubhsaëyu* said she was tired, Saidhan was obliged to halt well short of his goal, selecting a gentle hollow that gave a little shelter from wind.

His exasperation — or perhaps need to justify what might otherwise have been called poor choices — could be detected, as he described the unwieldy dimensions of his encampment, with its tents for the many servants and minor functionaries, its wagons, including two for wardrobe alone, its herd of draft, pack and saddle horses. These, under guard, had to be tethered outside the perimeter he formed with his four squadrons, each diminished by a file to give him a one-squadron reserve.

Then as now fugitive outlaws lived on Ní-Tilagh, occasionally ambushing a small riding of unprotected travellers; Saidhan was sure there could not be a band large enough to challenge his forces. In his report he confessed the notion of *jinzal*, seldom seen except in the Farther West, never occurred to him. In any event, though *jinzal* were said to be able to scent living blood miles away, rarely were more than two or three to be encountered together, and the troops would have been adequate to deal with that.

For two large hunting-packs to find the same prey was without known precedent. The first came crashing out of utter darkness near midnight, when the alarm was given by the watch on the north side of the camp. Saidhan used his reserve to put a close cordon about the royal tents, and in person led men from other positions to the point of attack, where soldiers had been killed, and others were hard-pressed, hacking blind at their fierce adversaries. Confusion notwithstanding, this assault had been virtually beaten off when, as he later ascertained, a second and larger mass of *jinzal* tore into the western side of the camp, where the horses were. These bolted, dragging pickets and snapping halters, and burst through the guards on that side, *jinzal* in their wake. They stormed through the encampment, trampling many, scattering watchfires, spreading panic. Painful to picture the terror and confusion, flame-blotched blackness filled with thunder of hoofs, shrilling of horses, clash of weapons and yells of fear, shouted orders of officers, though even those who kept their heads could not know how or where to rally or strike. Men and women died, *jinzal* too, one by running blind into a watchfire; the creatures feared and were often maddened by being near flames.

Saidhan, with what men he could collect, struggled back to the heart of the camp, where several tents were burning. Horses and *jinzal* had passed through like a storm, and it was astonishing some of the royal tents were left standing. But none of Saidhan's three chief charges, *rabhsaëyu*, Heir, and Laluvoi, could be found.

Many alarms, and muddled fighting went on (afterwards, Saidhan unhappily concluded from their wounds that because of night and panic fear, soldiers had assailed soldiers, and some of those they were supposed to be protecting). Long before he could be certain the attacks were finished, Saidhan, assembling the men and horses he could, went in the direction taken by the larger body of *jinzal*, using torches and lanterns to follow the swathe trampled by the massive creatures and the horses they had stampeded. The body of a serving-woman was recovered, and grisly fragments of other victims; one groom came out of the darkness unharmed but babbling. But soon the tracks began to multiply, branching in every direction, and Saidhan, for whom pursuit was impossible with the men at his disposal, made his dismal way back to what was left of the camp.

Laluvoi was there, trying to calm servants. Stunned by a falling pole and buried in the collapse of her tent, she was not otherwise injured. Saidhan wrote, the safety of Laluvoi and the unborn Heir, as objectives in his grasp, became his chief concern. Dolvid had heard from Merovas authentic-sounding words Saidhan did not include in his report, that sight of Laluvoi alive, and the knowledge he had a task ahead, were all that prevented him from taking his own life.

He had no field experience, and his age was even less than Shumat's at the start of the Narn expedition; understandably he was anxious to give the logic behind his decisions, which seemed astonishingly well-reasoned and correct at a distance of sixty years. When light came his tentative patrols encountered more bloody relics, scattered clothing and other belongings, a few additional chilled survivors, and the unmarked body of Thral-Sivu, who had died of a broken neck. Some wandering horses were recaptured, but the Heir, Valplakh, had vanished entirely, and strangely so had the Bronze Sword of Owan, actual sword of Yuvakh Martyr, ancient emblem of rule, which had been in Thral-Sivu's tent. Nothing, weapons included, was made by *jinzal*, but they occasionally picked up swords and spears of men they had killed, and Dolvid reflected that as he sat reading the Bronze Sword might be held in the clumsy clubbed fist of an aged *jinzai*.

With barely one hundred cavalry able and with mounts to ride, Saidhan could not attempt any real search for the Heir in the featureless and waterless wastes of the Ní-Tilagh. As he wrote, there was no certainty the *jinzai* hunting-packs would not come back; abandoning all but one of the supply-wagons, using pack-animals for mounts, he turned back, sending ahead his fastest riders to take news of the disaster to the north.

Most remarkable was his coolheaded decision to send sealed messages to Banak in the West, out of recognition those who had rebelled three times against Thral-Sivu and her predecessor might take this catastrophe as their opportunity. The legitimate succession was unclear, but Laluvoi's unborn child would be seen either as a prize or an unneeded obstacle by anyone seeking power.

These guesses were confirmed with startling promptness. Having crossed the border into Nîv, but still many hours short of the fortress of Kir, Saidhan and his remnant were met by messengers from Tobhsila baKargul, son of the Tolvan defeated by Banak in the War of the Royal Stud. He wanted to offer Laluvoi his protection, and it was understood that also included marriage, as soon as propriety allowed (and Tobhsila could dispose of his current wife).

Laluvoi (*with all courtesy*, the report said) answered she was already under protection of Banak, and of his captain, Saidhan. The couriers departed, and Saidhan made his best speed to Kir, where Laluvoi's small and feeble son was born, weeks before term. This was new for Dolvid, who had always heard the child was stillborn, but the three days he lived made little practical difference; by then the cavalry of Kargul had been unleashed, and other excuses for the war could be found.

Saidhan ended his report with Kir, its garrison well below strength, invested by many squadrons of first-class cavalry, a time when he could not know his actions had settled the eventual outcome of the war, and given Arbhal a new ruling house.

The common name for the war came from the fact that just as Thral-Sivu's son was Laluvoi's husband, so her daughter had been Tolvan's second wife. She was not Tobhsila's mother, and she had died eight years before the loss of her brother the Heir, so the struggle was between two not of Gabh'Owan blood, who had married into the royal house, and survived their spouses; hence, War of the Widowed.

Dolvid knew the rest. Saidhan, using auxiliary bowmen and lightning sorties by single squadrons, defended Kir, till with stunning speed Banak came at the head of a powerful army to raise the siege, and nearly capture the astonished Tobhsila. There was to be a further year-and-a-half of war before Saidhan, in single-combat, killed Tobhsila, but Kargul by then had no chance of winning; the other provinces had given no open support, Banak had married Laluvoi, and Lambarr had been born.

After so many years there were several puzzles left to solve. Banak's arrival at Kir was not merely a dazzling demonstration of his principle of the unexpected, but an apparent impossibility. Besides his own men from the West, that army had included Household squadrons, which meant he must have come by way of Kadon Dinul, scarcely allowing the time needed for crossing of Arnan by the normal southern passage, made not with the sharp-prowed vessels used for couriers, but in slower-moving transports, filled with troops and their *pefral*. Still less explicable was how Tobhsila baKargul had received word of the disaster in the Ní-Tilagh so rapidly his messengers could intercept Saidhan before he reached Kir. Quite likely Kargul had kept spies at the posts where fast-messengers changed horses, perhaps coincidentally Tobhsila had already been in the eastern part of his province, but even so he would have to digest the news and make his plans, and the conclusion he was prepared in advance would have been irresistible, if only the assault in the Ní-Tilagh had come from armed men — soldiers, for example, disguised as bandits. But no one could plan an attack by *jinzal*, and about the *jinzal* there was no doubt; three at least had been killed, and Saidhan described the bulk of the unclothed bodies, fearsome even in death.

Explanation could only be surmise: imaginably Kargul had meant from the first to take advantage of the *rabhsaëyu*'s absence, massing troops for an attempt on Kadon Dinul. The events in the Ní-Tilagh would then have come as an opportunity to accomplish the same purpose without a fight. Meanwhile, Banak, wary of what Kargul might try, could have had his men at Kamsilat, ready for instant embarkation. A cynical historian might even suggest Banak had been the one ready to seize Kadon Dinul, to prevent succession of the dimwitted Heir.

Trails led from Ní-Tilagh to now; not just the obvious one, that Saidhan and Laluvoi were still alive. The parallel was irresistible, between the former catastrophe that extinguished the House Gabh'Owan and the equally shocking Tan Lughsai disaster that had come near ending Banak's line. In the wake of those *jinzal*, as now after the fire, more common evils had come scavenging; greed, hunger for power, the desire to subjugate others.

He marvelled at how absolute he had become. This was not just a debate between eternally hostile points of view; Laluvoi with her allies, Dolvid among them, was struggling against simple evil. This he knew, not because he was good, but for the opposite reason. He remembered very well how *Menadhi* used to stir him with the glory of Old Owan, make him want to be a part of its rebirth, how grudgingly he had come to see it as a glory that reached for the mountaintops by standing on prostrate bodies. Even now his passion for justice had to struggle against the same unctuous Owani feeling of being better; he knew the greed and contempt because they were alive inside him, hungering. They would never be completely extinguished in his life, but that did not mean they would triumph.

The House of Arvus

"Have you heard the news? A very bad business." Coming to the Bronze Residence in early afternoon Faëdhal was unwontedly dishevelled; the day was summer storms, dark squalls lashing in from the west with sudden vicious rains.

Arvus, he explained, had been denounced to the *rabhsai*, no one said by whom, on the old charge, theft.

"This is preposterous," Dolvid erupted. "The same foul game they always try whenever they're afraid the Treasury might make them pay their fair share, the cursed Families. Your pardon, Faëdhal."

"Not in the least. In confidence, I frequently make use of similar expressions myself. Well, you yourself, we may say, are of the Families."

He withheld any answer; this was meant as a compliment. In Faëdhal's world, though a *rabhsai* might have been a tanner's grandson, that of a chandler did not attain the Families by marrying into them. But the allegation against Arvus was made more dangerous by his performance in the Council. "Has Laluvoi been told about this charge?"

"Rhunilat says she has demanded and been granted hearing of the case. The *rabhsai* immediately disqualified himself, it being well known he had differed in questions of policy with Arvus; very proper, if one may be permitted."

Dolvid was agreeably surprised, although in a perfect realm it would have been equally wise for Laluvoi to recuse herself for the opposite reason; her open alliance with Arvus would leave its taint on the acquittal there was sure to be. But it might be beyond the resources of the *rabhsayum* to find an official who had no prior feelings about the fiery little Deniant. "If Arvus has been making himself rich," adapting a remark Laluvoi had once made about him, "you'd think we would see some signs of it."

In Faëdhal's chuckle there was faint, lingering disapproval for the austerity of Arvus's life, adding so little to the splendour of the court.

Not an hour later Tellis came, cloaked through new lashings of rain. She was white-faced as she gave the news in a flat voice; her father was dead. As the tale had come to her, a contingent of Household had gone to the Treasury to take Arvus into custody, but found him instead at the neighboring Mint, closeted with his friend Mirrat. On hearing the accusations against him, this mad tale continued, Arvus began to implicate Mirrat, who drew a knife and stabbed Arvus to death. The Master of Coinage, a very small man past the fiftieth year of a life without a single warlike action, was then said to have tried to cut his way out past the Household soldiers, who were forced to kill him.

They listened to this recital sitting at the worktable in the Old Throne Room, and Dolvid found slight comfort in the utter disbelief of Faëdhal, usually inclined to first accept any story at face-value. This one was not made more credible by the supporting fable of a conspiracy between Arvus and Mirrat, said to have accomplished thefts amounting to thousands of plakhi in value, mainly jewellery and household articles of gold and silver, accepted in lieu of taxes. These Arvus was supposed to have taken to Mirrat, who converted them into perfectly genuine money, keeping one-third for himself.

But knowing these charges must be false, and completely rejecting the account of events at the Mint, did nothing to alter the terrible fact: Arvus was dead, with his friend Mirrat. Tellis had put her hand in Dolvid's, and while she kept her face stiffly composed he could feel her trembling with anger and grief.

"Of Household, who was in charge?" he asked, hoping painfully it was not Bolan.

"Acting-*Kímukan* Zhinladh."

"Yes," at the Council meeting, standing by the door, glowering when Arvus spoke up for smallholders against the magnates. For years men such as Zhival, Zhinladh's father, had wished Arvus dead, and at last they had a climate for their crimes. There would be an Owani at the Treasury, another at the Mint, and no Mixed among *bôdh'loikil*.

"Certainly," Faëdhal said, "the *rabhsai* can never be contented with this, if I may say it, grotesque tale."

"My father kept one horse." Tellis began weeping in huge, painful, childlike sobs. Dolvid left his seat to hold her by the shoulders. Soon, she turned her face to his chest, and he kept her clasped to him. His mind was crowded but clear; his friend and debating-rival was gone, and despite what Faëdhal said Dolvid was wondering sickly how much the *rabhsai* had been told in advance, whether he had commanded the killing — or, as it would be, hinted at its desirability. The bleakness of any future for a realm where murder was a thinkable part of policy, the unconsolable wounding of Tellis, and with it all a part of him outside rebuke felt how right it was she should be turned to him for comfort, how rightly they breathed together.

He had a new fear. "Is Arvat here at the Bronze Residence?"

Faëdhal began an answer, and the face of Tellis emerged, blurred with tears. "He knows, I've seen him. He went to the Library."

"He must be brought here."

"He wants to be alone," Tellis protested, and Dolvid stopped her with a look. He tried to worry it through, while a copyist went for Arvat. "You both need protection, but Arvat more than you. There is going to be a public outcry over this killing, and then you'll be in less danger."

"Surely — " but Faëdhal was out of his depth here.

"Whatever his orders or lack of them, Zhinladh is not on a short leash. He and a few of his sort among the Families think they see the chance for settling old grudges."

Tellis said, "Arvat has not done anything to the Families."

"He is Arvus's son. They'll be afraid he would be a name for vengeance to rally round." The familiar realm was a strange and savage country, but its rules could be mastered by instinct.

Arvat came, and he had been weeping, too, but was indeed hot for retribution, repeating over and again he must have a weapon. In slack hours Dolvid had occasionally taken apprentices outside to teach them rudiments of swordplay. No one had less aptitude for it than Arvat, whose feet and hands would not act together. On him he urged prudence, telling him that to find revenge he had to begin by staying alive.

"My sister — "

"You are in greater danger. Tellis has friends at the New Residence." Rhunilat in particular, but he could not protect Arvat.

"Tellis," Faëdhal said, when he realised Dolvid was taking charge of the brother, "if one may suggest, could be a guest for now at my house. You would not be disturbed there," he told her. The offer, from a lifelong bachelor who avoided the company of women, was a measure either of his high regard for Tellis, or the depth of his concern for her safety.

Nervous about how long it could be before fresh visitors came, Dolvid said they should leave now, by the old guardhouse door; the guard there was certain to be sheltering inside the side-entrance proper. By cutting through the Gardens of Kamzhinu, deserted in this weather, they could then take a side-street off Market Way, and stay off the Avenue entirely.

Tellis faced him, and he told her Arvat would be safe, not sure how it would be done. She thanked him, and it was natural to give her a comforting hug. She kissed him softly next to his mouth.

Senseless, perhaps dangerous, to send others with them,

though at least two of the apprentices would have been willing. He still had misgivings as he stooped at a small window above the main portico, and watched his two friends cross at the south side of the square, slender, erect form of Tellis, the bowed one of Faëdhal, cloaks whipping in the wind. They reached the gateway to the Gardens, and at once passed out of view.

At the same moment a file of Household riders emerged at Harbour Gate, Acting-*Kímukan* Zhinladh at their head, easily identifiable by his girth. They headed across the Square, passing beneath the Spear. Dolvid made an exasperated noise; this was the one place they could be making for.

Going back, he led Arvat through the Audience Chamber and Old Throne Room to his small sleeping space. He took his Froghuli knife in its sheath down from the side wall, where he had kept it ever since the night of the intruders, and strapped it on, mainly to keep it out of Arvat's hands.

"You should be safe enough here — " and he decided not to withhold any secrets. Going to the solid-seeming rearward wall, he found the movable blocks, reaching through the slot which became visible to push back a bolt. A man-high slab turned easily on a pivot to reveal a black aperture, entrance to a passageway, discovery he had not intended to share with anyone, the result of reading among documents from the personal archives of Plakhsila, followed by careful searching.

Arvat's mouth was open wider than the entrance. Dolvid gave him an *ôdu*-lantern and told him to step just inside. The air in the passage was good, but he should not wander away. While the latch-slot was open he would be able to hear what was happening, and if there were voices in the Old

Throne Room he could slide the bolt in.

"I ought to be facing my father's murderers, not hiding from them."

"You can face them when we have law again," pushing the young man inside.

A moment for brief words with the scribes and copyists, to send one of the apprentices down to the main entrance to bring a couple of the Household guards from there. Zhinladh would come by the side-entrance, and was sure to be using hand-picked men for his day's business; presence of others would leave less opening for a tale like the one from the Mint. On the same thought Dolvid started to take off his knife, then called his action to the attention of Orimat, most serious of the young apprentices. "Take note, I am laying this aside, and have no other weapon. I shall ask you again about this in a minute or two." Without overt understanding, Orimat nodded frowning agreement.

Zhinladh came in with only four men, two of them file-leaders. Bulk made him more than his thirty-odd years, but he moved surprisingly well. The nod with which he greeted Dolvid was dangerously self-satisfied.

There was no preamble. "Master, you may have heard about the incidents at the Treasury, or rather, the Mint?"

"I have heard about Arvus being accused."

"Isn't his son here?"

"Is Arvat being accused, too?" trying to keep the edge off his voice.

Zhinladh said, "Perhaps we could talk privately."

Dolvid gave offhand assent. "I took off my weapon,

didn't I?" to Orimat, as if absent-minded.

"Yes, Master. It's here."

"Then I must be unarmed, mustn't I?" fatuously. Though aware of danger from the first, till now it had not occurred to him his own death might be the principal purpose of this visit, Zhinladh tidying away all officials who had opposed the interests of the Families. The fat officer followed him into the Old Throne Room, and the two file-leaders, both Owanil, came with him. With the door open Dolvid called back quite loudly over his shoulder, "No day for riding," and Zhinladh agreed.

The door closed behind him, Zhinladh gave a summary of events at the Mint, exactly the story Tellis had heard, and the lanky file-leader to Zhinladh's right kept echoing his commander.

"Mirrat drove his knife into Arvus's heart, before we could move."

"Into the heart," the file-leader agreed. "Before we could move."

"He was killed instantly, nothing could be done."

"Instantly, nothing."

Any attuned ear could catch the note of men corroborating not facts but the agreed account. Yet there might be menace in that, as if to give notice there would not have to be a very good story to explain Dolvid's death, either.

"This year is nothing but griefs," Dolvid said.

"Aye, Arvus had many friends, who'll be shocked by it all. All of it, I mean. A man so trusted — what is it?" Two auxiliaries of the Household, part of the Bronze Residence guard, had come through the door. Seeing the officer, they halted in surprise, saluted, and said they had been sent for.

"As I was about to say," Dolvid put in, "I now see why Tellis Arvus-daughter came here looking for her brother. She was a pupil here, too, but I am afraid we may have lost her to the New Residence and Rhunilat." This chattiness was bizarre for one who had just heard about the death of a friend, but as Zhinladh recall where Tellis had allies. "I had these men brought. Arvat left with his sister, not so?" He was gambling neither of these men knew them by sight.

The younger one offered, "A man and a girl went across the Square not long ago — I'm sure they must have come from here. They didn't walk from the *Mankh'* today."

"As I thought," before any details of height or apparent age could be volunteered. "The Household, I assume — " he turned back to Zhinladh — "wants to give them protection."

"There is a lot of upset," Zhinladh nonsensically agreed, "about the whole business, the thefts." His face had the watchfulness of a stupid man who is aware he is being deceived in some complicated way. Not possible, as he was yet to work out, that the guards had been sent for to answer a question not then asked.

His notion Tellis and the supposed Arvat must have gone home would have been accepted if the auxiliary had not mentioned the pair he had seen had gone into the Gardens, wrong direction for Arvus's house, well north of the Avenue.

"Ah," sounding to himself more and more like Faëdhal at his vaguest. "They have kin, a cousin, as I remember, who lives somewhere near Market Gate hostelry." This was absolute invention.

"I never heard of any kin," Zhinladh said.

"Perhaps I am mistaken. At the Residence someone could tell you."

After ponderous consideration, Zhinladh fidgeted. "We'll find them. Arvat comes here every day, doesn't he?"

"Most days." Here Dolvid came very near letting his real anger go into a display of offended dignity: except in a realm gone mad, Zhinladh had no imaginable right to be questioning him in this way. It was as if the fear surrounding the man was a trick, an illusion the right word could make vanish. Just on the other side of the door Lambarr might be sauntering in with his cheerful opinions on weather, carpentry, the decline of the stonemason's craft.

Not satisfied, but apparently ready to leave, Zhinladh sent the two auxiliaries back to their post. His own two file-leaders moving off, he lingered. "I have heard you often spend nights here, Master."

"When we were working on the *True Song*. Not often now."

"You have quarters here, then?"

"Here — " hoping Arvat had the sense to keep the secret door closed, he led the way to the curtained alcove. "Not much to see, I'm afraid."

All was quiet. Zhinladh nodded as the curtains fell back in place. "Your pardon, Master, were you not formerly with the *Mankh'*?"

"That's where I learnt how to sleep plain."

The officer touched a thumb to his well-padded chest, Raëdh's sign. "A man could learn a lot there that would be with him all his life."

"A lot, also, *Kímukan*, that belongs to ages gone by."

"But you're of the Old Blood."

"We've got the common letters," blandly. "Only a madman would want to go back to the obscurity of glyphs."

Baffled, Zhinladh took his leave. As the doors closed behind him, Dolvid took a colossal gulp of air, and sat down, trembling.

When Arvat had spoken in the past of going to the Colony, it had been for the sake of finding faster advancement under Saidhan, perhaps a way of rebuking Dolvid for not giving him his due. "You must go there now," he told him. "They can find a place for someone trained, as a secretary or a record-keeper at the Great House in Kamsilat." Exactly what he had conjectured doing for himself.

"My sister needs me here."

"You can't help her. I promise you she will be safe."

"But you might be in danger yourself."

"Not really. But I am not the one who'll make Tellis safe." That was curiously bitter to say.

Fingering his straggly moustache, Arvat went through obligatory postures, saying he was no coward, that he would dedicate himself to vengeance, that Zhinladh should be the fugitive, and then, with a drastic descent, that he had never been farther than the Arcades at Bathrâd in his whole life.

"It need not be for ever. You'll find good people at Kamsilat, and the Heartland is going to see better times." And before that, worse, he did not say.

Saidhan had just returned from his long journey south. Dolvid meant to get word to him at the Residence, but when Faëdhal came back to report Tellis was safely installed at his house, he also gave the news Saidhan had left for Owan Sai last evening with his escort. There had been a rumoured fresh quarrel with Ban-Sila on old themes, the Colony's pressing need for supplies, the strength of the Army of the West, and its command.

"Not, I fear," Faëdhal said, "the weather one would choose for a crossing of Arnan."

True. Chances, in fact, were very strong Saidhan had not yet set sail. "We'll ride for Owan Sai after dark," Dolvid told Arvat.

The Warden of the Royal Port was another old soldier with recollections from the War of the Widowed, Narudhai, a tall, big-nosed man with a dry, barking laugh, frequently sounded. It was at his residence that Dolvid caught up with Saidhan, who had sailed early in the day, but whose ship, after clearing the Estuary, had been forced to put about and run before squalls, regaining the shelter of Owan Sai before noon. With gusts easing he expected to be under way tomorrow. He was drinking wine with Narudhai.

"*Bôdh'loiki*," in surprise. "Just the man I wanted to see, but I was afraid I'd have to ride back to Kadon Dinul."

With Arvat outside, sheltering behind the *pefrai* they had double-ridden, Dolvid did not wait, as he should, to hear what Saidhan wanted with him, but asked for private talk. Narudhai, ostentatiously discreet, left the room, and then Saidhan heard an account of the day's turbulent and frightening events, from the impossible killings at the Mint to Zhinladh's visit to the Bronze Residence.

He listened gravely. While in Kadon Dinul he had heard about the charges against Arvus, and had no hesitation about their origin. "Aye, I wasn't happy with how it went in the Council, and I could tell you one who was unhappier. This would not be his doing, but, Hrafi, his to prevent. The higher you are, the more careful you need to be — a lord in a bad mood says he is sick of someone's ways, and there's always a fool who guesses a little murdering is his way to favour. But Arvus! We can't spare such men. What about the son?"

After Dolvid explained what he had come for, Saidhan had the young man brought in. Before anything else, he said, "You want to be in my service, so I hear."

Arvat, a little bewildered, approaching exhaustion from the strains of the day, nodded, "*Asai.*"

Saidhan, calling Narudhai back in so he too could witness, took out a coin and gave it to Arvat. "This is against your wages, when we determine them. If anyone comes here to offer protection, or for any other purpose, Arvat is in Saidhan's service."

Arvat mumbled his dazed thanks, and Saidhan spoke kindly about his father, not caring what Narudhai heard. "A Deniant, he called himself, but there are not many true

Children of Yoëlladhu I'd trust as well.   Beliefs aside, g'*Asalladh'* Himself loved Arvus."

"Anyone honest had to," Dolvid's voice broke.

A servant was told to show Arvat a bed. "They may try to implicate him in his father's supposed crimes," Saidhan speculated.   "Well, one more bone of contention between Kamsilat and Kadon Dinul. How long do you venture it will be, before my grandson learns what a *rabhsai* can't do? Good breeding there, and it'll win out in the end."

Now he came to the reason he had been ready to ride back for a word with Dolvid. In the day's storms a ship had been driven onto the rocky coast of Arnan south of the *Mankh'*. No loss of life, but the cargo, a full hold of grain for the Colony, was past recovering.

One shipload, Saidhan allowed, might not be life or death, but the Colony was already struggling, and he had hoped the small amount of food he had been able to purchase here would be enough to carry them through to harvest. He could not say where more could be found.

"I can, not four hours from Kadon Dinul, though it has not actually been offered for sale. There are powers I have not yet invoked." The wheat Dolvid had in mind was Khelagh's.

"Will you have adequate support?" but Saidan did not press for details, and gave his personal draft with the amount left open. "There will always be a place at Kamsilat for you, too. Not the same for a married man, though, is it? and Laluvoi needs allies, all the more now."

In the morning he rode straight for Faëdhal's house. He had meant to come back last night, but Saidhan, protesting he had committed no crimes by bringing Arvat, said his best safety was to ride openly and in daylight. Narudhai brought a fresh bottle of wine, and they sat up late, the two old soldiers telling anecdotes, Dolvid wishing he could make notes.

Tellis, calm but pale, sat facing him. He always felt large and clumsy in Faëdhal's house, filled and perhaps overfilled with rare and fragile things, spindly tables, horses and birds of Kamanta glass, perched where an elbow seemed certain to sweep. In his narrow, exquisitely carved chair he was almost knee-to-knee with her.

"Were you not all-but promised to Rhunilat Rhunsilakhati?"

"So he wanted it."

"This is a good time to have Rhunilat as a friend. Would it be such a bad match?"

"He's not stupid, nor unkind," she agreed (if it was agreement).

"He has no enemies."

"He is wise to avoid controversy," suspecting the presence of irony.

"You don't want to be his wife?"

"I had heard," coolly, "Khalú might be ready to choose again. When you are away from Kadon, she is often with — "

"With another one who is well-placed," he interrupted. Tellis's calm admission shook him far beyond the news about Khalú, which was not news; when she first began calling him

Dol he could guess where it came from. Divorce was not difficult, where both agreed to it, and there was no dispute over property. He had even considered proposing it to Khalú, who had every right to be anxious over his future in the *rabhsayum* of Ban-Sila; she had not married him to be an outcast, and was not obliged to suffer for convictions she was nowhere near sharing.

He reached out to take both Tellis's cool hands, and they gratefully clasped his fingers. "You realise I could not offer you protection."

"He does not have to be *uzh'freladhai*, or wrestle the Families for food. We could follow Arvat to Kamsilat."

Was it possible? Of what he had on the Mainland he needed only clothes and books; Khalú could not object to a divorce leaving her with her lands and the house and grounds Laluvoi had given.

"I have to go to the Residence."

"The Bronze Residence."

"The New. I must speak with Laluvoi."

"Dolvid — " She had never used his name so, directly, without any title. "My father thought he was strong enough — " she nearly broke down, but regained control. " — to stand up against these changes."

"I don't." But there was stubborn resentment against letting Zhinladh and his crowd bully him from the scene, and the growing idea Saidhan's commission was chance for a rude gesture.

She was reading his mood. "You are no less of a man if you decide to stay alive."

"You don't want me to say anything to Rhunilat?"

"What are you going to do?"

He admired the vulnerability in that, and wished he could be as brave. "I have not decided. If I were not married to Khalú — " he remained guarded. "There is no one else I would want for my wife, except you."

"I have had a long wait to hear that. If you are going to follow my father and fight against the tide, I can't afford any more patience."

"Of course." They kissed lightly, and then in earnest.

He was not alone going to the Residence. His mind full of Tellis, the Colony, Khalú, he came out on the Avenue and there were dozens moving up the slope in twos and threes; up beyond the Disc of Aëlovoi they were thickening to a crowd. The morning was fine and bright, but it was not a happy gathering. The mood was ugly.

Seeing him on the big *pefrai* of the Household, one small group began shouting abuse at Dolvid, and from the other side a brawny hand grabbed at his stirrup. Bred to fight, the horse started a menacing caracole, till Dolvid brought him up.

"*Rabhsayani!*" He had never heard that used as a term of contempt.

"Killers of Arvus!" A rough-clad man brandished a stave.

"Murderers! Give us Zhinladh — " and this was taken up by others, till the name of Zhinladh became a chant. The news was out, and his prediction of public outcry had been more than fulfilled.

"This is *Bôdh'loiki* Dolvid," a small man bawled in the face of the large one holding his stirrup.

"They're all murderers."

"Zhinladh! Zhinladh!" Some boys, oldest not above twelve, were armed with stones in each hand.

"No, no," the little man insisted, a stranger to Dolvid. "He's one of ours. He'll tell them. Tell the *rabhsai*, Dolvid. Give us Zhinladh!"

"Aye — " a woman on his right took it up. "Give us the butchers!"

He had quietly resumed forward motion. He had no notion how this mob could know anything about his opinions, but was equally incredulous so many knew Arvus, even who he was, enough to be angry over his killing. These feelings were an infection, and the idea spread that Dolvid was not one of the enemy, so that as he came up to the Disc he had an unsought escort advising him what to say and do. Perhaps the one who yelled loudest was listened-to, and if someone had bawled out he was Zhinladh's friend, he would be torn apart by now. He was glad not to be, but did not want to be their banner, either.

Shouting for Zhinladh, the crowd at the foot of the steps was being held back by a double line of Household, pikes held crosswise (there was really no such thing as a Household pikeman; it was an unloved duty rotated amongst squadrons). The names of Arvus and Mirrat were also heard, but soon the rhythmic chant, *Zhinladh!* spread from the rear and pounded like a heavy hammer.

His escort left him, pressing forward with the rest, and with a sharp rightward wheel he was in the open. The crowd was not as big as noise and confusion made it, and away from the foot of the Steps the space in front of the Pefrai Gate was relatively clear. As he made for it, not sure whether he would be admitted, it opened to let out *péfrapravádal* of the Household, a strong force. He saw they were led by Kizhunai, a coolheaded officer, and though their swords were belted on, in their hands the cavalry were carrying nothing deadlier than the long, slender canes used to control Pledging crowds, till Bolan's special forces had substituted heavy staves.

As one contingent of Kizhunai's men pushed for the Steps to relieve the hard-pressed pikemen, the rest extended in the direction of the Disc with the object of enveloping the ugly-mooded crowd; he had to back away, and move almost against the wall of what had been Rhunsilakh's house. From there, across the heads of the crowd, he had a view up the small street which went past the Treasury and the Mint, with a branch leading to the main barracks. There, more troops were approaching, mounted on saddle-horses, and without the crispness of Household men. They would have no space to deploy, unless they meant to charge into the flank of the crowd. It was the special forces, but Dolvid could not see Bolan with them, nor any officer he recognised.

The shouting went on, with the struggle at the base of the Steps, where the object of the crowd certainly was not to mount up to the doors of the Residence, but the Household were obstinately determined to keep them off even the level where the Residence border was marked by the end of the reddish stone of the Avenue, and the beginning of the blue-grey paving at the Steps.

Leftward, other parts of the special forces had come down Market Way, and were extending just to the near side of the Disc. Two groups faced west to prevent any further townspeople from adding to the press by the Steps, but others in a continuous line, about a squadron, faced the Residence, completing encirclement of the mob. They were wearing swords, but had nothing in their hands, and were under the orders of a long-faced young squadron leader unfamiliar to Dolvid.

In a fresh surge at the foot of the Steps a man brandishing a rough length of wood was taken under the armpits by a strong cavalrymen, and pikemen behind seized and held the struggling, cursing figure. Instant shouts sounded for his release. The mob there pushed forward, while farther back, where bodies were not packed as close, one of the boys seen earlier drew back his hand, and threw a stone the size of a bunched fist. It clattered off the Steps, but the next clanged from the helmet of a staggered pikeman. Kizhunai, out in front of his waiting men, spurred into the crowd to deal with the boys, and then, leftward again, Dolvid saw an action that frightened him: the officer by the Disc gave `Draw swords' to his raw troops — the command could not be heard, but his mouth made the words, and blades came from their sheaths in ragged fashion.

For all the area between the Residence and the Disc he found he was the only one watching this contingent. In clear space behind the line of Kizhunai's men, he moved, then began to trot in that direction.

Just as he swung past the end of the Household men, the infuriated mob by the Steps drove a wedge between horsemen, knocked a pikeman sprawling, and came very near rescuing the captive. No longer reinforced from behind, the crowd, pushing forward, had made twenty paces of open Avenue in front of the squadron of special forces. Their officer was standing in his stirrups to observe events at the Steps. An expression between fear and battle-lust came into the long-jawed face, his right arm swung back flat, sword fiercely gripped.

He would give the Charge. Plain as a vivid memory Dolvid saw the results and heard them, the yells of pain and fear, howls of anger, crowd unable to retreat or scatter, the deep rose-colour of the Avenue splashed with brighter red. All this in no time, as he spurred in front of poised blades, and lunged to grab at the squadron leader's wrist.

"Fool," he was bellowing. "Don't." The muscled right arm stiffened and wrenched against his grip, but Dolvid had the better mount, and he braced in the saddle, so his adversary came near unseating himself. Fury flashed out amongst the nearest of the soldiers, but then Kizhunai was there, calling, "Sheathe swords. Sheathe swords.

"All swords — " emphatically to the officer, who was glaring in Dolvid's eyes, face mad with hate. Somewhat reluctantly Dolvid released the wrist. A waver, but a senior officer was there; the sword went across and down into the sheath.

Backing off and wheeling his horse, he did not wait to hear Kizhunai's reprimand of the officer. At the Steps the attempt to free the captive had failed, and there was a recoiling, jagged anger winding down to a muddled rumble. Above, the tall doors had opened, and Ban-Sila emerged, all alone.

His face was rigid. Even at that distance he was obviously annoyed, but also frightened, as he had a right to be. Yet he achieved calm, holding up a hand. The noise of the crowd swelled then diminished, took form, going from identification of Ban-Sila *Rabhsai* to new but less strident demands for Zhinladh. Detached cries accused the Household, denouncing Zhinladh as killer of Arvus and Mirrat.

Ban-Sila's mouth moved, and nothing could be heard.

"Hear the *rabhsai!*" was sounded in the crowd, and voices amongst the cavalry-officers gave the same shout. The noise dwindled, though to nothing near silence.

"My friends," Ban-Sila called. "The death of our well-loved Arvus, and of — " but the name of Mirrat was lost amid new shouts about murder, and Zhinladh.

"Hear the *rabhsai!*" from the cavalry.

"We — " Ban-Sila repeated the word twice more before he could go on. "We are looking into these deaths. If anyone is guilty — if anyone is guilty, he will be punished. Justice will be done, you have my word."

In its flat-voiced way Ban-Sila's brief address had its effect. Here and there in the crowd was a little patter of applause, and then a startling rendition of the royal salute came from trumpets over by Pefrai Gate. As the *rabhsai* turned and vanished into the Residence, he was replaced by Merovas, a familiar figure, and well liked. Quite undisconcerted, as if out for a morning stroll, he came halfway down between the lines of gilded statuary before getting set.

"Look — " his voice was powerful, and he could be almost conversational and still audible. "You've heard the *rabhsai*. We have to keep order. You've got troops on every side here — " this caused a stir of twisting heads, and a murmur. "If you don't go to your homes, sooner or later something's going to get broken. Go home." He raised a palm for quiet. "You have the *rabhsai*'s word, you know how it's done."

Dolvid admired Merovas enormously for hitting just the right, reasonable tone. There was muttering, some vehement, but also an ebb in pressure at the foot of the Steps. Bolan had appeared by the Disc, and was moving men to the downhill side, so as to shepherd the crowd up Market Way. Most of the mob would be from Old Town.

Kizhunai was next to him. "My thanks, *Bôdh'loiki*. I was too busy to notice that young fool. This could have been a butchery."

Dolvid nodded. "Can I get in at Pefrai Gate?"

"Oh, aye, you can. The password is anything but *Zhinludh*."

Pleased by the unexpected flash of humour, he made for the entrance to the courts. The crowd was perceptibly backing off. "But we'll have justice," a man bawled, unhappily accepting present facts.

Now it seemed blood would not flow, Dolvid was

quietly elated. They cared enough, the townspeople, about the two victims — or the ones who had marched not at all clear about who Arvus and Mirrat were, cared enough about what their deaths were emblem of, to risk death to show their anger.

Not that it brought back a friend. In the high-ceilinged hush of the New Residence, joy quickly evaporated.

Laluvoi's dejection was not less than at the loss of her son and grandchildren. "I killed him," she said, whispered, alone with Dolvid. "He believed he could rely on my protection, and I let him be killed, and poor Mirrat, too. I did not mean him to speak out as he did in the Council, but that was Arvus. I should never have brought him to that meeting."

Like Saidhan, Laluvoi was in no doubt why Arvus had died. Dolvid could not invent anything to lessen her remorse.

"Do you think the *rabhsai* knew?" Her tone was severe.

"Madam, I cannot believe so." A statement about *rabhsayum*, about himself, rather than the facts.

"Zhinladh's account, that will be the story. Oh, yes. We can't believe, either, that officers of the Household contrive murders for their own revenge. I asked you to stay beside me, Dolvidh."

"I have tried to, *Asayu*."

"A wise man would try elsewhere. I shall have to betray you, in the end. By my death, I mean. Saidhan has said he will come back soon." With the last she had gone again into private worlds.

"I had thought of making my home in the Colony."

Had she heard? Slowly, she looked up. "Soon?"

"Nothing is settled, *Asayu*. There would be matters to be disposed of, first." He was thinking of the commission from Saidhan, but would sound unfeeling if she took it to mean Khalú.

"You seem decided."

"I would need your permission, *Asayu*. I hold an official post at your pleasure." The sinecure.

"My pleasure is what pleases you. At the Bronze Residence, you'll leave a great deal unfinished, I suppose; the good Faëdhal has his talents, but I do not think the writing of history is among them. Well, after you sail we shan't meet again, Master. What you are escaping here can't last forever, but it may well outlive Laluvoi."

The change in her manner chilled him. Unwarned, she had raised a wall between them — and Dolvid, astonished, saw what it reminded him of: himself, a dozen years ago, when Valnoi told him she was going to marry. And then was puzzled by his determination to be finished with her, the coldness he used to mask hurt and prevent more: then Laluvoi, *the* Laluvoi, was proud and lonely, fearful as ordinary people to let her needs be seen?

"*Asayu*, if I do go, I shall seek an audience with you before leaving."

"So I would assume."

Coming out of her personal suite into the corridor he was waylaid by Bolan, who all-but dragged him away for *raminat* in his quarters.   He was pale-faced, and looked sleepless. "Kizhunai told me what you did by the Disc. You're a fool, but Zhôl be thanked for making fools — I'm going to have that young *jinzai*'s liver.   The city on the edge of an outright revolt — " he rocked a hand to and fro to indicate a delicate balance. "A bloodletting in front of the Residence, it's throwing lamp-oil to put out a fire. Who guessed so many knew Arvus, much less loved him?" Seeing Dolvid's face, he added, "I'm shocked, as I don't need to tell you."

"Has Zhinladh been arrested yet?"

Bolan ran fingers back through his hair, giving a windy sigh. "Out of my hands, Dol — the *rabhsai*'s taken charge. But how can you punish a man for doing his duty? Listen, Dol, have you any clue where Tellis is? No one can find her."

"Only Tellis? What about Arvat?"

"That idiot has run off to the Colony — we just had word from Owan Sai. He must believe this Deniant talk of a plot to kill his father. The Colony? He must be mad."

"The fact that the idiot's father was dead," acidly, "may have given the Deniant talk some weight. Zhinladh came snuffling after him at the Bronze Residence yesterday. If I had known where Arvat was, I would not have told him."

"Now, Dol. You're not saying a Household officer killed Arvus and Mirrat — by design?"

"Is that what the rumour is? With the crowd by the Steps, I simply assume there is something wrong, when a man gives offence to the *rabhsai* and the Families, and is killed while with a Household man whose father is Zhival."

"Do you believe this?"

"Tell me you can see little Mirrat running wild with a dagger."

Bolan was in a struggle that pained and frightened him. "But men when they're cornered do things you'd never imagine. They were doing it, Dol, they were stealing. We found a chest of coins, all mint new, gold and silver, hidden at Arvus's house."

"We? You mean, Zhinladh found it."

"No — " a small triumph for Bolan. "One of my men, my own squadron. After Zhinladh's lot had gone through the place and found nothing. They forgot that little cellar where he kept his fruit and wines."

"Put a different way, Zhinladh's men left the Mint and went to Arvus's house, and then yours went there and found this chest." This was sarcastic, yet there was pale consolation in seeing if Bolan was a dupe, he was not worse, and only a small faction with the Household was part of Zhinladh's scheming. But Laluvoi was right; Zhinladh's ramshackle tale was going to be propped up and made to stand.

"About Tellis, the thing is, the *rabhsai* wants her here at the Residence, where she'll be safe."

"Safe from what, if Mirrat killed Arvus? Where, you mean, she can be shown off to prove the goodwill of the *rabhsai*."

This contemptuous response scared Bolan more. Still, the fright the mob had given Ban-Sila meant there was no longer danger to Tellis. "I may be able to reach her with a message. She'll hear the *rabhsai*'s invitation."

"Soon."

"Today, certainly."

A long, troubled frown. "You're playing some risky games," then, "Have you seen Khalú yet? She's here."

"Here, where? In Kadon?"

"At the Residence. Your rooms in the Rose-Stone Wing." Bolan carefully explained. "I sent men to fetch her. She knows you're alive now, but she was frantic, with the killings and all the rumours."

She would have been more so if told what he had been doing yesterday and last night, and not all her horror would be fear for his safety. He thrust down a jab of guilt to concentrate on Bolan's folly. "At the *Mankh'*, we had an exercise called *knowing, not-knowing...* "

He gave it up; Bolan would never see his necessary faith in Zhinladh's story was incompatible with his solicitude over Khalú's fear. She, knowing the Families as well as anyone could, recognised at once what the deaths of Arvus and Mirrat meant, and Bolan, by his actions, without seeing he did, agreed with her.

"I'll go to her, if you have nothing else."

"Don't forget about Tellis."

Khalú had been weeping, and would again. "Dolvidh, you mustn't leave me with no word." She came into his arms, turning her face sideways against his chest. He held her, and felt tears in his own eyes. He could not go to the Colony with Tellis.

In a while she recovered her good humour, telling him the *rabhsai* wanted to see them both. "I saw him after Bolan went to make his report. He spoke highly of you, Ban-Sila *Deghi*, I mean. He was very pleasant, and said you kept me hidden away too much." She dimpled. "He said I am one of the realm's treasures. It was only a joke, but it's not as if there aren't plenty of lovely women, so it was quite flattering, really."

Telling Khalú he had to run an errand for the *rabhsai*, he went through quietening streets, many troops abroad, to Faëdhal's house.

"You are going to stay," Tellis, when she saw his face. "You'll stay with Khalú till she wants a change."

"There are those who have to stay."

"Let the big lords stay — Saidhan. He is in no danger, but he has gone off to Kamsilat, because his grandson irks him. Part of being a famous captain is to let troopers do the dying."

This hard anger was a new side of Tellis, but rooted in grief. "That's unfair to Saidhan. He won his fame in single-combat."

"You are going to end the same as my father, murdered by the law, or you will be sent to salt eels." She was weeping freely now. "Why, Dolvid? You can't love Khalú. She is a house-pet bred by the Families."

"Perhaps I can't love." If he loved Tellis, and he seemed to, it ought to make him callous about his wife, indifferent to the fate of the realm, or unfinished work Laluvoi had goaded him with. "I can get you a passage to Kamsilat, if you want."

"I shall marry Rhunilat." For this her manner was as near arch as he could imagine her: she was too generous for spite.

"No urgency. The *rabhsai* is offering you his protection." She made a sour face, and he told her of the mob, the glimpse of insurrection that had surely chastened Ban-Sila. A pained pride came into Tellis's face when she heard how the crowd had shouted out her father's name, and demanded the blood of his killers.

He also told about Laluvoi's grief, and Tellis fixed him with a strange, considering look. All at once bitterness came uppermost, and she spoke with an alien sardonicism. "I vow solemnly to be in the mob wanting vengeance for your death. The *rabhsai* is going to go carefully for a while, till he has made himself stronger. I should be safe, married to Rhunilat." She adopted a hard smile. "He would be better with dear Khalú, an adornment for any man who wants display. He is not the loser, though — " she moved her body in the long undulation of the cheapest week-wife attracting a customer. "I give much the better sport, so I have been told by men who have tried us both."

"Stop it." He hugged her tightly against him, marvelling at the greed that wanted everything, no matter who it hurt or killed. "If I had choice, I would choose you."

"It's not Khalú. You're not staying here for her. It's that wonderful old spider."

"Who?"

"Laluvoi. She has been sucking men's blood all her life, and can always find new prey to love her. She lives, they die." Seeing Dolvid's face, too incredulous to be offended, Tellis modified her singular assessment. "Oh, I love her too. She is a great woman, for the realm. She doesn't use up men out of vanity or for her own pleasure; the cause is a good one. But she's a hungry old spider, and you are the same fool my father was."

"The realm could use a few hundred more such fools." The rebuke was unnecessary; anger had dissolved again into its originating grief.

"I knew," weeping softly, a recognisable Tellis again. "I sat here thinking about Bronal's lyric of the Lamp and the Mirror, and I knew we were never going to Kamsilat together."

The endless day — it was coming nearer two days, with very brief sleep at Owan Sai — continued with the *rabhsai* putting an arm about his shoulder in a stiff attempt at cordiality. At the same time he awkwardly grasped the hand of Khalú, radiant with pleasure.

"Dolvidh' — " Banak's grandson carefully pronounced the aspirate. "We partly saw, and also were told of your bold action to prevent bloodshed this midday. Very courageous."

"I had no time for courage, *Deghi*." While still suspecting Ban-Sila's motives, he could not deny compassion for this stiff young man whose best simulation of warmth was this hollow heartiness.

"You must visit me often here." It was as if he was speaking a lesson. "Certainly, you are a busy man, and also you want to be with our lovely Khalú — who would blame you for that? But you are our *bôdh'loiki*, and still the *uzh'freladhai*."

Dolvid made deference. He was reconfirmed. Arvus was dead, but he had his titles.

"You play *zhabhu*, so I am told."

"Not well, *Deghi*."

"Oh, Dolvidh," Khalú reproached. True, he had beaten her father when, infrequently, they had played, but Khelagh was the kind of fumbling player no stroke of luck could rescue.

"You must give us a game soon."

He bowed again. Early reports of Ban-Sila's skill at *zhabhu* had altered to include the idea he might cheat; he was said to be a very bad loser, and if he played with Dolvid was certainly going to have no chance to show it.

"Mistress Khalú should also be here more — this court needs beauty, laughter." Ban-Sila was becoming bizarre: had anyone ever heard him laugh, except in scorn?

"We shall have — feasts," rather vaguely. "Music. A jewel such as Khalú needs a setting."

Khalú was ready to burst with modesty; long ago, in the reign of Plakhsila *Kímukoi*, and perhaps less long ago with Great Banak, such a speech by the *rabhsai* would have warned the husband to expect his wife's unexplained absences. Not so in the reign of the devoted Lambarr, and most certainly not in this.

After Ban-Sila, he left Khalú again for what he hoped would be the last meeting today, one he had arranged with Merovas in the Court of the Ram. Having exchanged compliments about their separate parts in holding down the riot, they sat together on a stone bench in late sun, sure they could not be overheard.

"Bolan wants to enforce a curfew," Merovas said. "But Bolan is a little out of favour just at present. He's been ordered to put his special forces outside the city, under canvas if there's no other way."

"I wish he had been told, dissolve them for good."

"Ah, well," pinching his lower lip. "Now they've found out how brave they are, riding together, I wouldn't want to say, goodbye, you're not needed — not unless we could scatter them all over Six Provinces, so's they couldn't meet each other again. That's the trouble with turning thieves into an army. But they're not being broken up, just put far enough away not to provoke anything, near enough if they're needed." The voice was lowered. "I could believe I'm watching the Burantal Marionettes. But the dying is real."

They spoke for a while about Arvus, and then Dolvid came to the commission from Saidhan.

"You have that much grain stored."

"Yes, but we can't run those stocks down. Add hunger to this city's mood, and we'll have blood running in the streets. I can tell you where we can find this much wheat ten times."

"Aye, you can. You've kept saying, wait."

"Till we had tried everything else. The *rabhsai* confirmed my appointment just today."

A cock of the head. "He told you you could seize stores from the magnates?"

"I did not go through my powers, point by point." He had no doubt what Ban-Sila would have said, asked for specific authorisation for what Dolvid planned.

"Should this be now? We don't want you joining Arvus."

"It is the best time. While the storm about Arvus keeps blowing, the Families can't hope for favours from the Residence."

"Who's to be the lucky seller, then?"

"Khelagh," watching the soldier's eyebrows go up. "He has the biggest stocks, and if I forced anyone else to sell, they would say I was favouring my wife's family."

Merovas mused, and with studied tact worked all round the suggestion Dolvid might achieve the same objective by having Khalú talk to her father, avoiding use of force. Equally indirectly Dolvid hinted he had tried without success to use family influence to make Khelagh more tractable. "Besides, we need a demonstration of the powers the law gives us."

"What are the plans?"

Dolvid asked him to provide two squadrons in full battle-gear, to be ready first thing in the morning. He would ride with them and compel sale of the wheat Saidhan needed.

The granaries he had in mind were to the north of the Great Stone Road, not far beyond Sennu Bridge, about midpoint between the city and Kred Bakali. For a year his father-in-law had been unlawfully moving goods outside the province, using a cart-track that led down to the Paowan River near where the Lurr Ferry used to have its landing, and loading big barges there.

To ride east, and act as Dolvid's escort, Merovas would give him a half-squadron from the General Cavalry post by East

Gate; with unrest here he could not spare more from Kadon Dinul. The rest would come from the Kred Bakali garrison, and would meet up with Dolvid's men near where they had to leave the main road. "I can give you Squadron-Leader Kennar, if he's acceptable."

"I have served with him. We were at the Pass of Perus together." A warm satisfaction in saying that, and he remembered Shumat telling him, in his revulsion after the battle, that he would come to have kinder feelings about the victory, about warfare itself. Whether he wished it or not, that seemed to be coming true.

"Good. He won't hear the reason why he's riding till you meet with him. The orders can be on their way in an hour. Aye — " Merovas rubbed his chin. "But I wish I could go myself. I daren't risk it, with the street-rats looking for blood, and those cutthroats in soldiers' tunics more than ready to oblige."

"Kennar is a good officer, and I do not expect a fight, when Khelagh's men see a hundred lances."

Merovas got to his feet, sighing. "All true, all true. But it's been ages since I had a bit of soldiering to enjoy."

Later it occurred to him that in their war-council the action had been his duty, help for the Colony, a timely demonstration, even a possible lark. Neither of them had mentioned what they both knew: this was token revenge for Arvus.

Shemugrân

Dolvid's Raid (as Merovas called it) went off with no real trouble. Khelagh kept armed men at his granaries, but as expected the appearance of so much regular cavalry cowed them, and beyond petulant, covered words about *thievery* they did nothing to interfere, as he oversaw loading of eight cartloads, sixteen *gruvai* to a cart, for which the market price was filled in on Saidhan's open draft, left with Khelagh's foreman. At the river end of the cart-track, barges, not Khelagh's, were already moored, and after sending Kennar back with thanks to Kred Bakali Dolvid embarked the seized grain and his half-squadron escort, and was carried downriver to Owan Sai, where Saidhan had arranged for a ship to be waiting. The entire adventure ended by evening with a tame ride up Harbour Way to the city.

For a week he braced for a summons from the *rabhsai* to give an explanation of the raid. It did not come. At the Bronze Residence they had quietly begun work on the *Tale of Songs*, briefer lyric appendage to the epic history of the Gabhanil. Except that visitors were rare now, for a while it was quite like the good days, when Lambarr reigned. As if to confirm the illusion a wonderstruck at-Dhanurai reported that *g'Asalladh'*, shrunken, altogether blind, His age variously reckoned at anything up to one hundred and ten, had once more pulled back from the final cliff, and was again dictating *Atarlum* policies.

Ban-Sila was practically courting his capital, showing himself often, and giving out a few minor honours to those who had helped plan his investing. The special forces were not seen in the city, and Household regulars kept order without excessive force. Easier to be cynical and say fear of fresh uprisings was responsible for the conciliatory mood; hope said the *rabhsai*, as foreseen by Saidhan, was learning the limits of his power.

Marvellously, Zhinladh's account of the two deaths became their history. Influential people, including Dolvid, were allowed a sight of the chest of mint-new coins from Arvus's cellar, while in drink-shops and the Market there were shabby men who had personal knowledge of the conspiracy between Treasury and Mint. These men were probably in Bolan's pay, leftovers from recruitment of the special forces, yet Bolan also appeared quite sincere when he proudly noted that in proof of the *rabhsai*'s displeasure Zhinladh had lost his acting-*kímukanum*. Reduced back to squadron-leader, he had been put in permanent charge of the rotating detachments of pikemen at the New Residence. Sardonically Dolvid saluted the additional benefit, that it kept Zhinladh off the streets, where his corpulently recognisable figure might cause outbreaks of anger.

Bolan made no direct reference to Dolvid's Raid, but on that same occasion he made a point of mentioning a bad-

tempered Khelagh had come for private audience with Ban-
Sila. No censure, or official comment of any kind, came to
Dolvid.

Khalú, however, white with fury, slapped him. There
was no warning, and the words came after, about her
humiliation, his lack of feeling for her, the deliberate cruelty of
his actions. Wearied rather than annoyed, he almost asked her
where was the unforgivable wrong? when in effect he had only
bought grain from her father at legal price. But that was both
true and dishonest; would the raid have given him the
satisfaction it had (and did), without the certainty Khelagh
would take it as an affront? He also kept unspoken another
question asking itself obsessively in his head: was she Khelagh's
daughter more than she was his wife? She became shriller in
enumerating once again all her wrongs, but his refusal, at last,
to make any answer achieved a cold and heavy silence.

Two days later he left. With warm days promising a
rich and early harvest, he had been planning extensive travels
in the province, making sure there would be transport where
needed to bring crops to market, mill or storage. This would
be, he had almost decided, the last official journey, and when
he came back he would resign the provincial post.

"Some weeks," he answered Faëdhal as to how long he
would be gone. Starting sooner, without the urgency there had
been when starvation was near, there would be leisure for a
little wandering. He gave detailed instructions about work
needed for the *Tale of Songs*, aware of quick, suspicious glances,
as if the old scholar was recalling an occasion years ago when

Dolvid, in a similar uncommunicating mood, had ridden off and vanished.

Or perhaps Dolvid was the one remembering; the Gardens of Kamzhinu were often in his mind, and he could not tell why that was so important, unless the parting with Valnoi had lessons to teach him, even now, about Khalú.

Merovas had warned him there were some Residence Quarter sons vowing to kill him; Khalú's brother Ghuradh, now a big-limbed eighteen or so, was among them, but their leader was the same Lavsila who had shouted abuse in the street a couple of summers ago. What then had sounded as impotent noises were changed by change into real threats; Zhinladh, or his impunity, had brought in the age of the bully. But he declined to be encumbered with an escort, leaving the main ways, riding through farmlands where fields were golden under deep blue skies, doing his best to leave the miseries of Kadon Dinul behind.

Reaching Burantal after meandering days, he stayed two nights with Untimarr and Morú, who listened greedily to news from the capital, but were all the surer they had made the right choice in coming home. He could have spent longer there, but his restlessness soon took him up into the hills, and he camped where he could. He was lonely, but the source of his unhappiness was not solitude, which he could relish: over and again he was tugged at by emotions that belonged to that memory from the Gardens of Kamzhinu, a bleak sensation of loss that could, he ventured, explain where he had come to.

By narrow paths along the flanks of Kafan Burantali, where his horse had to be led, he came once again to the desolation of Shemugrân.

The weather changed. Next day he toiled and skidded southward through the heart of the marshlands, leading his patient horse, no *pefrai*, a Sebira gelding of his own. The breezes shifted constantly, and showers were as frequent as his falls; he was muddied to the waist and tired to numbness when he reached firm ground, mounting steadily, and saw he had done what everyone said was impossible, passed through Shemugrân. He had little idea where he was, other than the southern Paowan, the peat country between the marshes and the great Kôbh River: a veiled sun had found threadbare patches in the clouds over to his right. Muddily mounting his muddy horse, he continued southward, where the ground with slender trees and clumps of bramble rose to a ridge. He would try to find a farm or village for the night.

With evening coming on he looked down into a gully, where, beyond a tiny stream and rank, tangled weeds of a long-neglected vegetable patch, a small stone house stood. Picking a way down, he dismounted to try the door. It resisted, then creaked open, and he was in the dim of a single-roomed dwelling, smaller but not unlike one where a farmer called Urnirr had made him welcome amongst ducklings and cats. The floor was flagstones, and he could make out recessed shelves, one amply broad for his bedroll.

There was a lean-to beside the house, sagging but not soon to fall; after clearing out piled wood which he carried into the house, Dolvid stabled his horse, who had been cropping long grasses. From his saddlebag, besides spare clothes and what was left of food Morú had packed for him, he took a bundle of short candles, and inside by light of a couple he found the close-tiled roof over dark beams was sound; there were no wet patches on the floor, nor on the rough stone table. This, he concluded, must have had the house built round it; there was no aperture it could ever have come in through.

The firewood was not altogether dry, but with the help of fluffed tinder-cord and a crumbled candle he got a fire going to heat a drink. Arranging sticks and larger billets so they could dry a little, he felt a flagstone to one side of the fireplace shift under his knee. It came up easily, the lid to a bricklined pit armslength deep, containing one hidden treasure, a grimed flask of excellent red wine, undoubtedly from Peframi Gorge in western Kargul. In its place he left money, far more than the price of the wine, although its owner, if he came looking for it some raw night, would not think he was overpaid. A marvellous wine, luxurious with cold rabbit, hard eggs, staling bread and several fruits. Soon, starting to hum happily to himself, he rolled into his sleeping-bag.

He woke knowing at once where he was, suffused with pleasure at it. Pallid light was coming through small and dirty windows. Outside, where his horse nickered softly, a dank mist was clinging. Dolvid relieved himself, then went down to the streamlet for a wash. He was shivering, but keeping back his breath so as to hold the sharp joy of the morning, beginning of a new world where everything could be different and nothing was impossible. A bird was piping on a clear note, and the sun came, slicing mist to layers of muted gold. He stooped, and the keen cold of the water was like something alive.

Putting a riding-gauntlet on he gathered nettles, and

after untying his horse so it could browse went back to the house to brew a drink and eat an unhurried breakfast. He would ride west. Though vague about just where he was, it seemed certain he could be in Nambalus, a port city he had meant to visit, in just a few hours, by making south and west; even spending an entire day winding and skidding through Shemugrân had cut off an immense loop of journey, eastward to Kanzan Tâl at the head of Entun Shelum, then back west with another long detour about an elbow of the Lovu. He had, in any case, no reason for hurry.

Nor indeed — the notion was perched and waiting on his shoulder — to go on at all. The house he was in was evidently abandoned, and he could take it for his own; he had its price in his purse if an owner or a landlord were to appear. By the rank growth it supported the soil of the vegetable patch was good; he could grow much of his own food. Somewhere near there must be a hamlet where he could buy his tools, a goat or two, some chickens.

The possibility grew, and its attractions. He could vanish, and so many questions with no answers would instantly do the same. The sad watch on large events he could not affect, his unhappiness at the centre of a realm set for madness. There had been a slight respite, but the Patriarch would die, *Menadhi* would come to the Golden Seat, Laluvoi would be gone one day, and Ban-Sila would call himself his own man at last, while faithfully serving, as surely he meant to, *Menadhi*'s dream, restoration of Ancient Owan. Not feasible; Dolvid had discussed this with Laluvoi, and they were together in seeing the new realm was too strongly rooted, and had too many champions: Saidhan and his son Sebhal, Shumat if he was driven to it, their battle-tried followers.

Your rebirth — he debated *Menadhi*, who had a puppet Ban-Sila for mouthpiece — will be the final death of anything left of Owan. Families, Great Families, would rally to the *rabhsai* and the *Mankh'*, but except for the *Adanum Plakh'* and perhaps Kargul the armed men they relied on were largely Others, and there would come a time when those would refuse to carry out orders leading to dispossession of themselves and their kind; the struggle might end when the last man calling himself an Owani was killed, or had fled to the Island, clearing the mainland for the next war, when victors fell out over the spoils. The Night of Owan had lasted six centuries, and for most of that, till the Gabhanil began to impose order, there had been war amongst dozens of tiny, shifting realms. Ordinary life, always with threat of murder and rape, must have been unimaginably impoverished, huddled into fortified towns, fearful of travel, too precarious for any arts or crafts or the civilised gifts of safety and leisure. What would stop that coming again, once present rule broke down?

Munching yellow cheese he speculated on about a life here. Not half an hour away he had passed recent peat-cuttings, and that was land belonging to no one; fuel was his for the carting, small game to be had from the wild, and when not working to feed himself or keep warm, he could write; most of what was needed for the history of the last Gabh'Owan rulers was already in his head.

He was thirty, and it might be a sign the last of his boyhood was gone, that he did not expect to be happy here, only tranquil, escaping the worst miseries. Surely, he did not owe any more of his life to the realm, which he had given the *True Song of Tales*, to a desire for justice, where all he could do was die as Arvus had, nor to Khalú, who had chosen. What was it, then, that made him feel guilty, as if it was a defect to desire freedom?

Again, the Gardens of Kamzhinu lingered in his mind, and a bitter sadness, not of the summer's day when he told Valnoi he was leaving Kadon Dinul, but long before, in mostly forgotten childhood. A dark midwinter's afternoon, and he had climbed the rock above the Grottoes to watch for the beginning of Fire Days. Snow falling, and he kept his body hunched, hands buried in his pockets. He was with Shumat, his friend.

No, not with Shumat, that was the whole focus of the memory. It was all exact in his head: the day he had come with the news about being invited by Kheval to learn the weapons, expecting his friend to be as excited as he was. Instead Shumat had used taunts to entertain the other boys, ridiculing not only Dolvid's pretensions, but also the dreams they had made up together about being renowned captains and winning back empire in the West. Well beyond mere mockery, treachery, and he had fled.

Now it led forward to that other parting, with Valnoi, when rancour had sent him, against his nature, to leave in search of wealth as an obscure revenge, and again, clearly, to betrayal by Radis that had been behind numb retreat to Irbat, and long apathy there.

It could not have begun with Shumat turning shared secrets into scorn; back even farther, out of any memory, he had already been taught the dangers of trusting. He could remember thinking, as he shivered alone waiting for the bonfires to be lit, how sorry Shumat would be if he died, and that he supposed was a thought common with children, who cannot compel loyalty, and whose only power is to wound by their absence. Or was that still the only sword he could invoke?

Perhaps he gave trust too entirely, and his disappointment was correspondingly more painful, but as an historian, in this instance of Dolvid, he could not make much of a case to justify the sensation of having been uniquely wronged: for anyone, living was being betrayed. As it was betraying. Tellis was to marry Rhunilat soon, and when Dolvid had seen her in a corridor of the New Residence, and stopped, expecting her to do the same, she had gone on with a firm and separate step; their instant had flickered and passed, and only her strong sense of what to expect from life prevented her hating him.

And Laluvoi, she thought he had abandoned her, or been ready to, as he could indeed, by vanishing without a word. No mitigation to say her age or the lesson of Arvus's end made it only prudent for him to stop trusting her: those were not the rules for friendship.

There was his wife, and if she had been less than his ideal ally, he had betrayed her, too, if not in the action against her father (which could be called necessary), then surely in the glee he had brought to the raid. He could have put it off a day or so to discuss it with Khalú, but then after bitter quarreling she would have warned Khelagh, not to have him give up the goods without compulsion, but so as he could spend all night shipping his grain across the river, where, even if the sacks were piled on the bank, Dolvid had no power to seize it. But to say there was no choice, that he had given his word to Saidhan, that law and justice beyond law were on his side, did not make it admirable to enjoy humiliating his wife's father. Or his wife. It occurred to him with a flush of shame that Khalú's deep anger did not necessarily prove her first loyalty was to her father; she could quite reasonably complain the raid had held up to the world (her world, the Families) how slightly Dolvid considered his wife's standing.

Rolling up his bedding, he went outside to recapture and saddle his horse. Mists were lifting; behind the house at the top of a steep gravelly bank where there might be a cart-track, a group of slender beeches stood with their leaves not touched by autumn, deep and glossy green in clear sunlight. These times, when nothing mattered beyond what was seen or felt in the instant ought to be enough, but were only interludes; the hour spent in a warm farmhouse, certain moments when a knot of translation came miraculously untied, the days with his Froghul long ago. As Laluvoi said, much work was unfinished, and not only at the Bronze Residence; she needed her allies, and though she had been distant since his talk of going to the Colony, she would call on him and confide in him again. He had come to this place by impossible ways, through Shemugrân, and that was his life, to answer riddles, not ride round them.

He would go to Nambalus, and return to Kadon by boat. Muddle was ahead, and danger, but it might be there were ways, after all, to find hope. Two small boys throwing stones at the Steps had made a change in Ban-Sila, perhaps only momentarily, but bigger dangers could do more. Better if they had a *rabhsai* who would act wisely out of his own wisdom, fairly from an inner passion for justice, but if fear for his rule and his realm produced the same effect, did it matter? Laluvoi would say, no. Once done, it could never be known: arguably Plakhsila had performed all his good works purely to preserve his rule through an appearance of virtue — the historian would rather believe in a good man, but that justice was advanced was the real point, not why.

From the top of the bank, where the expected track went winding off east and west, he looked back into the gully, filling with golden light, and the small stone house meant a simplicity he could neither have, nor stop longing for.

He came back up Harbour Way with evening coming on, and found Faëdhal working late at the Bronze Residence, filled with gossip from the New. As Master of Tongues he had been consulted about possible readings of a passage in the law relating to the royal captaincies, and understood from hints Ban-Sila was seeking a legal way to remove Saidhan from his post as Captain of the West, without yielding to the demand Sebhal be named as his successor.

Faëdhal was exasperated that as good a scholar as he knew *Menadhi* to be had wasted his own breath and Faëdhal's learning trying to persuade him a plain mistranslation was a valid variant reading, so as to change `proven acts of rebellion against the *rabhsai*' to `acts of rebellion charged by the *rabhsai*.'

"From Tellis, I heard Laluvoi *Asayu* told the *rabhsai* Saidhan would be within his rights to ignore an illegal dismissal, and it was worse than folly, these were her words, you understand, to issue commands that could not be enforced."

Tovakh baKargul and his wife Petakoi had been at Kadon Dinul, and the other part of the story was their abrupt, irascible departure, for which Ban-Sila's failure to retire his grandfather was assumed to be responsible. "They took their leave without taking leave, so to speak. Tovakh gave Rhunilat an oral message for the *rabhsai*, spoken with considerable heat, according to Tellis, which Rhunilat has been more than reluctant to deliver. A reference, one is given to believe, to broken promises."

Not the first time the nightmare idea of putting Tovakh at the head of Saidhan's devoted army had come up. "But Kargul will have to be given a captaincy one of these days. Now, have you managed to make anything of that pied passage in the *Lament for Okseti*?"

Faëdhal was astonished, and Dolvid laughed; they had changed roles, Faëdhal concerned with great affairs, he in the world of texts.

"We shall go on with our work here, till *Menadhi* reaches his *g'Asalladhum*, and is permitted to fill the Bronze Residence with *atarlal* again. Till they come to burn every word we have done."

"No small task, if I may say so."

"Here, we write histories; that is our work. Pardon me, I should say, that is what I mean to go on doing."

Faëdhal was genuinely mystified. "I myself had never contemplated any change of occupations."

In the morning, fine after brief showers, he rode for the Arbhu Hills. He climbed southward of the road, above shining fields already partly reaped, harvesters idling now, waiting for some of the moisture to go off into the bright air, stubbled swathe disputed by rooks and starlings. This was not far from where he had once met Khalú; he remembered the teasing excitement of that day, and the headlong race down to the Great Stone Road.

Soon he was on the shoulder of a hill, ridge ahead crowned by silver lindens with curled and drooping leaves that no longer showed their fish-white underbellies when the breeze stirred them.   Nearby a horsewoman was descending, negotiating the steep downslope skilfully, her body erect and untroubled. As she crossed low ground and began climbing to intercept his course, he thought of Khalú, but the figure was too long, and the hand raised to hail and halt him lacked Khalú's taut intensity. Linaëyu.

"They said you were at Owan Sai yesterday." She came alongside, and leaned over for her cheek to be kissed. "I was hoping I might see you."

"You're well?" She appeared so.

"You look a mighty traveller."

"You didn't ride out to sing about my sunburn."

She smiled. "Same Dolvidh. Is there a woman you trust?"

"Laluvoi."

"That's high enough, not what it used to be. I should not be talking to you, and you should not be riding alone. Can you guess what your name is now, among the Families? Nothing. It is too vile to speak."

"But you are here."

"They are fools. Profit! But you're a bigger fool, baiting them. And Khelagh is biggest of all. He keeps ranting about fighting you himself — he can't tell a cavalry-sword from a sickle."

Dolvid took a glad breath: Linaëyu's talk was bringing back carefree days.

"But I am here to warn you — Ghuradh will challenge you."

After a grimace, "Then there is one bigger fool than his father."

He had half-forgotten she was the mother. "He is very strong," with elaborate impartiality.

"And young."

"Don't forget his grand-uncle was the great Kheval."

"Kheval was my teacher."

Linaëyu changed to pleading. "You have to refuse him, Dolvidh. First get an armed escort, so his bullies can't reach you. But he says you are his kill, and Khalú could not bear it."

"I would never harm her brother, your son."

Linaëyu made a familiar flapping motion used to drive away annoyances. "Do not pretend to be an idiot. Ghuradh's dangerous. They're afraid of him in the Residence Quarter. I can't think how I ever gave birth to such a bully."

It was hard to keep in mind her fear was for him, not her son. "His reputation is safe; I shan't fight him."

"But you need an escort."

"I'll be careful."

"You promise?"

He was becoming testy. "I promise not to humiliate Ghuradh."

"Don't make stupid jokes." Pouting, she was so much Khalú he could have laughed, remembering when he used to see faint resemblances the other way. They had maintained a gentle walk up-slope, and were just short of the saddle between hills; in a few paces he would be able to look down and see his stables, with the house half-hidden behind green banks.

Linaëyu pulled up. "If I am seen with you — "

He reached to touch the back of her near hand. "My thanks for your concern." He was not going to tell her how absurd it was; Ghuradh might be strong, but had no experience with skilled swords; Dolvid, not counting a scuffle in the dark, had not fought for his life since the Pass of Perus, but at the Bronze Residence and on his travels had never missed a chance to cross blades with Household or General Cavalry, usually in answer to an invitation to show some of Kheval's style. Linaëyu, of course, had never seen any of that Dolvid, and had him defined as a scholar with a talent for bed.

She turned her hand over to hold his fingers. "Please, I don't want you killed."

"Once — " he began lightly, but saw it distressed her. He sat wordless regarding her, and she shifted self-consciously in the saddle. "Does it take so long to count my wrinkles?"

"I was remembering how good you are, have always been to me." Tears were behind his eyes.

She became arch. "I had good reason. No." She shook her head. "Old beddings were never as sweet as we pretend."

They touched hands, and he rode on down into the valley, his melancholy not altogether unpleasant.

By the stables Norlum was watching Bolan prepare to mount. "I was looking for you," he lied, toying with a stirrup. "You've heard that lumpy brother of Khalú's is bragging all over the Heartland he's going to chop you into pike-bait? That was a bad day's work, that raid of yours, and Merovas must be mad to have given you the troops. What in Shâl's name were you thinking of?"

"Food," dismounted by Bolan.

"Why couldn't you speak to me, before starting a private war?"

Coldly, "The Household was not concerned.   The authority and the decision were mine."

"Yes," becoming abstracted. "Listen, Dol, don't kill Ghuradh. Duelling is against the law, you may have heard."

"I don't plan to fight him."

Bolan began again, apologetically. "The *rabhsai* — well,

you've said often you wanted to give up this quartermastering, and the *rabhsai* sees the Bronze Residence as a better use of your gifts."

"Is the post to be terminated?"

"Not yet, and Merovas at his age has enough with the garrisons." Bolan was again adjusting his stirrup-leather, and confided, "The *rabhsai* asked me to look after the food supplies."

"You?" It was out before he could stop it.

"Nothing is decided. If it does come to me, there's things I'll need explained, the laws, and who I can rely on, and about the measures for corn, and so forth."

"You will have all the help I can give."

"You were always a good fellow."

As Bolan prepared to mount, Dolvid had a thought that worried him. "What troops will you use?" He already knew: his quartermaster force drawn from the General Cavalry, carefully selected, trained, constantly weeded out by Dolvid and Merovas, would be replaced by Bolan's cutthroat special forces, who would follow any orders. Assuredly they would not do anything to offend Bolan's friend Khelagh or Khelagh's friends, but would be useful in foreclosures against smallholders.

"Nothing is settled." In the saddle, he was a little thickened, quite unchanged, a man like many others, self-satisfied, standing for nothing, blown by the wind.

"Bolan — "

"I am due at the Residence."

"If you do get the provincial post, remember it began because there was hunger. And still is."

"I know that." With a shake of his reins, he moved off. Norlum, leading in Dolvid's horse, hawked and spat.

He had to listen to Norlum's detailed recounting of minor ailments amongst the horses, and had only just started for the house when riders came up, three of them, all heavily armed, with hunting knives as well as swords. He supposed they had been watching for his return, and then waited for Bolan to leave. A friend of Ghuradh's, another muscled young man of the Families who gave no name, also carried a heavy pike, which made both riding and dismounting awkward. Their leader was the rather older, less burly Lavsila, spoiling his looks with the habitual sneer as he put his horse in Dolvid's path.

Ghuradh, sullen rather than enraged, said, "You have insulted my family, my father and my sister both." His neck was red, but his face quite pale in the sunlight. He had dismounted on the sandy patch in front of the stables, and Norlum, a few paces away, was watching with interest.

Dolvid explained that paying a man lawful price for his wheat was not an insult. From the saddle Lavsila said, "Then so long as you give him a fair price, it's no wrong to seize anything you want from a man, whether or not he wants to sell, his house, his lands, his horses?" He had acquired or was affecting drawled tones to convey a generalised contempt born of boredom.

Before that debate could go on, Ghuradh said, in badly-pronounced Owanilú, "*I am going to kill you. Arm yourself.*" This was a formula.

"Go away and practise for a couple of years. Come back then, if you still want to fight." Ghuradh had wide shoulders and strong wrists, but none of his mother's grace, or the quickness that had come to Khalú from somewhere. Feet like a mired ox.

"If you were a real man — "

"Ask anyone, ask your father's friend Bolan, who would win if we fought."

Lavsila said, "He wants to hide behind the mongrel Captain of the Household." Dolvid ardently wished Bolan could overhear how they spoke about him in his absence, his flatterers from the Families.

"Only vermin won't fight," Ghuradh said. "We exterminate vermin."

"Mongrels, vermin. You swallow words and spew them up again. Do you want to be exactly the same as your great-grandfathers?"

"Oh," puzzled. "I don't doubt you would win in a fight with words. Men use steel."

"No, kinsman, children use steel. They may be fifty, with beards, but they are children if they think killing makes them right."

"I am not your kinsman, let us see who is the child. Where are you going to fight me. Or will we kill you?"

"Here," reluctantly. He would have to wound Ghuradh, not badly, but enough to stop the fight. He must keep his temper, but fight in earnest, otherwise there was an outside chance of being badly wounded or worse.

"Where are your shield-men?"

"Deputies, Ghuradh; shield-men are in the romances. I name one — Norlum, will you?"

Grimly, Norlum threw down a hay-fork, and reached up inside over the stable-door to take down a sword, a plain cavalry blade in an army scabbard.

"A stableman?" Lavsila questioned, "a Gabhani?"

His sneer was echoed in Ghuradh's face, and Dolvid silently warned him to take care, or he would have him fight Norlum instead. A deep pride for the Narn Campaign and the men who had won it rose, as Norlum, sword buckled on and ten years lifted off, came to stand at his side.

"My deputy is File-Leader Norlum Norrdus-son, of the Army of the Northeast." Lavsila did not offer a hand to Norlum, as Ghuradh did Dolvid. Ghuradh's weapons were too heavy, a broad slashing sword and thick hunting knife, nearly a second sword. Was nothing taught now Kheval was dead?

Lavsila asked if they agreed to the ancient Laws of Honourable Combat, and Dolvid nodded. Nothing was as savage as civilisation when it made rules about killing: under the laws they would fight to the death, or till one of them suffered a head, body or upper leg wound of *tak'bedal* proportions, meaning a hole two fingers could be thrust into to knuckle depth. Strictly interpreted, it meant there was no dishonour in hacking down a man after both his hands were chopped off.

They stood on packed sand and gravel, moist but not

puddled from the early rain. Taking the pike from the silent one, Lavsila inscribed a rough circle, and advised Ghuradh not to finish his man too quickly.

Solemn, he faced Dolvid. Each clashed his weapons together, Dolvid with a supple sword and the fine-bladed Froghuli knife.

Lavsila clapped hands for a signal, and Ghuradh promptly attacked, aiming a mower's sweep for Dolvid's legs. Stepping inside it, taking the forearm on his side, he slipped away before the big knife could be brought round. He could have killed Ghuradh in that opening second, but there had not been space for the superficial wounding he intended.

Turning clumsily, hopelessly straddled, Ghuradh came with a lurching series of fast jabs. Dolvid was content to turn them, then came up to parry a knife-slash that left Ghuradh's throat laughably unguarded. Three quick steps and a rapid pass, and Dolvid was behind the young man, in the centre of the circle.

As Ghuradh turned his wide face showed unmistakable conviction he was overmatched. He snorted in the air, and fear gave fury to a wild overhead slash. Dolvid stepped in, pressed down the long knife with his, and spun back to slice with his sword into the inside under-muscling of Ghuradh's right arm, knowing a horrible joy in the ease with which the blade did its work; Ghuradh gave a cry, dropping the heavy sword.

A confusion of sounds, a woman's stifled shriek, a shout from Norlum, ring of other weapons, and Dolvid whirled to find Lavsila making a brandishing run at his back. He sidestepped, and an irritated slash disarmed his second opponent. Dolvid rapidly took in Norlum, glowering at the other, burly one, who was holding a wrist struck so hard with the flat of a sword he had dropped the pike.

There was still his original fight; he parried an off-balance knife-thrust, locked hilts on his sword side, and held the Froghuli knife just under the chin of Ghuradh, who really expected to be killed. Again, a woman's cry came. Dolvid pushed Ghuradh away with knee and forearm, and kept him at sword's point. Lavsila was crouched over, bleeding knuckles hugged to his chest.

Ghuradh, defiantly, "It's not over. This is not — " and stooping to recover his sword, threw back his head and yelped at the stretch of his injured muscle. His sister said, "Don't be such a fool." They had been Khalú's cries; she was there in a long, light gown he had not seen before, her hair untied, colour coming back into her face. "Let's go to the house," she ordered her brother, "and I'll bind that wound."

Remaining wary, Dolvid collected weapons and handed them to Norlum, with thanks for his part. He told all three of his enemies to come up to the house; Khalú added *raminat* as an inducement; it was all courteous.

She came to him, breathing "Oh, Dolvidh," a muffled sob. She was soft and warm in his arms; he perceived she had been anxious, and now was excited, pupils huge, nostrils flared. Her body came against him with more heat than he had known in her.

He managed to grasp Ghuradh's hand and offer consolation; blood whining in his ears he saw binding of wounds delegated to servants, said jocular hostly words, made a weak joke about cups being better than cuts, at which two at least of his guests laughed much to excess. Khalú had gone through the archway and into their sleeping quarters, and he followed her.

Naked already, she closed to him in curtained dim, her mouth all greed. Not sport, but the shock of animals, tough, ferocious, impossibly tender, wanting to touch with all of themselves.

Bruised, panting, they became still. Soon he said, "I must go back and tend the cubs. A pity I had to hurt your brother," kissing her as he sat up.

"You were a master — you are a master." She held his hands, and began, "Dolvidh, you must, I — " but he kissed her again.

"No need," as she began gathering herself to come with him.

"I want to. They are such a nuisance, my family — the Families. Let's join with a band of travelling tumblers and escape."

This was so exactly her mother, he could not keep back his smile. "Tomorrow," he said. She had been going to tell him about Bolan when he kissed her to silence, to explain she had begun that out of exasperation with him, Dolvid, and now she would end it. He did wonder passingly whether he would have to wound half the Residence Quarter to bring Khalú to pleasure.

"Was he as wonderful as they say, my great-uncle?"

"He has only been dead five years," Khalú came in, freshly gowned. "You must remember him." Not caring what guests thought, she wound into Dolvid's arms, as he sat on a short couch, feeling slightly drunk, though he had only sipped at a cup of wine. Khalú had scented herself with violet, and he was astonished by her beauty.

"Yes, yes, I remember him," Ghuradh, testy with his sister. "I meant, as a swordsman. He wouldn't touch a weapon after he retired."

Dolvid tried to recall for him the greatness of the old master, the ease in doing the hardest things, even at eighty. "There is an officer in the Household, Dorrmas; it's a plainer style than Kheval's, but he has that same way of making everyone else seem to be sweating." With its owner, the name Dorrmas was not from Old Owan, and Ghuradh did not altogether approve of the comparison.

"He takes pupils, but while your sword-arm is healing, you might find someone to teach you some dance."

"Dance?" Lavsila said, but his rote scorn was losing ground with the two younger men.

"Kheval was always saying *feet, feet, how can your hands be right if your feet are wrong?* You have to get up off your heels."

"I've heard that before," the unwounded one said. "*Bôdh'loiki,* does he teach?"

Dolvid himself, now in respectful indirect address. "Dance?"

"No, weapons."

"He hasn't time. If you want to learn the scripts, you can

come to me at the Bronze Residence."

"Is it not strange," Lavsila, airily, "one so learned, with so much appetite for praising others, has so little regard for his own people, or the glory of his own history?"

With Khalú's head in his lap, her eyes gazing up at him, Dolvid gave more answer than was wanted, speaking at length of his love for what was best in Ancient Owan, quite deliberately taking Lavsila out of his depth with dates and eras, names of craftsmen, lawgivers and poets. As he spoke he found how true it was, he would never be anything but Owani, with as much pride in that as anyone who simply asserted superiority, without reasons why.

Then he went on to speak about the stature and the virtues of other peoples, and when Lavsila tried to interrupt, the other two hushed him, so Dolvid could go to his thesis, that the wholly natural conviction his race was best did not give any man the right to make underlings of others; the highest glory of Ancient Owan was justice, so using laws to deprive others of their rights dishonoured Memory, and lost what it claimed to be preserving.

Laluvoi, he reminded them, had always understood that; she was a great Owaniyu, rightly revered for her devotion to a realm where merit was rewarded and crime punished with no regard as to blood, shape of a nose or colour of one's eyes.

He was having a good hour, wrapped in a robe and self-satisfaction, voice filled with earned authority and the afterpurr of pleasure. Absurd that ability to use a sword gave weight to what he said, and he was not so sotted with present complacency to dream he was changing the beliefs of lifetimes, but he hoped two of his listeners might not speak exactly as their great-grandfathers had.

"We could be friends, or not unfriendly, Ghuradh and I. Nothing wrong with his courage," he told Khalú after their visitors had ridden off, two of them with wishes for future meetings, presumably without the array of weapons Norlum handed back. Lavsila had not surrendered entirely to the new cordiality, but then he had greater cause for loathing Dolvid. He might even be right in thinking he would have made Khalú a better mate, one more in accord with her ideas of what a husband should be. A sour thought, just when Dolvid had her undivided devotion, but somewhere on the farther side of Shemugrân, admitting his own share of guilt, he had lost the need to deceive himself.

She was gazing steadily at him. "You could be friend to all the Families, if you wanted. There is nothing you might not be — Captain-General, the *Bôdhrai*, richest man alive."

"I would rather be the man who brought out the *True Song of Tales*."

She touched his face tenderly. "Bolan says you would rather find out how Larghai buttoned his coat than reconquer the Empire."

Twilight had come, with a cool breeze dodging around the house, a profound blue above the faint rim of paleness outlining the hills. He was lying with his head in Khalú's lap. Tomorrow he would see Laluvoi and help decide what they were going to do to put everything right forever. He had not offended the Families for the last time, and there would be more differences with Khalú, future quarrels: even now, murmuring how happy he made her, it was and would be her nature to try to make him into someone else.

It did not matter. Soon he would take Khalú back to bed, but there was no hurry, in the warm memory of pleasure and warm certainty of pleasure to come. What happened was only itself, not a promise to be broken.

Dolvid

The End

Edwin Ahearn

The Arbhal Sequence

Appendix

Appendix

List of Personal Names

[Italic cap initials following entry, *D, AH, AW*, indicate volume(s) in which name appears; *Dolvid, Arbhal I (Hostages), Arbhal II (The War)*. Square brackets, as with *[D]*, indicate the character is *alluded to* but does not actually appear in the volume cited.
 C = *circa*, b = born, *fl* = flourished *d* = died, *k* = killed, *m* = married, *r* = reigned, *abd* = abdicated.
 Military forces: AP = *Adanum Plakh'*, AoW = Army of the West, GC = General Cavalry.]

I: Characters
[This lists all actual persons, living or recently dead, mentioned in the three volumes. Names in *light italics* indicate XRef to boldface **Main Entry**.]

Abdanai *AW*; *Faëdhal*'s housekeeper, C2942

Absivoi *AW*; *b* 2939, infant daughter of *Ghuradh*, w. *Khelagh* visiting New Residence 2942

Aëlu *[D],AH,AW*; *b* 2908, *nôd'yanu* 2925, *m.Sebhal* 2927, hostage at Drin b'Afon, aids Colony   refugees 2942; *m.Dolvid* 2942, mother of *Sebhal*'s posth. son, *Sedukh* 2942

Akaëkhai-kindhri (= "Market-Victor", *Bolan*)

Alkmas *AW*; fisherman and boat-owner of Voruni; carries *Âna*, &c, across Arnan 2942, briefly a   captive of the *Mankh'* 2942

Alli *[D]*; a farm-owner, NE of Yuvakh Din

Altis *D*; wife of *Urnirr*

Âna *AH,AW*; *b* 2922, mistress to *Sebhal* from 2941, in Kadon Dinul Expedition, captive of Kamin-   Tolagh, witnesses, and brings news of *Ban-Sila*'s death to *Rodlakh* at Frontier 2942, *m.Rodlakh*, becomes *rabhsayu* 2942

Antrovai *D*; *b* 2876, Officer of GC, at Yuvakh Din from 2912, commander there from 2917, *k* Narn Gates 2928

Arbhai-Navu   (surname adopted by *Banak* for ruling house he founded with *Laluvoi* in 2878)
Ardi *D,[AW]*; *b* 2905, son of *Ott*, leader of auxiliary bows at Narn 2928, *k* nr El'tuf 2942

Ardirr *[D]*; father of *Arvus*

Arlemirr *[AH,AW]*; (a non-existent farmer of the Paowan, *Âna*'s alleged father)

Arlimas *AH*; a farmer near Burantal, friend to Nentirr

Arodinal *[D]*; Household officer, *d* 2926

Arvat *D,AH,AW*; *b* 2918, apprentice under *Dolvid* 2931-6, serves Saidhan 2936-42

Arvus *D*; 2877-2936, "Deniant", *bôdh'loiki*, in charge of Treasury 2913-36, father of *Tellis, Arvat, k* by *Zhinladh* 2936

Asana *[AH,AW]*; *b* C2890, wife of Konat, mother of *Âna, Konir,* &c

Asdron *D,[H]*; a thatcher of S. Paowan, at Great Pledging 2914, uncle to *Neldron*

at- (prefix indicating *atarlai; see* following name)

Aud *[D]*; Froghuli herder

Aval (at-) *D*; *b* C?2870, *atarlai* of the *Manadilum*, teacher at *Mankh'*, C2910-

Bakir (= *Bolan*)

Banak-loi (= "Little Banak", *Ban-Sila*)

Ban-Sila *D,AH,AW*; 2912-42, third son of *Lambarr*, third Arbhai-Navu *rabhsai*, originally named Banak, takes new name at accession 2935, restores many Owanil privileges, outlaws Saidhan and his followers 2938-42, *k* by *Rheduban* at New Residence 2942

Bolan (Bakir) *D,AH,AW*; *b* 2899; officer of Household 2920, commander of Narn Expedition,*Narnai-Kindhri* 2928; Captain of Household 2928, *m Khalú* 2939, Captain-General 2937-42; defeated at Dônshei 2942

Bradhinal of Ân *D*; *b* 2909, second son of *Daënakh* & *Leghayu*, Household officer 2927, led Provincial auxiliaries with *Bolan* 2928; at Pass of Perus, Gates of Narn, &c. *m Sholu* 2934

Brodhai of Ân [*D*]; 2904-35, first son of *Daënakh* & *Leghayu*, Household officer 2926-8, *m Laloi*, eldest child of *Lambarr* 2933; *k* in Tan Lughsai Disaster

Daënakh of Ân *D*,[*AH*],[*AW*]; *b* 2878, *Nimu* of Ân from 2902, *m Leghayu* 2902, sons *Brodhai, Bradhinal*; helps identify ancient site of Luskran Bay atrocities 2928

Dal (= *Dalirr*)

Dalirr *AW*; man of *Galt*'s squadron, at capture of New Residence 2942

Darborr *D*; *b* C2884, *Dolvid*'s neighbor at Kadon Dinul 2913-16, business partner 2922-25, hus	band of *Radis*

Dhanurai (at-) *D*; *b* C2884, teacher at *Mankh'* C2915, at Bronze Residence 2929-34

Dheruli *AH*; Karguli soldier & groom, at Burantal with *Rheduban* 2942
Dhunival *AW*; trader of Ninkufu, witnesses *jinzal* preparations 2942

Dol (= *Dolvid*)

Doleni [*D,AH*],*AW*; *b* 2870 (Ninkufu), *m Saidhan* 2888, mother of *Saëdhu, Sebhal*

Dolvid(h) *D,AH,AW*; *b* 2906 (Ninkufu), Kadon Dinul 2912-18, at *Mankh'* to 2922. Joins *Bolan* in Narn Expedition 2928, appointed *uzh'freladhai* & *bôdh'loiki* 2928, *Song of Tales* 2929-32, *m* to *Khalú* 2931-38, provincial exile 2938-42, joins *Sebhal* &c in Kadon Dinul Expedition 2942, *Bôdhrai* to *Rodlakh*, recaptures Residence for him 2942, with *Shumat* at Dônshei, and *Kamin-Tolagh* at Lunu Tezh' Gate, Relief of Kamsilat 2942, *m Aëlu* 2942

Dorrmas [*D,AH*],*AW*; *b* 2909, Household officer 2929, renowned as swordsman, a leader of *Rodlakh*'s faction at Kadon Dinul 2942; in storming of Residence, at Battle of Dônshei 2942

Dravadhi *D,AW*; *b* C2905, pupil at *Mankh'* 2917-?   Captured by Shumat's forces, as spurious "True *Rabhsai*" 2942

Edarron *AW*; *b* C2910, officer in Sebhal's personal squadron, *k* at Drin Navuna 2942

Embhu *D*; *b* 2905, Islander, at Mankh' C2920, *nôd'yanu* at Luskran Bay 2928

Enikai [*AH,AW*]; a *pefrai*, given by Rodlakh to Dolvid 2942

Esodra *D*; *b* C2875, Vidukh's housekeeper (?and mistress) at Kadon Dinul, mother of *Radis*, goes to Dônshei 2915

Faëdhal *D,AH,AW*; *b* 2863, Master of Tongues in 4 reigns (Banak, Lambarr, Ban-Sila, Rodlakh) from 2901, friend to *Vidukh*, later to Dolvid, collaborator in *True Song of Tales*, advises *Rodlakh*'s supporters at KD 2942, *bôdh'loiki* from 2942

Falis *AH*; *b* C2900, Burantal, wife of *Nentirr*

Filuvakh [*AH*]; 2878-2940, nephew to *Laluvoi*, *m Radhoi* 2899, father of *Finú, Radaghi*

Finú *AH,AW*; *b* 2900, elder sister of *Radaghi* lineal descendant of *Kamâbhu Gabh'Owan*, allied with baKargul, C2942

Foi'kani (title) *AW*; at Dônshei, declines to acknowledge Rodlakh until after Shumat's victory 2942

Fonul *AW*;   Under-Captain of GC, Acting Warden at Owan Sai, relieved by Dolvid 2942

Forrlas *D,AH*; *b* C2886, served in GC, tax-gatherer 2931, afterwards magistrate, executed after alleged rebellion 2941

Freighanai *AH,AW*; *b* C2900, soldier of Kargul, *m Avedhoi* 2929, daughters 2930, 2932; leader of Kamin-Tolagh's personal squadron from 2936; at Kadon Dinul, in Jinzai War 2942

Fru-nam *D*; Froghuli herder, brother to *Ka-Nam*, at Great Pledging of 2921

ga- ("Blessed," prefix indicating Patriarch; for entries, *see* following name)

Galt *AH,AW*; 2909-42, bowman in AoW, squadron-leader 2942; a leader of the rescue at Drin b'Afon, commands troops with *Dolvid*'s return to Mainland, in storming of the New Residence; *k* at Dônshei, after crucial contribution to victory 2942

Ghuradh *D,[AH,AW]*; *b* 2918, son of *Khelagh, Linaëyu*, brother of *Khalú*; ineffectual duel with Dolvid 2936

Grenaspaluk (1) *D*; name ?or title, leader of invaders in Northeast, defeated (and killed) by *Bolan*   at Narn Gates 2928; (2) [*D*] a subsequent invader, defeated by Shumat 2931

Gula *D*; member of Froghuli clan at Great Pledging 2921, mother of *Tini-ra*

Guthdar *AH,AW*; *b* C2910, brother of *Noldar*, bowman of *Galt*'s squadron, first to scale cliffs at Drin b'Afon, in taking of New Residence, at Dônshei 2942

Happ *AW*; officer in AoW, commander at Banakit 2942

Haun *AH*; man of *Galt*'s squadron, gravely wounded at Drin b'Afon 2942

Hinn *D,AW*; *b* C2900, officer of GC; seconded to Quartermaster 2933, commander at Kred' Bakali,   brings forces to Dônshei 2942

Huro-nam *D*; elderly patriarch of Froghuli clan at Great Pledging 2921

Idmas *AW*; officer in AoW, commands part of rearguard at Banakit 2942

Iliukh *AW*; officer (of the *AP*), under-captain over *jinzai* army 2942

Indhil *D*; *b* C2890, officer of GC, *kímukan* at Yuvakh Din 2928

Inghi *D*; "Well-woman" and "Mocker" of Froghul clan at Great Pledging 2921

Iriban Baëtufi *D*; *b* 2869, hereditary warden at Irbat, welcomes *Bolan* 2928

Kaëfanai *AH*; under-captain of *Adanum Plakh'*, commands on Island, hunts Rodlakh, 2942

Kamanasalladh (ga-) (adopted name of eleven Patriarchs, 477-2936); **XI** *D*; ?2825-2936, *P* from   2897

Kambanal *AH*; *b* 2923, officer of Karguli cavalry, forced to lend *pefrai* to Âna 2942, fights in *Jinzai* War 2942

Kamin-Tolagh baKargul [*D*],*AH*,*AW*; *b* 2919, son of *Tovakh* and *Petakoi*; officer in provincial cavalry from 2936; at KD with Kargul' troops attached to Household 2941; abducts *Âna*, joins alliance against the *jinzal*, victor (with *Shumat*) at Lunu Tezh' Gate, wounded at Kamsilat, offered Household captaincy by Rodlakh 2942

Kamin-Tarú baKargul *AH*,*AW*; *b* 2924, daughter of *Tovakh* and *Petakoi*; offers herself as counter-hostage for Aëlu, aids Dolvid in seeking alliance with her brother 2942

Ka-Nam *D*; clan-leader of Froghul' at Great Pledging 2921

Keliukh (at-) *D*; *b* C2870; teacher at Paowanu *Mankh'* C2920

Kemunai *AW*; officer of AP, commander over *jinzai* army, *k* Kamsilat 2942

Kennar *D*; *b* 2905, officer of GC, Narn Campaign; Pass of Perus 2928, commands cavalry in "Dolvid's Raid" 2935

Khalú *D*,[*AH*],*AW*; *b* 2913, daughter of *Khelagh*, *Linaëyu*, *m* (1) *Dolvid* 2931 (2) *Bolan* 2939

Khazubran *D*; *b* C2872, master-enameller of Kadon-Dinul, father of *Ladhat*

Khelagh *D*,[*AH*],*AW*; *b* 2863, wealthiest of Heartland magnates, *m* *Linaëyu*, father of *Khalú*,*Ghuradh*, patron of *Bolan* (from 2927); negotiates with Dolvid after capture of New Residence   2942

Kheval *D*; 2837-2931, renowned swordsman and teacher, Master of Weapons at New Residence 2898-2923; uncle to *Khelagh*

Kizhunai *D,[AH],AW*; *b* 2895, with Household; *kímukan* 2925, escorts Victors of Narn 2928; as under-captain, contains riot 2935, joint-captain, with *Kamin-Tolagh*, of Household 2941, attempts to mediate dispute, comes over to Rodlakh, directs storming of New Residence 2942; Captain-Counsellor for Armies from 2942

Konat *[AH,AW]*; *b* C2884, landowner, S. Paowan, father of *Âna*, *Konir*, etc.

Konir *AW*; *b* 2918, brother of *Âna*

Kras *[D]*; Froghuli herder

Kuno *AH,AW*; a man of Galt's squadron, wounded in retreat from Drin b'Afon, takes part in storming of New Residence 2942

Ladh-Sivai *[D,AW]*; *b* C2880, major landowner nr Kred' Bakali, duels with Arvus 2917, candidate for magistracy 2932; father of *Lavsila*

Ladhat *b* C 2894, son of *Khazubran*, *m Valnoi* 2923

Laënakh of Nîv *D,[AW]*; *b* 2882, *Nim'* of Nîv, celebrated dog-breeder

Laloi *[D]*; *b* 2907, eldest daughter of *Lambarr* and *Saëdhu*, *m* Brodhai of Ân 2932, among those   *k* at Tan Lughsai 2935

Laluvoi *D,[AH],[AW]*;   2848-2940; *m Valplakh Gabh'Owan* 2865, survives Disaster of Ní-Tilagh,   2876, *m Banak* 2877, son *Lambarr* 2878, *rabhsaëyu*, joint-ruler with Banak 2878-2904, powerful influence thereafter

Lambakh *[D,AH]*; *b* 2916, fifth child and third son of *Lambarr, d* in the Tan Lughsai Disaster

Lambarr Owan-Navu *D*; 2878-2935, second Arbhai-Navu ruler, son of *Banak* and *Laluvoi; r* 2904-35, *m* Saëdhu 2905; father of *Ban-Sila, Rodlakh* and *Orbanak* (and eight others, the surviving six of whom perished, with their father, at Tan Lughsai)

Larghai (1) see Hist., (2) *AH*; *b* C2930, son of *Vedrughi*, a boy at the Summer Palace in Drin b'Afon 2942

Lavsila *D,[AH,AW]*; *b* 2914, duels with *Dolvid* 2936

Leghayu *D [AH,AW]*; *b* 2880, wife (and cousin) to *Daënakh*

Linaëyu *D,[AH],AW*; *b*?2892, *m* Khelagh 2911, mother of *Khalú, Ghuradh*; Dolvid's mistress at KD 2928-31

Malvan *[D]*; of Irbat, a leading dealer in fleeces, *fl* 2910-2940

Manda *D [AW]*; *b* 2910, *Ott*'s daughter, *m Shumat* 2929

Mandellis *D*; *b* C2875, nr Yuvakh Din, wife of *Ott*

Mansi *AW*; servant, at Kamsilat with *Kamin-Tarú* 2942

Manto *D*; a boy of the Froghuli clan at Kadon Dinul 2921

Marra *AH,AW*; a young serving-woman at the New Residence, *k* by *Rheduban* 2942

Mattin *AW*; *b* C2900, officer of GC, leader of mutiny against *Bolan* at Dônshei 2942

Menadhi (title for Head of *Manadilum*) *D*; *b* C2860; advocates reopening of *manal* 2914, abducts *Dolvid* to *Mankh'* as personal pupil 2918, accuses him of theft 2928, at celebration for *Narnai-Kindhri* 2928, at proclaiming of *Ban-Sila* 2935, raised to *P* 2936; see *Owan-Alladh XX*

Merovas *D*; 2859-2938; Household officer; in Ní-Tilagh 2876; fought in War of Widowed, Captain of Household 2920-28, of Armies 2928-37

Mirrat *D*; Master of the Mint for *Lambarr*, friend of *Arvus*, *k* by *Zhinladh* 2936

Morulis *[D,AH],AW*; *b* 2929, younger daughter of *Untimarr, Morú*

Morú *D,[AH],AW*; *b* C2897, wife of *Untimarr*, mother of Ondis, Morulis; well-known midwife

Muranak *AH*; seaman and fisherman of Kamsilat, with Sarnak; in assault on Drin b'Afon 2942 ***Narnai-kindhri*** o (= "Victor of Narn", *Bolan*)

Narudhai *D*; *b* C2854, veteran officer of GC, warden at Owan Sai 2929-40

Neldron *AH*; a boy of Lower Paowan, nephew to *Asdron*, warns *Dolvid* of hunt for him 2942

Nelutt *[D]*; man of the Lower Paowan, cousin to *Asdron*

Nentirr *[D],AH,[AW]*; *b* C2898, elder son of *Nettumar*, *m Falis*, Master of Burantal Marionettes from 2931, assists *Rodlakh* and his companions, Burantal 2942

Nerumas *D*; a pupil at the *Mankh'* C2920

Nettumar *[D]*; 2865-2931, Master of Burantal Marionettes 2895-2931

Noldar *AH,AW*; *b* C2907, mounted bowman in AoW, brother of *Guthdar*; in Drin b'Afon assault, injured in retreat, returns with *Dolvid* to Mainland, carries message to Shumat, at Dônshei, succeeds to leadership of *Galt*'s squadron, fights at Kamsilat 2942

Nolimas *[D] AW*; 2894-2942, officer in AoW, captain 2929, grievously wounded in relief of Shâl Mines, *d* at Kamsilat 2942

Norlum *D,AH,AW*; *b* C2880; GC officer in Narn Expedition 2928, stablemaster to *Dolvid* 2932-8, at New Residence 2938- ; Dolvid's deputy in duel with Ghuradh 2936

Nuril *D*; a horse of the *Mankh'*, used by Dolvid 2918-21

Ondir *[D],AH,[AW]*; *b* C2902, younger son of *Nettumar*, marionette-maker, treats *Sett* at Burantal 2942

Ondis *[D,AH],AW*; *b* 2925, elder daughter of *Untimarr* and *Morú*, sister of *Morulis*

Onebhal *D,AW*; 2871-2942, soldier of GC, officer with Narn Expedition, wounded at Pass of Perus 2928, remains in Northeast under Shumat, retires 2937, Shumat's emissary to Kamsilat 2941. 2942, with Shumat at Lunu Tezh' Gate, *k* at Kamsilat 2942

Oradhai (*at-*) *D*; teacher and librarian at Paowanu *Mankh'*, C2870-2935

Orbanak *[D,AH],AW*; *b* 2930, youngest son and lastborn of *Lambarr, Saëdhu*; early childhood in Telnavu, at Paowanu *Mankh'* 2940, liberated 2942

Orimat *D*; *b* 2920, apprentice at Bronze Residence 2932-36

Ott *D*; *b* C2866, clan-chieftain and rebel leader, nr. Yuvakh Din; alliance with Bolan 2928; wife *Mandellis*, sons *Ottar, Ardi*, daughter *Manda*

Ottar *D*; *b* 2896, son of *Ott*, leads bows at Pass of Perus 2928

Owan-Alladh (ga-) (adopted name of twenty Patriarchs 477-2942);
   XX *[AH] AW*; see also *Menadhi*; *P* 2936-42, encourages Ban-Sila's policies, after his death attempts to proclaim *Orbanak*, abducts Aëlu, closes the Straits, confronted by *Dolvid*, vacates Golden Seat 2942

Pedhival *[AH]*; Island landowner, brother of *Petakoi*, father of *Pedh-Sivai*

Pedhivan *[D]*; *d* 2937; Island landowner, father of *Pedhival, Petakoi*

Perimas *D,AW*; officer of Household; brings news of Tan Lughsai Disaster 2935; comes out for Rodlakh at Owan Sai, and is made Commandant of the Port 2942

Petakoi *D,AH,AW*; *b* Kamanta 2889, *m Tovakh baKargul* 2918, mother of *Kamin-Tolagh, Kamin-Tarú*; demands royal appointment for Tovakh 2928; plots with *Owan-Alladh' XX*; captured at New Residence 2942

Pir (1), (2), see *Historical*; (3) Name assumed by *Sebhal* in 2942

Pirron *AW*; Healer at Drin Navuna, treats *Rodlakh, Edarron, Nolimas* 2942

Pivrekhan *AH AW*; *b* 2919, officer of Karguli cavalry, gravely wounded at Kamsilat 2942

Pranuvi *D*; *b* C2885, officer, captains Cavalry of Ân till wounded at Yuvakh Din 2928

Radaghi *AH,AW*; *b* 2910, sister of Finú; *m Rheduban* 2935

Radis *D*; *b* C2889, wife of *Darborr "Rekh'Rabhsai"*; see *Dravadhi*

Rheduban [*D*] *AH,AW*; 2908-2942, Karguli captain, *m Radaghi* 2935, *k Sebhal* at Burantal, *k Ban-Sila* (and Marra), duels with *Dolvid*, *k* by *at-Zhâlai* at New Residence 2942

Rhonalai *AH*; officer of AP, *k* by Rodlakh at Drin b'Afon 2942

Rhonis *D*; a woman of Irbat C2928

Rhubani (at-)[*D*]; *atarlai* of Paowanu *Mankh'*, composed partial, unreliable Froghulú grammar

Rhunat [*D*]; 2841-2932; *Bôdhrai* to Banak, *Laluvoi* from 2885, *Lambarr* to 2911; father of *Rhunsilakh*

Rhunilat *D,[AH],AW*; *b* 2910, son of *Rhunsilakh*; *bôdhloiki* to *Ban-Sila* 2935, to *Rodlakh* 2942; *m Tellis* 2936

Rhunsilakh *D*; 2869-2935, son of *Rhunat*, father of *Rhunilat*; *bôdhloiki* to Lambarr, *Bôdhrai* 2921; *k* in Tan Lughsai Disaster

Rodlakh *[D],AH,AW*; *b* 2922, eighth child, fifth son of *Lambarr, Saëdhu*; childhood in Ninkufu,   takes Saidhan's side against *Ban-Sila* and is (unlawfully) exiled 2940; with *Sebhal, Âna* in attempt to reach Ban-Sila 2942; in rescue of *Aëlu* at Drin b'Afon, proclaimed fourth Arbhai-Navu *Rabhsai*; leads AoW against *jinzai* armies, and in Long and Short Retreat, saves *Kamin-Tolagh*'s life at Kamsilat, *m Âna* 2942

Rongar *AH*; a man of Galt's half-squadron, at Drin b'Afon 2942

Roti *D*; a girl of the Froghul'. Tini-ra's friend, at KD 2921

Saëdhu *D*; 2890-2940, daughter of *Saidhan, Doleni, m Lambarr, rabhsayu* 2905, mother of *Ban-Sila, Rodlakh, Orbanak* (the three to survive infancy and Tan Lughsai, of eleven births in all, 2907-2930)

Saidhan *D,[AH],AW*; *b* 2855; officer of Household 2873, saves *Laluvoi* in Ní-Tilagh, defies Tobhsila at Kir 2876, *Bolan*'s lieutenant in War of Widowed, kills Tobhsila in single-combat, 2878, Captain of Household 2878, of West and *Nim'* of Telnavu 2888, *m Doleni* 2888, daughter *Saëdhu b* 2890, son *Sebhal* 2895; raises "illicit" soldiery, c.2920, aids *Arvat* 2936, at Lunu Tezh' Gate, Siege of Kamsilat 2942

Sarnak *AH,AW*; *b* C2915, seaman of Kamsilat, with Galt's men at Tan Lughsai, navigates to lan ding on Island, among first climbers at Drin b'Afon, outmaneuvers enemy rammer, kills *Kemunai* at Kamsilat 2942

Sebhal *[D],AH,[AW]*; 2895-2942, only (legitimate) son of *Saidhan*, many legendary feats from 2911 with AoW, effectively its commander from 2925; *m Aëlu* 2927, rediscovers lost ruby-mines   2928, outlawed by Ban-Sila 2939, leads covert expedition, *k* by *Rheduban* in Burantal 2942

Selnoi *D*; *b* 2882, *m Rhunsilakh*, mother of *Rhunilat*; survives Tan Lughsai Disaster 2935

Sepivadhi (at-) *b* C2880, healer of *Ramadilum*, treats *Vidukh* 2916, visits Froghul with *Dolvid* 2921

Sett *AH*; *b* 2894, trader, uncle to *Âna* &c, with *Sebhal*'s KD expedition, injured above Burantal, stays with *Untimarr*, procures supplies for relief of Colony 2942

Shardirr *[AH]* a seaman of Nambalus in *Sett*'s crew 2942

Sholu *[D]*; of Sebira, daughter of Warden there, *b* 2912, *m Bradhinal* 2934

Shudarr *[AW]*; *b* 2930, son of *Shumat*

Shumat *D,[AH],AW*; *b* 2906, boyhood friends with *Dolvid* at KD, C2914, soldier of General Cavalry 2923, Household 2924; *Bolan*'s lieutenant in Narn Expedition, in victories at Pass of Perus, Odis Combe, Narn Gates; made Captain of Northeast, *m* Marra 2928; 2 daughters, son *Shudarr*; declares "Free State"; defeats Bolan and Tovakh at Dônshei, leader of relief for Colony, with *Kamin-Tolagh* wins victories at Lunu Tezh' Gate, Banakit, Kamsilat, becomes Captain of Armies 2942

Shurri *[D]*; father of *Shumat*, farmer and surveyor of the Angle

Silnath *D [AH]*; *b* C2867, officer of the AP, father of Sunabhal

Sovrai *AW*; *b* C2880, magistrate at Kreshavu

Stanni *D*: *b* C2895; former stableman for *Ott*, hired by Bolan's expedition 2928

Sunabhal *AH*; b 2919, son of *Silnath*, officer of AP, guard over *Aëlu* at Drin b'Afon, *k* in retreat

Svondais *AH* [*AW*] C2912-2942; a woman of Burantal, mistress to *Rheduban*, *k* after his death

Taësu [*D*]; 2887-2918, wife of *Arvus*, mother of *Tellis, Arvat*

Tam (= *Kamin-Tolagh*)

Tellis *D*; *b* 2913, daughter of *Arvus*; assistant at Bronze Residence 2932-36; *m Rhunilat* 2936

Telura [*D*]; 2920-35, seventh child, third daughter of *Lambarr*, *d* at Tan Lughsai

Tholat biArbhai-Navu *D*; 2908-35, second child, eldest son of *Lambarr, Saëdhu*, 'Prince of Paowanu Loi' from 2924, *d* in Tan Lughsai Disaster

Thuladh *AW*; brother of *Dhunival*; brings warning of *jinzal* armies 2942

Tini-ra *D*; Gulas-daughter, *b* 2905, with the Froghul at KD 2921

Torr *AW*; *b* C2926, a boy of Voruni, helper to *Alkmas*

Tovakh baKargul *D,AH,AW*; *b* 2886, son of *Tobhan* and *Faëlu*, *m Petakoi*, father of *Kamin-Tolagh*,   *Kamin-Tarú*; seeks royal captaincy 2928, at KD, leads forces against *Shumat*, defeated and wounded at Dônshei 2942

Truni *AH*,[*AW*]; a young slinger from the Lunu Tezh', with Galt's men, *k* at Drin b'Afon 2942

Tú (= *Kamin-Tarú*)

Udanak [*AW*]; a man of *Âna*'s kin, employed on her father's farm

Untimarr *D*,[*AH*],*AW*; *b* 2887, master-carpenter of Burantal, *m Morú* 2924, daughters Ondis, *Morulis*; at KD from 2929, works at Tan Lughsai, Bronze Residence, steward on *Dolvid*'s lands 2931, returns to Burantal, becomes City Elder 2935, shelters injured *Sett* 2942

Urnirr *D*; a farmer of the southern Paowan

Uttar *AH*; seaman of Kamsilat, with Sarnak at Tan Lughsai, twice wounded at Drin b'Afon 2942

Vadirr [*AH*]; a boat-owner of Nambalus

Vakhilat *AW*; C2918-2942, officer of GC in charge of levies at Dônshei, *k* by *Dorrmas*

Valnoi *D*; *b* 2904, daughter of *Vulakh*, *m Ladhat* 2923

Varr *D*; an auxiliary of the Household in 2921

Vedrughi *AH;* *b* C2870, Steward of Summer Palace at Drin b'Afon 2942

Vidukh *D;* 2869-2916, librarian at New Residence 2912-16, father of *Dolvid*

Vinilat *D [AH,AW];* *b* 2879, *nimu* of Dramal, first cousin to *Tovakh baKargul*

Vinosai *AW;* C2905-2942, Under-Warden and Patriarchal spy at Kamsilat, *k* by Rodlakh

Vol *AH;* alias assumed by *Rodlakh* in 2942

Vulakh *D;* *b* C2875, goldsmith and jeweller at KD, father of *Valnoi*

Vulnak *AH;* a man of the Lower Paowan, related to *Neldron*

Wanildhai *AW;* *b* 2975, officer with AoW, commander of Drin Navuna during siege 2942,

Yenughai *AW;* *b* 2913, officer of Kargul, half-brother to *Rheduban*; with *Kamin-Tolagh* at Lunu   Tezh' Gate, Kamsilat 2942

Yubhai *D;* a pupil at the *Mankh'* C2918-23

Zhâlai (*also* at-) *b* 2907, pupil at *Mankh'* with *Dolvid, atarlai* C2924, in Patriarch's personal retinue, at New Residence, friend to *Ban-Sila* from C2940, *k Rheduban* 2942

Zhinladh *D [AW];* 2900-42, son of *Zhival,* Household officer responsible for death of Arvus, Mirrat 2936, *d* of wounds suffered defending the

Residence against Rodlakh's forces 2942

Zhival *D*; *b* c2870, an important grower and horse-breeder of the Heartland, father of *Zhinladh*

Outline History

[*Among the various races of Arbhal only the Owanil possess a continuous written record, however self-serving, from earliest times. Their method of reckoning dates was generally adopted after the Return, and is used here.*]

Early Period

Time is held by the Owanil to begin with the *Descent of Yoëlladhu*, which also places the birthplace of their history as in north central Kamanta, where Yoëlladhu's Watch-Rock, a free-standing natural pinnacle, may still be seen. About the four centuries following this legendary event very little is known, except that the Owanil gradually gained control of the Mainland shores to the east of the Island.

477 Traditional date for founding of the Paowanu *Mankh'*, shrine, temple and Patriarchal seat, near the fortress of Drin Kaëdhu (future site of Kadon Dinul), proclaiming the permanence of Owani settlement on the Mainland. There had been (and still exists) an earlier *Mankh'''* (known as the `First' or `True' *Mankh'*) on the Island.

c.600 Owani hegemony over most of the area now making up the western Paowan, Dramal, Kargul and northern ("Old") Nîv. War-captains struggle for increased power: to this time the Patriarchs had been rulers as well as religious leaders.

c.800 Yuvakh, known as *the Martyr*, killed in wars between His patriarchal forces and religious dissenters, joined by rebellious soldiers. Empire of Owan now includes southern ("New") Nîv, western Aëni, and the Paowan beyond the Angle.

868: Hruval, Yuvakh's grandson, with large armies led by his brother, makes war on the *Aëni Confederation*, an alliance of various peoples of the Northeast with those Owanil rejecting patriarchal authority. Victorious, Hruval becomes both Patriarch and ruler, *Nímurai* (880), but is the last to combine both functions.

Greatest of all epics of Owan, the Frela'olurai Yuvakhatilai — *though composed many lifetimes after the events — gives the entire story of the bitter struggle against what became the Aëni Confederation, from the* Martyrdom of Yuvakh, *who "Great as was his suffering, died defiant, the primacy of the Fourfold One still laughed into the faces of his foes...", to the* Conciliation of Yubhsilai, *Hruval's Captain (and younger brother), who "Turned at last away from vengefulness, and spared his imprisoned enemy, chief of all enemies, moved by the noble courage and the beauty of his Petitioner — "* Noirúlu, *daughter of the captive chieftain, who afterwards became Yubhsilai's wife. Their son, Yuvsilâo, renouncing all civil power and eventually becoming Patriarch, accomplished the final separation of His office from that of the secular ruler.*]

c.1000 All the territories east of Arnan comprising the present realm (and including the now-deserted province of Ásekh) are under Owani control by this date. In the southeast war begins with the Empire of Vrobhan.

First Empire

(Age of the Shâl')

[*The two terms are used interchangeably, although strictly speaking the Empire was not proclaimed till the reign of Shâl IV. There were twenty-one rulers in the period, of which fifteen were named, or adopted the name, Shâl. Dates in parentheses, (), are of birth and death, in brackets, {}, years reigned.*]

1165 Accession of Shaëlai. Renewed war with Vrobhan, at first to recover lost territories.

1172 Overthrow and destruction of Vrobhan Empire. Shaëlai, later styled **Shâl I** {r.1165-1198}, brings many captive Vrobanil nobles and artisans to his capital, Undaëni Shei (Dônshei).

1302 Rhuval II {r.1292-1327} moves capital to Kaghedonu' Dinul. During his reign the armies of Owan establish footholds on the forested shore west of Arnan, especially at the mouth of the Navu River, and fight with the untamed forest tribes.

1328 Accession of **Shâl IV** {r.1328-1407}, founder of the Western Empire, first ruler to style himself (from 1347) *Nímuraibáki* ("Emperor"). Crushing victories over confederations of western tribes, especially by his Captain, **Larghai** (?1335-1430). The frontier in the Northeast is also extended in war with Gabhanil.

[*Though they later adopted the name for themselves,* Gabhanil *is of Owani origin, used to describe a hunting and trapping people (*Owanilú gaëbhu, *pelt, hide) or related group of peoples, probably coming from across the Eastern Ocean, but already established in the Northeast by c.800. Recovering from their defeat by Hruval in the ninth century, they had pushed westward, and under the great warrior-chieftain,* **Pir Perus** *(fl. 1350-80) were able to resist and even reverse the Owani advance.*]

c.1380 Final defeat and death of Pir Perus, Mutilations at Luskran Bay. Empire of Owan resumes expansion to Eastern Ocean.

1384 Shâl IV brings about the deposing of the Patriarch Kamanasalladh' II, and the installation of a Patriarch more to his liking, thus laying claim to supreme authority, even over the *Mankh'*, a question not to be settled for many centuries.

1494 With the submission of Tufani the Empire (including "protected" territories of the Farther West) attains its greatest extent. The lands of the Vrobanil have become a waste, but the Empire stretches from beyond Flamûrai in the West to the Eastern Ocean at Naënai Aëlva (now Narn).

1500 Traditional central year for *Shud'rai baSibadhum*, the so-called Blossoming Age (c.1420-1580) when Owanil arts, architecture, song, dance and decorative crafts are all held to have attained their highest perfection.

1550 Yuval III {r.1502-1550}, on his deathbed, fixes the westward boundary of the Empire at the head of the Great Gulf, Flamûrai.

[*Yuval, 110 at his death, had long been alarmed that the resources of the Empire were being drained by the vast length of its frontiers, and the constant need for increased armies to defend it. It is probable the effects of a long-term change in climate, with diminished rainfall throughout the West, were beginning to be felt, with consequent widespread hunger and unrest. At about this time also,* jinzal, *first recorded c.1475, began to appear in increased numbers.*]

1604 Shâl VIII {r.1584-1639}, unable to defend Yuval's Frontier, abandons much of Tufani, now arid and unproductive, and establishes the new frontier along the western edge of Landegh, constructing extensive walls and forts.

1703 The Frontier of Shâl VIII, overrun at many points by nomadic raiders and by *jinzal*, collapses. During this reign, that of Shâl IX {1702-1717}, most territories west of Arnan are lost.

[*The final six rulers of the First Empire, all named Shâl, presided over a rapid decay. Because of scant rainfall the great western plateau of Landegh was no longer capable of supporting the armies needed to defend it. Later, the drying of Shemufegh' Rai, the Great Salt Marsh, permitted enemies for the first time (c.1725) to enter the Old Realm, passing north of Arnan.*]

1728 On the Island the great mathematician-astronomer Patriarch, Owan-Alladh IV *Kirova-Kindhri* (`Star-Conqueror') begins construction of **ga-Tembúrai**, the Great Hive of Mysteries, adjacent to Yoëlladhu's Watch-Rock. Not completed till 1815, the edifice incorporates in its proportions and dimensions many astronomic observations and mathematical laws.

1750 Shâl XIII killed near the present site of Irbat, while leading his army against tribal invaders.

1771 Accession of **Shâl XV**, known as *Ifradhi* (`the Last'). During this reign control over the remaining lands east of Arnan becomes intermittent, and communication with the remaining enclaves of Owani resistance is uncertain. About 1800 the Patriarch Owan-Alladh VI offers Shâl XV refuge on the Island, if he agrees to acknowledge supreme patriarchal authority. The invitation is renewed at intervals during the confused decade that follows.

1809 Shâl *Ifradh'*, defeated in battle near Shelum, makes a difficult retreat to the Arnan shore, and with what remains of the aristocracy and the army embarks for the Island.

The Night of Owan

(1809-2477)

[*This period is named as in the only continuous record, although Owani
history for these six centuries is confined almost entirely to the minor events
of the Island. Shâl XV left no direct heir, and after his death (1815) the line
was regarded as extinct. After some early raids on its shores the Island was
largely left alone, and, with no need for a great captain, could be and was
ruled by a long succession of patriarchs, mainly concerned with preserving
Owani tradition, regarding the outside world as having lapsed into disorder
and darkness. It wasn't until late in this period, when the stability of the
Island realm began to be troubled by internal dissent and by invasions,
threatened and (in more than one case) actual, that new leaders outside the*
Atarlum *began to emerge.*

*On the Mainland minor pockets of Owani rule persisted in the southern
enclave of Ninkufu, in western Kargul, and for a time at the fortified city now
called Dônshei. With the disappearance of the armies of Owan from the
Northeast the Gabhanil at intervals resumed the westward extension of their
power, much of the time under clan chieftains, who chose a supreme leader
only in extreme circumstances. They possessed their own runic alphabet, but
the few accounts descending from before 2000, concerned mainly with
individual deeds and isolated struggles, do not lend themselves to the
construction of a coherent, detailed history. By 2000, however, it is clear*

*Gabhanil settlements were established in Dramal, trading and sometimes
warring with many petty local warlords and self-styled kings. More often
than not the Gabhanil formed alliances with the remnant Owanil, whose
learning they admired, and upon whom in return they exerted considerable
influence, especially in weaponry and methods of warmaking.*

*In speech, the Gabhanil were always notably ready to borrow and adapt, and
as they became more dominant a form of their language, altered by contact
with the Owanilú, became general east of Arnan, spoken even by the Owanil
of the Mainland, with whom the Old Tongue became a ceremonial and
religious language. Intermarriage between Owani and Gabhani became
common, though discouraged by the Island* Mankh'*, which, by c.2240, had
renewed communications with pacified regions of the Mainland, and
reasserted its claim to primacy, at least in religious questions, with the
Mainland Owanil. Patriarchal insistence on Owani preeminence caused
friction with the Gabhanil chieftains, but there were Owanil among the
following of the Gabhani* **Pir Kallikuk** *when he entered Kadon Dinul in
2430, and began its rebuilding.*]

2430-2477 Traditional (Owani) dates for the *Wars of Cleansing*, though
the process of reordering the lands once included in the Old Realm
had been carried on by the Gabhanil for most of the two preceding
centuries.

[*While it was under the captaincy of Pir Kallikuk that the critical battles were
fought and won, the* Mankh' *histories place great stress on the advice and*

assistance he received from leading Owanil of the Island. Nevertheless it is likely that the new realm which emerged would have been dominated by the Gabhanil, but for the coming of Konúrai, *the Great Plague, which decimated the ranks of the Gabhanil nobility. All peoples suffered from this terrible illness, but the Owanil seem to have been the least susceptible, and were also helped by the* ramidul, *priests of the Healing Order, who were sent from the Island.*]

2464 Pir Kallikuk goes to the Island to plead with the Patriarch, Kamanasalladh VI {P. 2460-2495} that He order the *ramidul* to minister to the sick irrespective of race or belief.

[*According to the* Mankh' *account, it was during this visit Kallikuk caught a glimpse of the young* **Plakhat**, *and recognized the future ruler of a restored realm. The truth seems to be that Plakhat, tracing a tortuous descent from Shâl XII, had already been chosen by the Patriarch, who made reestablishment of an Owani aristocracy His price for healing. This hard bargain was at first rejected by Pir.*]

2472 Alarmed by renewed ravages of *Konúrai*, Pir Kallikuk returns to the Island, and opens negotiations for a restoration of the Owanil which will at the same time preserve Gabhanil rights.

2476 Having provisionally approved Plakhat's elevation to the monarchy (with safeguards for his own people), Pir Kallikuk himself succumbs to illness. Treaty of the Wind Caves divides power between Plakhat and the *Mankh'*, without reference to the Gabhanil.

The Return

[*The surname* Gabh'Owan *chosen by Plakhat at the founding of his House was seen as a good omen by those of Other Race, since it appeared to combine the names of both major races. Those who feared the racial and religious exclusivity of the* Atarlum *were further encouraged by Plakhat's abrupt rejection of patriarchal tutelage. As Pir Kallikuk's lieutenant in the final campaigns of the Wars of Cleansing he had an army behind him, and once sure of widespread support from the Owani aristocracy he proclaimed the powers of the* Mankh' *were to be strictly limited and defined as quite separate from those of the secular ruler (whose title was now to be* Rabhsai*). Though war for a time seemed probable, Kamanasalladh recognized He could not find sufficient support and the rival leaders met in southern Dramal, where they negotiated the famous Treaty.*]

2476 Treaty of the Wind Caves grants or reaffirms many patriarchal prerogatives, while virtually depriving the *Atarlum* of any sovereign power, except over the Island; the Patriarch's armed forces to be limited to a small bodyguard (the *Adanum Plakh'*).

2477 The Return. Installation and investiture of **Plakhat Gabh'Owan** at Kadon Dinul {r.2477-2514}. With the remnant Gabhani leadership in disarray he moves swiftly to reestablish the Island aristocracy, and to place those of the so-called Old Blood in positions of power and authority; all provincial overlords, most high-ranking army officers, and all but a very few magistrates, tax-assessors and other local officials.

2480-85 Promulgation of the doctrine of *Preference*, denying high rank to all those without required knowledge of Owani language, customs, history and belief. While the *manal* (schools) of the *Atarlum* are said to be open to all, their prerequisites for entry virtually exclude all but the children of established Owanil families. Increasingly from this time the Gabhani-Mixed majority were ruled by a numerically far inferior Owani aristocracy, and denied entry into many of the skilled crafts.

[*Thus, in the first decade of his reign Plakhat I established the basis for the bitter resentments and often brutal struggles of the next four-and-a-half centuries. It was later observed that while the* Gabh' *element in the surname of the ruling house was the same as that found in* Gabhani, *it also relates to* gâvu, *"shield," and it was as the Shield of Owan that Plakhat and most of his successors ruled.*]

Gabh'Owan House

(successors to Plakhat I)

Kamsila, son of Plakhat {r.2514-2567}. Became *rabhsai* when his father, at the age of 70, abdicated. Continued most of Plakhat's policies, but chiefly remembered for reestablishing a foothold on the western shore of Arnan (popularly attributed to his insatiable appetite for the oysters of the Navu estuary). Flattered as a new *Nim'raibaki* (Emperor), Kamsila never made use of the title, perhaps fearing ridicule, when the "Colony" was measured in acres rather than miles. The port city of *Kamsilat* preserves his name.

Kanavakh, his (younger) son {r.2567-2576}. The elder son of Kamsila was Plakhan *Rhaëli* ("The Lost"), of the celebrated Bride-Quest and subsequent disappearance. Kanavakh thus became Heir, and in his brief but terrible reign amply earned his cognomen, *Vakh'biSegh* ("Bloody"). His many cruelties helped establish (or renew) the legend of the True *Rabhsai* (here thought of as his vanished brother) who would return out of the West to cure the ills of the realm.

His forced abdication was brought about by a conspiracy among the provincial overlords, the army, and the Kadon Dinul Families, concurred in (and perhaps fostered by) the Patriarch Owan-Alladh XV, who agreed to invest Kanavakh's only son.

Plakhval {r.2577-2652}, son of Kanavakh, whose long reign is remembered chiefly for its hopeful beginning, when nearly one hundred prisoners condemned to a variety of lingering deaths by his father were set free. The rule was without large events, but patriarchal influence was at its height, and the complete victory of Preference drove the Others deeper into poverty and despair.

Kamzhinu {r.2652-2667}, the first *rabhsaëyu* (woman reigning in her own right), elder daughter of Plakhval, who outlived his only son. She abdicated at 75, and was succeeded by her nephew, son to her younger sister, Kamnâvu

Plakhat II {r.2667-?2732}. His dates are misleading. Due to unpopular measures and his weak character this reign was plagued by factionalism and attempts to depose him, in favor either of his aunt and predecessor, Kamzhinu (who lived to 2689), or of one of his sisters, especially Kamâbhu, married to the *Nim'* of Kargul. After his second flight from Kadon Dinul (2698) Plakhat II lived mainly in Ninkufu, and is known as *Arnaël* ("The Exile").

Plakhan, his son, recaptured Kadon Dinul from Kargul' usurpers for the Gabh'Owan lineage in 2707, but while he was acting for his father his own supporters prevented the Exile's return; Plakhan was thus *rabhsai* in everything but title from about 2708, but declined to adopt the style till after his father's death; the official dates for his reign are therefore: 2732-2737. He died young (51), especially for an Owani.

Plakhsila, his son, succeeded (under a *Moradhilum*, or Protectorship) just short of his twelfth birthday. Once of age he emerged as one of the most powerful, popular and effective rulers. He attained the age of 106, and his reign {2737-2831} falls only six years short of living up to his sobriquet, *Kímukoi* ("Century").

Plakhsila believed the underlying cause for the unrest of the past eighty years was to be found in the undue influence of the *Mankh'*, and the system of Preference. This was all-but abolished, and a series of "agreements" and "understandings" arrived-at with the *Mankh'*, more strictly defining the limits of patriarchal power, were in fact largely Plakhsila's dictates.

He also undertook to rebuild Kadon Dinul, clearing much of the plague-ridden Old Town, laying out the Avenue of Treaties, and constructing the New Residence. The so-called Bronze Residence which had served his seven Gabh'Owan predecessors was small for its function, and had the added disadvantage of standing (as it still does) outside the city walls. Plakhsila occupied the New Residence from 2800, though work on it continued for many more years.

The reign was notable for widespread prosperity. The quarrelsome province of Kargul was curbed, unrest quelled on the northeastern borders, and the westward frontier of the Colony advanced to the old First Empire fortress of Drin Navuna, which now began to be rebuilt. Though sometimes accused of excessive vanity Plakhsila remained generally admired, and firmly in control till his peaceful death.

Plakhat III {r.2831-51}, son of Plakhsila, was sixty-seven at his accession, and is known as *Plakhat `Afoi'* ("The Old"). He was always in poor health, and during his twenty years of reign the Patriarch Owan-Alladh XVIII won concessions restoring some of the privileges lost in Plakhsila's reign. Plakhat abdicated in favor of his son.

Dromladh {2851-2859} was fifty at accession, still with his lifelong interest in the building of ships. He is credited with the idea for the slender, swift, oar-driven rammer, and with many innovations in methods of construction, hence the irrepressible but erroneous belief that the ship in which he and the Heir were both lost in a sudden squall on Arnan was of his own design. His cognomen, *Prafu* ("Ship") thus has somewhat sinister connotations.

Thral-Sivu {r.2859-2876}, Dromladh's elder sister, was a widow of 60 at her sudden accession, and might have declined the rule, except for the feeble physical and intellectual qualities of her son, Valplakh, who now became Heir. During her reign the ambitions of Kargul were reawakened, and their growing military strength openly displayed for the first time; she was fortunate in possessing a captain as resourceful as Banak (b.2825), who demonstrated outstanding courage and leadership on the western frontier, and in the three civil wars in which Kargul, with the covert but generally suspected support of elements within the *Mankh'*, tried to seize supreme power.

*[The marriage (2861) between Dalsinu, Thral-Sivu's daughter, and Tolvan baKargul was part of the attempt to heal this rift, but Dalsinu died suddenly in 2868 without issue. The Heir, though widely regarded as half-witted, was more fortunate in his choice; **Laluvoi** (b.2848), married to him at 17, was already a young woman of remarkable intellect, charm and force, and a celebrated beauty. Though descended from ancient Owani blood, she was soon loved and admired by all the races, to whom she showed impartial favor. Childless through more than ten years of marriage, she conceived in early 2876, and decided she would bear the child in the milder climate of her native*

Ninkufu. That journey, accompanied by her husband and his mother, the rabhsaëyu, *ended in the* **Disaster of the Ní-Tilagh** *(2876), amply described elsewhere, and the extinction of the Gabh'Owan line.*]

Valplakh {2876} appears to have died somewhat later than his mother, thus becoming, for a few hours the twelfth, and (discounting the unnamed male child born prematurely to Laluvoi at Kir) shortest-reigned and last of his House.

The War of the Widowed
The Arbhai-Navu Rulers

[*After the Disaster the initial prize for the warring factions was the unborn Heir, but when it was learned a child (as was for many years believed) had been stillborn, the conflict became one between the two survivors of marriage to the children of Thral-Sivu, Tolvan baKargul and Laluvoi, championed by Banak. It was a brutal and bitter war, but the young captain,* **Saidhan** *(b.2855), Banak's apprentice, whose swift actions after the Disaster had, by ensuring Laluvoi's safety, begun the war, also ended it with his famous killing of Tobhsila baKargul in single-combat. By then (2878) Banak and Laluvoi were man and wife, with an infant son.*]

Banak and Laluvoi {2878-2904} are the only recorded joint-rulers, Laluvoi both *rabhsayu* and *rabhsaëyu*, and Banak was the first *rabhsai* with admixed heritage (his paternal grandfather, Rodelam, was of Mixed descent). Although Banak was inevitably accused by many Owanil of favoring those of Other race, the policies of this joint reign were in fact a resumption of the evenhanded course set by Plakhsila *Kímukoi*. Unsuccessful in their proclaimed object of ending all conflict among the races, Banak and Laluvoi took great strides in making both justice and high office available to all the people.

Banak's health began to fail around 2900, and he and Laluvoi decided on joint-abdication in favor of their son when he reached 25.

Lambarr {r.2904-2935} was betrothed to and soon married Saëdhu, the daughter of Banak's lieutenant and great friend, Saidhan (who, in 2894 had become first *Nim'*, hereditary overlord, of the Colony). Lambarr, a well-loved rather than powerful or decisive figure, is chiefly notable for the mildness of his reign, and his devotion to the *rabhsayu*. She bore nine children in the first fifteen years of their marriage, and eleven (or ?twelve) in all.

[*The realm was fortunate in continuing to benefit from the prestige and wise guidance of Laluvoi, widowed in 2906, who lived on to great age, with little diminution of her powers. Details of the latter reign of Lambarr can be found elsewhere; he, together with the Heir and five others of his offspring were lost in the* **Tan Lughsai Fire** *(2935), and he was thus unexpectedly succeeded by his second son.*]

Ban-Sila {r.2935-2942} was originally named after his grandfather, Banak, but in his youth became universally known as *Banak-loi* ("Little Banak," by contrast with *Banak-rai*, Great Banak). Being short in stature he decided at his accession to rid himself of the slighting suffix by changing his name. It was remarkable that he chose a new name in Owani form, but an accurate harbinger for a reign which the *Mankh'*-educated Ban-Sila devoted to the restoration of Owani supremacy, notwithstanding the Mixed element in his own paternal heritage.

[*The results of the policies pursued by Ban-Sila, and his eventual assassination, are dealt with at length elsewhere. He was succeeded by his younger brother.*]

Rodlakh (b.2922) came to power after victory in the **Great *Jinzai* War** (2942). Upon investiture he married Âna Konats-daughter, of common birth, but with uncommon gifts of intellect and character; with a new and more conciliatory Patriarch, he assented to, some say, imposed a Second Treaty, which, with Rodlakh's own stated policies, appeared to promise a fresh and more equitable future for the realm.

Adanum	*	"brotherhood" (of the Patriarchal
bodyguard)		
aën'modha	*	"distant vision" = "Enlightenment"
Angle	geog.	the wide bend of the Paowan R.;
the area (eastern		Paowan) so enclosed
anib'anu	*	"homosexual"
Arbhu	geog.	Hills east of Kadon Dinul
as'loi		
asai		
Asalladh		
a		
Asprandha		
asumanai		
asumu		
at'ai		
atarlai		
Atarlum		
b'akhi		
Baëdhral	**"Ministers"	
baKarguli		
balakim		
baRadhum		
baSibadhum		
bedai		

betufi

betuloi

bikradha

bikradhapaghai   *"oath of death" (sworn by the Adanum
Plakh')

bôdh'loiki   * "lesser counsellor"

bôdhal

bôdhrai   * "great counsellor"

brona'dodhi   * "oak-leaf" (a verse-form)

Colony   geog. Telnavu

dabhai

danulurai

dazhai   * "fear, awe"

deghi   * "high one" (as an honorific)

Dônsheyai

edhradu

Edhrodilum

Encompasser

Epranda

eviscerator

filso   * geog. "straits"

finnal

foi'kani

frel'afoi

frela'olu

frela'olurai

Froghu

Froghul

Froghuli

Froghulú

g'Asalladh

g'Ati

Gabh'Owani

Gabhani

Gabhanilú

Gabhaniyu

gaëbhu

glyphs

gruvai

Heartland   geog.; the northwestern Paowan

Hradhi

Hrafi

Hranakh

Ifbleni

ifnaku

ifradh

Ifradhi

iftaki

Irvati   a salty cheese of Irbat

Jalef   an early name of ?Zhól

kaël'rolai

Kamanasalladh

Kamintolaghi

Kamsilatai

Karganprova   * "rowan-tree"

Karguli

Karguliyu

keghu

kematakhi

keshai

kezhul

kímuko   * "one hundred" (also an obs. measure)

Kímukoi   * "Century" (style of Plakhsila)

kolukezh'

kolukezhal

Konúrai

Lalaru

Larghayi

Lekh'Owan

Lekh'Owani

Lekh'Owanit

Lon

Lovi

mai

Manadilum

manadu

manadubalaki

manai

manayit

Man-mani

margul

margú

Menadhi

modhum

moradhilum

murutrakha

Naëdhi

Naënai

navu

Navuna

Navuni

nim

nim'asai

nim'loiki

nim'raibaki

nim'raibakim

nimu

nimuraibáki

nímurai

Nivu

Nôdhilum

nôd'yanu

Nôdhilum

olu'rai

olúdhanai

olútaloi

Owanai

Owani

Owanilú

Owaniyu

ôdu

Paowanu

pefrai

plakh'

plakha

plakhi

pledging

rabhsa'dhanai

rabhsaëyu

rabhsai

rabhsaidakradhai

rabhsaidakradhi

rabhsayani

rabhsayin

rabhsayit

rabhsayu

rabhsayum

Raëdh

Raëdhi

raëdho

raf'yalu

Ramadilum

Ramidhai

ramidu

raminat

ramminai

Rehk'rabhsayum

Rekh'Rabhsai

rhaël'olu

Rok'olul

Sebhali

Shaëlil

shan'loi

Shâls

Shei'Owanai

Shei'Owani

Shu'sai

Shud'rai

Shuda'sai

shuzi

tak'bedal

Tembúrai

tobhai

tra'munu

traëvu

uzh'freladhai

vadh'oloi

van'naëdhu

van'odhoi

vanu

Vrobani

weekwife

Yagha-yeghut

yali

yalit

yalol

yalum

Yoëlladhai

Yoëlladhani

Yoëlladho

Yoëlladhu

Yoëlladhuyil

Yoëlu

Yoëlut

zhabhu

Zhavukindhrai

zhin'paghai

zhin'pefrai

Zhinzhappa

Abfekh, Tâl: Village, Central Paowan, on Burantal Road
Abfekhi (Hill):   Site of above village
Aëni: Former name of *An*
Allistead: Farm, eastern Ân, north of Yuvakh Din
Angle, the: Region of Northeastern Paowan within elbow of the
river
Arbhal: The Realm (Six Provinces, enclaves of Ninkufu and
                   Narn, later with the addition of the Colony and
                   Protectorate) after the Return, 2477
Arbhu Hills: East of Kadon Dinul
Arcades, the: (see *Bathrâd*)
Arlemirrstead: Fictitious farm of central Paowan
Arlimasstead: Farm nr. Burantal
Arnan: The inland sea of Arbhal
Ásekh: Defunct province east of Paowan, largely desert,
                   source of minerals
Avenue Of Treaties ("The Avenue"): At Kadon Dinul, laid out C2775
by Plakhsila, a broad way of rose-colored stone, running eastward
straight from Harbor Gate to the New Residence
Ân: Northeastern province, seat *Sebira*
Antal Iravulin: (see *Iravulin*)

Bakali: (see *Kred B.*)
Banakit: Town, central Colony; seat from 2947
Basegh Din: Largely derelict town, northern Ásekh, former seat
Bathrâd: Town, Paowan, on Royal Way, known for covered
                   market (the Arcades)
Bérovan: Hamlet, central Dramal, known for sweetmeats

Places

Bronze Residence:

> Former royal residence (to 2800), by Harbor Gate at Kadon Dinul; also *Old Bronze Residence*; important library, joint-property of *Rabhsayum* and *Atarlum*. After 2942, administrative site for *rabhsayum*

Burantal: City, Paowan, famous for its Marionette Guild. Sebhal k., 2942

Burantali Gap: Betw. Burantali and Lughsai Hills, site of above city

Burantali, Kafan: Hills, eastward of Gap, forming northern border of Shemugrân

Colony, the: Usual name for *Telnavu*; seat *Kamsilat* (to 2947), thereafter, *Burantal*

Daëni Tâl: Village, east coast of Kamanta, on Klam Nampai

Dakani, Drin: Fortified town, western border of Ân, on Dakbân River

Dakbân (River): Boundary between Dramal and Ân Provinces. Upper reaches of river famous for steelmaking

Danulurai: (at Kanzan Tâl) (the) Great (`Golden') Walls

Disc of Aëlovoi: Monument of carved stone in the circle where Market Way crosses the Avenue, Kadon Dinul

Doniftu: Port and headland, western Kamanta

Dônshei: Nominally sovereign city, central Dramal, capital (under former name, *Undaëni Shei*) of Old Owan to 1307; former site of Schools, Battle 2942, Tovakh and Bolan defeated by forces loyal to Rodlakh

Dônshei Bridge: Town, Paowan, and bridge across Paowan River, south of Dônshei

Dramal: Northwestern province, seat *El'tuf*

Dramaru: Heathlands, central Dramal

Drin b'Afon: Fortified city, central Kamanta, Patriarch's Summer Palace; the deposed Kanavakh `Vakh biSegh` confined there from 2576 (*d*.2580); successfully assaulted by Rodlakh, to release Aëlu, 2942

Drin Navuna: (see *Navuna*)

Dromladh's Canal: In Dramal, linking the Arnan at Irbat to the Tufa R., hence to the Northern   Sea at Eltuf. Completed 2850

East Gate: Start of the Royal Way, at K.D.

Ekhladi =? *Y'ath*

El'tuf: Port, Dramal, on northern sea, provincial seat

En'tesh: Lake, settlement, Lunu Tezh'

Eshaël Asumun: Lost city of Farther West on Landegh, nr. ruby mines rediscovered by Sebhal in 2928

Filso Kamantani: Strait betw. southwestern Kamanta and Lunu Tezh'

Flamûrai: Great western gulf, for Old Owan demarcating Farther and Farthest West

Forbidden Road, the: North central Kamanta, betw. Doniftu and Pavani

Froghushei: Peninsula east of Flamûrai, largely incorporated in "Empire" of Kargusai, 2942-51; see also *Hrinani*

Frontier, the: (usage) Westward border of the Colony with Landegh, anchored at *Drin   Navuna*

Gabhan: A Mainland realm (or confederation) of indeterminate and shifting extent during the Night of Owan, 1809-2477

Gardens of Kamzhinu: Shallow ravine on the south side of K.D., west of Market Gate;   public place of recreation, planned by and named after the *Rabhsaëyu* Kamzhinu (r. 2652-67)

Grâdhasumi: Natural lake of tar, northern Ásekh

Grân (or *Grânu*) River: Of the Lunu Tezh', flowing south through En'tesh to Arnan

Great Stone Road: The *Royal Way* between K-D and Kred Bakali

Heartland, the: Populous and fertile region, northern and central Paowan province

Hlaod =? *Y'ath*

Inilu (River):   Central Kargul

Inilun Barabhi: City, central Kargul, provincial seat

Inner Islands: *Iravulin Laëdhaki*, more northerly group of *Antal I.*, off southern coast of   Kamanta, known for eel fisheries

Iravulin, Antal: Minor islands of Arnan, southward of Kamanta, comprising two main groups, *I. Laëdhaki* (see *Inner Islands*) and *I. Naënaki* (see *Southward Islands*)

Irbat: Arnan port, Dramal, center for fleece trade

Island, the = *Kamanta*

Jinzalladhiyu, Lunu: Natural depression in Farther West, site of *jinzai*-breeding (to 2942)

Kadon Dinul: Greatest city of Arbhal, capital from 2477, of Old Owan (under former name) 1307-1809, capital and provincial seat of Paowan after Return

Kadonu, Shufloi: Minor stream east of Kadon Dinul

Kaghedonu: Version of former name of *Kadon Dinul*

Kamanta: "The Island;" Patriarchal preserve in Arnan

Kamanta, Karg':   Mountain, central Kamanta, sacred to Raëdh

Kamsilat: Port, Colony, at mouth of Navu, seat (to 2947); besieged by *jinzal*, battle, won by Rodlakh's forces 2942

Kanzan Tâl: City, southern Paowan, site of the Great Golden Walls

Kargan baDulfu: Loftiest mountains of Arbhal, southern hem of Kargul

Kargul: Province, south of Arnan, seat *Inilun Barabhi*

Kargusai, Abu: New name for *Lunu Jinzalladhiyu* after 2942; Kamin-Tolagh's northern seat 2942-50

Kazha Face (rock formation): on Landegh nr. Drin Navuna

Kir: Fortress city, Southern (New) Nîv, defended by Saidhan when unsuccess fully besieged by Tobhsila 2876

Klam' Nampai: Bay, eastern Kamanta

Klam' Owan: Bay, southern Paowan

Klamuru Gap: Low pass in hills southward of Irbat in Dramal

Konatstead (farm): Southern Paowan, east of Nambalus, birthplace of Âna

Kovilanu: Easternmost region of Kargul, ceded to Paowan, renamed *Paowanu Loi* 2878-2942

Kôbh: Greatest river of Arbhal, boundary of Paowan with Kargul, Nîv

Kred Bakali: Town, northern Paowan, due east of Kadon Dinul

Kred Taknai: Town, southern Kamanta

Kreshavu: Town, western Colony

Kufshei: Lands of Farthest West, west of Flamûrai

Lambarr's Way: The Tan Lughsai Road from Kadon Dinul

Landegh: Great plateau, long barren, west of Colony and Protectorate

Lovu: River, southern Paowan, flowing from Shelum to the Kôbh

Lughsai, Kafan: Hills, continuation (north and west of the Gap) of
Kafan
       Burantali

Lunu Tezh':   1. The "hidden" valley of *En'tesh*; 2. (by extension)
               "The Protectorate;" wide protected lands west of
               Arnan southward of the Colony
Lunu Tezh' Gate: Complex of high passes betw. Colony and
Protectorate, south of Banakit and Navu River; Battle 2942, won by
Shumat and Kamin-Tolagh over *jinzal*
Lurr: Stream of Dramal, tributary of Paowan R.
Luskran Bay: North central Ân, on Northern Sea; murder of Pir
               Perus and mutilation of his followers C1380

Mankh', the: (1) "True" or "First" *M.*, central Kamanta, overlooking
               Lunu Midhi;   (2) Paowanu or Mainland *M.*,
               Paowan, west of Kadon Dinul, shrine, temple,
               headquarters and school of *Atarlum*, Patriarchal seat
Mainland, the: (1) Arbhal, excluding Kamanta; (2) (in usage) Arbhal
               south and east of Arnan, excluding the Island, and
               westward lands, the Colony and Lunu Tezh'
Midhi, Lunu: Valley, central Kamanta, site of True *Mankh'* and ga-
               Tembúrai
Minshei: Lands of Farthest West, never incorporated in, but
               tributary to, First Empire, after C1475
Moon's Road, the: (1) Of the First Empire, the (conceptual)
               Imperial Way between Larghamit   i n
               the Farther West and Naënai in the extreme
               northeast; (2) A remnant east of Larghamit,
               still visible C2842
Moranti, Tanu: Headland, western side of Filso Kamantani
Mountain, the =   *Karg' Kamanta*

Naënai Aëlva: Former name of *Narn*
Naëni: Former far northeastern province, long desolate
Naëniyu, Gronu = Owani name for *Pass of Perus*
Nambalus: Arnan port, southern Paowan
Nanakh (River):   Eastern Kargul, westward border of Kovilanu
Narn: (1) City, extreme northeastern Arbhal, Battle 2928, won by
        Bolan over invaders led by Grenaspaluk   (2) (Enclave) its
        immediate hinterland
Navu, River: Flowing eastward into Arnan, the great river of the
Colony
Navuna, Drin: Frontier fortress and town, Colony; site of Rodlakh's
                accaliming, 2942, withstood *jinzai* siege (until its
                evacuation) 2942
New Residence: Admired edifice at Kadon Dinul, built by
                       Plakhsila *Kímukoi*; occupied (though still
                       unfinished) by him after 2800, seat for every
                       subsequent *rabhsai*; recaptured for Rodlakh
                       by loyalists 2942
Ninkufu: Southern Enclave of Arbhal, and its peninsula
Nivu Din: City, central Nîv, on Nibhfoi River, provincial seat
ní-Tilagh: Unclaimed wilderness between Nîv and Ninkufu;
                Gabh'Owan ruling house extinguished in *jinzai* attack.
                2876
Nîv: Province lying to the south of Paowan, north of the
                ní-Tilagh, seat *Nivu Din*

Odis Combe: Vale, Naëni, west of Narn, battles won by Shumat
                2928, 2933
Old Town: (1) Lowlying northwestern quarter of Kadon Dinul,
                larely rebuilt (and rid   of plague) in reign of
                Plakhsila C2770-95;   (2) At Zelkova in Kargul,

waterfront section noted for its hostelries and drinkshops

Ottsvale: Clan country, western Ân, nr. Yuvakh Din

Owan: (1) The realm founded by Yoëlladhu, eventually comprising the entire First Empire (to 1809) (2) Among the Owanil, name for the realm after the Return, proscribed by Plakhsila in favor of *Arbhal*

Owan Sai: Royal (Arnan) Port on Paowan Estuary north of Kadon Dinul

Paowan, the: (1) The Royal Province, site of Mainland *Mankh'*, and of the *rabhsai's* seat at Kadon Dinul (2) River, forming the border between the Paowan and Dramal

Paowanu Loi (see *Kovilanu*)

Pavani: Port of Kamanta, eastern end of Forbidden Road

Peframi: Town and river, western Kargul

Peframi Gorge: Western Kargul, famous for winemaking

Perus, Pass of: Eastern Ân, frontier of province and realm proper, Battle 2928 won by Bolan's lieutenants over rebel confederacy

Porrhaven: Harbor, Colony, south of Kamsilat, with dry-dock facilities

Preghala Ravine: Paowan, north of Tan Lughsai

Protectorate, the = *Lunu Tezh'* (2)

Rekhsepa: Rapid stream rising within Kadon Dinul

Residence Quarter, the: Southeastern section of Kadon Dinul, south of New Residence

Rhutalai: Hamlet, Paowan, on Tan Lughsai Road south of Kadon Dinul

Royal Way, the: Between Kadon Dinul and Thenimala in Ninkufu, especially the improved section

Places

betw. K.D. and Kred Bakali (the *Great Stone Road*)

Rufeni (River): Southern Nîv, forms Arbhali border (with ní-Tilagh)

Sebira: (1) Port city, Ân, provincial seat, celebrated for the beauty of its situation; (2) *Bay*, on the Northern Sea, admired site of above city

Sennu: Minor river, tributary of Paowan, rising in Arbhu Hills east of K.D.

Shâl Mines: Familiar name for Landegh ruby-mining settlement (? corruption of *Eshaël Asumun*) after 2930; successful evacuation after investing by *jinzal* 2942

Shoals, the: Wide band of islets, rocks and reefs, many cross-currents, northward of Kamanta, a danger to navigation

Shelum, Entun: Lake, south central Paowan, betw. Kanzan Tâl and Shemugrân

Shemufegh Rai: Borderland salt marshes, northern Dramal, north and west of Irbat

Shemugrân: Extensive marshlands, west central Paowan

Shuburu: Stream, rising nr. Burantal

Shuf'Oëladh: The "Stream of Being," Kamanta, flowing through and from Lunu Midhi, a place of pilgrimage

Shumu Shan'loi: Underground stream at K.D., emerging and flowing west to the Arnan south of the *Mankh'*

Southward Islands: Familiar name for *Iravulin Naënaki*, outer group of *Antal I.*, southern Arnan

Talbronu: Market town, northeastern Paowan, at the Angle

Tan Dramali: Northern headland of Dramal

Tan Lughsai: Cape and peninsula, Paowan, Lambarr *Rabhsai* and several of his offspring *k.* in disastrous fire, 2935

Telnavu = *the Colony*

(ga-)Tembúrai: Temple-observatory, Lunu Midhi (Kamanta), conceived by Patriarch Owan-Alladh IV; completed 1815, after His death

Thenimala: Port city of Ninkufu on Southern Ocean, birthplace of Doleni, Dolvid

Thramai Rubha: (former name of *Dramaru*)

Tomb of *Kirova-Kindhri*: (Spurious) shrine overlooking upper Peframi Gorge in Kargul

Tufa (River):   Northern Dramal, reaching Northern Sea at El'tuf

Tufani: Extensive lands of the northwest, incorporated in First Empire 1494-1604, little known after the Empire's dissolution

Undaëni Shei: (former name of *Dônshei*)

Utalai Course: in Burantal, a celebrated, curving avenue

Vonn: Hamlet, central Colony

Vonni's Jaws: Defile west of Vonn, defended (by Vonn) against armies of Owan, C1380; (by Rodlakh) against *jinzal*, 2942

Voruni: Fishing village of Paowan, west of Burantal

Vrobhan: (1) Former empire adjacent to Old Owan, defeated and eradicated by Shaëli C1165-72; (2) Peninsula far to the southeast of the present realm, heart of the former empire, now sparsely populated and little known

Y'ath: A lost realm of the northeast (in northern Naëni); also called (?) *Hlaod* or *Ekhladi*

Yoëlladhu's Spear: Natural rock spar erected outside Harbor Gate at Kadon Dinul

Yoëlladhu's Watch-Rock: Lofty isolated natural pillar, Lunu Midhi, Kamanta

Yuvakh Din: City, eastern Ân

Yuvat: Town, central Kargul

Zelkova: Arnan port, largest city of Kargul, on Kôbh Estuary

Zelu Bablakhi: (see *Bablakhi*)

Zhanu bi-Nimraibákimai: see *Moon's Road*

Names (Religion and Myth)

Adhi o (r) *Edrodhi* (= "The Grower"), Owani Creation Myth, one of Four Ministers, associated with fecundity, the direction South, the *Edrodhilum* (Growing Order of the *Atarlum*), the middle-finger.

Aëlovoi o (r) *Yoëlu* (= "The Giver"), Owani Creation Myth, consort of *Raëdh* and mother of *Zhôl*.

Aroptil g (m): brother of *Okseti* in two of the Odi Kukkuk stories in *The Song of Tales*.

Azakit g (m): beautiful sister to *Dalakim* in the Odi Kukkuk tales

Dalakim g (m): Evil sorcerer (apparently associated with spiders) in the Odi Kukkuk cycle

Draha (r) "Rock-lord"

Edhrodi o (r) (= "The Grower", *Adhi*)

Enardak g (m): Mysterious bull-horned sorcerer in the *Odi Kukkuk* cycle

Encompasser o (r) (= *Hrafi*)

Fiunuvoi o (r) "Flood-Tamer"

Hradhi o (r)

Hrafi o (r)

Hranakh o (r)

Hrâmi o (r)

Jalef v (r), said to be a god of the Vrobhanil (? = Zhôl).

Kukkuk g (m) (*see Odi K.*)

Maëdhi o (r) *Maëdhu* (= "The Wise"), Owani Creation Myth, one of the Four Ministers, associated with clarity, the direction North, the *Manadilum* (Teaching Order of the *Atarlum*), the index-finger

Odi Kukkuk g (m) Eponymous, unconquerable hero of a Gabhani cycle of legends

Okseti "Jester" g (m): The hero's frequent trickster-companion in the *Odi Kukkuk* cycle

Raëdh

Yoëlladhu o (r)

Zhavukindhrai o (r): (= "Gale-Victor"); a style of *Zhôl*

Zhavukran o (r)

Zhinzhappa

Zhôl (r)

Zhunoi

*Yagha-Yeghut Owani nursery tale; a frog

(Yoëlu)   "Giver" (Yoëlladhu)

www.ingramcontent.com/pod-product-compliance
Lightning Source LLC
Chambersburg PA
CBHW020324180626
46812CB00001B/43